Jen

People are the ~~ too!

Maybe the Bird

Will Rise

Susan Helene Gottfried

[signature]

West of Mars, LLC

Editing assistance from Peter Senftleben at PES Editorial

Proofreading by April Bennett at The Editing Soprano

Book Cover by Croco Designs

Print only author's photo by Rustbelt Mayberry Photography

Shot on location at Tall Pines Farm, Darlington, PA

Print only author's makeup by the Rainbow Room, Ellwood City, PA

First edition 2023

Author's Note

A large part of the *Tales from the Sheep Farm* project is about racial justice. To that end, most of the characters you will encounter do not have their race identified. Only a few must be entirely white, and it should be evident who they are. Likewise, only a few must be other races or ethnicities. It should be evident who they are, as well.

The rest? That is up to you.

And if you feel inspired to tell a story of your own in this world, or if there's a character you want to know more about, I am accepting proposals so that you can come play in this world and help advance the issues of racial and social justice.

Your voices matter. Your stories matter. This story, hopefully, lays the foundation for my firm belief in that.

That also means that any mistakes are my own and if you gently point them out, I will own them.

One

September 8

Tess Cartieri tried not to think about where she was. It was just an old, unloved, rundown stadium, just a set of crumbling concrete stairs that demanded her attention as she picked her way down them. She tried to convince herself she'd never used this route as a shortcut across campus and met anyone special, never come out to the field down below with a blanket and a boyfriend so they could look for the Milky Way, never taken off her shirt and lain back on the metal bleachers that were dented even then, their coolness against her back a startling contrast to the heat of Mack's body above hers.

"No, no, no," she chanted in time with her steps. Forty rows.

She knew this place all too well. If a place could know a person, it knew her. Or, rather, it knew who she'd been. It had known a Tess who was full of hope for a future she'd thought would be hers: Architect. Mack's wife. Urban renewal expert.

Two out of three. She'd made her choice and, she told herself, she had no regrets.

Time hadn't just changed her, it had changed the steps too, and she stumbled on a piece of loose concrete. She reached out for the nearest bleacher, trying not to flash back to the day she'd done the same thing, landing equally as awkwardly back then as she did in the present.

That was the day she'd met him.

She paused, breathing heavily. Every time she'd ever set foot in this place, she'd worried she would put a foot wrong and would wind up hurting herself somehow. Back then, she'd been through here often enough that she'd known all the tricks to stay on her feet, unharmed, unscathed. By the stadium, anyway.

In every project she worked on, every piece of property she renovated and turned into something new, she paused and asked it what secrets it held. What old secrets she would discover, what new secrets she would build into it. In this one, she knew some of those secrets. But there were more to be discovered. There always were.

She scuffed her toe through some debris that had fallen under the bleacher in front of her. Leaves. What looked like weathered trash. A crushed beer can, long abandoned, its wrinkles pressed almost smooth. Something plastic.

Her reverie was broken by a disc that sailed through the air and landed underneath the row of bleachers in front of her. Just as it had done all those years ago.

"No," Tess said again, although this time it came out with her breath.

"Hey! Mind bringing that down? Don't throw it; the wind's not right."

Tess closed her eyes and covered her face with her hands. He'd remembered. How had he remembered? It had been one moment, one eyeblink in all the time they'd spent together.

Of course, he was Mack. When he wanted to remember something, he did.

"Tess?" She heard feet on the stairs, running up, scrabbling on the disintegrating concrete. "You okay?"

She forced herself to lift her head and plaster on a smile as she pushed her hair out of her face. He stood there, in front of her, life-sized, breathing, dusting off his hands as if he'd used them to help his quick ascent. Emerson Mackenzie. "Mack. I... hadn't expected you to be here. What— Why— Oh, no. Don't tell me you're the client."

"You didn't pick up on it? When I had my assistant ask for Tess to come to the consultation? Just Tess?"

"No," she said and let her eyes rove over him. He looked good. Too good. Entirely familiar and still heart-stoppingly dear, his dark hair cut short, his eyes that strange dark blue, his body less exploding with muscle but still flat and toned—but broader through the shoulders and hips, as if he'd filled into himself. "We were worried you were some creep who was going to assault me. I've got the whole office waiting for me to check in. In fact," she said and pulled her phone out of her pocket, sending the quick text.

"I am not a creep who's going to assault you," he said gravely.

"No," she said, looking up at him, shading her eyes so she could see him. He wore a pale yellow collared shirt with stripes the color of the sunset across the chest—Tess picked up the orange in it, of course. He'd left it untucked and hadn't bothered with the buttons. She tried not to stare at the exposed skin and chest hair, tried not to remember the feel of it, his warmth, the silkiness under her fingertips. With effort, she pushed the memories aside and took in the rest of him: a pair of casual black pants and black sneakers. He looked less like the athletic trainer he'd hoped to be, nothing like the corporate CEO he'd chosen to become, and entirely like a guy who'd just turned thirty-one and had a day off. "I'm glad."

Her phone buzzed. She replied to her boss, Red, briefly. *Old college buddy. All good.*

But what an understatement that was.

"So tell me why I'm meeting you here," she said. "I hope it's for more than a stroll down memory lane."

"It is." He nodded and sat down, straddling the bleacher in front of her, putting his knee down on the concrete beside her feet. He played with his phone, turning it end over end, and she cocked her head, watching. There was something he wasn't saying.

"Kelsey died two months ago."

Tess paused. "Kelsey?"

"My wife." He looked up at her, looked away just as quickly. "Gotta be the good Mackenzie man, right? Marry the woman they tell you, spit out some heirs, get on with your life." He closed his eyes and shook his head. "This wasn't supposed to happen."

"I'm sorry," she said softly, wondering why they were *here*, at this dilapidated old stadium that she had long dreamed of bringing back to life. Was this a convenient reason to see her? Or did he truly want to renovate this old place?

He smiled weakly at her, a smile that didn't touch his eyes. "The official story is that she had an undiagnosed heart condition. And it's true. Her heart *did* stop beating."

"But not because of an undiagnosed condition."

He turned and stared out over the field. So did she. The time since she'd been here last hadn't been kind to it. Poor field.

Poor Mack. He didn't deserve to have lost his wife.

"Last week," he said, "Krista told me the timing was right to stop talking about buying the naming rights to this place. It's time, she said, to force the university to finally fix it up. I think she's tired of watching me just kind of go through the motions. That's... about all I've been able to do, and it's not good for our long-term plans. She and Logan had to move back into the Manor when things got weird with Kelsey," he said, looking up at Tess again, his face laced with pain, his eyes begging her for something. "Yes, it took my mother to figure out what was going on," he said, his voice thick with bitterness, "and she confronted Kelsey, who was scared, so scared." His voice changed, and so did his expression. The bitterness was replaced by… desperation? "So we called security in. Did everything we could to protect her. Eyes on us both every second when we weren't in our bedroom, but in the end, they just watched her stop breathing and didn't even know it."

"Oh, Mack." She couldn't help it; she touched his shoulder. That hadn't made complete sense, but it sounded traumatic and horrible. And it was so bad that Krista and Logan had moved in? Who wanted their mother and her long-time lover living with them and meddling in their spouse's issues? Not the Mack she had known.

He put his hand on hers. "I didn't love her. Not like I loved you. I took care of her, I tried to protect her, I tried to care for her the way she deserved, but she didn't think she deserved it. Not from me."

She tightened her grip on his shoulder. He, in turn, tightened his on her hand.

Tess watched as he took a deep breath, then let go of her hand, giving it a lingering pat.

"So Krista did the motherly thing and told me to come do this. Ask you to fix the field so I can hang my name on it. Make good on a promise I made us both."

"That's a very old dream. Are you sure?"

He lifted himself off the bleacher and moved to sit beside her, but only after grabbing the disc beside his downslope foot. "I'm still not sure the school's on board with this idea, to be honest. I've tried dangling money in front of them, and they tell me they'll take the money but can't promise the field. I figured this time—okay, *Krista* figured—that if I am serious about seeing this happen, I should show up with a full plan, drawn up by experts, and make it easy for them."

"So there's a chance you're going to pay our fees for a site plan and it'll still get shot down?" She wasn't sure why she was surprised. It happened often.

He shrugged. "Krista's right. I need something to distract me from what happened."

"Something? Or some*one*?"

He gave her a sidelong look. In it was a tiny hint of the mischievous look she knew all too well. "You'd have to ask her, but I'm not complaining. I've missed you. I…" He shook his head again and the disc bobbled in his hands. He caught it and she let herself look at his left hand. He still wore his ring and she wondered why.

Then again, two months wasn't very long.

She ran a hand along her neck, under her hair, over her tattoo. Two months most certainly wasn't very long when you loved someone. And even though he said he hadn't loved this Kelsey, Tess wasn't sure she believed that. She knew Mack. He would have gone all in on a marriage even if it wasn't to his ideal woman.

"I bet you haven't kept up with the wacky world of Ultimate at all since we broke it off."

"I have not," she said, tucking her hands between her knees and leaning forward. The impulse to lean against him, to touch him, to go back to who they'd been together was too strong, even after nine years. No wonder no other man had stuck. "Do you still play?" She wasn't sure why she needed to hold her breath when she asked the question. It felt risky somehow.

"Yeah. They've tried to get me to quit, to make me focus on the company more, but it's my stress relief. You know."

"I do."

They fell silent.

"Tell me what you want for the field," she said, feeling as though for a minute there, she'd forgotten why they were here. "Spill your vision."

"What's possible? I mean, beyond the obvious," he said, his foot tapping the bent metal bleacher in front of them. "This place needs some basic TLC, but more than that? I don't know. Figured you'd know more about it than I could."

"What's your budget?"

He shrugged again and, once more, stared out over the field. She had the sense that if he were wearing a jacket, he'd put his fists in his pockets and hunch his shoulders. "You tell me. Start with the basics, and we'll see what I feel like shelling out on top of that."

She wanted to tell him that wasn't how it worked, but someone like Mack probably didn't understand that. Besides, she'd met and worked with plenty of deep-pocketed people who'd operated under the same method. They just hadn't been so explicit about it.

"I'll have Charley bring a team out to do a preliminary site study."

"No. You."

"Mack," she sighed and brushed her hair out of her eyes, the wind just strong enough to play with it. "My expertise is in workspaces. Corporate towers, small buildings—it doesn't matter. Not outdoor spaces. And this," she said, gesturing at the field in front of them, "is an outdoor space. To do it right, we need the outdoor space expert. That's Charley."

He eyed her. "Is he nice?"

"She, and yes. But before you ask, yes, I'll remain as team leader. I'll be your contact, I'll be the one at the top. Okay?"

He tapped the disc on his knee, as if thinking, but Tess knew better. He was stalling, trying to save face. "Okay," he said at last.

"So let's talk about some basics," she said, confident in this part, at least. "Will the field be used for other sports?"

He shrugged. "When I was here for an alumni weekend last spring, the current players were complaining that they aren't allowed out here anymore and sharing field space with every other team is a nightmare." He stood up and took a step forward, onto the bleacher in front of them, then looked over his shoulder at her. "Let's go down. See how bad it is."

It was a good idea, so she stood up. He put a hand under her elbow as they descended slowly, their feet ringing with each step, each bleacher's particular bends and rips making what sounded like a different note. Thankfully for their route, all the bleachers were intact, even if some of them had been damaged so badly they slanted, usually forward.

"Does it look to you like someone tried to set the field on fire?" he asked as they got to the bottom row of bleachers.

"Yes. And that hole in the turf over to the left... Seriously. I can't believe they haven't barricaded this place off, padlocked the entrances, and started filling it in."

He snorted softly. "What else do you do with a hole in the ground if not put a stadium in it?"

"Lots of things, but this *is* the university, and ignoring it while it deteriorates is kind of on-brand." She took a deep breath and turned in a circle, taking in the devastation, feeling the project begin to work on her. Replace the turf and all the fencing, none of which stood straight, fix the steps and bleachers... She narrowed her eyes at the press box. What could Charley come up with for that beast? And lights. They'd need to add lights, preferably solar powered.

"Question for you," she said.

"Let's hear it." He crossed his arms over his chest, spreading his feet a bit wider.

"I'd need my team to measure to make certain, and we'd need the university to confirm this would be an Ultimate-only field, but what do you think of shrinking the field to regulation size and putting a track around it? Teams can use that for track workouts, right? And, again, we'd need to measure, but that area over there," she pointed to the right, "could be a sheltered area of some sort. Something to keep your gear dry, maybe."

He was nodding, and some of his sadness had left him. "Yeah. All that would work. Do you have other ideas?"

"Not off the top of my head, but Charley will. Do *you* have ideas?"

He shrugged. "Again, what's possible?"

"It may not be about what's possible so much as what's *functional*. Bringing this up to basics might be painful. We might need to keep it simple."

"I'm not sure I want to put my name on simple."

She turned and looked up at the seating area. From here, it didn't look so bad, but it was as forgotten and forlorn as any other property she made an initial visit to. It cried out for love, was embarrassed by its neglect, and it tantalized with its past history.

In some ways, she'd been getting a similar vibe from Mack.

"We absolutely can put your name on simple but well-done," she said. "No shame in that. But," she added as he opened his mouth, "simple doesn't mean we can't do something like look into running a water line. Or seeing what's under the bleachers and maybe adding spaces for locker rooms. Or maybe we don't even get that ambitious and instead spend some cash on really swanky fencing. But no matter what we do, it'll be a safe field for the teams."

She hoped the field heard her. It was stupid, she knew, but it was a ritual she'd developed. Telling the project that its days of neglect and disrepair were over. That she was there, she saw it, she was going to help it. To her, it felt like the first step in the process.

"We'll see what your team learns. A whole team, Tess?"

"Yeah," she said and smiled, feeling the pride in his gaze. "We work in teams. Charley, Sanjit, and I head them up. Red's the overwatch and the director. He makes the connections with the city's politicians and movers and shakers, thank God. And Anchey runs the stuff no one sees—from the front desk, of all places. He loves that people see him first but unless they know us well, they don't realize he's the co-owner, and that changes how people treat him. So if you ever walk in, remember that. The business would fold without the dude at the front desk."

"Always." He snorted softly. "I may have the fancy title, but I'd be lost without my assistant. It's those invisible people who are the most important."

She eyed him and ducked around the broken fence so she could walk out onto the field, wanting to see the spot that had been set on fire. Why hadn't it spread?

Mack followed, going back to spinning the disc on his finger again. "Is this your dream job?"

"Mostly."

"Mostly?"

"Nothing's perfect. If I loved every aspect of it, something wouldn't be right."

He nodded. "Perfection would be boring?"

"You know it." Of course he did. How many times had they both said that to each other?

"And what *is* perfect, anyway? What does it mean?"

"Mack—"

He spread his hands out in one of those gestures of surrender. "You see why I had to do this *now*. I needed to see you, Tess. I need to know..." Again, he looked over her head at something distant. Tess was half-tempted to turn and see what he was looking at, but she doubted there was anything actually there.

He sighed. "I need to know if there's a way out of this mess."

"I'm not your savior," she said.

But he laughed, a sharp, brittle, pain-laced laugh that she'd never heard from him before. "Of course you're not," he said. "I am. Except I'm doing a lousy job of it and if things don't turn around, Tess, I'm going to drown in my own attempts to save myself."

"I can't help you," she insisted.

"I know," he said and gave her such a sad smile, her heart tore in half. "Like I said, this is on me. And this," he added, gesturing around the field, "is part of it. You're going to lead the team who restores this field, and then I'm going to name it Field Emerson, and then I'll find the next thing that used to be important to me. And once I put that right, I'll go on to the next. And maybe in there, I'll find my soul again."

"The devil drives a tough bargain."

"I never went down to the crossroads. That was Tristan and my grandfather Cullen, and maybe Great-Grand Patrick, but if anyone alive remembers him, they refuse to talk about him. I thought I was okay, but sometimes I think I might have been buried with Kelsey." He turned away and coughed.

Tess pretended not to see him swipe a finger under his eyes—or the way his wedding band glinted as he did.

"Losing her doesn't have to be the end of everything."

He tapped the disc against his leg. "Maybe it does. That's what this is about. But if so, maybe I can at least save someone else's future."

Tess thought about the Mack she'd loved. Unless he was studying, he couldn't be still. He had to be moving, exploring, experiencing life. He was the guy who drove without the top on the Jeep and turned his face up to feel the wind and the sun. He was the guy who sailed through the air to catch a piece of plastic. It made sense that he'd start here, on his old field, in this quest.

"We'll get to work on this immediately."

"But you're my contact person," he insisted.

"I am," she confirmed again, starting to understand. She couldn't save him, but she could hold him up as he saved himself.

Two

I t felt like everyone at the company was waiting for Tess' return, although it was only the company principals—Charley, Sanjit, Red, and Anchey—who were in her office when she got back. They were the heart of Urban Renewal, and they'd been together for long enough now that she wasn't surprised they wanted to hear about this new client, her *old college buddy* and what that meant.

"So let's hear it," Red said, tilting his chair back on two legs and taking a drink of coffee. The light reflected on his bald head but wasn't bright enough to turn his shirt transparent enough that they could see his tattoos.

Tess was glad she hadn't given in to the temptation to fall apart on the drive back to the office. Mack was a mess, and the contrast between their lives had never been more obvious. In a way, it had been a confirmation that she'd been right to walk away from him.

But if she hadn't, would he be in this place?

"The field's in *terrible* shape," she said, allowing herself to sink into the comfort of work. "Charley, wait until you see it. We've got our work cut out for us."

"Define *terrible*," she said. "Did you get pictures?"

Tess froze. She always took pictures. She'd even bought herself a relatively nice DSLR camera too. But she'd been distracted by Mack and the camera had remained where it was. "Yeah," she said, more than a touch ruefully. "I completely forgot."

"So this is more than an old college buddy," Charley said, giving her the once-over as if she were looking for evidence that Tess and Mack had found a place for a quickie.

"It was enough of a surprise that it threw me off," Tess said. "He left a clue, but I hadn't picked up on it."

"Should you have?" Red asked, setting his chair flat. There was something protective in that gesture, something that Tess appreciated.

"If I had, I doubt I would have believed I was reading it the right way." She paused and set her bag down on her desk.

"What was it?" Sanjit asked. He blinked when Charley threw him a look. "What? So if he does it again, we'll know."

"He's the only one who calls me Just Tess."

"Just Tess?" he repeated. Everyone else stared.

"The first time we met, he asked what Tess was short for. First time we met, right? So I didn't think anything of replying *Just Tess.*"

Red chuckled. Sanjit groaned.

"Okay, so if you've got nothing until we get over there in an official capacity, and since you're obviously okay after that mysterious summons, let's break this up and get back to work," Red said, taking another sip of coffee and setting the mug down so he could gather his tablets into a pile. He swept them up and grabbed his mug, but paused. "Tess. We owe Councilwoman Salveggio and a couple of the investors an update on Woolslayer. Want me to do it so you can get started on this?"

"Yes, please. Tell them things are *great.*"

With a nod, Red left, the door slowly closing, leaving Tess and Charley alone in Tess' office.

"Okay, what aren't you saying?" Charley asked.

Tess took a deep breath and pushed the power button on her monitor. She called up a browser and opened a fresh tab, then typed *Emerson Mackenzie* in the search bar.

Charley's mouth fell open at what followed. "CEO of PharmaScience Technologies, young heir to the throne, latest in the Mackenzie family to run the company..." She took a step closer to the computer and pointed at a picture. "Click on that one."

Tess did—and realized she hadn't been prepared for a picture of Mack in a tux, a gorgeous, slender blonde on his arm. As she fought to breathe, she checked the date; it had been earlier in the year. That must have been Kelsey.

She slipped a hand beneath her hair and touched the tattoo.

"Well, I'd do him," Charley said and paused, turning to Tess and studying her for a long minute. "You did him."

"I did."

"More than once." It wasn't a question, and it encompassed more than a statement about sex.

"Breaking up with him was the hardest thing I've ever had to do. And remember: my dad died when I was thirteen."

"So *he's* the one who got away."

"He's the one I set free." Why that was such an important distinction, she wasn't sure.

"Hmm." Charley turned back to the screen. "Quite a beauty for a wife. What did he say about her?"

"She died two months ago."

"Oh."

"Yeah." She Xed out of the picture before Charley had finished looking at it, then sank into her desk chair. Charley hit the button to lower Tess' desk, and waited for it to stop so she could sit on the edge of it.

"So he's technically available again, although two months is way too soon."

"Even if it wasn't, the underlying problems are all still there. I didn't want his life—they are at least multi-millionaires, Char, and a big part of society up there in their swanky New York town. You know me. That life isn't for me. I..." Tess stared out the window and rubbed her arms. "I'm a Tennessee girl from a working-class background. I had to make a choice."

"And you've been waiting for someone like him ever since."

"No. Well, not deliberately."

Anchey buzzed in. "Tess, your new client's on the line. Can you pick up?"

Charley arched an eyebrow, but Tess answered, "Sure thing. Send it through. Hey," she said to Mack as she picked up the receiver.

"Hey. I don't have your cell or I'd have just texted you. After you left, I went and rattled some cages. Krista was right and having you officially on board makes all the difference. Your team's got full access to the field, no worries, no issues, and if you get in touch with them, they'll give you the VIP treatment. All of a sudden, they're interested in getting this done." Already, his voice had more energy.

"Good," Tess said, fluttering her fingers at Charley for a piece of paper and a pen. She wrote down what he'd just said, then asked him for his number. "I'll be in touch," she said as Charley slipped out of her office.

"You sure?" He sounded scared, maybe a little desperate, and she wasn't sure why. She took a deep breath, reminding herself he wasn't hers to fix.

"Promise."

"Okay, then I need one more favor."

"If I can."

"I don't have to be back at the airport until later. Where should I go for lunch?"

THREE

Krista was waiting on the couch in the family room when Mack got back to the house after his day in Port Kenneth. It was late, but of course she'd stayed up. She was still keeping a motherly eye on him, and he appreciated it. "And?"

"She looks good," he said, knowing she wanted to hear about Tess. He gave her an air kiss beside each cheek, then sat down on the same couch, pushing into the corner so he could turn and face her better, but it was Tess he was seeing: the way her jeans had fit and held her ass the way he used to, the hiking boots, the lightweight dark purple sweater she'd worn that had followed her curves without being as tight as those jeans. And silver dangling earrings, of course. "She's more... womanly?" he said. "The tips of her hair are lavender and I don't know," he added on a sigh, trying not to think of those brown eyes that had locked onto him, the Cartieri bullshit detector, he'd once called them. One thing he knew not to mention was that Tess had a way of keeping him honest that surpassed any technique Krista had ever used.

She nodded. "And the field?"

He told her about his victory with the university. She answered with a "hmph" and then asked how it was, being back. As if he didn't go back every year for the team's alumni weekends. As if every time he'd gone back, he hadn't hoped he'd run into his Tess.

"It's a great little city. I had time to explore a bit of downtown, and it's begging for serious development. I don't know," he said, shaking his head, "but it's almost as if something about the place calls to me. Pulls at me. Like I belong there."

"Emerson. It's a city. It's not alive."

"Maybe it's just nostalgia." But he didn't think that. He couldn't remember ever going downtown when he was in school, so the idea that he'd felt at home there made no sense.

"Maybe you should take some time and learn your Mackenzie history already."

He eyed her. "What does that mean?"

"You are overdue to understand more than company details, Emerson. Some of what you learn about the Mackenzies might surprise you."

"Does it tie into Port Kenneth? Mother, it's hundreds of miles from here." He shook his head. This was more than he could handle. The day had been long, and seeing Tess and talking to her about Kelsey had hurt. He wasn't even sure what he'd told her. Had he even been coherent?

But, as he'd known she would, she'd understood. Her soft East Tennessee accent had held the same caress as the air, soothing him somehow.

"Tell me about the office," he said. "What did I miss today?"

"Well, our respective assistants had another spat."

"I'll talk to Taylor," he sighed. "But let's face it: Among her other issues, Meryem hates that Taylor is nonbinary."

Krista blinked and jerked her head back slightly. "Do you really think that?"

"Of course. PharmaSci is the domain of the old, straight white man, and Meryem was the most diverse hire at corporate until I brought Taylor in—and hiring an LBGTQ assistant opened the door to everyone else. Meryem's lost her crown, she's lost the power she had when you were more hands-on running things, and Taylor was the one who dethroned her, both in terms of diversity and power. And don't deny Taylor's an issue. You've heard Thomas' comments."

She pursed her lips slightly but didn't say anything.

"It's been a long day. I'm going to go lift for a bit, then go to bed," he said, bending down to give her another air kiss and immediately starting out of the room.

"Emerson?"

He paused, his back to her. "Yes?"

"Will this be a good project for you? Will it," she paused, and Mack pictured her licking her lips as she got too close to talking about those distasteful things called emotions, "will it help you heal?"

He closed his eyes briefly, picturing the surprise on Tess's face when he'd thrown the disc at her feet, the way she'd settled into understanding exactly what he wasn't able to tell her.

"Maybe," he said, knowing it wasn't the answer she wanted, but unable to give her anything more than that.

Four

October 6

The day had been crazy so far. Tess was working on three projects besides Field Emerson, and although each was in different phases, all three had decided that this was the day to be problematic. And she needed to get over to the Woolslayer neighborhood where, with Red's help, she ran a business incubator for the local women.

So when Tess' phone buzzed with yet another text and she saw it was from Mack, her stomach sank. They'd texted once a week about the field and she'd sent him the first major update, which was that they'd been to the field and were working up the initial site study. It was where she expected to be four weeks after the initial meeting, maybe a little ahead of schedule.

Just Tess! Had a thought. Does your team know enough about Ultimate? I know you personally do, but the rest of them?

Send me links? she replied. She'd been able to explain the basics: the size and dimensions of the field, the way the players hung out on the sidelines and their unique contributions to the play, seven players for each team on the field during a point. It had been basic and brief and hadn't touched the heart and spirit of the sport.

I can do that. Want video, too?

Only if it's of you. She hit send before she realized what she'd typed, so when she saw it pop up on her screen, no longer something she could edit, she knew her eyes got big. She closed them and hoped that if she opened them again, it would be gone.

It wasn't.

I can do that, he replied, with no emojis or anything that would give her a hint about how he'd taken it.

She set her phone down and mentally kicked herself. What was she doing? They had ended things—*she* had ended things—years ago, when he'd committed to going back to Lakeford and, with his mother's help, overthrowing his father and taking over the family business. As if something as large as PharmaScience Technologies was a *family business.* It was the antithesis of the women she worked with.

Her phone buzzed. *I'll have my assistant send those links over. Their name's Taylor, yes their pronouns are they/theirs, and don't freak out when they refer to me as Emerson. Remember: I sold out.*

Their pronouns? Are you sure you sold out?

Positive. I didn't set out to hire a non-binary assistant, but wait until you meet them. Which you'll do when they send you what you asked for.

Got a lot going on, she answered, *or afraid of how it'll look if you send me a ton of links all featuring the great Mack?*

Buried. This CEO stuff looks easy from the outside but that's a lie to make people actually want to do this job.

Tess didn't respond at first, trying to envision what his life could possibly look like. Probably the suits and ties he'd always dreaded. Meetings upon meetings.

Hey, Just Tess? Her phone pulled her out of her thoughts.

Yeah?

Now that we're talking again, can we agree to Google stalk each other?

Like you haven't been doing that all along?

Only a little bit. I had to find where you were so I could make sure I could hire you, but that was as far as I got.

Mack showing restraint? You really did sell out.

I warned you. Yes or no? Let the Google stalking begin?

Tess took a deep breath, her eyes closed. She held the breath, then opened her eyes and breathed out. *Yes,* she answered.

You have no idea how much I've missed you.

And her phone went quiet, letting her turn her attention back to the more immediate fires. The quick break, she noticed immediately, had been good for her. She'd needed it. Sometimes the famous Cartieri laser focus wasn't a good thing.

The rest of the day went quickly until she had to head over to Woolslayer. Once a month, she sat down with everyone renting space from her and discussed any problems they were having, either with the building or their business in general. She and Serenity Williams, one of her tenants and a life coach, had taken responsibility for setting up workshops for not only the other building tenants but any interested small business owner. They were getting a good reception about those, and Tess couldn't always believe it, but people in Woolslayer seemed to like having her around.

Sometimes she looked around and wondered what she was doing, the token privileged girl in the diverse group—as if the daughter of a high school art teacher and a manager at the glass factory was so privileged. What made her any different than they were? The fact that she had a college degree and a day job that paid her well? Well, some of them had college degrees and with her help, they'd all have jobs that paid them well.

At times, it felt like they built her up as much as she tried to give them the tools to build themselves and each other.

"So what else do you want or need?" she asked them once they'd gone through their agenda for the night. She had a list of issues in the building: a broken thermostat, a bird nest in a gutter on the roof, and more about the constant plumbing issues. Tess wondered if it came from little kids in the babysitting center flushing things they shouldn't. Two of the women needed desks, and Rivka, the psychologist, was getting rid of her starter couch in favor of something that was actually purchased new; did anyone want it?

No one did.

Tess frowned. Usually, they were more forthcoming. That meant at least one of them was sitting on something big.

"Let's hear it."

"We need something to bring us and the community together," Serenity said, looking around at the group. Tess noticed there were a few nods, but also a few of the women looked down at the ground.

Janeesa, the real estate agent, shook her head. "I don't agree. We *are* the community. What are you looking for, exactly?"

"Clients," Serenity said. "We should be serving the Woolslayer community."

"That's what I am here to do," Janeesa said, her frustration coloring her voice.

"I serve the neighborhood," Binh said. "There's no other day care or babysitting in Woolslayer."

"Other than you," Serenity said to Binh with a regal nod, "how many people in the community are educated about what the rest of us do?"

"So you need help with marketing," Tess said before Serenity could stir the situation up into something heated. "That's not so hard."

Gerri, who insisted she was the only Puerto Rican to get a Reiki certification, snorted. "Girl, you do not understand. Who's going to listen to a bunch of women?"

"You all have websites, right? Those are gender-neutral."

She was met with blank stares.

"Okay, there's our starting point." As mouths opened to protest, she stood up, holding her hands out, her coffee cup still clutched in one. "Hold on. Trade Creation already has a web person. Of course, if we can find a neighborhood someone to handle all of us, including TC, that would be better, but maybe that's a goal to work toward." She paced to the back of the room and spun. "But for now, let me talk to the woman I've already got in place." She paced back to the front. "This would be a great opportunity to freshen up my home page, too, so let's think about getting together for group pictures, as well. Every one of you should be featured on the Trade Creation site. You are *all* success stories I should be bragging about."

The women didn't look sold. Tess understood; most weren't online much, if at all. But if they started with web content, maybe they could then put together press kits, and from there, maybe they could find themselves a media contact and build a solid foundation for the business incubator as a whole and each woman and her business individually...

She could see how it would all work, and she explained it to them. "Anything else?" she asked when the conversation had exhausted itself. She stifled a yawn. "It's been a long day and I haven't gotten to work out yet, either." Honestly, instead of the gym, she'd rather take a walk. If it weren't dark and getting cold, she would. There was an intriguing trailhead only a few blocks from the incubator, and she had been wanting to check it out for some time now.

This wasn't the time for it, though. The last thing she needed was to be one of those women who showed up on the news, stupid enough to go walking alone in an unknown area after dark.

But wow, that trailhead called to her.

Once back at her place, she changed into leggings and an oversized t-shirt and settled on the couch with her tablet and a cup of tea. Now that she and Mack had agreed to Google stalk each other, it was time.

Finding information about him wasn't hard. PharmaSci was often in the news, but now, it was nice to see most of the news was positive. Before Mack had taken over, the stock had been stagnant, going back to a controversial drug, SH-34, that they had rushed to human testing. Seven people had died from it, including Tess' father. The company had been able to stop the stock from plummeting farther than it had, but once Mack's father had stepped down and Mack had taken over as CEO—in his twenties, which, Tess figured, went to show how awful Tristan had been—the stock was rising again.

The youngster CEO had turned himself into the thing he'd sworn he'd never be: a good Mackenzie man.

Tess tracked the changes he'd made at PharmaSci, including pulling out of some of the more risky and controversial drug development his father had loved so much. There had never been any doubt he'd do that. Not after they'd had some very hard conversations that essentially went *Your dad killed mine and now you and I are lovers and what's wrong with this picture?*

He'd made good on another promise, too, Tess saw: He'd restored the company's mission away from profit and back toward wellness. She wasn't sure what that meant, exactly, given that they were a company that focused on drugs for sick people, and wondered if it was worth her time to dig further.

First, though, she wanted to know about this mysteriously dead wife. Tess found the picture she and Charley had discovered. Kelsey had been as expected: as blonde and beautiful and close to a physical clone of Mack's mother as possible.

But as Tess looked at the pictures, she paused. There was something *off* about Kelsey. Her expression was blank, like she was drugged or had checked out, mentally.

Tess wondered which it was. She texted the link to her best friend.

Something's not right there, Jamie texted back. *She looks traumatized somehow—and not in that Mack's-having-too-much-fun way. But he sure looks good. He also looks like he's very solicitous of her. Like he cares, but I'm not seeing love between them. I saw Mack in love. I know what it looks like, and this isn't it.*

He told me there wasn't any.

Wasn't?

Tess related what little she knew of the story. With a deep breath, she closed all the sites with information about Mack. She'd seen enough. He had become exactly who she hadn't wanted to be with.

Tess?

Yeah?

You okay seeing all this? Working with him?

Yeah. It's over between us. He's living that life I refused to have.

Doesn't mean you can't or won't still have feelings.

I'm not Mrs. Mackenzie material. But she looked around her condo and wondered just what sort of material she was.

Five

October 7

"Tess," Red said when she got to the office the next day.

She knew a summons when she heard it.

"How'd it go with the business ladies last night?" he asked when she shut his office door behind her, pausing to make sure the clear glass turned opaque.

"I have a list of repairs and things they need."

Red held out his hand for it and fluttered his fingers when she wasn't immediately forthcoming.

"You can't keep doing this," she said, holding her tablet to her chest. "It's my problem to solve."

"It's *our* problem to solve. I'm your overlord."

She tried to hide the grimace that wanted to come out. "Believe me, I'm not going to forget that so fast."

"You sound resentful."

"No, not at all." She paused, looking out the window. Red had the best view of all of them, which was fitting. Sometimes, Tess thought if she had that view, she'd barely get any work done. Then again, she rarely looked at the view she *did* have. "I'm just stressed. I've been putting in more time here, as you know, and I feel like I'm not taking care of the Woolslayer ladies the way I need to. And now I need to get everyone websites and update the Trade Creation site."

"You're doing fine."

"It doesn't *feel* fine. It feels like I'm juggling a set of really precious and fragile gems and if I drop one, I'll stop being your golden child and live in shame and infamy the rest of my life."

"You put too much pressure on yourself."

She cocked an eyebrow. "Ya think?"

Anchey stuck his head in the office. "Tess, you didn't tell me Emerson Mackenzie was coming in for an update. There's nothing on your calendar and the conference room has Charley and some of the juniors in it..." He gave Tess a bewildered look, which she returned.

"What's he doing here?" she asked.

"He said you'd want to see him. I tried to tell him he needed an appointment, but he told me you'd make time."

"That's true, but..." She looked to Red for help, but he was watching the conversation unfold, his coffee cup in one hand, frozen halfway to his mouth.

"Small conference room?" Tess asked, feeling like her eyes had grown huge and had, maybe, gotten stuck that way.

"Felicia's spread out in it. She might be working on his field, in fact. I'm not sure."

"Okay," Tess said, closing her eyes and looking deep for patience. "Let's go get him. I'll take him to my office if you'll check with Felicia to see if she's got anything for him." She turned to Red and widened her eyes even more at him as Anchey left.

Red finished lifting his coffee to his mouth, the lines at his eyes crinkling just over the edge of the mug as he sipped. "This sort of spontaneous disruption might be exactly what you need," he said.

Tess whipped around, her hands at her sides, her eyes narrowing. "Not *this* kind!"

Red chuckled and set his mug down. "Send me that list of repairs and I'll get someone on it. Oh, and don't close your office door. Or if you do, remember the rules."

"Red!"

"You good if I send Reggie the plumber over to look at the water issue?"

"He's ignored the last three calls I've put in to him."

"I'll talk to him about that, too," Red said with a frown.

"Just Tess?" Mack's voice was loud and echoey, like he'd left reception and was in the hallway.

"Mackenzie?" Red asked her as she fought the urge to cover her face with both hands and weep.

"In all his disruptive glory," she said.

"He is just what you need."

"Red. Stop and think, will you? His wife's been gone for what? Three months now? And *I* dumped *him*. The reasons I did that haven't changed."

"Just don't shut your door, Tess. Or if you do, remember the rules," he repeated.

"Oh, you!" With a head shake, Tess left Red's office, making a beeline for Mack. "Wasn't expecting to see you today," she told him in greeting, stopping just out of range in case he wanted to hug her.

She couldn't bear being hugged by Mack, let alone while she was in front of her coworkers. It didn't help that he still looked good, in a green collared shirt and tan dress pants—very expensive dress pants, she noted. She wasn't sure if it was her imagination or if some of her coworkers were giving him appreciative looks of their own.

He shrugged. "I had to get out of town. And I like it here. Port Kenneth, I mean. It feels like coming home somehow."

"Next time, let us know so we can be ready for you." She started toward her office, deliberately putting her back to him so she couldn't see his expression. She'd put a little chill into her voice and she was willing to bet he was kicking himself for not thinking about her needs.

At least, the Mack she knew would have.

"I just figured you'd like the surprise," he said in a small voice and fell into step beside her. He craned his head to look at everything he could, she noticed. "This place is pretty cool."

"Thanks," she said and motioned to her office. "You're the client," she sighed when he just stood there. "You go in first."

"Oh," he said and started forward. "I guess that makes sense. I'm not used to being the client. Sorry." He shook his head.

She motioned him to the small table to the right of the door, but he either didn't see her or was ignoring her because he got busy examining the art on the walls.

She decided to take the time and clear off the table so they'd have a space in which to work. "Mack, it's a bad day, isn't it?" she asked softly.

He turned to her, surprise on his face melting away as he took her in, head to toe. She had worn black leggings and a loose magenta camisole, with a rose-colored long jacket over it, and ballet flats. It was her usual in-office look, but his smile made her think he liked something about it. "I should have known you'd see through me." He grimaced and looked up, over her head, rubbing the back of his neck. "I didn't love her, Tess. Why is it so hard?"

"Jamie's the therapist, not me, but I suspect she'd say you're either denying the fact you did love her, or you feel guilty you didn't love her the way you loved me."

The quick, electrified way he jerked his hand away from his neck told her it was the latter.

"I figured, in time... it'd grow, you know? I thought we had our lives in front of us." He snorted and turned his back to her. "Then again, I thought other things about you and me that turned out not to be true, so why do I keep coming back to the idea that Kelsey and I were going to get old together?"

"You hoped," Tess told him, wishing she was bold enough to reach out and touch him. Instead, she folded her arms over her chest and hoped she didn't look like she was hugging herself. "And that's okay," she continued.

"It's been months," he said and sank onto her couch. He braced his elbows on his thighs and cradled his head in his hands and again, Tess wanted to go to him and hold him.

"Give it time. I know that's the worst answer ever, but it's really all you can do. And go easier on yourself for not loving her. You need to do that, too."

Anchey knocked at her mostly closed door before sticking his head in. "Yes to Felicity working on your project right now." He looked from Tess to Mack and back at her again, raising his eyebrow in a question. She dropped her arms and lifted her chin, ready to defend and protect Mack, but he stood up, so Anchey continued. "She said it might be easier if you go to her since she's spread out in there."

"Let's go," she said, motioning to Mack, who was frozen in front of a black and white photograph of a shattered glass door that she'd taken about a year ago, the light catching the shards, darkness filling the spots where the glass had fallen away.

"This," he said softly.

Tess motioned to Anchey and went to stand beside Mack. He put his hand on her shoulder, gently, like he was afraid to.

His hesitation wasn't why she let it stay.

"Who's the photographer? Think they'd make me a copy of this?"

"I am, and it's no big deal. I got lucky."

"When did you turn into a photographer?"

"I didn't. Like I said, I was on site and this caught my eye and I got lucky."

"I doubt that," he said and tilted his head toward the door. "Lead on."

She did, and Felicia mercifully had information for them. They spent so long poring over the plans that Anchey stuck his head in. "Shall we order in for a late lunch?"

"Is—" He gulped. "Tess, can we— It's probably too far out of the way—"

"English, Mack."

"Burger Emporium? Any chance?" He looked so hopeful, giving her the best version of his puppy dog eyes that she wondered how she'd ever built up an immunity to them.

Just as fast, he regained his composure, sitting back, one hand on his chest like he was holding his tie in place. Tess cocked her head, recognizing the gesture. Holding his tie... she'd never realized that's what he was doing. It was such an ingrained habit in him that she'd wondered, of course, but back then, no one had worn ties. They were college students.

And he'd been a kid who'd grown up in an environment where ties had been required.

"No," she said heavily and at length. "No chance."

Felicia looked between them. "Burger Emporium? What's that?"

"*Was*," Tess said. "Used to be our favorite place. It was out in Covington."

"Best burgers I've had," Mack said. He sighed heavily and shook his head, his eyes closed. "Just Tess, pick something."

"Have your tastes changed?"

"Gotten snobbier, I'm sure," he said with another sigh, then stood up. "On second thought, maybe you're right and this wasn't such a good idea. I should get back home, see what's tried to blow up while I've been gone."

Before Tess could get up to guide him out, he left the conference room.

She had to chase after him; he'd gone the wrong way. "We still have things to discuss," she said, eyeing him. "About the field. Let's bring in sushi and get back to work."

He leaned against a wall, in between two pictures, his eyes squeezed shut. "Maybe this was a bad idea. The whole thing. You're right; I know better than to show up uninvited. Just... you get so used to everyone dropping everything when you walk in that I wasn't thinking."

"Mack?"

He smiled slightly, but Tess thought it was tinged with sadness. "Man, I miss being Mack."

"Yeah? I Google stalked you, you know. Looks like you're doing good things."

"Yeah, and it's Emerson who's doing it. I didn't entirely lose Mack, but it feels like he's in hiding or something. I was hoping if I showed up, good old spontaneous Mack..."

Tess grabbed him by the wrist and pulled him back to the conference room. Felicia hadn't left. "Fe, would you and Anchey come up with some sushi for lunch, and we'll get back to work in a few?"

"Sushi? Good thinking. Soup or salad?"

"Sure," Mack and Tess said in unison. They locked eyes and for a second, Tess forgot where they were.

But then the unhappiness slid back over Mack's eyes and the spell was broken.

Six

October 14

A week after his impromptu trip, Mack met his mother for lunch, greeting her with the proper air kisses, holding his tie in place so it wouldn't hit her as he leaned forward and down. If he'd ever dared to roll his eyes at her, this would have been the perfect time, since he knew perfectly well she would stand up to greet anyone else. And for anyone else, he'd have skipped the tie.

"Sit, Emerson," she said. "We have much to discuss."

"Go ahead," he said, glancing at the small plates covering the table as he took a seat. She'd remembered and asked them to go easy on the balsamic drizzle over the fresh mozzarella.

She surprised him with a smile. "I heard from Tristan. He has bought property in Tahiti now and still has no intentions to return or interfere with our project."

Mack couldn't help it; he grinned as he put his napkin on his lap.

But his mother was frowning. "Removing him from our lives was only one step in a long process. Don't start getting cocky." She gave him a long look. "*You* are the current Mackenzie. He understands that."

He wondered what parts of her soul she'd had to give up to make sure of that.

"I always thought getting me to take over was his only mission. That, and trashing the company so thoroughly, I'd have no company *to* take over. As if Cullen hadn't tried that already." He paused. Krista hadn't liked his grandfather; she'd never made a secret of that. But he'd lately wondered if that was because Cullen had recognized her ambition and been threatened by it. PharmaSci was, after all, the *Mackenzie* family legacy. Only a Mackenzie could be at the helm.

Certainly, his former father-in-law had wanted it, regardless of that rule. That's what had led Kelsey to...

He cut that thought off and focused on his mother.

"If Tristan or Cullen let it spiral out of control, it's only because they would never listen to my input."

"Which has been golden. Thanks for that."

Krista's one-shoulder shrug was cool and elegant, but Mack watched her fight a smile. He and his mother had never had much of a relationship until the day he'd demanded Tristan set things right with the families of the victims of experimental drug SH-34. That had triggered something and Krista had come for him, although, to be fair, when she laid it all out, it wasn't a hard decision to make. It was losing Tess that had been excruciating.

It was a genuine coincidence, so far as anyone seemed to know, that one of the seven families involved with SH-34 had been Tess's. But learning that had set everything into motion: he'd forced Tristan to set it right, Krista had showed up the very next night, and Mack had begun seeing and appreciating a whole new side of her. His mother was *savvy*. Tristan was all the bigger fool for not seeing that and valuing it.

This was the first time in all the years that he'd thanked her. She'd guided him, helped him curry favor with the board and gain their approval to overthrow his father, and now she was helping him reimagine the business that had been passed down through generations of Mackenzie men.

"That's the first thing," she said and led him through a quick discussion of other outstanding issues they'd been working on.

"And one more thing," Mack added when she finished, tapping his napkin to his lips.

"Go ahead."

"I've been doing rough cost comparisons, and do you know how much money we'd save if we moved the corporate headquarters to another city?"

She set down her fork and paused, her hands returning to her lap. "PharmaSci has deep roots in Lakeford."

"And it's incredibly expensive to be here. If we moved to one of these up-and-coming cities that's offering massive tax breaks, put in as many green features as we could, and even paid to move every employee in the current corporate headquarters, we'd still save a nice chunk of change every year. And that's just *preliminary* figures."

He let out a breath when she cocked her head. "Let me look into it," she said at last, picking her fork back up and spearing a grilled artichoke heart. "Now," she said after she'd chewed and swallowed, "this may not be the most welcome of discussions, but we need to have a serious talk about your status as a widower."

Mack set down his water glass and sat back in his chair, eyeing her. Part of him knew he should have expected this, but that didn't mean that made it an easier discussion. "You said six months, Mother. We're not there yet."

"I did, but something happened today that we need to discuss."

Mack groaned.

"Yes, it's that bad," Krista said, folding her hands in her lap and tucking her feet, crossed at the ankle, underneath her chair. "I ran into Alyssa Schoenstrom today. She seems to fully expect to be your next wife."

There were no words.

"Emerson? Now, I am sure you'll agree that Alyssa would barely be a suitable partner for you. I don't think she would stop to consider your needs and wants."

"Mother, Alyssa's the girl who slept with everyone in our high school class *except* me. Guys, girls, she didn't care so long as I knew how much contempt she had for me."

"High school wasn't your best self."

"You noticed?" He cocked an eyebrow at her. "I know you'd like to see me and Tess together. But remember, she walked away because she didn't want to be part of this world. She didn't want the money, the power, the games—none of it."

"But you just told me you want to be where she is. Why, if not to be with her?"

"Maybe I just want her as a friend. If you haven't looked lately, I don't have many."

"You've been busy, your attention on PharmaSci."

"That's not likely to change anytime soon. And neither is Tess's attitude," he said, wondering what it would take for her to understand.

"Well, tell me how the field is coming."

"Do you want to hear about the field," Mack asked tiredly, "or more about Tess?"

"What's the difference?"

Seven

October 15

R ed paused, his coffee cup mere centimeters from his lips. "Tess, in my office," he said and took the sip that meant the daily status meeting was over.

Tess paused to talk to Anchey a minute before following Red. "What's up?"

"Reggie went out and took a look at your building. The problem's not the babysitting business. Good choice with the toilets in there, by the way. He says they'll flush pretty much anything."

Tess smiled.

"The building is sound. You did a good job replumbing it, except—"

She braced herself. They'd had to gut the old building; it had stood empty for so many years, the roof had started to rot, water had gotten in, floors had fallen apart. It had probably been a week away from being condemned when Tess had bought it. Maybe that's why the city had sold it for a song. Or maybe it had been Red's influence. Either way, she was grateful.

Red tapped a pen against his coffee cup. "The problem isn't the job, or the building."

Understanding hit and Tess winced. "It's streetside."

Red nodded.

"And that's city property," she continued, thinking out loud, "which means... oh, Red, just shoot me now. Don't tell me I have to deal with it."

"We're not done," he said, holding the pen up as if to focus her attention. "That entire block, at a minimum, needs attention."

"In a working-class, highly diverse area that most people like to avoid."

They fell quiet for a minute, Tess telling herself not to panic. There was going to be a solution to this. There had to be.

Good thing she had Red at her back.

He started tapping his pen against his coffee cup. After a long minute, he stopped and said, "Think there's a photographer in the neighborhood who can capture some beauty and vibrancy around the area? We need the best of what your building and the rest of that block can give. Let's hit the city council and the mayor's office with every possible reason to take action, and fast, before we're looking at a worst-case scenario."

"We should just accept that's where we're going to end up."

"And the hope is that if we can take action and get the city to prioritize this before it's a problem, it'll save them money in emergency repairs and a longer closure later."

"Do we really have the clout to do this?" Tess asked. She stared out the window, looking in the direction of her building. Although it was walking distance away, she couldn't see it through the rest of the fringes of downtown Port Kenneth. Her beloved building—and the people who occupied it. They deserved for her to do battle for them.

"Us? No. That's where the court of public opinion is going to come in. And maybe a city councilperson or two." Red shot her a quick grin, the one that told her he was already two steps ahead.

"Why do you keep doing this for me?" But she was beyond grateful, and they both knew it.

"Bunch of reasons," he said and picked up his coffee cup. "I don't want to lose you, I think you can be more than the excellent self you are for us here, and you make the company look good." He held his cup out in a sort of toast. "And it's fun. But right now? Get busy so I don't have to fire you for being a slacker."

"That'll be the day," Tess laughed as she turned to leave, already coming up with a game plan.

Unfortunately, it would have to wait. She had a full day of projects already, and she hadn't heard from Mack since his visit. She was overdue to talk to him.

Two days later, she was still waiting for Mack, but she had managed to make time to sit down with Serenity. They could have done it over text, but Tess loved it when she could spend time in the neighborhood. It was a comfortable place to be, where people knew each other and talked to each other, unlike where she lived. "Do you know someone in the neighborhood who is good with a camera?" she asked and outlined why.

Serenity took a minute to think. "There's that young woman who takes pictures every day and puts them on social media," she said after the pause had started to get long. "But she's left the neighborhood and is adamant about not returning. Let me talk to people, and then we'll go to war." She patted Tess' knee. "It seems like a lot, but it's not more than you can conquer."

"On the one hand, I know you're right, and this is actually going to be a fun fight that fits with our idea of being more visible in the neighborhood, but on the other hand, I hate that we're all going to have to put resources into this."

"These are the things that pull a community together."

There was no argument for that. And since she was back in Woolslayer, she decided to go check out that trailhead she'd been curious about.

Just as she got there, though, her mother called. The trail, once again, would have to wait.

Good thing it wasn't going anywhere.

Eight

October 22

"You needed this," Jamie told Tess the following weekend after they'd snuck away from Jamie's husband and twins and headed out along that trail that Tess kept trying to explore.

"So did you," she agreed, picking her way along. When they'd gotten up to it, they'd discovered it wasn't actually a trailhead and now that they were probably a hundred steps in, it was nothing more than a deer trail. They had debated bagging it, but Tess had been too curious. "What if it's something?" she'd asked Jamie. "And we're together. What's the worst that happens?"

"We find some creepy axe murderer who's fast enough to take us both out?" Jamie answered and motioned Tess ahead.

"I'm not sure if we needed the time away from everything or just an adventure in general," Tess said, holding a branch out of her way.

"Well, I needed the excuse to sneak away from Hank and the twins. I will admit that freely."

"If I didn't know any better, I'd wonder if you liked them," Tess teased. The trail took them along a fence, one of those traditional wooden split-rail fences. On the other side, the grasses had grown knee high and looked undisturbed. Interestingly, even though the side she and Jamie were on was forested, there were no saplings of any size inside the fence.

Tess paused for a minute, studying what was in front of her. Was the area enclosed by something she couldn't see, and some sapling-eating animal was stuck inside? How could there be zero trees inside the fence and a forest outside? Even right along the fence line, where you'd expect the two different habitats to mingle, there were clear lines.

There were spots in the city where trees had been planted on the edges of the sidewalk. The concrete in spots had been upended and any available soil nearby was often full of renegade trees.

This made no sense. She opened her mouth to ask Jamie what she made of it, but Jamie had continued walking—and talking.

"They're twins: they're rambunctious, they're cute, and they're mine, so I'm stuck with them," Jamie was saying, "and the scary part is that I don't mind. Good thing; I don't think the baby store takes returns."

Tess chuckled at the idea of a baby store and scrambled to catch up. "And how's Hank? I haven't seen him in eons."

"He's Hank. Solid, dependable, the love of my life."

They followed the trail along the fence line. Nothing changed: forest outside, grassy plain inside, and not a clue as to how or why.

"Marriage is hard," Jamie sighed at length, just as Tess was about to ask her opinion on the strange vegetation.

Tess stopped walking. "Marriage is hard? What gives?"

Jamie grabbed at a long piece of grass underneath the bottom piece of fence. "Tell me about you and Mack."

Tess snorted. "There *is* no me and Mack. We're working on a project together. That's it. That's all it *can* be."

"Yeah, but... You said he's widowed. What else?"

"I have no idea. We haven't talked about much beyond the field."

Jamie's eyes got huge. "What? Tess? For real? You and Mack not talking about every-thing under the sun?"

"For now. I'm okay with it," she said although she was struck by a pang that might have been a bolt of lightning, and she glanced at the sky. Still blue and beautiful. Not a storm cloud in sight.

"Talk to me," Jamie said.

"Why? Don't you get enough of people talking to you all day at work?"

"Yes, but this is you, and besides, I don't want to think."

"That's not a good sign." Tess turned and started walking again.

"Hank's thinking of quitting his job and going the start-up route. But at the same time, what he really really wants is to be a stay-at-home dad to the boys."

Tess froze at that bombshell. "Can't say I blame him," she said after a breeze had fluttered their hair and the trees around them, a few red and orange leaves fluttering past them. Even the grasses inside the fence bowed. "They say kids are little for such a short time."

"And that's my issue," Jamie said, finger combing her hair. She let out a big breath. "We have savings and I'm making a good salary. But on the other hand, we have preschool tuition for two coming up and we should be saving for college *now*, and then there's the day-to-day costs of taking care of four of us..."

"It sounds like you're expecting him to stay home."

"I kind of am. He really wants to, and it's only another year until they're in preschool, which will give him a couple hours a week to work on a start-up or as a part-time consultant." She glanced at Tess. "I think it's the whole idea of a start-up that scares me the most. One salary, we can manage... for a while. Consulting isn't as steady, but that's about networking and being available when you're needed, and Hank's always had great timing."

Tess nudged her and Jamie chuckled.

"Business, Tess."

"I didn't say anything."

"A start-up just seems so... *big*. Risky." She looked out over the grasses. "Like it could rip your heart out and eat it while it still beats."

They were quiet for a minute, watching the grassy area behind the fence.

"Why aren't there any trees in there?" Tess asked.

"What?" Jamie turned to her. "Where did that come from?"

"Look. There's no trees. But think about the city. Trees do everything they can to grow in the middle of all that concrete. Why? What's going on?"

Jamie shrugged. "Maybe it's the type of tree. Maybe the city trees like close quarters and that"—she pointed to the pasture—"is not close quarters. C'mon. Let's go."

Tess started forward once more, realizing that she could only see the trail to the corner of the grassed-in area. Did it continue around the corner?

It did, and when she rounded it, Tess skidded to a stop, Jamie squealing and knocking into her from behind. "Tess! What did you do—oh, hello."

An elderly man stood in the trail, which still wasn't wide enough for one person, let alone for Tess and Jamie to have passed him. His hair, what there was of it, was white and bushy. His eyebrows matched, and he wore a sweatshirt that said WOOLSLAYER JUNIOR HIGH in faded grey letters that once might have been silver.

"Didn't anyone tell you two this is no place to be?" he asked, squinting as he looked them over, as if he needed glasses.

"I tried—" Jamie said, but Tess nudged her quiet.

"No," she said. "I was curious what's here."

The old man nodded toward the fenced-in area. "That's what's here."

"So I see. But what *is* it? And why are there no trees in it?"

"Used to be a farm. A sheep farm, of all the cockamamie things."

"A sheep farm?" Tess tilted her head down so she could look up at the man. "For real."

"For real. And you shouldn't be here. For that matter, I shouldn't be here, but at least I know what I may find."

"And what's that?" She crossed her arms over her chest and waited, acutely aware of Jamie shifting her weight, probably expecting the guy to pull out an axe and chase them.

"I don't know if you hold with any of the old beliefs, but this land has seen more than its share of human misery, and it's held on to it. This land cries out for love, but no one can get near it long enough to love it and exorcise the blood and the deaths."

Tess gazed at the overgrown pasture. As she looked at it, she could feel something, something dark, threatening, and creepy—or maybe she was telling herself to, since the man was telling her that it was there. But if he was right, maybe it explained the lack of trees? "Who owns it?"

"No one's sure. There's lots of stories, but they're just stories."

"No one's been down to City Hall to look at the records?"

The man shrugged. "Most of us try to stay away from that place. Most of us try to avoid this place, too."

"Most. But not you."

He turned and looked out over the field. "Every so often, I like to come out this way. I hear them, you know. The spirits. They talk and I listen." He turned his light brown eyes on Tess. "You probably think I'm just some crazy old Black man."

"I'm not sure what to think except that I doubt your being Black has anything to do with it."

"Well, take it from old Harald. Being Black has *everything* to do with it, but that don't mean this is a place to spend your time. It works on a person, gets under their best intentions."

"It is creepy back here," Jamie said.

"You're lucky you ran into me. You girls should head back. No sense in bad things happening to the both of us if the spirits get stirred up."

Tess opened her mouth to argue, then closed it. There was no doubt he believed what he was saying.

"Yeah," she said. "We should go." She pointed over her shoulder.

"Good idea," Jamie said and was halfway to the bend in the trail before Tess and the old man stopped staring each other down.

"What *was* that?" Jamie asked when Tess had caught up to her. It wasn't easy; Jamie wasn't exactly dawdling.

"Ten times better than an axe murderer?" Tess asked, and the two of them chuckled, more out of relief than because Tess had been funny. "But beyond that, I'm not sure." She gazed at the grass... had this been a sheep pasture at one time? And what was that about human misery? And why hadn't the forest encroached?

"I think that puts you up one," Jamie said, her pace not slowing any. "You have this place and Mack, and I only have Hank's situation."

"Why are we counting?" That was one of Jamie's cardinal rules: no keeping score.

"Because it's that or scream as I run back to our cars."

"We're fine," Tess told her. "Slow down. Nothing happened. I mean, not really." She glanced over her shoulder, half-expecting the old man to be watching them, but he hadn't followed them.

She wasn't sure how she felt about that.

"You were telling me about Hank staying home with the boys."

Jamie glanced at her, almost as if she resented Tess steering the conversation away from anything potentially creepy. "There's just so much to work out. Like days like this, for example. I can't be running out on him if he's the parent on duty most of the time. I'll be stuck at home with the boys every weekend." She eyed Tess. "You should come help me. You can be Aunt Tess."

"Me? I'm awful with kids."

As they came into the clearing at the trailhead, Jamie gave her a mischievous smile. "But you need to learn, now that Mack's back in your life."

"First off, he's a *client*. And second, he'll probably just hire nannies."

"Mack? Nah. He'll be crawling on the floor with those kids and you'll be wondering how many adults are in the family."

"Sounds like Hank."

"He is a fantastic father." Jamie hugged herself. "I just don't know..."

"Do you have to decide now?"

Jamie eyed her, but Tess shrugged. So what if it had been the question Jamie would have asked, if the situation were reversed? It was a good question. The therapist didn't own a monopoly on good questions.

"It'll work out," Tess said. "Even if, yes, I have to come over on some Saturday morning while Hank's out doing guy things and we let the boys make messes with syrup after we make them pancakes."

"They're a little young for that."

"Nope," Tess said. They stood between their cars and Tess felt a pang. She didn't want this adventure to end, even though she was dying to see if she could learn anything about a strange sheep farm on the outskirts of town. "But for the record, I was probably the kids' ages when my dad got me started with his weekend rituals." It was her favorite memory of her father: his French maid's apron, his weekly attempt at pancakes, grabbing her mother first and then Tess and dancing them around the kitchen until the pancakes burned and they all went out for a big breakfast buffet. Usually he'd take the apron off, but every so often, he'd declare he *had* to wear it so everyone could see the evidence of how hard he'd tried to provide for his wife and daughter. "The perfect family," he used to say and would grab Tess' mother for another waltz around the kitchen while Tess laughed and clapped.

No wonder she'd fallen so hard for Mack. He'd had that same spirit.

"Thinking about Mack again?" Jamie asked. "And don't deny it. You always get this expression when you do."

Tess shook her head. "It doesn't matter. We should probably get going."

"Nice avoidance technique. Don't be afraid to embrace the inevitable return of Mack in your life."

"Can I declare him off limits?"

Jamie produced her car key. "You can try, but don't expect to succeed."

"You're as bad as he ever was," Tess muttered.

Nine

October 29

Mack paused before he opened his bedroom door. Krista would be in the house somewhere, lying in wait for him, and he wasn't in the mood. He was already on the verge of being late for practice, and being late for practice meant the whole team did extra sprints.

Because of him, the whole team did extra sprints fairly often.

He tried sneaking out through the kitchen, but *lying in wait* meant she had all exits covered. He really needed to look into an escape route out one of the windows in his rooms. It was a two-floor suite. One of the windows on the ground floor was bound to be in the right spot that he could jump through it from time to time.

"Emerson?"

He pulled out his phone and sent a text to the group. *Late again.* He checked the time; he had about a minute to spare before the notification was considered late and they'd run sprints anyway, with extra for him. He'd just made it so the whole team wouldn't suffer. Only him. He always got the extra.

"Emerson? I know you're there."

With a propriety he didn't feel, he turned to his mother as she appeared in the kitchen, leaning in to give her the proper air kisses. Her hair was up in its twisty thing, her outfit was her usual: light pants and a navy blue shirt with matching sweater buttoned over her throat. "Good morning. Can it wait? I have practice."

"I was just wondering where you were last night."

"At the gym until seven, and then here, like you asked. Where were you and Logan?"

"At the benefit for the environmental center, as you requested of *us*. Colleen Mayes was asking about you, by the way. I believe she's single and interested, and she had a friend with her as well. Did you talk to Tess?"

"Not about dating her," he said, trying to remain calm. "Not to change the subject, but why did Tristan go so utterly bonkers about my going to Kenilworth?"

"Well, it's not Yale," she said slowly. She turned as Logan entered the room and gave her air kisses, his hands possessive on her elbows, then greeted Mack as he turned to pour coffee.

"I wouldn't have come out of Yale with my ATC."

Krista wrinkled her nose. "I still have reservations about my son designing workouts all day."

"You know there's a lot more to being an athletic trainer than that, Mother," he said, giving her a dark look. "I loved the science behind it, I loved knowing I could help people, and don't think it hasn't come in handy a time or two at work."

"Oh, I know," she said, waving him off. "And from that standpoint, your reasoning is solid. It's just," she paused, studying Logan for a long minute before turning back to Mack. "How you help people matters."

He eyed her. "What does that mean?"

"It means you're doing a larger amount of good for a larger amount of people where you are. And that is much, much more important than designing workouts."

Mack snorted. "Sure. When the average, ordinary people who need our drugs can't afford them, we raise prices and make them choose between food and medicine. Or rent and medicine. Or all of the above." He glowered at her. This had been one of his pet peeves. That and those stupid coupons you had to be lucky enough to get your hands on. "That's not exactly doing good. Not the kind we *should* be doing."

"While I'm glad to see you returning to the company's historical emphasis on wellness, you are forgetting—again—that you are ahead of your peers on these subjects. You have to coax them along."

"How?"

She gave him a look. "Slowly, Emerson. You can't simply walk in and turn the entire industry on its head."

"Why not?"

With a sigh, she looked up at the ceiling. "We have been over and over this. If you want to have a company to run, tearing the industry apart will not allow you to achieve that goal. Some things," she said and pierced him with a look, "you need to tackle slowly, step by step, so that the people around you aren't so aware of what you are doing. Look at Flemming's actions with Kelsey. That may be an uncomfortable situation, but there's much to learn from how your former father-in-law handled you both."

Mack snorted. "How he *played* all of us, you mean."

"Perhaps." She stood up and held a hand out to Logan. "But if you can strip the emotion out of the situation and look at it clinically, you will see the perfect roadmap to achieve many of your goals. Slow, Emerson. Stealthy. Learn the Mackenzie-PharmaSci history. And don't forget to employ a full dose of charm."

That was worth considering, especially because it was a direct contrast to how his father had approached his own tenure at the head of PharmaSci. He'd killed seven people with his SH-34 experiment. Mack, fourteen, pimply, and hormonal, had seen the pictures.

He'd never been the same—and not just because it was the moment in which he'd forged his alliance with Krista. Of course, he hadn't known that for a few more years. He'd only known there was absolutely no way he would let himself turn into his father. No one was going to die like *that* on his watch.

"Speaking of charm," Krista went on, looking Mack over, "tights again?"

"I hear they show off my legs."

"To all the men on your team."

"They bring their wives and girlfriends. Sometimes. Rarely," he said, feeling sheepish. "But there are other people around in the park," he offered.

"I'd sooner see you with Colleen Mayes."

"*You* would sooner see me with Tess. And unless we figure out how to get me down to Port Kenneth, Mother, there's no hope."

Krista considered him, her eyes narrowing slightly. "*Mother,*" she said in a horrible imitation of him, "*if we move the corporate office, we can save a ton of money.*"

Mack opened his mouth to respond, but the truth was that she had him. "Slow and steady with that, too?"

"Oh, Emerson," Krista said as she leaned against Logan, Mack blinking at the rare contact between his ever-proper mother and her longtime love, "slow and steady is the *only* way."

TEN

November 4

Tess stopped in front of Anchey's desk and glared at him. "I am going to go out to grab a coffee. The line is going to be very long. You are not going to disturb me, and I will be back when I am back, regardless of who is looking for me."

"That kind of day, huh?"

"Aren't they all?" she asked and tossed her hair over her shoulder as she opened the glass door to the office and paused in the atrium.

Anchey followed her. "Just so you know, Cartieri, I didn't go to Princeton so I could hold your phone calls."

"Hate to break it to you, Anchey," she answered, "but you didn't go to Princeton."

"Exactly!" he called after her as she went outside and paused, feeling the afternoon sun and the humid, early November air. It had started to cool off, which was both good and bad. Good because weather like this was her favorite, maybe because it never lasted long. But bad because it meant the city would probably cite the changing seasons as a reason to put off the work in front of her incubator.

She and Red were leaning on the city as much as possible, and they'd recruited the other businesses directly on the street to help. Reggie had offered his diagnostic skills to anyone in the area in an attempt to determine how far the problem ran, and they'd found it was a good three blocks, ending at what had once been an old firehouse and was now an empty lot.

That made the potential fix easy, Tess had thought. But the ownership of the lot had wound up being in dispute, and the city refused to dig until they had at least figured out who was supposed to pay: taxpayers, or the owner of the lot, or the city, or the people who owned all the buildings in the affected area, or... They kept coming up with longer and longer lists of people who could potentially pick up the tab.

Red had laughed at the Woolslayer councilwoman, Rheda Salveggio, and the mayor's office. "The people who live and work in that neighborhood are about to unleash holy hell on you," he'd told them.

And they were in the middle of doing just that. Serenity had found Tess' photographer, a junior in high school with a secondhand camera and a principal who was trying to find ways to keep the kid in school. With Georgie's photography skills, they had gotten busy quickly, too quickly to organize the way Tess would have wanted.

Janeesa had helped them basically hijack an abandoned butcher shop at the far end of the block from Tess' building. When they got inside, Tess had asked how it still smelled like blood. Serenity had shaken her head and laughed at her. "The pampered white girl," she'd said with a sad smile, but Tess hadn't backed down. The place *stunk*.

But it had the perfect windows for an impromptu art gallery.

Sanjit at Tess's office had made posters explaining the issue, and they'd hung them along with Georgie's pictures. Neighbors were coming to see the activity, but so far, the media had been scarce.

They needed the media.

On a whim, they changed the pictures to feature a spontaneous neighborhood party that had happened during trick-or-treating. Sanjit changed his posters, as well, and the community finally understood what was at stake. They were on borrowed time, and if they wanted more fun parties, they had to fix the water issue.

And at last, media had finally come around.

Red beamed at Tess like a proud papa.

She'd never been more exhausted. Invigorated, too, especially as she got to know more people in the neighborhood. But at times like now, the exhaustion overrode it all and sneaking out of the office was the only way to get through the workday.

The coffee shop wasn't nearly as busy as Tess had hoped, so once she had coffee in hand—complete with extra whipped cream because she deserved it, dammit—she slid into a seat beside the window and watched the people walk by. They were definitely different than in Woolslayer: whiter, more professionally dressed, striding with a purpose, their faces closed off. Many were, of course, sunk into their phones.

And none of them looked any happier than she currently felt.

With a sigh, she propped her cheek on her fist and stared instead at the surface of her coffee and the whipped cream that was melting into it.

"That bad?" someone asked.

She jerked her head up, startled, and gave the man who was speaking to her a polite smile. "Have we met?"

"I doubt you've even noticed me, but we pass each other here at least once a week."

"Oh." She scrounged the energy to cringe.

He shook his head and pointed to the chair across from her, his eyebrows raised. She nodded. "Don't feel bad," he said as he took a seat, not pulling the chair in toward the table and immediately sitting back, as if he were carefully giving her space. "Most mornings, I don't feel like saying hello to anyone, either."

"Is this where you say creepy things like seeing me helps brighten your entire day?"

He laughed self-consciously and adjusted the lid on his take-out cup. It was a refillable one, Tess noticed with approval, and took in the rest of him: light brown hair in a longish little boy cut, brown eyes, a demure tie over a white shirt with just the edge of what was probably a smart watch showing, no rings on his hands and no visible tattoos or piercings. "I hope not," he said. "And don't think I've become the office coffee boy because I'm hoping to catch a glimpse of the cute brunette who seems so sure of herself, she'd never give the time of day to someone like me."

"Two thirteen," Tess said with a wink.

He smiled and nodded. "Thanks." He stood up. "I should get back. I envy you, that you can sit here and decompress."

Tess took a deep breath, as if that could fortify her for what was waiting at the office. "I actually can't," she said.

"Can I be forward enough to give you my card?"

"Please," Tess said and smiled. She had no illusions this would go anywhere—it rarely did—but it was nice to think that it might.

He set the card on the edge of the table and left the shop as if afraid she wouldn't take it. Or maybe, she realized as she noticed him outside, trying to look like he was simply getting his bearings, he was watching to see if she'd reach for it.

She did and read it, turning away from the window before he could see her reaction.

He worked in the mayor's office.

It figured. It really did.

She wondered if he'd known who she was when he'd approached her. For all that certain people around town knew her name, most didn't know her face. She certainly hadn't recognized his—but then, Red was the one who knew people at the mayor's office, not her.

If there was a way to make this work in favor of her building and the neighborhood, she was going to figure out it—and use it.

But in the meantime, she had to get back. She was willing to bet that four different fires were waiting for her. And she, of course, would rise to the challenge.

Some days, she wondered why she'd chosen this life when she could have picked something else. She'd been at a different firm when Red had invited her to come work for him. If she had stayed where she was, how many of the buildings that she'd helped save would have been torn down?

She wouldn't have been able to live with herself if she'd been responsible for that much destruction of perfectly good space. Those old buildings didn't need to be torn down and replaced with slick new eye-catching marvels. They were the city's history, both good and bad, and there were ways to modernize them, green them, reduce their carbon load and remind people of just how far Port Kenneth had come—although, to be fair, they still had a long way to go.

Just like that, an idea for Mack's stadium popped into her head.

"Is Charley busy?" she asked Anchey when she got back inside.

"Wasn't my turn to watch her," he said with a shrug.

She nodded and went to find Charley. Why they hadn't thought of this earlier, she wasn't sure, but at least they were still in early stages. The university had gotten back to them and requested certain details, and they were supposed to video conference with Mack about the stands and the locker rooms he'd decided he wanted. It was time to see how far they could go on the funds already committed, and they would probably have to play the game to see how much more he was willing to invest.

Charley liked her ideas about the university's requests and launched into some of her own, but Tess got lost in her thoughts, toggling between memories of Mack on the field, physical, fast, and ferocious, and a man with light brown hair who left his business card on a table, hoping she'd take it. There was a cruelty to it: two men to potentially let in her life, and both had serious disqualifying traits.

"Tess? Hello? What happened to the famous Tess Cartieri laser-sharp focus?"

"It wore out," she said.

"You and me both," Charley said. She glanced around. "You free for dinner tonight?"

"Yeah," Tess said slowly, hoping this wasn't a pretext for a bitch session. Some complaining, she could handle. But not two hours of it. "Come get me when you're ready."

"Girl, I am ready *now*."

"Me, too, but it's a bit early yet." It was just after four. "Come get me after six. But we're not spending the whole time talking about Mack."

"Buzzkill," Charley said, but Tess ignored her and turned from the field project to something else. She wasn't coming back to the office after dinner; it was yoga night, and afterward, probably another hour or two fruitlessly trying to dig up information on that weird sheep farm she and Jamie had found.

Eleven

November 17

There was something about the clarity that good exercise gave a girl, Tess thought two weeks later as she wiped down her bike after spin class. It was almost as good as the clarity that came with really good sex, but truth be told, it had been so long since she'd known that state that she'd almost forgotten it existed.

Her exercise-induced clarity was telling her it was time to reach out to the guy at the mayor's office.

No time like the present, she told herself.

At home, she showered and pulled her wet hair into a ponytail. No one outside of the house ever saw her like this. Okay, Jamie and Mack and their other roommate, Mary, used to, but that was a long time ago. At least Mack hadn't screamed the first time she'd done it, like he'd apparently done to Mary the first time he'd seen her in the morning without her makeup on. Even though Tess hadn't been there to see it, she still chuckled at the idea.

Mack had, it seemed, grown up seeing his mother always turned out to perfection, regardless of the time of day, and hadn't realized that wasn't how women worked. But that sheltered upbringing didn't warrant screaming first thing in the morning. Then again, he was Mack. Pampered, sheltered—and, at least in college, trying to break out of those molds. Now, she didn't know how much he'd changed or who he really was anymore.

She picked up her phone and Philip's business card. She reached out like this so infrequently, she hoped she was about to do it right.

Hey, coffee shop boy?

She didn't have to wait more than a minute for a reply. *Who's this?*

The woman you tried to pick up in the coffee shop. Or... am I not the only one?

For a second, it felt like texting Mack. This was how they bantered.

She missed it with a pang that made her gasp. This. This was what she'd been missing. Just the casual, flirty way they'd talked, like everything was possible.

Umm, no, came the response. *I don't usually walk up to women in coffee shops. Is this really you? Brunette, with the purple streaks? Looked like you were being buried in the cares of the world?*

It's really me, Tess texted back, biting her lower lip. The purple streaks had been a whim, something she'd debated the professionalism of, but everyone had liked them, so she kept refreshing them each time she had her hair trimmed. Clearly, they'd made an impact. Besides, she liked them.

Glad you reached out. I was starting to think you wouldn't.

Just been busy. You?

Same. So who are you?

Well, that might be a problem, Tess answered, wincing as she did.

Why?

Know the business incubator in Woolslayer? She held her breath.

Wait. I finally met Tess Cartieri? And without meaning to?

Yeah.

He didn't answer for a long minute, and Tess took that time to convince herself that he'd realized what a minefield he'd stepped into and was trying to come up with a graceful exit.

I've been wanting to meet you. I want you to know, up front, that I really like and admire what you're doing with those people.

Tess frowned. They weren't *people*, and they especially weren't *those people*. They were women. Mostly minority or immigrant, but they absolutely weren't *those people*.

Thanks, she texted back. *Should we knock heads and solve my water problems?*

I'd love to, but I'm constrained by the boss on what I can say.

That didn't surprise her. *But are you,* she replied, *constrained by the boss on what you can DO?*

Sometimes. In this, definitely.

Her frown deepened. Talking to him felt like pulling teeth. That wasn't a good sign for *any* sort of relationship, one with or without flirty banter.

Let me see what I can do and get back to you. Work hours okay? he asked.

Yes.

She set her phone down on her leg and closed her eyes. She'd imagined a million different scenarios, and not one had gone like that. *Those people.*

He was in politics. Surely he hadn't meant it like that.

In the morning, she was still disgruntled and unsatisfied. Maybe that's why she showed up in Red's office before the morning meeting and hooked a leg over the corner of his desk the way he sometimes did. "So I met this guy in the coffee shop a couple weeks ago," she said.

He looked up at her, his mouth slack.

She understood; she'd never before pulled his own power play on him—or discussed the men she'd met.

"And?" he managed, pulling his coffee cup toward him but leaving it on his desk.

"Turns out he works for the mayor's office. Made it clear he's constrained in anything he can help us with." She folded her arms over her chest, aware she wasn't angry with Red and hoping he'd pick up on that.

"Ahh, yeah." Now he did take a sip of his coffee, standing up as he did so. "That's very true. Who did you meet over there?"

"Philip. He had one of the most respectful pickups I've ever had the pleasure of, but as soon as he learned my name, he sure got cold fast."

Red nodded once and took another sip of coffee, watching her over the rim. He stood by the door, but Tess ignored the signal. "Know anything about him?" she asked.

"He and I have gone across the dance floor together more than once."

"And?" She fought the urge to tap her foot at him.

"I don't always win," Red said heavily. "And this problem you've got? You need to win."

Tess cocked her head and thought about that. "But you get things from the mayor's office all the time."

"Things. Not necessarily what I set out to get. I've been trying to get behind this problem, see all the angles, be ready for whatever they throw at us. I'm fairly certain the city's got a weak position. If you meet with him without me—and you're certainly welcome to—make sure he doesn't take advantage of you."

"What would that look like?" Tess asked carefully. That statement of Red's was packed: that he was willing to share a contact, that he trusted her to handle herself, that she needed to be careful and educated.

He was shaking his head. "He's a good guy, Tess, if a little *too* loyal to the mayor. I have no beef with him. But I also think he'll do whatever it takes to put the onus on Trade Creation, not on the city even though, by all accounts, this problem originates on city-owned property. They *should* bear the brunt of this."

Of course *should* didn't always translate into what they *would* do. It was something she and Serenity had discussed. Woolslayer wasn't affluent. It wasn't majority white. Those two facts created immediate obstacles.

Serenity had suggested offering some neighborhood fundraising of their own in an attempt to show the city they were worth the investment.

Tess had gotten angry. They didn't need to show they were worth anything. They paid their city taxes. They deserved what every other city dweller got.

"But what if," Serenity had asked, cocking her head in that regal way she had, "we hand them a grant from someone bigger? Something to match funds?"

Tess had wanted to kiss her. She shared the conversation with Red.

He leaned against his office door, his eyes unfocusing as he thought. "That might be good leverage." He nodded. "That works a lot better than a demand to fix it and give the neighborhood a handout."

"A handout? Is that some slur against the stereotype of the neighborhood?"

"Not from me, but you sure don't want anyone at city hall or in the press looking at it that way."

Tess took a deep breath. Red was, like usual, right. Truth be told, all she wanted was to keep her head down and do her thing: create buildings and spaces, and take care of her women. Why did her life keep trying to push her in this same direction, which she explicitly didn't want to go toward?

TWELVE

November 23

"Emerson," Taylor said somberly, standing in the doorway between their offices, hands hidden behind their back, "you might want to sit down for this."

Mack looked at his assistant for a long minute, taking in their light blue dress shirt and black dress pants that didn't need the braces holding them up, and a pair of light blue low-top Converse sneakers, then made a show of looking at his desk, his lap, his feet on the floor, his hands on his desktop. "I think I beat you to that *sitting* part. What's going on?"

"Well, you might want to brace yourself, then."

Mack groaned, understanding why Taylor had their arms behind their back. It was another newspaper article. "How bad, what now, and have you called PR to deal with it?"

Taylor held the article up and Mack groaned even louder at the headline. "Me? I'm the Mackenzie treasure?"

"*Five months after the untimely passing of his wife due to a heart problem, many single women will be giving thanks this week for not marrying young,*" Taylor recited, their voice rising and dipping and taking on a cadence like a TV news anchor.

He covered his face with his hands, bending forward to gently bang his head on the desk. "Tell me you're kidding."

"I would never tease you about something so personal."

That was entirely true. Mack had to give Taylor credit for that. The two of them liked to tease and play, but when it came to either of their personal reputations, Taylor was a total pit bull. Mack figured it came from practice defending themselves; it had to be tough most days to be nonbinary. "Does it get worse?" he asked with a low groan.

"I'm afraid so," Taylor said kindly, now as gentle and nurturing as Mack had often wished Krista could be. "I won't read it to you, and if I may be so bold, I'd advise you not read it yourself, either."

He hadn't moved. He didn't want to move. He wanted to wake up and not be the subject of some sick gossip. Didn't these people know he still couldn't sleep in the bed he'd shared with her? That in some weird way, he missed her?

He wondered what she would say if he could tell her that. She probably would have pulled away and told him to stop saying things that weren't true. And then she'd have sat and gazed at nothing for as long as he'd let her.

Oddly, he missed that, too. And he hated himself for not figuring out why she did it.

"Emerson? If I may be so bold?" Taylor asked quietly and Mack made himself look at his assistant, at the way the light caught their hair, turning it golden. Taylor had earned his trust a million times over, and he reminded himself that they had come to the house that early morning, when everything had been chaos.

Taylor *knew*.

"Let's hear it," he said.

"The company holiday party is in three weeks. It might be a good idea to make your first public appearance at that time, and perhaps with a lovely old friend on your arm to help hold you up."

Mack looked at Taylor, feeing strangely punched in the gut. "Not you, too."

Taylor blinked and took a step backward. "Not me too?"

"Trying to get me and Tess back together."

Taylor laughed nervously but spoke softly. "Far be it for me to pry like that, but I know you think highly of her and trust her, and that might be just what you need to get through the night. If you'd like me to tender the invitation, I would."

"No, it's for me to do." He grimaced. "Just... Ugh. I have to discuss it with Krista." He bowed his head, shaking it. "That might be worse than the damn article."

"People have odd ways of caring, don't they?" Taylor asked, the softness dropping away and a bit of their usual shell returning.

"What do you mean?"

"If no one cared about you, they'd just ignore you, not speculate about you."

Mack hadn't thought of it that way. "I'm not sure that *care* is the right word."

"In this case, I suspect you're right and it isn't meant with affection. Just nosiness."

"Is there any way to shut it down?"

"I'm afraid I have yet to find one."

Mack let out a sigh, which Taylor echoed, then vanished back into the outer office. From his desk, Mack could hear the phones ringing, probably with members of the board who had seen the gossip and wanted to suggest women they knew.

He picked up his phone.

Talk later? he texted Tess. *Not work related.*

Sure. After nine-thirty okay? I want to get to yoga.

Reach out when you're ready.

If it was all he could do, at least he could do it on her schedule.

THIRTEEN

*Y*_{*ou there?*} Tess had gotten home from yoga, showered, and combed out her hair. She climbed on the couch with a cup of tea and flipped on the TV for background noise, although as she waited for Mack to reply, she debated between a home improvement show, a cooking show, and a travel show about Iceland.

Iceland won out. It had the prettiest scenery. In fact, it was amazingly gorgeous. She'd have to find a travel buddy. Maybe Charley, although Sanjit would probably want to tag along, and what would Red do without the three of them in the office?

Probably close it for ten days and join them. Assuming his wife could get away.

The idea made her smile. It would be fun.

Yeah, Mack finally answered. *Just got in, myself.*

Late night at work?

Off-season track workout with the team. I was actually on time for once.

Tess wasn't sure if she could praise him for that or not. It all depended on why he was usually late.

It was a strange way to be reminded she knew so little of what his current life was like.

So what's up? she asked, unfolding her legs and stretching them out, letting her head fall onto the back of the couch. It was time to unwind for the day, and she covered herself with a blanket. She felt warm, snuggly, cocooned.

He texted her a link, then immediately said, *I actually haven't read it. Taylor gave me the gist of it and told me to leave it at that.*

Tess clicked and was immediately sorry.

Mack's a side of meat, huh?

Brutal, Just Tess. But true.

She supposed he *was* a catch: a young CEO of a global company, good looking, a widower with no kids or reputation of playboy tendencies. Not to mention the family money that went back generations.

So... Why are you sending me this?

It was Taylor's idea—

Never yours. Ever notice that?

What?

Krista told you it was time to make good on the dream of the field. Now it's Taylor telling you what to do.

Last time I did something on my own, I played hooky from a day of important meetings, jumped on a commercial flight—coach class, thanks—and showed up in your office without scheduling a meeting. We might be better off to let everyone else make decisions for me for a bit longer.

Only for a bit longer?

However long it takes to get over her.

Tess bit her lower lip. She hadn't been thinking along those lines, hadn't stopped to consider that Mack was such a mess that he had to simply follow the lead of the people he trusted.

She wanted to kick herself for that. Except, she reasoned with herself, she didn't know much about Mack at all anymore, and especially not how he was dealing with his grief.

Fair point, she replied. *So what's Taylor's idea?*

Be my arm candy for the PharmaSci holiday party? Taylor said I need to show up with someone I can trust. Krista said I have to be there, that I only get six months to hide. And you just saw how people are talking.

"And you asked why I walked away from you," Tess muttered to her empty condo, sitting up straighter and running her hand through her hair to see how wet it still was.

Tess? I scared you off.

It's... you know how I feel about this stuff.

Every company has holiday parties. I can return the favor.

She frowned, unsure of how she felt about this. While it wasn't strictly the sort of society event she hated—he was right that holiday parties were part of office politics—in Mack's case, it was close enough to a society thing, wasn't it? Either way, it meant she'd be putting herself under the microscope that she hated so much.

Red would tell her to go and start every sentence with the company name.

Can I think about it?

Of course.

She texted Jamie. *You still up?*

Yep. The boys are asleep and Hank and I are on two totally different couches in the same room and about all the talking we're doing is asking each other to pass the wine.

Ouch.

He's tired. Hates his job. Still wants to stay home with the boys. I'm caving.

Tess wasn't sure what to say. She thought if it were her, she'd let him stay home. He *wanted* to. That had to count for something.

Anyway, what's up?

Mack asked me to be his date for his corporate holiday party.

Yikes.

What do I say?

Do you want to go?

Yes. No. I don't know. All of the above. And it gets worse. He said he'd return the favor.

Mack and Tess. Together again. Keep him this time, will you?

It's not like that.

Maybe it should be.

Tess mulled that over. Since he'd shown up that day at the field, she'd asked herself more than once if this was their second chance. If they got one, if they deserved one, if things could be different and his obligations to the society set didn't have to spiral to include her. If she could still be Tess Cartieri at the same time she was Mrs. Emerson Mackenzie. If she could stay grounded with all that money at her disposal, if she would stop relating to the women at the incubator, if she'd have to quit her job to be a proper society wife, if, if, if.

Tess hated the word *if.*

Send the date, she texted Mack.

Fourteen

Tess didn't sleep well after that, genuinely not sure how she felt about agreeing to Mack's request. Sure, she'd promised him she would have his back, but she hadn't intended that to include needing heels, a slinky dress, a pasted-on smile to go with impeccably proper behavior, and a weekend under his roof.

Maybe it was that last part that bothered her the most. It was certainly the part she least wanted to dwell on. And even though he hadn't said as much, Tess knew it would be the worst insult if she even mentioned a hotel.

At least work was a distraction, with a conflict between a client and a contractor—Reggie the plumber—that needed to be dealt with. Reggie had somehow learned that the client's chairman of the board had a personal history that was, as Red put it, problematic.

"What does that mean?" Sanjit asked, blinking quickly.

"Either a slave owner, ties to the Klan—past or present—or both," Charley told him. She had one leg tucked under the other and wasn't sitting quite straight, busy drawing on a notepad in front of her, and she didn't look up as she spoke.

"Can we ever get *past* this?" Sanjit asked, looking around at them all. "Tess? What's the temperature about this down in your neighborhood?"

"The one I live in, or the one I take care of?" She tilted her head to one side, then the other, as she made the distinction. Not that it really mattered. Race issues in Port Kenneth as a whole were problematic of late, and Tess had privately wondered how much of that, if any, came from her incubator. After all, there were still plenty of people in town who thought the incubator's tenants didn't deserve to be successful. Skin color, religion, gender... it didn't matter. They weren't white men, and that made them problematic.

"I see Reggie's point," Charley said, "but is this the right hill to fight over?"

"That's a good question," Red said. "I'll talk to him, but if he won't reconsider, we need to call the second-choice contractor and make sure they are still interested. Who is that?"

Sanjit checked his notes, but Tess knew. "Of all people, it's Jessie White." She didn't want to react to the horrible irony of how his name echoed actions he thought no one knew about, but she wasn't sure she could hide her grimace.

Red passed his hand over his mouth, wiping off a smile. "Figures."

"At least he won't have issues working for the client," Tess said and Charley gave her a sympathetic look.

As the meeting broke up, Charley followed Tess down the hall. "What's with you and the guy at the mayor's office?"

"Please. That's one relationship that can't go anywhere unless he gets a better job, and you know it."

"I love how you set the rules."

Tess blinked in surprise. "What do you mean?"

"*He* has to quit his job."

"Well, I sure refuse to."

"Let's lunch and talk about this."

"There's nothing to talk about."

"How about your hottie and his field?"

Tess let out a breath. "Fine. We can talk about *him*." Maybe Charley would have an insight into this whole holiday party dilemma, but once they got to lunch and Tess explained the story, Charley's insight was simple. "He's your friend, right? Why are you even thinking about this? Sounds like everyone agrees he needs you."

"Does he, or is this a way to get me back in his bed?"

Charley stared at her. "Do you really think he's ready to just pick up where you guys left off how many years ago? Tess, you know I know grief. He's probably not even *thinking* about his dick right now."

Given his inability to make decisions, Tess had a feeling that might be true. Then again, this was Mack they were discussing and for a second, she flashed back to how it had felt when he'd been in her, above her, on his back watching her, the feel of his body between her legs, his back under her hands, his chest under her palms, his lips hot on hers...

She told herself to stop thinking like that and focus on the subject at hand, which was that she could argue Mack's grief-stricken sex drive either way.

"Hey. Hello?"

"It's impossible. He's there. I'm here. Neither of us can move."

"Famous last words," Charley said.

And despite herself, Tess hoped they would be. That hope flared again late that afternoon, when Red summoned her.

"Know anything about this?" he asked, shoving his tablet at her. It was opened to the local business gossip, and right there, at the top, was a story that made her jaw drop.

PharmaScience Technology Scouting for New Corporate HQ?

She knew her mouth had just gone slack and hoped she wasn't drooling, but nodding was about the extent of her brain's capacity at the moment. She couldn't even command her hand to check for drool.

"Tess?"

She blinked twice, fast, and managed to shut her mouth. "Sorry. I... had no idea." She reached for the tablet, but Red turned it toward him.

"It says *discreet inquiries were made just an hour ago*. And the story's barely twenty minutes old. Like they were waiting for most of us to clear out for the day."

"Clearly, they weren't discreet enough."

Red shrugged. "You get the right people in your pocket—or know who to avoid—and you can play the press like a fiddle."

"Think that's what this is? A trial balloon to see what the city will offer?"

"You're the one who knows the guy."

Tess pulled out her phone and texted Mack. *Scouting my town for a new HQ? You really must want me to come to that party of yours.*

Will you?

Only if you tell me if this is true or not.

Sort of? Mack answered. Tess nodded at Red, but her phone buzzed again with a series of replies. *We're surveying a bunch of cities. See if it would be cheaper than here. It will be, but the question is if we can make uprooting families worth it.*

I thought Emerson Mackenzie sold out. You're not supposed to care about the people who work for you.

I'm a new and improved Mackenzie man.

I bet your board loves you.

You can meet them all at the party. I'll have Taylor help with flights. Plan to stay at the Manor.

"And?" Red asked. He had a smile playing about his lips and he placed his elbows on his desk, his hands clasped in front of his face in an attempt to hide the smile. He'd rolled his sleeves up and his tats were on full display. They made him seem less like a boss, somehow, and more like a... Tess had to consider that some.

"We're not the only city he's looking at." She looked up at him. "But what it all actually means is anyone's guess. I know he had an agenda when he ousted his father, but this seems a bit extreme, even for him." She paused, thinking, wondering if this was another of those bad decisions he said he kept making—and wondering if this meant she couldn't use their lives in different cities as a reason to put him off. "And by the way? Getting that out of him cost me dearly. I've got to be his date for his company holiday party." She wrinkled her nose.

Red beamed. "Like I said, he's the disruption you need."

"You going to come dress shopping with me?"

"No, but I bet Christine will. And," he said, holding up a hand, "before you grouse that if we'd had a full-on party, you could wear it more than once, let me remind you that when we do a just-us lunch, no one's partners fight and no one gets drunk."

"Yeah, there's that," Tess said. "And the dress code is better."

"Maybe we should go formal this year, just for you."

"No. Hey, speaking of parties, Woolslayer's having a New Year's celebration. Food trucks, the new beer truck, the whiskey truck. No fireworks at midnight, but it should be a good time. This is the first time they've done something this big, so I'd like to see them succeed. Since our October campaign didn't do much except bring people together."

Red sobered. "I'm working every angle I can find. Leaning on Councilwoman Salveggio, as well. She's sympathetic but new enough to politics that she doesn't have a lot of clout yet."

"Anything helps. It's just that every day that goes by, we get that much closer to disaster."

"Believe me, I know," he said and looked down at his tablet. He frowned. "The article just refreshed. Now it says they've gotten official word that PharmaScience Technologies has no intention of moving and any so-called inquiries were done by someone not affiliated with the company."

"Mack moves fast," she said, wondering if his assistant had been reading his texts over his shoulder.

"He'd better not move too fast for you," Red said, giving her a long look.

"Thanks, Dad. I've got it under control," she said, but he continued to glower. "What happened to him being the disruption I need?" she asked, but he merely shook his head, his grin sneaking back out.

Fifteen

December 20

Even though Krista had all but forbidden him, Logan had laughed at him, and even Marisela had looked up from making lunch and invited him to distract himself by helping her, Mack waited outside for Tess. Part of him couldn't believe she'd agreed to do this, but the bigger part of him was relieved to be seeing her again. Too much of this field project had taken place long-distance.

And waiting for her, keeping the focus on Tess and not the damn party, kept his mind off making his first semi-public appearance since Kelsey. He still wasn't sure he was ready for it.

Juan must have been surprised when he found Mack at the main entrance, long since unused. "Are you sure about this, Emerson?" he asked when he pulled into the long circular drive.

"I want Tess to have the whole experience," Mack said, leaning in the passenger window, not terribly surprised to find her there and not in back. He paused, breathing her in, feeling steadier already.

"The whole experience?" she said, stepping out of the car when he opened the door for her.

When she was out and standing beside him, and Juan had driven around to the garage, he motioned to the house, trusting her architect's eye to kick in.

It did. "Mack. This is..." She shook her head, closed her eyes, gave them a quick rub, and opened them again. "Twelve-foot first floor?"

Despite himself, he was impressed.

"Perfect symmetry," she said, drawing shapes in the air with her hand, "tall windows that match, the wide porch and corresponding overhang with the columns... Mack, you have to be kidding me. Tell me I am not looking at an almost perfect representation of what we now call a Southern plantation house, circa 1860."

He beamed, but it dimmed as he realized she was hesitating. "Uhh, you are."

"Hmm." She frowned.

"It's that old, too," he said, wondering if he should start to panic.

She looked the house over again, but he could tell she'd lost some of her appreciation for it. And then she confirmed it by saying, "You're telling me it's some weird coincidence? That the family tree that spawned a bastard like Tristan lives like this—"

"I... guess," he said, rubbing the back of his neck and wondering if he should have expected this. "We can ask Krista when we go in. She'll probably tell me it's time I learned this stuff myself." He ran his hand through his hair this time, stopping at the back of his neck. She would definitely tell him that, and she was right. Learning the family history was one duty he'd been neglecting. "Do... do you want to see the inside? I hope the door still works. The other day, Juan and I were in most of the rooms we don't use, but we came in through our living space."

"Yeah, let's go in," she said, but he thought she didn't sound thrilled. He said so, and she smiled. "Oh, Mack. It's... it's a very mixed message."

His heart sunk, and he wasn't sure why. "How so?"

"You have a Mexican couple—"

"Nicaraguan."

Her smile was watery. "You have a Nicaraguan couple who are your housekeepers and your house is... magnificent despite the lifestyle we all equate with it, but you're... the complete opposite of who you *should* be for growing up surrounded by all this."

"Maybe," he said quietly, feeling thoroughly chastised, "having you come up wasn't such a great idea."

She turned to him, her eyes somber. "I'm being hard on you, and that's not fair because you *are* the one fighting against and defying the stereotypes. I'm sorry. It's just... well, Mack, I *do* live in the South. I work with minorities. Maybe I'm too sensitive to the issues."

"But they're real issues," he said

"They are." She glanced over her shoulder at the house. "And I *am* curious what it's like in there."

He produced the key and was relieved when it worked. The house was most impressive from this angle, even if Tess couldn't let herself be impressed.

Her mouth fell open as she looked at the grand staircase, into the parlor on the left and the ballroom on the right. "An entire ballroom?"

He led her in. This, more than anything, was what he'd wanted to show her.

She walked around, craning her neck to look at the ceiling, looking out the windows at the views, running her hands over the frames. When she turned back to him, he bowed and held out his hand to her.

Her eyes went huge and she took a step backward. "What... what am I supposed to do?"

"Take my hand." She hesitated. "Just take my hand, Tess. I feel like a fool."

"Look like one, too," she said, but smiled and did as he asked. He straightened and drew her in, closing his arm around her waist and holding her maybe a little too close, raising his other hand. She put hers on it, her fingers seeking to twine with his, but he shook his head and kept his fingers clamped together.

"Are you comfortable? Can you trust me?"

"Yes, and that's a strange thing to ask."

"Just let me do the work," he said and swept her into a waltz, his steps wide. Her eyes were wide and her mouth open during his first pass through the room, but then she relaxed in his grip and moved with him instead of making him do it all, and she tipped her head up and laughed and he sped up, confident they were in sync.

They did two more circuits of the room and then he stopped. He had to; her laughter had been light and airy and delighted and he couldn't help but share in it, too.

She rested her forehead on his chest, breathing hard. So, he noticed, was he.

"Is this one of those moments where I look up and you kiss me, like some movie?" she asked.

"That's not what I asked you here for," he said and switched his grip so he held her loosely at the waist, half-expecting her to pull away but hoping she wouldn't. "I asked you here to have my back tonight."

"Just don't ask my opinion of the exterior of the house," she said and lifted her head, looking up at him, her eyes dancing. "This room, at least, is pretty magic."

He beamed.

"Are we going to dance like this tonight?" she asked.

He shrank a little, but it was her turn to tighten her grip on him, as if she knew where his head had just gone. She waited him out, and finally, he produced a soft "Maybe?"

"Well, the decision is yours, but if you can handle it, I'm game. I've got your back," she added gently. "You're going to be fine."

He told himself to relax. It was his company, not some society party. The guest list was closed. There'd be no media, although that didn't mean a lack of gossips. It was as safe as it could be. And he had Tess, and his mother and Logan, and all the people he worked with on a daily basis, including many of his board members. She was right. It was going to be fine.

"Can I confess something?" he asked, shifting his weight, surprised when she still moved with him.

"Go for it."

"Ever since I was a kid, I'd sneak in here and dream of holding a beautiful woman in my arms and dancing like that."

"You never did it..." She broke off, as if afraid to say Kelsey's name.

He thought he appreciated that. "No. She wouldn't so much as come in here. She said it was creepy."

She let out a deep sigh. "Oh, Mack, I'm sorry. You deserved someone who'd dance with you in here." She wrinkled her nose. "Even if it's built as an homage to white supremacy."

"It's not, Tess. Or, maybe it was, but you said yourself that I'm making sure it's not that anymore. This part of it isn't even used! C'mon. I know Krista's waiting to say hello." He led her through the big, open rooms with their high ceilings, letting her stop and look when she wanted, always aware that he still had an arm around her waist and that she had fit herself up against him, holding him up, strengthening him for the upcoming party.

"Oh, hello. There you are," Krista said when they entered the kitchen. "What did you think of the house, Tess?"

"She thinks it's an homage to white supremacy," Mack said before she could answer.

She did chuckle, though, and slipped away from him to give Krista her air kisses.

His mother surprised him by actually embracing Tess. "I suppose it does seem that way," Krista said when Tess had seated herself, Mack only moving to hold her chair for her when his mother frowned at him. "But one thing to know about the Mackenzies is that they were historically neutral. In fact," she continued, giving Mack a look that he was willing to bet meant he should have known this, "PharmaSci got its start during the war. The Mackenzies of the time realized they had the ability to produce the medicines that were so needed and in such short supply. It is my understanding they sold them to both the Union and the Confederacy, although of course, the Confederacy ran out of funds quickly and selling to them was problematic, just for their stance in regards to humankind."

"I thought you just said they were historically neutral?" he asked.

She gave him a long look. "If you consult historical company sources, Emerson, you'll see how that was handled. It was quite fascinating. And so," Krista said, turning back to Tess, "I tend to think that the architectural style of the house, especially because it is so unique to this area, is really a Mackenzie forefather winking at us, reminding us to be *more*. PharmaSci—which back then was simply named Pharmaceutical Sciences Company—was a *good* thing that came from all that ugliness."

Mack considered all that, wondering if it was too easy, if Tess would think it was too easy, but she nodded and simply asked if Krista would help her decide which of two dresses she should wear.

He figured he should be grateful that she was letting it drop. But then, he reminded himself, she'd come to have his back, not be the one leading the charge against him.

Sixteen

December 28

"So how's our boy?" Jamie asked the Monday after the party. She'd had a couple cancellations, which was odd for a Monday during the holidays, so she had dragged Tess out to lunch.

"He's good," Tess said. "Rocky, still, but better than he was."

"And? Where do things stand with the two of you?"

Tess shrugged and looked away. "They are what they are," she said, although she knew Jamie wouldn't be satisfied with that lame explanation. "I'm here, he's there, neither of us are willing to give up our jobs, he's still making noise about moving the entire company, but he'll be the first to tell you it may not happen." She shook her head, her eyes closed. Unbidden, the image of him when she and Krista had made their grand appearance, ready for the party, came to mind. His eyes had lit up and he'd seemed so happy, if only for a few seconds, but then he'd turned away. Krista had winked at Tess, and she'd wondered if Mack was doing some quick adjustments or merely hiding a fresh wave of grief.

"Go on," Jamie said, as if she knew Tess' thoughts.

"If only things were different," Tess said and sat back as their lunches were delivered. "What's with you and Hank? He still want to work from home?"

"Well, things got interesting," Jamie said, pouring dressing on her salad. "The decision's been made for us. Hank's a stay-at-home dad at least until his severance runs out, and all of us are happier than I thought we could be. We're barely even having an adjustment period, and I'll tell you, Tess, there's nothing better than coming home and seeing two little toddlers come at you full speed, yelling your name."

Tess smiled. Jamie *did* seem happier, and that was nice to see.

"Did you sleep with him?"

The question almost gave Tess whiplash. "Of course not." The words were out of her mouth before she could censor them, which had been Jamie's intent.

"No opportunity?"

"Oh, there could have been plenty of opportunity," Tess said, flashing back to being in the ballroom at the manor, to being tucked under his arm, to falling asleep on him on the couch he'd been sleeping on since Kelsey's death, unable to face the bed he'd shared with her. "But we set the rules before I went, and you know Mack. He'll obey them if it kills him."

"He's a good guy."

"He is," Tess agreed. "Not to change the subject away from him *again*, but are you bringing Hank and the boys to the Woolslayer New Year's Eve gathering?"

"Don't tell me Mack's coming up to be your date."

Tess snorted. "I don't need a date for this, but it was actually Philip I tried to con into doing the honors. He needs to get down there and see the people he's screwing around with. But," she added, holding a finger up, "Councilwoman Salveggio is going to be there, and that's an improvement, even over our efforts back in October. Maybe she can finally ease the logjam."

"Hope so," Jamie said. "I'd like to go, of course. Hank's a little iffy. He... Don't take this the wrong way, but he's worried about safety."

It was a common misconception, one Tess had shared when she'd launched the incubator project. She did everything she could to set Jamie's fears aside, but in the end, she wasn't sure if Jamie had been convinced.

That was, she thought as she drove to the party, one of the biggest battles she had yet to figure out how to win. Maybe if she met the councilwoman, they could have a conversation about that.

She parked in front of the building, as always, in the space a couple of the artsy high schoolers had painted and marked *Miss Tess only*. It always made her smile, especially since it seemed that everyone respected the space and no matter how few parking spaces were free, hers always stood ready.

As soon as she got out of the car, she was swarmed by neighbors coming over to say hello and ask her to stop in at the old butcher's shop, which had somehow become the neighborhood art gallery. But they also wanted to thank her for being there, to encourage her to be sure to hear the bands and see the dancers, most of whom were made up entirely of Woolslayers, as they'd dubbed themselves.

Some good had come out of the otherwise fruitless October campaign, Tess decided. The neighborhood was ready to party into the new year.

Best of all, she thought, it wasn't too cold and the night was clear. In fact, the weather was as perfect as Port Kenneth got this time of year, as if it, too, wanted to party.

For a second, she compared the Woolslayers to Mack's employees. They had seemed glad he stopped by every table to say hello, although they had remained at a distance. "I'm the boss," he'd said with a shrug when she'd asked him about it later, when they were back at the house and Krista and Logan had gone to bed and she and Mack were sitting around in flannel lounge pants and sweatshirts. As for his vice presidents, he'd only said, "I'm the boss who's *younger* than they are. They don't seem to realize how much I listen and let them lead, but they will. I hope."

Maybe it wasn't a fair comparison. But they were the last group of people Tess had encountered.

The Woolslayers looked relaxed. They were smiling, laughing, talking to each other. Tess thought she'd rather be around them than most of Mack's people, and she reminded herself to thank Red for keeping their holiday duties to an employee-only lunch.

"Tess!"

She turned and there was Red, arms wide for a hug, his wife at his side. He hugged Tess, waited for her to hug Christine, and then hugged Christine.

"How many times has he been to the whiskey truck?" Tess asked Christine, who laughed.

"Only once, believe it or not," Red said. "I'm just glad we're out of the house, not downtown in that crush, and can be home in bed at a reasonable hour."

"You sound like you're getting old," Tess said.

"What's old about having my wife home for once instead of having to crawl into an empty bed and wish she was there with me? Besides, I didn't say anything about sleeping." He winked, Christine shook her head, and Tess laughed.

"You solo tonight?" Red asked, peering around as if he expected someone to show up from someplace Tess couldn't see.

"Yep," she said and put her hands in her jacket pockets. "How long have you guys been here?"

"Long enough to look at the whiskey truck menu and then wander back to see if there was a certain blue car in *Miss Tess'* space. Who calls you Miss Tess?"

"Mostly the kids. Georgie, our photographer. Oh, he's got new stuff up at the old butcher shop."

"Don't tell me you're going to make that an official art gallery."

"They did it without me." Although Tess had to admit she didn't know how *official* it was. "The deal with Georgie is that if he gets his grades up, I'll help find him a mentor. Right now, that's not looking so good for him."

"Running with a bad crowd?"

"I'm not sure what he's doing, other than walking out of school to take pictures and not coming back. He just doesn't *care*." She took a deep breath, reminding herself that if he didn't care, she shouldn't. But as she and Serenity had discussed, it wasn't so easy to stop caring about a kid like Georgie. He had so much talent; he just needed to make the smart decisions—although Tess had asked if they were truly the smart decisions or if they were the decisions she and Serenity wanted him to make. Surely there were successful photographers who hadn't graduated high school.

Still, she argued with herself as she led Red and Christine over to the old butcher shop, a high school degree opened doors. So did a college degree, but one thing at a time with a kid like Georgie.

Anchey and Sanjit both found them looking at the art.

"Tess, how much of this did you do?" Sanjit asked, his eyes bright behind his glasses.

"I rented the organizing committee the office space for fifty bucks and fed any leads I got about the food trucks to them."

"Fifty bucks?"

"It was a short-term deal, but if this goes well, they are talking about maybe going into party planning." She smiled. "It's like I've inspired *everyone* around here. Like they're finding dreams they thought they'd never get to realize." Her smile got wider, but so did her emotion. "It feels good. It feels *right*."

"Just don't be quitting your day job," Red grumbled.

"We have a deal," Tess reminded him and jerked her head at the row of food trucks lined up around the greenspace. "Let's go check out the other food trucks. I'm hungry, and I've been told I'm not allowed to miss the dancing and the bands on the small stage."

"They set up a stage?"

"Behind the trucks, in the space that used to be the firehall. If we ever get the water line issue fixed, I'd love to see it turned into a playground."

Red chuckled. "There's my ambitious girl."

"Red, don't encourage her," Anchey said. "We need her at the office too much."

"Maybe the ideas I have here will inspire more ideas at the office," Tess said, linking her arm through Anchey's, then offering her free arm to Sanjit. "Come on, boys! Let's see what goodies are here tonight."

They had just gotten over there and were debating between the wood-fired pizzas, the barbecue, something more traditionally vegetarian for Sanjit, and the super long line at the taco truck when the ground rumbled, both audibly and physically.

Sanjit and Anchey grabbed Tess, who grabbed them in turn, and they all stopped and stared as a geyser of water erupted just in front of the beer truck.

People screamed and ran, the adults away from the new addition to the party and the kids beelining for the edges of the water, which was spraying on the pavement like a summer splash park. A violent, unwelcome splash park.

"Well," Tess said as they all dodged inside the ring of trucks, "I guess the mayor's office just ran out of time to fix our problem before it all goes to hell."

Red threw his head back and laughed.

"Tess!" It was Serenity. "What do we do now?"

"Get the people out of the way, move the trucks to someplace safe and dry, and keep partying, I guess," Tess said, peering between two trucks, not surprised to see the police already on the scene. "But it looks like you and I don't have to worry about that. Let's find Patricia and Ebony and see what they need."

"I like the way you think," Serenity said.

Tess turned to her coworkers, who were nodding at her and telling her to go.

"This is the best party I've been to... maybe ever!" Anchey said, his eyes wide as he watched the influx of people into the smallish square. Unbelievably, they were still smiling and laughing, even as most of them were wet, although a few looked a little scared.

Ebony and Priscilla appeared on the stage, and Tess called her group's attention to them. "This wasn't how it was supposed to go," Priscilla said, the PA system crackling. Tess hoped the water and the electric weren't going to be a bad mix. "But I guess this one's so good, it took something like a broken water main to top what we put together for you tonight! As long as the police will let us, we're going to stay out here and party and perform for you, so Happy New Year, everyone!"

SEVENTEEN

Tess later told her mother and Jamie both that it turned into a New Year's Day unlike any other ever would be again—just as New Year's Eve had been. But while the water main break had somehow added to the party, dealing with the aftermath was worse than a nagging hangover, and Tess had thought she'd left *those* days long behind.

She woke to her phone. It was Philip, which surprised her.

"Uhh, Tess? I wanted to give you the head's up in case you've heard from anyone down in Woolslayer and are thinking about yelling at me..."

Pushing herself up so her headboard was her backrest, she cocked her head. "You're the first who's gotten to me. What's going on?" she asked over one of those sharp intakes of breath, the kind people make when you've surprised them. She glanced at her clock. Ten.

She blinked. Ten?

"Okay, good," he said, then rushed on. "The water main break wasn't fixed overnight."

"Well, because of the holiday, right?" So far, things weren't adding up. Why would Philip call to tell her this when it was common sense?

"No. It should have been fixed overnight. This... well, look. Ever go into a project expecting it to sail smoothly and then you take a closer look and it's so far off the rails, you have to stop and redo all your plans?"

"Of course." It happened more than she liked, but that was part of the challenge of adapting old buildings to new uses.

"Yeah. That."

She took a deep breath. "How bad?"

"I... probably can't tell you that yet. Can you be in my office on Tuesday? Give me a day to work on this and get more information for you. Things are, needless to say, going to be relatively shut down today."

"How shut down? I mean, Philip, if there's no water... That main supplies the entire street."

"We've already got the crews bringing in water buffaloes and trying to get to residents with instructions about flushing toilets and taking showers and all that, but... well, we're kind of hoping you can help us out here. An awful lot of those people don't like us government types and don't want to listen. Someone suggested it might be different if the word was coming from you."

Tess let out a heavy breath. Her first thought was to wonder why her, and her second was that she wanted to know who that *someone* was.

"Tess? Can you help with this?"

"Of course," she said, kicking at the bedcovers. "Let me grab a shower and something to eat and I'll head right down there."

"I got you up." He sounded chagrined, and Tess appreciated that.

"I had to get up at some point," she said, wondering how she'd managed to sleep so late. Yes, she'd been out late, but she had never been one to sleep in. "What time on Tuesday, and can I bring Red?"

"How's eleven, and yes."

"Done. See you then."

From there, the day spiraled into non-stop activity, punctuated by a text from Jamie around three. *Good thing we skipped last night. Ryan's got a stomach bug.*

Tess signaled to Serenity to finish talking to the scared woman who had been complaining to her. Apparently "bring your own container for water" didn't work so well when you didn't have containers.

A few people had shown up with gas cans and got angry when they were turned away.

An hour later, Jamie texted back. *Both boys have it.*

Tess texted her regrets and looked up from her phone, freezing. A man who looked like the man she and Jamie had run into by the sheep farm had turned and was walking away.

Tess took a step to start to follow him, but was stopped by someone else who needed help, this time carrying full containers of water back to their car. Water, it turned out, was heavy. And, of course, by the time she was done, the man had disappeared.

By five, Jamie had texted that Hank had the bug, too, but at least wasn't projectile vomiting. *Need me to pick up some soup for you guys?* Tess asked her.

Can you?

Yep. I'll call The Reuben Deli; they're usually open today. One quart? Two?

Play it safe. Get three.

Tess chuckled and called her mother to see if she was free for dinner. A stop at The Reuben Deli was always worth the indulgence, and always better when shared.

By the time she got home, it was close to nine. But the soup was delivered, Jamie said she thought Ryan was either completely empty or over the worst of it, and Hank and Tim were curled up together on the bathroom floor. It would have been cute, Jamie said, but for the puking and the fact that Hank had given up on pants for both of them.

Her mother was fine, too. Nothing new there, and she thankfully wasn't overly interested in talking about Mack. They had wound up making cookies after dinner, and Tess had a fresh batch of oatmeal raisin cookies that she'd probably have to freeze instead of attempting to eat before they went stale.

She picked up her phone to check on Jamie again and noticed a text that had been waiting for her. Mack, wishing her a happy new year.

Hey, she texted him as she settled on the couch. *Just saw this. How was your night?*

Mother, Logan, and I did the rounds. Alyssa chased me from one party to the other until I finally hid in a bathroom. Logan had to run interference and I got sent home after that. For Alyssa's safety.

Tess giggled, then checked the time stamp on his initial text. Yep. Right at midnight. *She wants you.*

Not interested. What had you too busy to check your messages?

She told him, ending with *I love the people and don't mind doing this sort of thing, but on the other hand, I wish they didn't need me to do it. There are a million people better at playing the games, building the bridges. Hell, I don't even work for the government. Why do I have to make it okay for a community I don't live in to talk to a city hall I don't work for?*

It was, really, the biggest part of why they'd broken up. As Mack's wife, she would have had to deal with the expectation of being a community leader of some sort. She didn't want to be a leader; she wanted to be left alone to live her life, and that didn't mean mixing with a bunch of rich women who thought their investment portfolios gave them privileges.

Mack belonged to a level of society she didn't want to get near. Back in college, he'd shared that opinion—until he'd chosen it over her.

The buzz of her phone pulled her back to the present.

Because you've got an opportunity. Don't think of it as an obligation.

It figured he'd look at it that way, she thought with a frown. He'd grown up knowing these sorts of obligations were part of what it meant to be a Mackenzie.

Opportunity? To play political games and make nice to people who want to step all over me?

Yes.

She held her breath, expecting him to tell her she'd always been too cynical about this stuff. There was no doubt she was.

I just want to be an architect and adapt and reuse the city's amazing buildings, and work with clients to realize their visions for new spaces in the city.

And your incubator?

That, too, she answered, frowning. Maybe, when she hadn't been looking, life had gotten more complicated. *Working with them is like...* She had to stop and search for the words. It was a good feeling, like she was full of goodwill and possibility. Even helping with the water, and helping residents figure out how to manage until the main was fixed, and introducing them to Councilwoman Salveggio when they wanted to be heard, had left her exhausted but... *It's a sense of fulfillment different from work.*

That's why it's an opportunity. Yeah, you're the middleman, and being in the middle can be uncomfortable sometimes.

All the time. She stuck her tongue out at her phone.

Welcome to my life, Just Tess.

You're welcome to it ALL.

Nah. You're right where you should be. Keep taking care of that neighborhood.

I'm trying, but it's getting harder.

Opportunity, not obligation.

She sent him a raspberry emoji.

He responded with a laughing emoji. *Look, I went through this, too. It's part of being a leader. At least, that's what Krista would tell me.*

I don't want to be a leader. I want a nice, quiet life where I just do my own thing and my work speaks for itself.

I know. Tess wasn't sure, but she thought she could hear his chagrin in his text. *That's why you dumped me. I haven't forgotten.*

So now I'm a hypocrite?

Nope. Just realizing that the things we want in life sometimes aren't the things we get. And the things we get make us dig deeper into who we are. You're rocking this.

I don't feel like I am.

Did you help people today?

Well... yeah. Sure. At least, she thought so.

You seized the opportunity.

Tess looked thoughtfully at her phone for a long minute before sending back a quick *I guess so. Thanks* and hoping that he would leave it at that.

Because the thing that was nagging her now was that she was helping people much in the same way that she helped her buildings. And if she took the time to get to know the history of her buildings, it was time to get to know the history of Woolslayer.

Which reminded her that after she'd discovered the sheep farm, she'd tried to reach out to local historians about it, but had let that ball drop.

Time to fix *that*. She yawned.

In the morning. She'd make time during the workday. Red wouldn't mind.

Eighteen

January 2

M ack hoped Tess wouldn't mind two conversations in two days, that she wouldn't think he wanted to continue the discussion from the night before, or that he was coming on too strong. But he had to laugh with her.

"So, Krista apparently is now reading the newspapers in Port Kenneth," he said when he got her on a video chat. It was late, and Alyssa Schoenstrom had showed up at the gym midway through his run and made eyes at him, but even she hadn't been able to dampen his mood.

"Oh?" Tess asked, a lightness to her voice that told him she knew exactly what he was getting at.

"Just Tess, seizing the opportunity to... I don't know. Were you trying to take a shower in a geyser?" The photographer had caught her, face raised to the spraying water, hands out in a helpless gesture, wearing a bigger grin than he'd ever seen on her face before. And he'd seen some big grins from her. Been responsible for a number of them, too.

"Yes. Fully clothed and everything." She chuckled. It was fat and satisfied, and he wanted more of it. "And wait," she went on, her eyes widening slightly. "I *knew* the photographer was there. It wasn't Georgie, the kid we've been trying to help, either. It was the legit photographer from the paper, covering the party and getting a nice bit of action instead. I thought they'd run a better picture."

"I think they picked this one because it looks like you're having fun, despite everything turning into a shitstorm."

"There wasn't any shit, just the water main break." She paused for a beat and he faked a groan before grinning back at her, feeling like the shared smile stretched an eternity. A comfortable eternity. "I still can't believe the cops let the night go on mostly as planned," she went on. "The food trucks got moved, the beer truck was almost a casualty but wasn't, the entertainment went on as scheduled, and everyone in town's talking about how they missed *the* party of the new year. That's what I'd call a happy ending. What's new with you?"

"Why the good mood?" he asked, hoping she wouldn't call him on his dodge. "This was your worst case, and you weren't this happy about things last night."

"Because now the city can't dodge *fixing* it. And everyone's talking about Woolslayer in a *good* way."

"How's it feel to be called *community activist*?"

A shadow rippled over her face, as he'd expected. "I am anything but."

"Like I said last night, those people are lucky to have you." He stretched out on the couch, hooking one arm behind his head and thinking how true that was. Those people were *damn* lucky to have Tess advocating for them. She just needed to stop fighting it and get busy doing it.

She'd get there. He was confident that she would.

"Maybe next time you're in town about the field, I'll take you down there and you can see what it's like."

"No regrets about walking away from me even though you've wound up here anyway?" he asked softly, a knife slipping through his defenses and into his guts. The memories surfaced, so he closed his eyes and welcomed them even though they hurt. He remembered the fallout after Krista had come to get him at school, all those hours he and Tess had spent, trying to figure out if there was a way to dodge the rule that a Mackenzie had to be at the helm of PharmaSci or it would end, how bad the threat was if they just left Tristan there... He hadn't wanted to take over, but the alternative had been ugly: thousands out of work and even more without access to medicine. Sure, people could find new jobs and the patents for the drugs would all have been bought out by other companies, but in the end, neither he nor Tess had been selfish enough to do that. PharmaSci was just too big.

And besides, once he'd gotten into the swing of things, he'd surprised himself by really liking the work. Maybe it wasn't taking care of people the way Tess currently was, and it sure wasn't the sort of work he'd gone to school for, but it was still making people's lives better.

If only it hadn't cost him the thing he'd loved best in the world.

He squeezed his eyes closed even tighter, that damn knife slicing through all the walls he'd put up. She was back, she was on the other end of a video chat, but what the hell did it mean?

"Question about the Mackenzie at the head of the company thing," she said, as if she were thinking the same things he was. He didn't doubt that she was. "And I know we probably talked about this, but it's been a long time. Does it have to be a direct line of succession after you, or can cousins step up?"

"Direct unless no one's alive. Then there are rules about how it passes. But Tristan ran off all the cousins anyway and they haven't been real receptive about fixing that. We spent Christmas with part of Krista's family and part of Logan's. That was weird. *Hi, you're my mom's lover's family. Merry Christmas.*"

"Yeah, no thanks."

"Tell me about it," he said with a slight grimace. "I know one thing, and that's this time around, I want love. Real, hot, complicated, enduring. I'm not settling again just to make her happy."

Tess drew back a little bit and her lips thinned, and he was convinced he'd said too much, but she said quietly, "Me, too."

"Yeah," he said and they stared at each other for a long minute, the knife slicing a new trail up toward his heart. "So," he finally said, breaking the unusual silence, "think we can set up a meeting for sometime soon? For the field?"

"Sounds like we need to," she said, turning thoughtful. Her hair fell in front of her face and she shook her head to move it out of the way. "If only so you have an excuse to get down here and see the hole in the ground. It's epic, and there's some complication, so it's not going away so fast." She frowned and again, he could all but read her thoughts: It should have been fixed.

"When you get a minute, check your calendar," he said.

"I'll coordinate with Taylor."

"I'll tell them to expect you."

"And then, I guess I'll expect you." Her voice got breathy and now he wondered what she was thinking, afraid to hope.

"Guess so." With a start, he realized he'd echoed her, and that knife twisted, refusing to let him ignore it. As if he could. She was Tess, and if he were honest with himself, he'd never stopped loving her.

Nineteen

January 2

Just Tess? My bed's too big.

Tess looked at her phone and melted. Even through the text, she could feel his pain. But she couldn't let him know that.

You decided to face it, huh? she asked.

If you can spend New Year's Day helping people find water, I can sleep in a stupid bed. Or, I thought I could. Took me two days to work up the nerve just to decide to.

I know you can. And I know the first time's going to be the hardest.

Nimisha said I should have stopped sleeping on the couch months ago. But there hasn't been a single night that I've been in this bed without Kelsey. How?

She never went away without you? Tess texted back, intrigued despite being grossed out by her voyeurism, not to mention curious about who or what a Nimisha was, although the advice was something she agreed with. When she'd been there, he hadn't seemed inclined to leave the couch.

Not without me. Guess Daddy made her stay close in case I left behind any juicy information that would lead to my downfall.

Tess closed her eyes, debating various responses. In the end, she settled for *What do you mean? You haven't told me much about what was going on with her.*

My dear father-in-law was actively working to undermine the Mackenzie legacy. He thought he could stage a coup and seize control of PharmaSci.

What about the rule that a Mackenzie has to be CEO or the company folds?

I didn't say the guy was smart. He also believed the old rumors of the Mackenzie treasure. Hold on.

Her phone buzzed with the second video request of the day. "Okay, explain all this," she said as she connected, studying him, but other than looking tired, he seemed as fine as he had earlier. Maybe, she thought, a little subdued.

"Rumor is that there's this Mackenzie treasure somewhere, probably buried on the grounds. He had Kelsey hunting for it." He closed his eyes and, for a second, he looked so old, so tired, that Tess wanted to reach out and touch him. It was hard to do over a phone.

"Krista and Logan," he went on, "moved into their townhouse not long after Kelsey and I got married. We had a place, so Mother talked briefly about actually selling the Manor, but Kelsey went bonkers. We *had* to move in here. So I renovated the rooms that used to be Tristan's. And Cullen's. And Patrick's. And every Mackenzie man since the dawn of time, and we moved in. I never gave Kelsey the idea to move into the wife's rooms; I figured they were still Krista's until she told me otherwise. And besides, Kelsey was my wife, right? What did she need her own rooms for? This isn't the Victorian era, or whenever it was that they used to do that."

"Okay," Tess said slowly, trying to understand it all and also trying to keep from pointing out that Krista and Tristan had slept apart—Hell, Krista had been apparently sleeping with Logan in the wife's rooms ever since Mack was an infant. Clearly, it wasn't all that long ago that *they used do that.*

"When Kelsey's behavior got *really* weird, Mother and Logan moved back in. Krista knows all the hidey-holes in the house and just happened to video a conversation between Kelsey and her father. When she called Kelsey out on what she heard, that's when all hell broke loose. Kelsey was—" Mack tightened his lips and looked away.

Tess waited. It wasn't lost on her that Krista had *just happened* to overhear a private conversation and then confronted Kelsey about it. Krista could be a fierce protector; Tess knew that firsthand.

"Terrified," Mack went on, his voice breaking slightly, "that her father would come after her for letting us know what was really going on. She fessed up to everything but then just... I don't know. Dissolved? She *swore* he would know we'd found out what he was up to, how he was using her, and that he'd come and kill her. So we did the only thing that would calm her, and we brought in security. Right there, that night. Eyes on her unless we were in our bedroom."

The things you can do with money, Tess thought.

"And that night," Mack went on, his voice hollowed out where a minute ago, he had been angry. Even his eyes, she noticed, seemed emptier, "she got up around one and went outside to look at the stars. The security guys had eyes on her the whole time. I fucking slept through it"—the anger, Tess noted, had come back, just that fast—"and her heart stopped. Just... stopped. That easy."

"That's a little..."

"Convenient?" Mack spat the word. "Especially when everyone came in my room, woke my ass up, and we found the empty pill bottles in our bathroom. She wanted to beat her father to it, I guess."

"Oh, Mack." All of a sudden, his inability to sleep in his own bed made sense.

"So here we are," he said. "And Nimisha says I need to sleep in here again. No more couches. Mother replaced everything she could: the mattress, the sheets, the pillows. She took all of Kelsey's things out of here so I don't have to look at them." He looked down at his hands, then held one up. A simple gold link bracelet was draped over his fingers. "I kept this. It was my wedding gift to her." He looked up at the phone, a new desperation in his eyes and spreading across his face.

"Oh, Mack." Tess wanted to kick herself for not being able to say anything else, but really, there wasn't anything else *to* say.

"But I didn't love her," he went on, staring again at the bracelet. "Not like I loved you. I cared for her, I cared *about* her, I tried to take care of her. And she told Krista she loved me, but then she went out to look at the stars..."

She waited.

"Why are all these sick fucks so damn twisted?" he went on after a minute, again looking straight into the phone so it felt like he was piercing Tess across the distance. "Is it the money? The lust for power? What is it, and am I doomed, or is there a way to avoid it?"

This, she knew, was really his concern. It always had been, and after this, it would of course come roaring back. "I think," she started, not sure if he actually wanted an answer, but he asked her to go on. "I think that it's all about what you're after. Power? Then yes, expect it to eat you alive. But you aren't in this to grow your bank accounts, and you're not in it to be the most glorified CEO out there, and you're not in it so you can walk down the street and have people point and stare in awe."

He snorted and looked away. She wondered what he was thinking.

"Sorry," he said after a minute. "Krista was on me for my tights again. She says people point and stare."

Tess grinned, remembering college Mack and his tights. "They used to make your legs look *good*."

"Yeah?" He brightened.

"Only when you wore the three-quarters, though. That's what set off your calves."

"Keep going."

"Can't," she said with a shrug that she was willing to bet came off as total flirt. "I haven't seen them in years. And no, do *not* stand up and drop your pants so I can fix that." Although, truth be told, she wouldn't have minded. At least he wasn't fixating on his bed.

"Dammit, Tess. I'm trying to have a pity party over here."

"And you're allowed, but it needs to end at some point. Hey, who's Nimisha?"

"Friend of Taylor's. She's..." He licked his lips and looked away. "A grief counselor."

"I knew I liked Taylor." Right then, she could have kissed Mack's assistant. He never would have reached out for help on his own.

"Do you still miss your father?" he asked.

She paused. "Every day." In another three years, it would be the twentieth anniversary of his death. She wasn't sure how she felt about that. He'd missed so much of her life...

"Not what I was hoping you'd say."

"Too bad."

"Way to help hold a guy down."

"You asked me to have your back," she said. "I'm just doing what you asked." Although, she had to admit, she'd gladly keep him down if it meant pinning him to a bed and having her way with him until he forgot about sleeping. If only there weren't so many miles and a huge lifestyle adjustment between them, she never would have been the proper house guest and gotten up after she'd fallen asleep on him at the Manor.

"Well, have my back on this one," he said. "How am I supposed to sleep?"

"Lie down. Close your eyes. Let your body do the rest."

"It's not that easy."

"What have you been doing on the couch all these months?"

"Not sleeping much."

"Well, then you're due. It'll be okay, Mack. It really will be."

"When?"

"One day."

"That's the best you can do?"

"It's the best any of us can do."

TWENTY

January 11

Tess didn't hear from Mack much again after that for the next week and a half. In a sense, she missed him, but figured he was as busy as she was. He was, after all, the head honcho.

That gave her time to investigate more about the crazy sheep farm, although details on it were sketchy. The people she had reached out to initially hadn't gotten back to her, so she decided to go to Serenity. Maybe, she reasoned, the old-timers in the neighborhood knew something.

Maybe Serenity would know more about Harald, the man Tess had met.

"He is the self-appointed caretaker of that old chunk of land." Serenity's lips pursed, like she'd tasted something sour.

"You think it's cursed too?" Tess asked.

"I know so," Serenity said. "If you go there at night, you'll hear the screams and moans. They have never stopped and they never will."

"Now it's haunted as well as cursed?"

"Always has been." Serenity folded her hands in her lap and waited while Tess thought it all through.

"How old is that farm?"

"Old." Serenity nodded, and Tess understood. Maybe Harald had been right and the land was something to stay away from.

But if Tess had learned one thing from working with Red, it was that property didn't like to be abandoned. It wanted to be occupied, to be touched by human lives, as crazy as that sounded. Red swore to it, and Tess had grown to think that maybe he could be right. Why wouldn't an old sheep farm have the same needs?

She wondered what would happen if she made time on a weekend to go over to the land, explore it, get to know it, see if it really was cursed and haunted, see if it could tell her what it needed.

As Tess left Serenity in Vera's, the corner café and bakery that was one of the heartbeats of Woolslayer, she knew the truth: She didn't have time for another pet project. The incubator was enough of one and she had to spend at least the next few weekends working with her tenants on their websites—the upcoming weekend visit with Mack excluded. And Philip still owed her answers about why the city was taking so long to fix the water main break. He'd had to cancel their meeting after New Year's.

Which was why she and Red were walking over to an old-style Italian restaurant that Tess had always thought had mob ties. It was *that* sort of old-style.

"This is a strange place to meet," he said.

"It is. I feel sort of sleazy."

He chuckled. "I know what you mean."

"You thought the same things I did?" She was surprised. Maybe it wasn't such a far-fetched idea.

"Almost everyone Christine and I know do. But I suppose it makes sense that it's a safe place for government types to meet." He motioned her inside, where a hostess showed them to a back room.

"This better not be some wild goose chase," he growled after the hostess had left. Even the stubble on his shaved head was bristling. "We both have other things we should be doing."

Tess took off her coat and slung it over the back of a chair, looking over at Red, but he kept his puffy vest on. The room was nice enough, with dark paneling on the walls, an industrial carpet, and a buffet table set up along one wall, chafing dishes waiting, their cans of Sterno closed.

Philip breezed in. "Okay, good. You're here." He shut the door and glanced around the room. "I'm told it's secure in here. We'll have to trust that."

Alarms went off in Tess' head. "Why?"

He took a deep breath and motioned to the chair beside the one she'd put her coat on, taking a seat before she or Red did. "When the crews went in to start to clean up the hole—really, it was a pretty basic break and we should have had it fixed in a few hours, but, well..." He took another deep breath and stood up, shaking out his pant legs. He started to sit again but must have thought better of it because he walked around the table.

When he stopped in front of Tess and Red, who were both still standing, he blurted, "There were bones down there."

"Bones?" Red repeated, blinking rapidly. Tess thought he looked like Sanjit.

"Yeah," Philip said and rubbed his arms like he was cold. His gaze flicked around the room. "Lots of bones. About three dozen bones." He held one hand out, the other still folded around his upper arm. "We had them analyzed immediately. Some are human, some are dogs, some are sheep? Sheep? And there's some raccoon and skunk and maybe squirrel—we're not entirely certain about some of the smaller bones. There's nothing like a full skeleton of anything, and if the human remains weren't there, we'd write it off as some kid's collection or something, but." He nodded, and Tess figured she and Red were supposed to finish that sentence for him.

"That makes no sense," Tess said, although the mention of sheep bones at least wasn't completely surprising. The trailhead to the old sheep farm was near enough to the old firehouse that it maybe could be explained. "It's too random a collection."

Philip tossed his head, flipping his hair off his forehead. "That's what has us tied up. What's it doing there? *Why* is it there? Did we find them all, especially the humans? So the bad news is that the water can't be restored so fast. Not until we excavate the area and see if there are more bones, more pieces to the story. But," he said, holding up a hand as Tess opened her mouth to mention the sheep farm, "I've got my engineers looking into getting service back by tapping into the line farther down, away from the old firehall lot. That might happen faster, but..." He took another deep breath. "It's going to be a long haul, Tess. I may need your help to keep the people from rioting."

She arched an eyebrow at him. "Rioting? Really?"

"Everyone needs water, and we're looking at... well, I don't know how long. The mayor's pulled everyone possible in on this, and not just because he knows you'll be breathing down our necks, Red. This is... it could be huge. And I'd appreciate the help keeping it out of the press."

"When have we ever—" Red said, shaking his head. It was his turn to fold his arms over his chest, his biceps straining at his sleeves, some of the vibrant colors of his tattoos seeping through the white fabric.

"I know, but don't start now, okay?" Philip said in a rush, taking a step back. "This is the worst sort of nightmare any of us could have expected. We really thought we'd have had this fixed."

Tess cocked her head, wondering if that could be true. This was Woolslayer.

Then again, if they fixed it quickly, the people would shut up and go away—and could be ignored some more.

"I'll keep you two in the loop," Philip said, reaching for his coat and slipping his arms in. "But it may need to be on the down-low like this. And anything you can do, Tess, to keep the peace down there will be appreciated."

"One thing that I know will help," she started, holding a hand out as if to stop him from leaving.

"Yeah?"

"Maintain a presence down there. Move machinery around. Have people there. If it *looks* like people care, your workers can be sitting in that hole watching Pornhub on their phones and no one will think they're not working. Hear me?"

Philip nodded and met her eyes, holding them as he said, "I do. Not my thing, but I hear you." He rushed out of the room.

Red looked at her for a long minute.

"What?"

"Pornhub?"

"Hey, I don't judge."

"Let's keep this one between us." He nudged her. Tess took it as a sign to reach for her coat.

"Define *this one*," she said. "We've had a lot to keep between us so far today."

"That we have," he said. "Let's get back to the office and put our attention on design."

Tess took a deep breath. "That is music to my ears."

"Can I ignore the easy Pornhub joke?"

"Please."

TWENTY-ONE

January 15

M ack sat up in his bed. He'd given it two full weeks, but he still couldn't sleep in it. Hell, he could barely breathe when he lay down in it.

Part of his guilt, he knew, was that he'd done everything he could for Kelsey—except for the one thing that had mattered the most: He'd forgotten that her father was a ruthless bastard with an agenda that went beyond marrying off his daughter.

He knew his mother was also kicking herself for not thinking ahead. But they'd both been so focused on their goals for the company, they hadn't stopped to think that Flemming wasn't willing to wait for them to transform PharmaSci into a strong, viable company. Mack didn't know if he'd wanted to do that himself, or just sell off the pieces. It didn't matter. PharmaSci was safe.

For the first time, he wondered if PharmaSci had ever been threatened before. The answer to that was probably in the journals all the Mackenzie men had kept, nice thick leather-bound books that were in a safe behind his desk downstairs, his on top of the pile. This was probably the safest time he'd ever have to go read them.

He wondered if Kelsey had known about them, and if she'd told Flemming about them, as well. The tradition held that she shouldn't have. It was supposed to be one of those quiet things, a legacy handed down from Mackenzie man to Mackenzie man, the entire history of PharmaSci there, written down as it unfolded.

Some part of him must have known Kelsey couldn't be trusted because he'd never taken those journals out when she was home.

He snorted softly. He should have done better by her. He should have heard her.

No matter what Nimisha said, he shouldn't have gone to sleep. He should have stayed awake, held her, helped her face whatever it was Flemming had been doing to her. After all, if he was an expert in anything, it was the level of asshole that fathers could be. Tristan had been angry, brooding, and argumentative about everything. If he told Mack to get a haircut and Mack said okay, he'd get angry and shout that Mack was too compliant. But if Mack had refused the haircut, he'd be labelled as a rebellious disgrace to the Mackenzie name. There had been no way to win.

And that's why he'd gone snooping in his father's office that day, the day he'd found the paperwork about SH-34. He'd used it as ammunition, to make a stand that he wasn't going to turn into a man like Tristan.

That's when he'd started going by Mack, and he'd blazed his own path. After all, if his father was going to call him a rebel, he may as well have acted like one.

Looking back at it, he was surprised to realize how little resistance Krista had put up to his rebellion. She'd been calm in the face of every choice he made. Fortunately, he hadn't done anything *too* dumb. Maybe that's why she'd been so accepting.

He squirmed.

Tess had been wrong when she had told him to just close his eyes and let his body remember how to sleep.

He pushed himself up, then swung out of bed. Could he even say he had a side of the bed anymore? Weren't they both his now?

Krista wouldn't appreciate him wandering around as he was, so he pulled on a pair of flannel lounge pants and went downstairs, to the safe. Inside it, on top, where it was supposed to be, was his journal. Under it was Tristan's, then Cullen's, then Patrick's.

He paused, eyeing it, and set the top three journals in their own stack beside the others. Patrick's was now on top. Maybe it held the story of why Cullen had been such a lousy steward for PharmaSci, and he picked it up, running his thumb along the page edges, listening to them rustle. He opened to a random page, immediately realizing that the problem with handwritten journals was the effort needed to decipher some of his ancestors' penmanship. Great-Grandpa Patrick—who Mack had never met—clearly hadn't worried that his words would be legible for future generations.

Maybe that was a clue.

He closed the journal and set it back on top of Robert's, but left the smaller stack where it was. He'd come back in daylight and see what he could make of Patrick's journal.

For now, though, he was restless, his thoughts cycling back to Kelsey.

He wanted to sit where she had that night last summer, to see the stars she'd looked at. Maybe he'd understand why she'd chosen right *then* to do this, right when they'd uncovered the truth and had prepared to rally around her and free her from her father's games.

But he paused when he got outside. For one thing, it was colder than he'd realized. It was, after all, January, and January in Lakeford meant cold. He hadn't even bothered with a shirt or shoes, so he popped back inside to grab a jacket. It still wouldn't be warm enough, but that was okay. He deserved to be cold. Kelsey certainly was.

For another thing, looking at the chair brought it all back. The yelling; the security guard who'd kept him inside until he'd threatened to deck the guy because dead or alive, that was his *wife* and he was going to see her; the chaos as the paramedics had come, then the police; Krista's comment that she was glad this was happening under cover of deep night when even the drunks and wandering spouses on their way home wouldn't be likely to happen by and see the vehicles that had arrived, of course, with lights and sirens off.

The patio was quiet now though, the chair still there. He'd had to ask for it to remain; the idea of the patio without it had been too much, even though they put the patio furniture away every winter. Juan had wound up leaving it all out.

Mack sat where Kelsey had, his back against the same mesh or nylon or whatever it was that hers had been cushioned against. He felt like it was the place to break down and cry, and maybe his face was a little wet, but he wasn't able to break down. Maybe he'd waited too long to be able to. Maybe he hadn't loved her enough.

And for that, he felt guilty. She'd deserved more. At the beginning, he'd thought he'd be able to give her more, that she'd wanted more, but she'd only pulled away from him. Like she was trying to protect him.

Maybe that was the job they'd each had: protecting each other.

But she'd succeeded, and he'd failed.

"Emerson?"

"Yeah," he said, surprised but not that Krista was there. Krista was *always* there.

"I can't sleep either," she said and sat down in the chair beside the one he was in. She blinked at him and tucked her hands into her lap. "Aren't you cold?"

He shrugged. She was, of course, in a fur. Her hair was down, though, sitting on her shoulders like an artist had arranged it. Always proper.

"Why did we get rid of Tristan if he wasn't half the bastard Flemming is?"

"In his own way, he was worse," Krista said.

"Did he—"

"Yes. But the day I told him I was pregnant with you, I also told him that if he touched me again in any sense, even a kind one, I'd cut his testicles open and slice his penis off and hide it so it couldn't be reattached, and then I showed him the knife I'd bought to do it with." She paused the barest of beats and smiled. It wasn't a kind smile. "Well, as you know," she continued, "your father's not the most courageous of the Mackenzie men."

Mack turned to her, his jaw hanging open. "You threatened to..."

"Oh, it wasn't a threat, Emerson, and he knew it. I knew his exact dose of sleep aids, and, well, I was carrying you, so clearly I had *some* idea of male anatomy. He had no doubt that not only did I know what to do, but how to do it—and that I'd bought the right knife for the job, too."

"He didn't try to take the knife?"

"Of course he did. But I reminded him that if he tried, that constituted touching me and his genitals were mine, and if he tried to find where I'd be keeping it, well, good luck because I know *all* the secrets of Mackenzie Manor, including where he was hiding the gifts for his various girlfriends."

Mack shook his head. "Why are men such shits?"

"Logan isn't, and that's why he was a fixture in your life as you grew up. Think about it. Your father was the role model you rejected. Logan is the role model you emulated."

He took a deep breath and, as he did, shivered. He wasn't sure, but he thought the temperature might be dropping.

Served him right.

He turned his face up to the sky and asked, "Why do I feel like I was never anything more than a pawn?"

Krista turned to him, surprise etched across her face. She raised her perfect eyebrows. "Well, of course you are. Just as I was, just as your father was, just as your wife was... we're *all* pawns. The question is how you choose to live out your service—will you give in to the corruption or will you rise above?"

Mack understood. Part of him always had, but sitting here now, getting to the point where he could neither stop shivering nor hide it from his mother, he understood it with more clarity.

But he had one more question.

"Why didn't you just take over PharmaSci yourself? You probably could have argued that you had to until I was ready."

She laughed, a light, tinkling laugh that suggested she was more frivolous than she actually was. "Because, dear, I'm not a Mackenzie."

"And because you were worried that if you did, I wouldn't?"

"Emerson, dear, I have faith that you're going to be a greater man than I could ever hope for." She grabbed his chin, holding him. He crossed his arms over his chest, like that would help keep him warm. "Now, go inside and get in your bed and pile on some blankets until you warm up. No more couches, even for part of the night."

Mack waited for her to let go of his chin, but she searched his eyes for a long minute.

"Emerson?"

"Yeah?"

"I love you beyond words."

It was the first time Mack could ever remember his mother saying anything like that to him.

TWENTY-TWO

January 16

It was a rare Saturday that Tess didn't have anything to do. The Woolslayer women were working with her web designer. They'd taken pictures for their various sites—including the incubator's main website—on New Year's Eve. Jamie and Hank were busy with the twins, and Tess' mother was off at a B&B with her boyfriend for the weekend.

No one needed Tess. For anything.

She grabbed a jacket to wear over her fleece quarter-zip, a pair of gloves, and sunglasses and headed out to the sheep farm. She wanted to see more of it than just the fence and those overgrown grasses. And maybe Harald would be there and she could find out what else he knew about the place.

At the incubator, her parking space was waiting for her, and as she walked around the temporary fencing around the hole in the ground at the water main break, she waved to a good number of people. Maybe she wasn't the barely tolerated white girl anymore, she thought as Ebony stopped to chat with her about the events she and her partner, Patricia, were working on now that New Year's had been such a success.

It was only three blocks, but Tess thought she'd said hello to at least ten different people and stopped to talk to not only Ebony but a few others, as well. Jayson had stopped her to tell her what the special of the day at Vera's was, and Tess made a note to stop in before she headed home. But first, she wanted to explore what she could of the sheep farm.

She half expected to run into Harald when she rounded that first fenced corner, but he wasn't there. Tess kept going, kept following the path along the fence. It went on for some distance, still looking like a common path used by deer, which made her wonder if the land really was haunted. Wouldn't deer stay away if it was?

She gave herself a shake. Hauntings weren't real. Ghosts weren't real. Land wasn't cursed. It was all a lot of superstition. She'd seen it before, of course. More than once, Red had told them they'd been hired to work on a haunted building.

The first time, Anchey had hired ghost chasers to try to confirm the haunting. They had tried very hard to find something, and then tried to manufacture a ghost.

That had been the end of that.

Tess paused to take in the area inside the fence. It looked a lot like it had the last time she'd been out here. Less green, more brown and yellow, and a lot of the tall grasses had bowed as winter had taken hold, but that was all, cosmetically. And it was still too quiet; she could see where the idea of it being haunted had come from.

Five more steps ahead, she came across an almost invisible break in the fence, just wide enough for a slim person to slip through. Glancing both ways, Tess held her breath and hoped she wouldn't rip her jacket.

It was immediately creepy inside the fence, as if the birds had stopped singing and the wind had stopped blowing. Tess folded her hands in her jacket pockets and stood still, three steps into the field, and looked to the right. She'd come from that direction and it looked exactly like it had from the other side of the fence.

But to the left was another fenced-off area, and as Tess narrowed her eyes to study it better, she realized there was a person on their hands and knees in it.

Carefully, she walked in that direction. "Hello?" she called, her hand wrapping around her phone.

The person turned to look at her, holding up a hand to shade their eyes. "Who there?"

"My name is Tess. Can I ask who you are?"

"You can ask. Doesn't mean I gotta answer."

Tess took two cautious steps forward, toward the person. "You were here the last time I was out here."

He straightened and slowly got to his feet. "You were told to not come back."

"Well, I did. Serenity thought you would be able to tell me about this place. I want to learn. I want to hear its history."

"Just like that? You show up where you were told not to be and say you want to learn and throw my friend's name around like it's going to open doors, and you expect answers, just like that? Like I should know who you are and why the story of this place matters to you? Girl, the world don't bow to you, and it don't need to. Some stories don't belong to the likes of you."

Tess paused, but his rebuke had awoken an anger. "The likes of me? Harald, I *collect* stories of old places. And then I do my best to make those old places into something new, something better."

"Leave this old place alone. It's not for the likes of you."

"There you go again. *The likes of me.* What? Because I'm white? I don't belong here because I was lucky enough to be born with paler skin than you?"

He narrowed his eyes like he was studying her. She raised her chin and waited. A breeze kicked up and pulled at her. It felt like it pulled the hair away from the back of her neck and gathered in a point, right at the spot where she wore a tribute to her father.

Maybe, she thought, the place really was haunted. Because that was entirely too creepy a thing to happen if it meant nothing.

Harald raised his own chin but kept studying her. A few brown leaves rustled and came to rest against the black iron fencing he stood within. He glanced down at them and then nodded, as if talking to them. "If you say so," he sighed, and Tess had a feeling he was.

She waited until Harald went on. "She don't look like much to me, but Serenity speaks highly of her." He paused, then scratched the top of his balding head. "Okay, Miss Tess, I'm telling you what."

Tess cocked her head and waited.

"The spirits around here, they seem to think you're important somehow, so you've got three questions. Make them count."

She took a deep breath. On the one hand, this was ridiculous. But on the other, she knew Harald believed the land was haunted. Even if the spirits were confined to his head, he believed they were real, and he was their caretaker. At least she could get answers, even if it meant playing games.

"Whose farm was this?" she asked.

"Very bad people. They got run out of town by their own disrespect for the human, you know what I'm saying?"

Tess bit her lower lip and nodded, assuming he was referring to slavers. "When?" she asked.

Harald shrugged. "Not soon enough for the spirits who are stuck here." He paused and looked down at the leaves again. "Okay, fine," he said with a sigh. "They say to tell you that the owners left years and years ago, but the farm was open and working until around the middle of the—what's that? They say what sounds like the nineteen eighties. Lots of us remember back then. You could get fresh lamb and mutton in the butcher shop right here in our business district." He raised a hand and Tess tensed, but he waved her forward.

She took a few steps closer, but when Harald frowned, she closed the distance between them, stopping on her side of the fence.

"That's better. We don't need to yell. They don't like it. Sounds *angry* to them, and they've had enough of *angry*." He shook his head, his eyes closed. "They are the angry ones. We don't need to be. You asked about when. I don't rightly know when the owners left the land. But they left people here, and those people were good. They hired from the neighborhood, paid a fair wage, never missed a paycheck. Then one day, they gave everyone three months' salary and said they were shutting down. A week later, no one was here. Just the spirits. And me, from time to time."

"And that was..." Tess prompted.

"You asking me? That your third question?"

"No. But like I said, I collect histories, so to me, the year is important. And it's part of what I asked in my second question."

He *humphed* and shook his head. "I told you. It was the middle of the eighties."

"The exact year might be important."

"Why?"

She shrugged. "Sometimes, it is. The little details matter."

Harald bent down and pulled some long grasses away from one of the fence posts. "They like you."

"Thank you."

"You still got one question."

"I do," Tess said, putting her hand back in her jacket pocket and strolling to the far edge of the fence. She paused at the corner, taking her hand out and touching the fencing. As expected, it was cool to the touch, like it hadn't absorbed any of the sun's warmth. Not that there was a lot of warmth in the winter, but, she thought, it was still warmer in Port Kenneth than it was, say, in New York, where Mack was.

Briefly, she wondered what he'd think of Harald.

"This, in here," Harald said, motioning to the fenced-in area, "is where some of them lie. I'm not the one who takes care of it in here. Someone else does. I don't know who. I've never seen them."

Tess nodded, thinking. She only had one question left, but if Harald was going to fill her silence with more information, she would let him.

"So you're not the only one who cares about this place."

"That a question?" Harald gave her a sharp look.

She forced a smile. "No. It's me thinking out loud. You and someone else take care of this place."

"This *cemetery*," Harald said. "The rest of the land, I can't speak to. Or the house."

Tess bit back another smile. A house, too? "Can't be easy," she said, "with the spirits talking to you."

"I don't know why they like you." He shook his head slowly, an exaggerated motion.

"Maybe for the same reason they like you."

He *humphed*. "They like me because I care."

"I'd like to care, too."

He *humphed* again. "Only so's you can turn this into something."

"Maybe. Or maybe… I don't know," she said, turning in a circle and looking out across the area. If there was a house nearby, she couldn't see it, but there were trees blocking her view of the top of the nearby hill. And was that another wrought iron fence, just uphill from this cemetery? If so, why were there two? And why was only this one tended?

That, maybe, she could figure out herself.

"I like it here. It's beautiful land." She turned to look downhill once more, this time looking out over the land, toward Woolslayer. All she could see, though, were the trees on the outside of the fencing. "I'd like to come back. Would the spirits mind?"

"That your third question?" He narrowed his eyes at her.

She nodded.

"No," he said. "No, they would not mind. Like I said, they think you're important."

She glanced around the purported cemetery. "Thank you," she said to the land, knowing there was nothing to the spirits beyond an old man's beliefs, but it never hurt to play along.

TWENTY-THREE

January 25

"I can't believe you called me to the principal's office," Tess told Serenity as she walked into the main office of Woolslayer High. She also couldn't believe she'd come, but this was for Georgie, and he was worth a summons to the principal's office.

Since the end of the October campaign, they'd left Georgie without a project, without an incentive. She hadn't realized she'd need to sit on him so hard, and she told Serenity that.

"How much experience do you have with teenage boys?"

"Fair enough," Tess said and smiled at the life coach. "How is everyone's business? Have the street closures been a problem?"

Serenity waved her off. "If I can't video chat, I go to my clients or we meet at Vera's, like you and I usually do. There's something fun about it, like we're taking our work public where others can see it—and that gets back to what we'd talked about earlier. Letting people know what it is we do. They're *seeing* it, Tess. Maybe this has been a blessing in disguise, although don't you fret. We *need* that private office space, too. It's not good business to be having a discussion that someone's paid for when some freeloader at the next table is eavesdropping."

Tess hoped things would continue to go well. All she'd heard from Philip in the last week was that they'd found some more bones. Not many, and no more human. They were, for some reason, carbon dating the human bones, which was news that had sat in Tess' gut like a bad dinner. Some sixth sense warned her that they weren't going to be recent.

"Harald said he was impressed with you," Serenity said.

"Thanks," Tess said and was about to ask another question, but her phone buzzed.

If I walk down the hall right now, am I going to find you?

No, but I'll be back soon, she replied to Red. She'd told Anchey she had Woolslayer business as she'd left. Maybe he hadn't passed the message along.

Things okay down there? Red asked.

So much for doubting Anchey. *Think so. There are crews in the hole. I'm not sure if they're doing real work or, you know, on their phones.*

The door to the principal's office opened.

It turned out Georgie had found a new project on his own, documenting the saga of the water main break, which he swore was taking up all his time. But the actual truth came out quickly: He'd decided that being a star social media reporter about the neighborhood was much more interesting and important than school. He wanted to drop out. His mother had. His older brother had. People had bought some of the pictures he'd hung in the old butcher's shop, so he had money. He didn't need school anymore.

"Want a mentor?" the principal asked. "Want these ladies to keep supporting you? Want to learn how to run a business the smart way, so you're successful?"

Georgie looked at Tess and Serenity, the guilt deep in his dark brown eyes, and mumbled a yes and made new promises to stay in school. He had sprawled in his chair, all knees and elbows, somehow looking defeated, but he promised to stick it through.

After the meeting, Tess went back to the office, where she jotted a note to herself to stop putting off the search for his mentor. Maybe they'd have to hold that over his head a little more firmly until he got himself straightened out.

Right as she started to get ready to leave for dinner at Jamie's, her office phone rang. She almost didn't answer it, but something insisted she did.

"This is Tess."

"You love me, right?" Mack asked.

She closed her eyes and took a breath. "Of course. What's wrong?"

"The whole world is conspiring against me."

He didn't sound as down in the dumps as he could have, so Tess figured he was just being melodramatic. "How so?"

"The meeting we scheduled with the university? Seems like it overlaps with something major going on in town and I can't get a hotel room for anything. And I mean *anything*, Tess. You should see what Taylor's tried. They've done a deep dive into all the private rentals and Airbnbs and even called our local reps and a couple hotel chain owners. That was weird, let me tell you, and not the sort of thing I want to make a habit of, but Taylor doesn't let anything stop them when they're on a mission."

"So we reschedule." It wasn't her ideal, but these things happened. She wrote a note to find out what was going on in town. It was almost February, for crying out loud. The city got quiet for the first month or two of the new year.

"Tess? I don't want to reschedule. It doesn't fit with some stuff I have going on up here."

"Oh. Well, I don't know what to tell you, Mack. What's wrong with flying the corporate jet in and out on the same day?"

"This isn't a corporate project," he said. There was a finality in his voice that she recognized. "And we'd talked about making a weekend out of it. So I had a thought…"

"And that was?" She knew. Of course she knew. This was *Mack*.

"You have a guest room, right?"

"Oh no." She wanted to ask why he was willing to bend rules and stay with her when he wasn't willing to bend rules and bring the jet, but she had a feeling she knew the answers—and they weren't all financial. Or that staying with her was bending any rules. Sure, he was a client, but…

"But you do. Right?"

"I do, but this is a really bad idea."

"Want to push this whole field project off another six months?"

"If we have to."

"We don't have to. Not if you let me crash in your guest room."

The problem—the whole, entire problem—was that of course she wanted to say yes. She wanted to spend the time with him and get to know the adult Mack. It felt like they'd had so little opportunity to do that, and it was a huge reason why he was planning to stay for the entire weekend.

One thing she knew for certain: If he wasn't willing to bend the rules and take the corporate jet, he hadn't fully gone over to the dark side.

"Optics, Mack," she sighed.

"Who's going to know?"

"Combine it with scouting sites for the new PharmaSci headquarters and take the damn corporate jet."

"But we're not close to scouting sites yet. We're still in information-gathering mode. Krista and I are supposed to get together about the whole relocation thing, but we've been too busy to really talk about it."

"All the more reason to push the field project back a bit. It'll let you free up your time and put us more firmly into better weather."

"What does weather have to do with finalizing plans?"

She closed her eyes. He had her there, and she wasn't going to bring up the idea that better weather meant he could wear shorts or his tights and show off his legs.

"And wouldn't it be better to finalize the plans now so you can start to get bids for the work and we can set construction schedules that'll maximize good weather?"

He was sounding like her, and he probably knew it.

"No, I'm just afraid of the optics becoming a problem if you stay with me." She was also afraid of what would happen if she let him stay with her. Would he actually sleep in the guest room, or would she invite him into her bed? Was he even ready for that, after losing his wife so recently? Was *she*?

"Who's going to see, and what is there to see?"

"We both know Krista will worry about gossips and pictures showing up online and—"

"Tess. No one cares about either of us. Sorry to hurt you, but down there, I'm one CEO out of millions, and you're... well, okay. Sounds like you're big shit, but when was the last time you wound up in the papers for who you were seen with?"

He was right again.

"Besides," he went on, "Krista will love this. You know she wants you to be," he cleared his throat and dropped his voice as he said, "the next Mrs. Emerson Mackenzie."

Tess hung her head and rubbed her forehead with the hand not holding the phone to her ear. "Next time she starts in, tell her you'd rather be Mr. Tess Cartieri."

His chuckle was fat and satisfied. "I will. So it's settled, then? I'm taking over your guest room for a weekend? And you'll show me the famous hole in the ground?"

"Oh, you," she said, already plotting revenge. There *would* be revenge. "Nicely played, Mack. Nicely played."

TWENTY-FOUR

From the moment they hung up, Mack felt bad about coercing Tess into letting him stay with her. He could see how it sent the wrong message, but the truth was he just wanted to be near her. That was all.

And hotels were so damn impersonal. Not to mention all booked.

Krista had committed him to some social event, so it wasn't until he got back that he made the time to text Tess and apologize.

I feel like I strong-armed you earlier.

You kinda did.

He considered the fact that she'd let him do it. Tess never let him pull shit over on her. *Just out of options*, he sent back, wondering what she would say to that. It wasn't true, and they both knew it.

No such thing, she texted back. *There's always the pay-by-the-week joint out near the airport. They're never full. Cheaper than a night in a CEO-quality hotel, too.*

He chuckled and kicked off his shoes, sitting on the edge of the bed. The goddamn bed. It still poked at him and refused to let him sleep. *Don't people die in that place?*

Not often.

Nice to know what you think of me.

He couldn't resist. With one hand, he loosened his tie and unbuttoned the top button on his shirt and with the other, he sent the text over to a voice call.

She was laughing when she picked up.

"That's me," he said, slouching in self-defeat. "Hours of entertainment."

"What I keep you around for," she said through a few last gasps. "You *know* there will be revenge for this." She gave him a side eye that dissolved into a grin.

"Same answer," he said. "Hours of entertainment." He returned her grin. He'd missed talking like this. "So long as you don't make me walk over the doorstep of that place. No, on second thought, we're not going within a mile of the property."

"Gonna be hard to get from the airport, then. You go right past it."

"Are you picking me up now?"

"Wasn't planning to."

Somehow, that was a letdown. "Optics?" he asked.

"That, and I'd guess you're arriving in the middle of the work day, and if I have to be out of the office, no offense, but Woolslayer needs me more. You can grab an Uber."

Mack paused. It was one of those things he'd never done. He either drove himself or Juan drove him, and business trips always had a car and driver arranged for him through a service. Every time he'd gone to Port Kenneth the past couple of years, he'd simply rented a car and, okay, gotten lost a few times once he'd left the area around campus, but it had all worked out.

But this time, he didn't need a car. Not if Just Tess could drive him around.

"You okay with that?" she asked, and with a start, he realized he'd let the conversation drop.

"Yeah, fine," he said with a small shake of his head. "I'll have Taylor set it up for me."

"Oh, Mack," she said with a heavy sigh that told him he was being stupid for some reason.

"What?"

"You sound like you're incapable of doing things for yourself. You don't need Taylor to set this up. Download the app. Fill in the information it asks for. When you get here and need a ride, open the app and follow the instructions. It's basic smartphone."

"I can do basic," he said, but it came out sounding as underconfident as he felt.

"You can do more than basic," she said.

"I'm a busy man, Just Tess," he said, feeling even more lame and on the verge of whining. "And everyone does everything they can to make my life easier and more focused on work."

"Do you do anything *but* work?"

"Well, I have the team. And I have all of Krista's social obligations. But other than that? No time. Between us? It's one of the reasons I want to move PharmaSci. Krista won't come with us, so I'll be free of all her social stuff and can have a life. And friends! And don't say it, but you were right about Krista and her social life. It got old *fast*, and now, without Kelsey, it really sucks. Everyone wants to express their condolences, their sorrow, and the single women..." He ran his free hand through his hair and closed his eyes. "Krista and I have had more than a few fights about it. She always tells me to put in an appearance and leave early, but they won't let me. They attach themselves to me like they're my dates. Alyssa's been the worst."

"Still? Tell me about her."

"Nothing to tell. I went to high school with her. She... has delusions."

The way Tess laughed, like it exploded out from between her lips, made him grin. "Don't tell me," she said through her laughter. "I don't think I could take it."

"Maybe, but I bet you could take her in a fair fight."

"Oh, what's the fun of fighting fair?"

"I doubt Alyssa would know, and not just because she'd lose. She'd go down and dirty from the get-go."

"Can't wait to meet her. Next time I come up, can you invite her over for dinner?"

He froze at first, but her laughter calmed his paranoia. He got up and started pacing anyway. "You *do* realize what she'd think of that, right?"

"Of course," Tess said. "She'd show up in some come-hither outfit, expecting a night of high romance and hot sex, and walk into an ambush instead."

"Krista would kill us."

"Be worth it."

He stopped pacing and leaned against the wall, realizing he was staring at his bed. His nemesis. Except it suddenly didn't seem so evil. Not with Tess planning the destruction of Alyssa Shoenstrom's romantic obsession.

"Hey, question for you," she said, and he thought he might be relieved she was shifting the conversation into safer territory.

"Ask."

"When you're here, are you okay with Indian food? Sanjit wants to use your being in town as an excuse to get us all together for his famous curry."

So much for her moving into safer territory. "Who is *us all*, and will it be a problem?"

Tess named the principals and the two owners. "And Red's wife."

"And you're showing up with a client."

"We've wined and dined clients before. Just not at Sanjit's house."

"And why are we wining and dining the great Emerson Mackenzie?"

"Because we've got one project of his and if he relocates his corporate headquarters like rumors say he might, we want the job. Maybe regardless of whichever city he picks."

Mack got quiet for a minute, trying to swallow the panic that rose at the idea of dinner with her coworkers. "Maybe another time." He didn't understand what it was about, but he didn't like it.

"What's wrong?"

"I'd better go. Again, sorry I strong-armed you." He started pacing again, faster this time, but he couldn't outrun the panic. "Don't feel like you have to do anything special for me."

"Mack." It was an order and it scared off the emotion, leaving him immediately drained.

"I don't know, Tess. I just don't know."

"Okay," she said, and her voice changed. It smoothed out, all the laughter gone. "Too early. I get it."

"It's been seven months!"

"Grief doesn't have a calendar. I wish like hell it did, but that's just not how it all works."

"That's what everyone says," he said heavily, leaning against the wall again. This didn't even feel like he thought grief would feel. There was too much *guilt* in there.

"So it'll be just us over the weekend, and Sanjit will pick a different weekend for his curry extravaganza."

"You okay with that?"

"Yeah. I mean, this way, I won't have to worry about you. Although warn me if I have to worry about you hiding in the men's room. I'd hate to have to ask some random man to rescue you. That could be awkward. Of course, if we're at Sanjit's, it'll be less so, but harder for you to save face once we get you out of there, so... yeah. No Sanjit's."

He smiled and sat back down on the bed. "Does this ever feel any better?"

"Eventually, but that hole's always there. And sometimes you stop noticing it, and at first you feel guilty for not noticing it, but then you realize that the only way to feel better is to stop noticing it, and you can either get caught up in the cycle of guilt or you can remind yourself that they wanted you to be happy and to move on and do great things with your life—"

"I don't know about that. I'm not sure she thought of me at all in any of this."

"If she hadn't, she'd have sold you out and stolen everything you own, and you'd probably be living on my couch until you could reestablish yourself as an athletic trainer."

"Is it totally wrong that sometimes, I wish she had?"

"Yes. Because either way, you'd have wound up without her."

"That wasn't what I was thinking of."

"Don't go there or you're paying for a seedy hotel room by the airport that rents by the week. You can be there with the newly separated men who don't know where else to go now that they've been locked out of their own houses, a bunch of junkies, and a few prostitutes."

"Sounds like fun." He laughed softly. "Either way, my life pretty well sucks."

"Except you've got an Ultimate team you like, you're being successful with your goals for PharmaSci, you're buying naming rights to a field, and after all these years, we're talking again."

"Just Tess, how can you always see the good in things?"

"Practice. And you should start."

TWENTY-FIVE

February 1

G etting out of the office on time proved difficult throughout the next week. Everyone wanted to confer with Tess and get her take on their projects—which, as team leader, they were supposed to do and which was fine, so long as they did it at a more reasonable time during the day. Anchey had to intervene the night she was due down in Woolslayer.

On arriving, everyone wanted an update on the water main, but Tess had nothing to say. If there was news, Philip wasn't sharing.

"Why are things so messed up here?" Gerri asked. "I get that people don't care so much about most of us. We're not rich, we're not college material, many of us weren't even born in this country—"

"And not all of us came here willingly," Serenity added, and Tess caught her eye and nodded acknowledgement, thinking back to her bizarre discussion with Harald. But she also considered the fact that Port Kenneth had been welcoming refugees from the various world crises of the past ten years. Those people hadn't come here all that willingly, either.

"You know what?" she asked, meeting as many eyes as she could. "I don't want to say where we all came from doesn't matter, because it does. But right here and right now, in this room, with this group of women, what matters more, I think, is that we help each other. That we all strive to be everything we can be, that we redefine what people think of us, and that we do it by our actions and by being successful with our businesses."

"It's about time you acknowledged you're a businesswoman, too," Janeesa said, exchanging looks with Serenity.

"Of course I am," Tess said, trying not to roll her eyes. "Thankfully, you guys are a labor of love."

That got a ripple of approval. And truthfully, with Red and Serenity both helping out in various but dependable ways, juggling two jobs didn't seem so impossible.

"I want to make my job pay me," Serenity said, "enough that I can have a car like yours. *That* is my goal for the year." She placed her hands on her thighs as if to show emphasis.

They spun into a discussion of their goals, but kept circling back to the water problem; goals were hard to achieve when there was no water and, as a result, no occupancy of their workspaces. Thankfully, no one mentioned that there had been a water main break downtown just the other day, and it had been repaired within three hours. Maybe it was better to let them think the problem was that they were in Woolslayer, and not that there was a bigger issue. It didn't feel right, but until they knew what was going on with the bones, she had promised to keep her mouth shut.

The next morning, she engineered a chance encounter with Philip in the coffee shop. He was two people behind her, and she let them go in front of her so she had Philip all to herself. "We need to talk," she told him. "Face to face."

"I'm under orders to dodge you," he said, giving her a weak smile and holding a hand up to block his face.

Tess crossed her arms over her chest. Not only hadn't she had coffee yet, she'd moved *back* in line. "Whose orders are those?" she asked, speaking a heck of a lot more calmly than she felt. What she really wanted to do was start screaming. Maybe creating a scene in a coffee shop wouldn't work against her.

"Tess... Look," Philip said, glancing carefully around the shop. "I want to say more. I can't. Do you read me? So let me say this: It's not as easy as it should be. This could affect the mayor's reelection campaign—"

"Since when does one working class neighborhood have that much power?"

He glared at her, as if telling her to think about it.

She stiffened and leaned close, grabbing his wrist. "Are you telling me there's a serious infrastructure problem, or is it entirely that weird collection you found?"

"I'm not telling you anything."

"Of course not," she said, wondering if the people she'd let in front of her would let her have her spot back. The first one was almost at the counter. "Hey, Philip," she said casually. He stiffened, but she smiled. "I saw that profile of you that the *City Central* did."

"What about it?" he asked, his eyes darting back and forth so fast, Tess wondered if he was actually registering anything around him.

"Well, is it true you walk dogs at the shelter?"

"Yeah. Of course. Why?"

She stayed facing straight ahead. "I've never met anyone who does that. Tell me about it."

"Why?"

"Because I'm curious. My best friend had a Golden when we were kids, but I'm not much of a dog person." Jamie's mom's dog had been a therapy dog, and Tess had spent a lot of time crying into Chloe's fur when things had gotten bad—and then worse—with her dad. "Are there trails you can walk, or do you just walk your doggos around the parking lot?"

"Tess, are you serious?"

"Yes." The first woman she'd let in front of her had made it to the counter and was ordering.

"Well," Philip said and again, he looked around like he was expecting someone to jump out of a hidden spot and yell at him for talking to the enemy, "there are trails. Do you really want to hear this?"

"Yes. Do you walk big dogs, little dogs, what?"

"Why?"

"Because in case you missed the memo, the only time we've talked about something other than Woolslayer was the first time we met. Time to fix that."

Philip was quiet for a minute. "And if anyone asks, we're not talking business."

"Well, that too. So come on," she said as she stepped up to the counter, where she was able to hand over her travel cup with a smile. The perks of being a regular. "Big dogs or little dogs?"

Philip stepped up beside her and did the same with his own cup. "Any, depending on who most needs a cage break. There are a few I've learned that I'm not the best handler for, and I have some favorites, but how can you even care about this?"

Tess held her phone over the payment machine. "I've thought about getting a cat, but not a dog; I don't think I'm home enough to give it proper attention." She raised her eyebrows as if the explanation settled everything and stepped aside so he could pay.

He made an aggravated noise and slipped his card into the machine. "I'm glad you're aware that dogs take work. That's why I walk them. Well, that and my landlord doesn't let us have dogs. Only fish in tanks no larger than twenty gallons and snakes. I don't know why they let snakes in an apartment building, so don't ask."

"Wasn't going to," Tess chuckled. "What kind of a pet do you think a snake is? I mean, can you pet a snake?"

For the first time, he softened and almost chuckled. "You are nothing like I thought you'd be, based on your reputation," he said, stepping beside her as they waited for their drinks.

"My reputation?" She hadn't known she had a reputation.

"Yeah. Kind of wildly creative and impulsive. You're a lot more focused and driven than I expected. Thoughtful, too."

"And that's a good thing," she said, hoping he wouldn't try to argue with her.

"It is. Until our agendas cross."

"I'm trying to uncross them, but you're not exactly helping."

"Trust issues," he said and, again, scanned the room.

"Are you looking for anyone in particular? You keep doing that."

"You know if anyone sees us together, the mayor's going to have my ass."

"Why? We're talking about walking dogs at the shelter. What about the fighting dogs?"

"What about them?" he asked uneasily, shifting his weight from foot to foot.

"Well, are they mean? Are they protective? What? And when someone goes to adopt one, what do you tell them?"

"I don't tell people anything. I show up, read the board and see who needs to go out, pick a dog, mark it on the board, and go walk the dog. Nice and easy. I come back and make notes afterward so the next person who walks that dog knows what I know about it."

She wondered what his notes about this conversation would look like.

"You make it sound almost zen."

"Some days, it is. I'd invite you to join me one day, but you have to go through training."

"To walk a dog? Seriously?"

He smiled. It finally touched his eyes—just barely, but it did. "You'd be surprised." He motioned as the barista held Tess' cup up. She signaled for it and took her first sip, sinking into the flavor.

"That good?"

She paused, loathe to tell him she'd been waiting for him and was almost in coffee withdrawal. "Yes." She looked over at him, but his attention was on the barista who was approaching with his own cup.

As he turned to her, his guardedness returned.

"One more question for you," Tess said, holding her coffee in both hands and cocking her head at him.

He gave her a weary look. "What?"

"Do you believe in ghosts?"

He closed his eyes and shook his head. "Tess... For real?"

She shrugged. "I work on old buildings. A lot of times, there are stories of hauntings, but we've never seen any proof. An office in a building as old as the city building... I can see that having a couple of ghosts."

He bought time by sipping at his coffee, then tilting his head at the table where they'd met. Neither of them sat once they got to it, though. "I've heard rumors, but no one's ever had proof. Like you said. So honestly? I don't know if I believe in ghosts or not."

"Thanks."

"I probably don't wish I knew what this was about."

Tess smiled. "Just making conversation." She winked and told him she'd call him later for a formal update, but right then, she had to get to the office for the morning meeting.

He was, she was sure, utterly confused about what had just taken place, but that was okay. He didn't need to know all that much, especially that he'd spilled more than he'd realized.

TWENTY-SIX

"Good job," Red told her after the morning meeting. She followed him into his office, recounting the story as they walked. He entered his usual way: butt first, tablets stacked and held in one hand, braced against his waist for stability, his coffee mug in the other hand. "So a serious infrastructure problem or some truths about the bones?"

"He wouldn't confirm or deny, but he also admitted he plays favorites and stays away from the problem dogs."

"Problem dogs?" He set his pile of tablets on his desk and moved to sit down.

"I got him talking about his volunteer work at the shelter. He walks dogs."

"And has favorite dogs and those he avoids," Red said, looking at her thoughtfully. He sipped at his coffee. "Interesting leap you're making there."

"We need to make Woolslayer his favorite."

Red flicked his gaze at her, then turned to his monitor. He ran his finger over the control panel and frowned. "Okay, let me deal with this and think about your issue. Who's going to rattle cages over there today? You or me?"

"Why don't you?" Tess said. "Since Philip's been told to dodge me." She rolled her eyes. "Because I'm such a threat."

"You certainly can be. Christine runs into this all the time, too."

"Runs into..."

"Men who can't handle a smart woman. A word of advice? Make sure Mackenzie appreciates how smart you really are."

"It's not like that. We're just old friends."

"Old friends who show up without an appointment and wander through the halls, yelling for you?"

"That," she said, not bothering to try to stifle the smile, "is classic Mack. You get used to it after a while."

"I'm not sure I'd want to."

"Aren't you the one who once said you didn't want to fix the brakes on your car because you were used to them? And bad brakes can kill you, Red. I've known Mack a long time and don't think my life's ever been threatened."

His laugh followed her out of his office and back to hers.

The rest of the week passed in a blur. Jamie insisted she change her scenery and come help with the twins instead of staying home to clean, then laughed at Tess' worry, pointing out that first, Mack was a guy and wouldn't notice if the condo wasn't sparkling clean and second, what did he even know when he had people who took care of everything for him?

"You know," Tess said to her, "I've owned it for five years and this is the first time I'm using the guest room." She shook her head. "That means this is the first time I'm glad I didn't get the one-bedroom after all."

"It's not your home office?" Something crashed in the twins' playroom and both women turned toward it, but it was only a stack of blocks.

"No way," Tess said. "If I had an office at home, I'd never disconnect. I need the separation."

"Even for all the Woolslayer stuff?"

Tess held up a finger. "Ahh, but Red gives me as much company time as I want for that, since Trade Creation is entwined with the firm. Remember, I'm the non-profit, look good, feel good part of the company." She hoped Jamie wouldn't go for the *community activist* label, but one of the boys chased the other out of the playroom and into the kitchen and the two adults had to spend a few minutes wrangling.

Hank got home just in time for baths.

"You're good," Tess told him.

"That's what Jamie said... up until she went into labor, anyway," he grinned. "Now she reminds me that being good has consequences."

Tess laughed while Jamie shook her head at her husband and handed Tim over to him. Ryan followed along, chattering incomprehensibly about something.

Jamie and Tess retreated to the kitchen table and a bottle of wine. "So... Mack's spending the weekend. Does this mean—"

"Honestly? I don't know what it means."

"Then be careful. I don't want to nurse you through another breakup with him."

Tess opened her mouth to answer, but shut it before any words could come out. She thought for a minute, Jamie waiting patiently, and then said, "Last time was so different. I just... I couldn't believe that after everything, he'd drop it all and go running when his mother told him to." She smiled faintly. "In some ways, I still can't. But he says he likes the work."

"So what does that mean for you as a couple?"

"What's wrong with us just being friends? Why can't I have his back right now as he deals with all this widower stuff?"

"Are you going to be satisfied with that? With him next door in the guest room that's never been used, when he could be right there with you?"

"Why are you fixated on the fact that the guest room has never been used?"

"You're not answering the question," Jamie observed, raising the bottle to offer Tess a refill.

She shook her head. She had to drive home yet.

"Are you going to be satisfied being his friend?" Jamie repeated.

"It's not that easy, and you know it."

"But it really *is*," Jamie said. "You're not willing to move up there to be with him. You don't know if he's going to be successful at moving the corporate headquarters. And neither of you are the type of people who can be weekend spouses."

"But the sex would be amazing," Tess said weakly.

Jamie laughed and shook her head, then held her wine glass up in a toast. She drank, then looked at Tess in such a way that Tess wanted to squirm and go hide under something. "And what happens when the sex gets old? When one of you starts keeping company during the week with someone else? When you have to stop having weekend sex and start doing things in public, and one of you is *always* the outsider in each other's world?"

"I know. You're right."

"So. Are you going to be satisfied being his friend?"

"If I have to, then yes. These past few months, since he first brought up the PharmaSci holiday party, we talk all the time. We can do friends. It's not that hard."

"Except this weekend, he won't be on the other end of his phone."

"Jame..."

She refilled her glass as Tess watched, then said, "Proximity changes everything, Tess. And on some level, you know it."

Tess knew it on almost every level, but she wasn't going to admit it. Saying it to Jamie meant she had to say it to herself at the same time, and darn it, but denial was a nice place to be for the time being. "I need to get home," she said quietly, knowing Jamie would see through her—and probably call her on it, too.

"We'll talk later, but remember one thing?"

"What?" Tess sighed. This wasn't going to be pretty.

"Sometimes, safe sex isn't only using condoms. Sometimes, it's taking care of your heart, too."

"Ugh. Do you really say that to your clients?" She had started to brace her hands on the table in preparation for getting up, and she paused, waiting for Jamie's reply.

"When the situation warrants. And Tess, I know you don't want it to, but it *does*."

"I hear your concern about what's going to happen this weekend," Tess said. "I appreciate it. I do."

"Good," Jamie said, standing up and walking with Tess to the door. She gave her a hug. "Because if he hurts you again, this time, I *will* kill him."

Tess laughed and thanked her for caring. Maybe, she mused as she walked down Jamie's front steps and to her car, that's how it was: Jamie had her back, she had Mack's. Maybe that was all she could ask for.

But when she got home, she had a text waiting from Mack. *Krista says I have to bring you a hostess gift since you're giving up your weekend for me.*

You are gift enough, Mack.

I told her that. She didn't agree. She also tried some Valentine's Day ploy, but I shut it down.

Tess laughed, imagining the look on Krista's face when Mack did that. *By the time I—* She stopped typing when another message from him arrived.

I found out what's going on in town.

Oh? She sank down onto her couch and pulled her shoes off. Being with the boys had meant play clothes—and shoes. Hank had figured out that if the adults wore shoes, the boys were more likely to, and that meant fewer stubbed toes and tears.

The annual Barbie collector's convention.

If you ask me what a Barbie is, I may have to hurt you.

Ha. Kelsey had a few. She had her wedding dress made for one, and she put it in a clear box. Flemming and I fought over who got to keep it. I won.

Oh. Wow.

Is that stupid?

No, she answered. *It's kind of sweet. In a macabre sort of way.* And it was, but it also made sense. Mack had a sentimental side he tried to deny, and keeping not just a token of his wife—which he had in her bracelet—but something from their wedding, when he'd been hopeful that it would be okay, that they'd be happy...

It made sense.

You're not going to make me look at Barbies, are you?

Only if you ask nicely, Tess replied, closing her eyes with her laughter. There was no way he would... Her phone vibrated.

Yeah, no. I can't even make a joke about you being a doll 'cause you'll slug me.

You got that right.

See you soon—

Tess held the phone to her lips for a minute, thinking. *Safe sex means guarding your heart, too.* Jamie's words came back to her and Tess bit her lower lip, knowing that this weekend could be dangerous.

TWENTY-SEVEN

February 12

When Mack's plane landed and he turned on his phone, he was met with a slew of texts, voice mails, and emails from Taylor and his mother. He ignored them all, ordered his car, and turned his phone back off. Sitting in economy class on a plane wasn't exactly the place for corporate shenanigans. That was why he'd chosen economy and pretended he thought he had to pay for in-flight WiFi. He'd wanted some peace.

He turned the phone back on. They'd know he was dodging them. Besides, he needed to make sure he got into the right car.

The board was furious with him and Krista. Well, not all of the board, just the hard-liners who wanted to eke out the most profit while they still could. Then again, he and Krista were trying to do an awful lot at the moment, including lowering prices—and therefore diminishing those precious profits—on specific women's health-related drugs, most notably their flagship chemo drug. They'd gotten board approval by saying they were doing it in Kelsey's memory, but that didn't mean the vote had been unanimous.

Funny that PharmaSci had wound up creating a highly effective chemo drug after all and without the risky trials that had doomed Tess' father. And it felt even more ironic that they were lowering the price by a couple bucks in memory of a woman who'd had no need for it. Cancer hadn't been what killed Kelsey. Not literally, anyway.

Mack was trying very hard not to think about how mercenary that made him. Using Kelsey's memory as a means to an end... But on the other hand, like Krista had said, Kelsey would have appreciated knowing she'd done something good in the world.

He tried to focus on that.

The board was also upset about the idea of moving the corporate headquarters. They didn't see any sense in uprooting so many families and going to a cheaper city when they could have a brand new, totally green headquarters right there in town, and who cared if the rent was higher than they were currently paying? They'd have presence. They'd be seen. They were a pillar of Lakeford society.

Mack didn't care about that, and that pissed them off even more. They claimed he didn't care about the company, and they were threatening action against him and Krista.

Let them, he answered the four board members who were worried about the threats. *This is why we changed the company mandate back to its original wording and why we brought you all onto the board. Enough of these archaic attitudes already. We have a future to plan for.*

And a large part of that future hinged on this weekend and being with Tess. Was it going to be as easy as everything else up to now had been with her? What were the chances they'd part on Sunday, realizing they hated who each other had grown into and were going to just finish off the field and he'd stay in Lakeford after all, no matter how expensive it was compared to Port Kenneth?

When he got to Tess' office, Anchey greeted him with "Good to see you again."

Mack started to reply, but he was caught by a vision of Tess. Her office door was open and she was standing at her desk, her head bowed over something, her dark hair falling so he couldn't see her face.

He drank in the rest of her: She wore a simple brown dress that fit without being sexy, a colorful scarf looped around her neck, and—God help him—thigh-high flat boots. It was the best combination of professional and perfectly Tess, and such a contrast to Kelsey and her simple, proper daytime wardrobe choices that for a second, he couldn't breathe. Being near Tess was like coming alive again.

He couldn't help the hard swallow. He figured Anchey heard it, too, but the other man didn't say anything. He just called out to Tess, who raised her head, giving it a slight shake to settle her hair, and grinned. "There's the man of the hour!" she called out. "C'mon in. Charley and I were just going over the project."

That was when he noticed the woman on Tess' left. To be fair, she'd been hidden by Tess.

She was like a buffer, keeping their greeting more formal, although he gave both of them air kisses out of some habit he hadn't realized he'd adopted, most likely compliments of his mother.

Tess looped him into the conversation and he stared again, this time at her screen, marveling at the renderings of what he hoped would be the stadium that would soon bear his name. It looked good, with smooth turf and fences that were straight.

"Okay?" Tess asked at last. He nodded dumbly, still unable to tear his eyes away from the field. "Hello? Macadamia nut?" She grabbed his arm and gave him a shake.

"Huh?" He blinked, only to realize she was in his face. He leaned back and blinked again, trying not to get lost in her screen again. "Sorry. Just... we might actually pull this off." He took a step closer to her and leaned forward, giving in. "Tess, look at it. This is going to be a *safe* place for the teams. No more risking injury, no more fighting other teams for crummy timeslots..." He closed his eyes and inhaled deeply. He let the breath out, acutely aware of Tess and Charley staring at him, Charley like he was nuts but Tess like she understood. "I did need this," he said.

"I'm glad to help you get it," Tess told him, touching his arm gently, probably to make him move out of her way because when he stepped back, she moved into the spot he'd been in and started closing down her screens.

He was sorry to see the renderings go. Before he could say anything, his phone buzzed. He pulled it out of his pocket, looked down at the screen, and frowned. Krista. Again.

"Need a few?" Tess asked. "But only a few. We've got to get moving."

"If you don't mind. This will be fast."

She and Charley left him in her office, and he watched her go as he answered the call. He missed her something fierce, missed her practicality, her vibrancy. That was something else Kelsey had lacked.

"What's wrong?" he asked Krista, moving away from Tess' desk, not wanting to accidentally touch anything and mess it up.

"I can't find your hotel information."

"That's because I didn't leave it and I told Taylor not to give it to you."

"Emerson, now why would you—oh."

"You're wrong but I love you, Mother. I have a meeting to get to." He hung up before she could ask if he'd brought a ring with him or reminded him to practice safe sex.

Catching up to Tess and Charley in the foyer, he put a hand on Tess's waist and bent to her ear. "Thank you. And by the way, did you mean to make me nuts with those boots?"

She stiffened and was probably blushing, he figured, but her hair was covering her face. "No, but I do have promises to keep, don't I?"

He groaned and followed her and Charley out. They did have a meeting to get to. He hoped it would be the best part of the business day. Then again, he had Just Tess with him at last. How could it not be?

TWENTY-EIGHT

The meeting, Tess thought, went well. She reminded herself she shouldn't have been surprised at how Mack handled himself; he wasn't the headstrong, full of himself, privileged college kid he'd been. He was a quick thinker, willing to explore alternatives when their contact at the university confirmed for one final time that there was no way to get water into the stadium, no matter how much money he offered to make it happen.

"Going over to the dark side wasn't necessarily a bad thing for you," she said over dinner. They'd picked up Chinese food and were eating it straight out of the containers, sitting on her couch, just like they'd used to. It wasn't the same now that it came in plastic containers and not cute boxes, but they were making do.

"Truth be told, I have more of my soul at this point than I thought I would," he said, wincing as a dumpling fell from his chopsticks and into the sauce, which splashed. Fortunately, it didn't get the couch, just him, but she wasn't even terribly worried about that, as he'd changed into a t-shirt and lounge pants, no longer the rich young donor to the university.

"You are allowed to use a fork," she said, watching him fumble with the chopsticks as he tried to pull the now-soaked dumpling out of the sauce. "Some skills atrophy with disuse."

He chuckled, his attention still on the dumpling. "You should have seen the first time Tristan took me out for lunch with a bunch of the bigwigs. I picked up the chopsticks like it was no big deal and every mouth at the table fell open and they all stared at me. Tristan chewed me out later for trying to appear multicultural when there was no need. I tried them again on a date with Kelsey, and she simply asked what was wrong with a fork. And..." He shrugged but the look he gave her spoke of helplessness.

"It sounds like a very different world," she said.

He held his chopsticks in the air, tips upward, dumpling forgotten in the sauce. "Another reason why I want to get the hell out of that environment and back here."

"I'm not sure you'll find it's as idyllic as you remember. This is still a fairly conservative town, still mostly industrial and manufacturing, and still with deep racial issues. The gossip I've heard is that people would rather have you bring in manufacturing because that means jobs. They don't want a bunch of stuffed shirts running up the property values and making demands on their schools—although frankly, the schools could use it. They're not nearly as good as the university is."

He listened, his eyes briefly unfocused. "Nothing's set in stone yet. Manufacturing happens regardless of where headquarters is, so if that's what the city needs, it can still happen. So can research and development. Really, the whole thing's stupid. Why bother with a corporate headquarters at all?"

"Because you need an address *some*where, and a place everyone can look to as the mothership. So to speak."

"I don't know. This is the twenty-first century. The company should be about where the talent is, not something that people can point and gape at."

"You're consolidated into one spot already," she pointed out.

He shrugged. "So we go to a better spot. A spot where we are more in touch with the people who we're trying to serve. Lakeford's too insulated and besides, we *have* to cut costs if we're going to survive."

"People will always need medicine."

"And there will always be really smart people who figure out how their business can put mine under. I have to be ready for all that. Besides, don't you want me around?"

"I'm not the one talking about moving an entire corporate headquarters just to be near their ex-girlfriend."

"Not *just* to be near you, but even if it were, can you blame me? I know you can't uproot. Well, you *can*, but it's not fair to ask you to."

"So you're going to uproot *how* many people instead? Mack, that's amazingly selfish."

He paused and studied her for a long minute. "When we buy companies, that's what we make their people do. Taylor and I have been talking to as many of our people as we can. Most everyone under thirty whose kids haven't started school, or who don't have kids, are into it. Then you get the people who've got kids, and they get more cautious as the kids get older. And then the people who're over fifty and starting to think about retirement are a lot less flexible; they don't want new mortgages at their ages, and I can't say I blame them. So then we raise questions of moving fewer people and letting others work remotely, with periodic travel so we can see each other's actual faces."

Tess propped her arm on the back of the couch, then rested her head on her hand, gazing at him. On the one hand, this was the Mack she'd fallen in love with. But on the other, he was a stranger.

Worst of all, she liked that stranger. He was savvier, more caring, and he seemed to be seeking something better than what he currently had.

He finally got a grip on the dumpling and managed to get it up to his mouth, leaving a trail of brown dumpling sauce down the front of his shirt.

She chuckled and shook her head.

"You're not eating," he said.

"I'm full."

"Forgot you eat like a bird. So did Kelsey."

"I don't eat like a bird, and I bet neither did Kelsey. You're just comparing us to the bottomless pit that is your stomach."

He paused, setting the dumpling sauce down and picking up his beer. He swallowed, took a drink, then looked at Tess. "Is it weird if I talk about her?"

"Only because I can't imagine what it must be like to be married."

"Think about when we were living together, only not so much fun. And in her case, add in the abusive father who wanted to destroy me and the whole family legacy... Hunh. Maybe it *was* fun," he said, shaking his head and pointing his beer bottle at her, then setting it back down. "Sure you don't want any more?"

"You finish what you want."

He picked up various containers, then set them all back. "I think I'm okay." He stood up and walked around behind the couch.

Tess shifted so she could see him. He was standing in front of the door to the balcony, stretching, his arms overhead. His shirt was long enough to keep from exposing a strip of skin at his waist. "We can go out if you want some air," she said.

With a nod, he worked the lock and opened the door. Tess paused to grab the blanket on the couch in case she got cold, then joined him out there.

He took the blanket, draped it over his shoulders, then wrapped his arms around her, pulling her back against his chest, huddling around her. She pulled at the edges of the blanket so they were almost cocooned, like he'd intended, she was sure. "Sometimes lately, the whole thing with Kelsey feels like some sort of dream," he said. "Like it didn't happen, or it happened to someone else. And then sometimes... I get this pang, like I fucked up. And that's when I realized that I don't miss her the way I should."

"According to who?"

He took a deep breath, holding her tighter. She put her hands on his arms, wrapped around her waist. "Me," he admitted after a minute.

She leaned her head back, trying to get a look at his face, but because neither of them had turned the light on, he was in shadows. She looked out at the street instead. It was a relatively quiet side street, but there was some traffic, enough to focus on and be absorbed by.

"You come out here a lot?" he asked.

"Yeah, actually, especially on weekends. My version of porch coffee."

"I swear, there are whole days when I'm outside long enough to go from the car into the building and back again."

"It's the price of being the important guy."

He snorted. "I'm not the important one. Not like you'd think. I'm just the one who holds all the reins and directs all the jockeys in the way I want them to move their horses around the track."

"Nice metaphor for a Frisbee boy."

He smiled. "By the way, I did bring my gear."

"Good. Want to hear the agenda for tomorrow?"

He groaned, lifting his head and rolling it from right to left. "Agenda? Tess, it's the weekend. I deserve time off from scheduled activities."

"If we don't have a rough schedule, we won't get you to pickup on time."

"How rough?"

She heard the wariness in his voice. "Rough. I'd like to take you over to Woolslayer, but not before nine, so you can see what's going on over there and what the neighborhood's like."

"And see the hole in the ground?"

"And see the hole in the ground."

"What else?"

"I thought I'd take you through the different neighborhoods. I don't know what exactly you've seen, or where you're looking to put the office, but we can drive through it all, walk some of it if you want, and get you to pickup at three."

"You'll stay and watch?"

"You mean heckle?" But she'd caught the note of hope in his voice, and she wondered, not for the first time, if what he most needed was attention.

He buried his nose in the back of her head. It would have been overly intimate if it hadn't been such a familiar thing.

"I need to tell you some things," he said. "But let's go inside. I don't want you to get cold."

TWENTY-NINE

February 13

Tess woke the next morning still reeling over what Mack had said when they'd gone back inside.

When Krista had come to him his senior year of college, he had initially been in favor of letting the company die, but she had pointed out how many people were employed, how many people relied on their products, and how big a reverberation around the world it would create if those people lost something they needed, in some cases quite literally, to stay alive.

Mack had been stuck. He couldn't have that on his hands. And Tess had agreed.

So he and Krista had decided to restructure the company, starting with ending the risky research Tristan had been so in love with.

And then people in government had started making serious noises about universal health care. Mack had smelled the opportunity to position the company for an uncertain future. Krista hadn't been so sure universal health care would pass in Mack's lifetime. They were still debating that situation, but Mack was also working toward alliances, intending to take a stand against the predatory insurance companies if it came to it. Universal health care *was* going to happen.

More specific to PharmaSci, lowering overhead was one of his first goals, and now that he'd fallen for Port Kenneth, he'd begun learning about the city, looking for opportunity. Despite the desire for more manufacturing, it was starting to die out, and the university was starting to struggle with dropping enrollment. Kenilworth had always been strong in the sciences but lousy with marketing itself. In some ways, it was a surprise Mack had even heard of it to pick it for his college rebellion.

And so he was making his move. Now that he had opened discussions with the school about the field, he would soon be suggesting an exploration of how the university and PharmaSci could work together, finding job opportunities for pharmacy and chemistry students, funding research—and even, Mack hoped, enrollment incentives for the families who were relocating.

There was even more beyond all that. It was a huge plan, with so many different parts to it that Tess felt like she hadn't slept much; she'd been too busy trying to get her brain around it all.

It was the sort of thing he'd never have let himself dream of, let alone work toward, if he'd stayed in town and remained an athletic trainer—and married her.

He really had become a very different man. If he was right about all this, and if he could pull it all off, he might even be considered a visionary.

Maybe he wasn't Mack anymore, Tess mused as she hauled herself out of bed, intending to get breakfast started. She hadn't had time the night before to make real cinnamon rolls—and hadn't intended to have that time, not with him staying with her—but she could still make a spread. She poured her first cup of coffee of the day and turned Spotify on her phone as she reached for her father's apron and tied it around her waist.

The bacon was in the oven, the raw eggs beaten and sitting, waiting to be poured into the skillet, and the waffle iron full of batter when Mack stumbled out of the guest room, still wearing the same clothes from the night before, complete with dumpling-sauce-dirtied shirt. His eyes weren't quite open, his hair was a mess, and he had more stubble than he'd had the night before.

He was, she had to admit, adorable.

And achingly familiar.

Best of all, he'd clearly *slept*, like his battle with his bed and with sleep in general had been left behind in his snooty corner of upstate New York.

Wordlessly, she slid a cup of coffee across the counter to him.

"No single cup machine?" he asked after he'd had a sip.

"Charley would kill us all. This is shade-grown, completely organic, environmentally friendly, keeping natives employed... all the politically correct stuff, except it's damn good. Makes me wonder why I spend so much in the coffee shop near the office."

He nodded. "It is good." He took another sip and his eyes came entirely open. "Just Tess... what's with the apron?"

"It was my father's," she said, smoothing it, and told him the story: the dancing, the burned pancakes, the breakfast buffets. She flipped the waffle and held her hands out, wiggling her fingers at him. "C'mon. Let's dance."

He tried to protest, but even as his mouth was flapping and making excuses, his body was pushing away from the counter and coming around to take her in his arms, just like he had in the grand ballroom of the Mackenzie Manor.

Their first step shoved her into the counter, and he grabbed her tightly, pulling her away from the waffle iron. "Not a lot of space," he said, glancing over her shoulder with a frown.

"No. Not like your ballroom."

"In my pantheon to white supremacy," he said, taking smaller steps, his hand strong on the small of her back. A smile touched his eyes but not his lips.

"Ooh, *pantheon*. Nice word."

He shrugged and looked over her head. "I know a few."

THIRTY

Tess gave him space for his thoughts, but when the song ended and something up-tempo started, he looked down at her again. "I don't want to let you go."

"That's how Dad always managed to burn the pancakes. But today, at least, can I not do that?"

"Yeah," he said, releasing the pressure of his hand on the small of her back but not letting go. He didn't want to let go.

"Mack—"

"I know," he said, searching her face for something, but he wasn't sure what. "I just feel really safe here with you. Thank you."

With that, he broke away and slid around the edge of the counter, back onto the stool he'd staked out.

"Should I start the eggs?" she asked.

"Please," he said, feeling like a guest.

She did, then pulled the fruit out and turned back to the waffle maker, sliding the second, slightly overcooked, waffle out and pouring the batter for a third. "Is it a waste of my breath if I ask you to cut the fruit?" she asked.

"I think I can manage that—whoa, okay, I lied," he said as she handed over a... something. He pulled back, hands raised, terrified by the prospect.

She froze in mid-twist. "Have you learned how to do *anything* in the kitchen?"

"No." He didn't even have to fake the sheepish look he gave her, and she chuckled.

"That's gotta change if you truly want to be a normal person and not a pampered executive type."

"I have a better understanding of the hows and whys these pampered executive types wind up unable to do something like cut"—he eyed the fruit—"whatever that is."

She paused, peering at him. "Are you serious?"

"What? That I work during the time normal people are cooking? Yes."

She wiggled her fingers, a signal to return the round fruity thing. He rolled it across the counter and she gave him a long, measured look. "Stop abusing the fruit," she said as she plunged her knife into it, halving it quickly and setting the knife down and reaching for a spoon.

"Tess," he said, half-standing. "You just fucking decapitated it and you're yelling at *me*?"

"I didn't decapitate it," she said, scooping some gross innards out and putting them in a bowl. "I cut it in half."

"Eviscerated, then." He was watching what she did, so he wasn't surprised when she pushed the second half and the spoon at him, then turned to the skillet and held a hand over it. She adjusted the heat and added oil, which she swished around.

He got busy, doing exactly what she'd done.

"See? I'm trainable," he said when he finished, setting the knife down with a strange feeling of relief.

She added the eggs to the pan. "Then cut it into slices, Mr. Trainable. Both halves, please." The waffle maker beeped.

He contemplated the half—it was orange, so he was assuming it was a cantaloupe—while Tess flipped the waffle and tended to the eggs. "Uhh, Tess?"

She sighed and grabbed another knife, then demonstrated how to cut it into crescents. "Then cut it off the rind. You want to get it as close to all green on one side and all orange on the other."

"I..." He tried to back away, but she wasn't having it.

"Will be fine," she said, her attention on the eggs.

The oven beeped. Mack's head jerked up.

"Didn't know that was on?" she asked as she squatted to take the bacon out.

"No. And I will remember to appreciate Marisela all the more after this. She makes it look easy."

"It just takes coordination. I had thought you'd sleep later or I'd have more of the fruit sliced."

"And here I thought I'd slept enough," he said with a sigh.

She paused to give him a long look. "I'm just glad you slept."

"Me, too," he said on another sigh, wondering why he hadn't thought of trying to sleep under a roof that wasn't his.

THIRTY-ONE

Once they'd cleaned up, Tess walked Mack through the Woolslayer incubator. "You did all this?" he asked.

"Most of it. Red helped get the funding, but I own and run it. And although we've got some open spaces here and women do apply for them, I'm still looking for the *right* people. You have no idea the proposals I've seen. Some clearly are headed by a woman only to get the benefits of being a woman-owned business, others aren't ready to move out of a kitchen—and even those that are shouldn't be *here*. Most should be in commercial food settings, which isn't something Red or I want to get involved with. Too much risk," she said as Mack pulled his brows down and opened his mouth to ask. "I suspect that might change at some point, but we'll see. Right now, I want to help these women launch themselves. Even Janeesa would like to break off from the parent company she's tied to and go out on her own, but for now, she's establishing herself as the expert Realtor in the area." She grabbed his hand and started down the stairs.

As they got to the first floor, Serenity opened her office door. "Tess! I thought I heard you."

Her eyes dropped to Tess' hand, fingers entwined with Mack's. Tess decided to ignore it. "Just giving a tour."

"Do you have a moment? I got a phone call yesterday that I haven't had time to discuss with you."

Tess glanced at Mack, who dropped her hand and motioned her into Serenity's office. They paused in the doorway for introductions, and then Tess pointed Mack to a seat on the couch. She joined him, all too aware that their thighs were pressed together, and not because the couch was small.

She was sure Serenity noticed that, too, as she sank into her chair.

"I know you recall that temporary fix and rerouting for the water lines you had told us to expect. The city hasn't been here the last two days. So I spoke to some people I know, and sure enough, the crews have been temporarily reassigned. To the Shadow Avenue area."

Tess groaned and covered her face with her hands. "Tell me it's an emergency."

"If being white and wealthy counts."

"That's one of the areas I want to show you," Tess said to Mack.

"Business?" he asked, perking up.

"Mixed. Small businesses and amenities like dry cleaners, coffee shops, some restaurants, a Whole Foods... Kinda like where I live, only newer and trendier."

Mack nodded, frowning. Tess decided to give him time to think and asked Serenity, "What's the issue over there?"

Serenity repeated that she didn't know. "I was hoping you'd heard something."

"No, but I'll..." She pulled her phone out of her pocket and frowned at it. "Is it rude to ask today? It's the weekend."

"Doesn't stop a chunk of the people I work with," Mack said, hiking his hips so he could pull his own phone out of his pants pocket. He frowned at it and excused himself to the hallway.

"Tess?" Serenity asked.

"I know. We deserve answers," she said, still eyeing her phone. "He might be walking his dogs over at the shelter." With a shrug, she decided to send the text. If Philip got offended, too bad. The entire neighborhood probably was angry about this, and there were more Woolslayers than there were Philips.

"Tess," Serenity repeated, her voice a hiss.

She looked up, surprised. "What?"

Serenity cocked her head.

"Oh." She closed her eyes and the feel of Mack's hands on her in her kitchen flooded her. She wasn't sure why. "Later," she said as she heard Mack say goodbye to whoever he was talking to. She wasn't sure if it was Taylor or Krista, but she was fairly confident it was one of them.

He didn't look sheepish or chastised when he came back in, so she doubted it had been his mother. Taylor, then.

Her phone buzzed. Philip.

What? Shouldn't have happened. Let me look into it.

She texted a thanks back, passed the news on to Serenity, and stood up. "Keep me posted. If I hear anything more, I'll let you know immediately."

"Hey," Mack said. "Before we go, I have a question."

"Of course," Serenity said with a regal nod.

Tess eyed him, not sure what he was about to come out with.

"Why is this area called Woolslayer? And Tess, why do you live in Wood's Ears?"

"Well," Serenity said, and Tess sank back down onto the couch. Mack joined her. "Woolslayer is because there used to be a sheep farm nearby. Our business district here was developed while the farm was still active, and the name was not meant to be a flattering reflection on the farm's history. Most everyone believes the land it's on is cursed."

"I've been meaning to tell you I ran into Harald out there," Tess said with a gasp, kicking herself for forgetting until now.

"He told me," Serenity said. "Your respect impressed him." She turned to Mack. "As for Wood's Ears, I am honestly not sure."

"To be honest, I never thought about it," Tess said with a grimace. "And I'm the one who collects stories of all the buildings I work on. Maybe I need to expand that to include neighborhoods, too."

"Now, I hate to end this," Serenity said, "but I do need to get over to Vera's, and I have a bit of work I need to finish before I can."

"Gotcha," Tess said, standing up again. She turned to Mack. "That's our cue to go check out the hole in the ground."

"Thanks for the talk," Mack said to Serenity. "A cursed sheep farm? Hunh."

"Thanks, Serenity," Tess said. She tilted her head at Mack. "I think you've given him something to think about."

"Oh, honey, I hope so. Now, you two enjoy your weekend," Serenity said, her gaze roving over Mack's back as he started to leave her office. "I have two more clients I'm waiting on today. One is new, and I will be meeting him over at Vera's."

"Smart," Tess told her and gave her a hug. "Be safe."

"Always. Terrence will be joining us, too."

Tess paused and looked at her. If she had asked her husband to join her… "Trust your instinct, Serenity. Sometimes, you need to turn away a client if they don't feel right."

Serenity nodded. "I thank you for that wisdom. Now, go enjoy your weekend." She looked up and down at an imaginary Mack and winked at Tess, who couldn't help but grin back.

THIRTY-TWO

Out on the street, Tess pointed toward the hole left by the water main break. Mack didn't try to take her hand again, and she wasn't sure how she felt about that.

"So that was Taylor. They'd run out of time to reach me yesterday and wanted to get me today," Mack said as they strolled. "Turns out I'm having a catered lunch on Monday with my research department about—"

"Miss Tess! You gotta see this!"

"Hi, Georgie," Tess said as the boy ran over to them. "Tell me you're going to show me two weeks of perfect attendance."

"Call the principal. He'll tell you. No, you need to see what's in the hole."

"Do I want to?" She glanced at Mack, who just looked confused.

"Tess, does everyone here know you?"

"Yes," she said. "But Georgie and I have a deal: he gets his ass to class and raises his grades and I find him a mentor."

"That F in math... it's gonna be hard," Georgie said, shaking his head. "I really don't like math. Come see what we caught!"

Tess' stomach sank as she and Mack followed Georgie to the hole, slipping between the jersey barrier and a traffic cone to get close. She peered in and let out a yelp, jumping back. "Tell me you've called the game commission. That's an alligator!"

"The who?" Georgie asked as Mack took a step forward and started to laugh.

"Did you get pictures?" Tess asked Georgie.

"Here," he said, holding up his camera to let her see the view screen. Tess had him text one to her, and she sent it to Philip.

Not again. You sure that's not a caiman? he texted back immediately.

A what?

A caiman. Legal in the state, but meaner than the Flaherty family.

I'm an architect, Philip. Not a zookeeper.

Mack kept laughing. Tess looked at him cautiously. Something about the situation had set him off. His face was turning red and she took a step closer, peering up at him.

Yes, she decided, she was seeing tears forming. That wasn't normal. Not for Mack.

Her phone buzzed. *Hey, Tess? Think you can keep the media away from this one? And if you're in the work area, get out of there.*

"Hey, Georgie? Have you uploaded any of your pictures of this guy to your social media yet?"

"Yeah, Miss Tess. I did a bunch right before I saw you. Why?"

"Because I was just asked to keep this out of the media," she said and when Georgie went a few shades lighter, she told him to relax. "This is too much fun not to share!"

Mack nodded his agreement, calmed, wiped his eyes, and looked in the hole again. "You know, Tess, I bet I could go in there and get it."

"No."

"It'd be easy."

She folded her arms over her chest, her phone still in her hand. "Despite what an amazing photo op that would be for Georgie, don't you fucking *dare*." That gave her an idea, though.

Know who's here with me? She texted to Philip and beckoned Mack to look over her shoulder.

Georgie pointed his camera at them, but she was too focused on Philip to think about it. Or about Mack's hands on her upper arms as he watched.

How would I know that?

Emerson Mackenzie, CEO of PharmaScience Technologies. You may have heard he's thinking of moving his company headquarters here. He wants to jump down into the hole in the ground and take a selfie with our friend.

Tell me you're joking.

He's bigger than I am. Emerson, I mean. The alligator's about two feet long, I think. Maybe three.

"Just Tess—"

"Yeah?" She turned at Mack's wheedling tone. He started to laugh again as he looked toward the hole, then let go of her and went back to the edge.

Tess, seriously! You can't do this to me!

"You know I could do it," Mack said. "I could jump down there and grab it right behind the head... it'd never know." He stepped closer.

"Yeah, man," Georgie called, shutter clicking. "I bet you could!"

"Mackerel! Don't you dare!" she yelled as Mack crouched to jump.

"Hey, dude. C'mere. Let's get to know each other." He bolted upright, and even from the back, Tess could tell he'd gone pale. "You know, I probably shouldn't." He took a step back from the edge of the hole and rubbed the back of his neck.

"It noticed you?"

"Its mouth opened up and it turned." He returned to Tess' side, his eyes wide. "Do alligators hiss? I thought only cats hissed, so maybe there's a cat down there, too. Something's hissing."

Tess, I've notified people. They're on the way. Get out of the work area if you're behind the barriers.

Wasn't that a line from Les Miz? she texted back. *Behind the barricades is there a world you something something...*

"If it's a cat, won't the alligator eat it?"

"Only if it's hungry," she said, frowning at her phone. "Philip says people are on the way."

"Philip?" Mack asked, turning to her but throwing a look over his shoulder, as if afraid the alligator might jump out of the hole on its own. "Seriously, Tess. Do you know *everyone* in this damn city?"

"Well, I don't know who left an alligator in a hole—or a caiman, or whatever it is. So... no. And we should move to the other side of the barriers before people arrive. They won't be happy to find us in what's supposed to be a restricted area."

Mack started to laugh again. "Can... you... imagine that?"

"Yes. And I can imagine the work you'd have to do with the board when your mug shot got out 'cause you got yourself arrested for jumping into a hole that the city had barricaded off."

"And abandoned," Mack said, all his laughter suddenly gone. "Seriously. They're getting off lucky with it only being an alligator in there. What if it was a dead body?"

She froze. That's where the bones had been. "Hold on. Are you implying—"

"No. Absolutely not. Well, unless you're about to ask if I'm implying that someone would be so stupid as to think that'd be a good place to dump a body."

"Someone thought it was a good place to dump an alligator."

"Hey, friend of Miss Tess? It closed its mouth again. I think its smiling 'cause it got the best of you," Georgie called. He was leaning over the opening, snapping away.

"Friend of Miss Tess," Mack said softly in her ear, nuzzling her hair at the same time. "I like that."

"You're okay with me telling the mayor's office you're here?"

"That was golden. I bet the mayor himself will be here within... half an hour?"

"Probably." She was all too aware of how close they were standing, that she had one hand on his forearm while the other clutched her phone to her chest, her arm brushing his chest, and that his hands were on her waist. She was so close she could smell him: male, familiar, *hers*.

Except, he wasn't. Not anymore.

"I should've gone for that selfie," he said. "You know Krista won't believe this happened."

"I don't believe this happened, and I'm in the middle of it. Should we get out of here before the mayor gets here or wait for him?"

"Oh, you need a minute in the spotlight," he told her. "If only so you can use it for leverage later to get the proper asses in gear to fix this already. It's a mess around here, Tess. You're right: these people deserve better."

"You barely know them."

"So? They're people, and that alone makes them deserve better. But more than that, *you* like them, they like you, and that says it all so far as I'm concerned."

THIRTY-THREE

Although they spent the rest of the day exploring the city—even if, for Tess, it was hardly exploring in the classic sense—nothing could top the fun with the alligator. After they'd posed for a few pictures for the media, the game commissioner had let Mack and Georgie take the alligator—its mouth securely duct taped shut—and do another photo session.

As he watched Tess shake her hair over her shoulder and reach for her turn with the alligator, he felt something in him release. Something about looking in a neglected hole in the street and finding a hissing little buddy left him feeling like this was what life was supposed to be, if that made any sense.

He wasn't sure it did.

"Why is life always more fun when you're around?" he asked Tess as she drove him toward the field so he could join a pickup game of Ultimate. Apparently they played year-round here, even though Tess had said the day was cold.

"I wonder the same thing about you," she said, then asked, "What do you want for dinner?"

That brought him up short. What did he want for dinner? How was he supposed to know?

"You know, I can't remember the last time someone asked me that," he said slowly, thinking it through.

"How... how do you eat?"

"Put food in my mouth. Chew. Swallow."

She smacked his leg, hard enough that it made a cracking sound that reverberated through the car and caused him to reflexively lift his leg in protest.

"Okay, serious answer," he said, grabbing her hand before she could smack him again. It had smarted pretty good. "People just... put food in front of me and I'm expected to eat it. Unless we're out to dinner, and then someone hands me a menu and then I pick something." He shrugged and twined his fingers through hers. "But no one asks what I *want*. Just what I'm *choosing*."

"Well, I'm asking," she said and gave his hand a squeeze.

He stared out the window. They were on the highway for the first time all day. "Pizza," he said at last.

"Okay. What kind?"

"What *kind*? What kind of question is *that*?"

"There's the traditional, there's deep dish Chicago style, there's Detroit style with the airy, more bread-like crust, there's—"

"Wait. That. With the crust."

"You up for one last adventure of the day?"

"Uhh—" Truth was, he was tired and two hours of Ultimate—not to mention meeting a bunch of strangers—was only going to make that worse.

"This one's easier than an alligator and all the political games that spawned, I promise. Jamie and her husband and kids have this place they love. Maybe they can join us."

"Jamie? How is she?" He perked up, unable to stop the grin.

"I'm offering you a chance to see for yourself."

"Do it," he said. He'd met Jamie before he'd met Tess; she'd been working at Burger Emporium and had insisted he meet her best friend. Afraid of messing up his standing at the restaurant, he'd put her off. It was sheer luck that he'd met Tess.

Jamie had been right: Tess was perfect for him. She was probably more perfect now than she had been then, but he couldn't tell her that. Not yet. Not after a day like this, so crazy and outside their lives, it probably felt to her like they had stepped out of time. It did to him. And hoo boy, did he need it.

He'd never look at an alligator the same way again.

It came crashing back down once at the field, though. After he'd modeled his tights—three-quarter length, to which she responded with wolf whistles and other cracks that soothed his ego—he took the lock off his phone and told her to let him know if either his mother or Taylor needed him. Anyone else could wait.

"I'm trusting you," he said to her, touching her gently under the chin.

She rolled her eyes at him. "Like I'd do anything to mess up your work? Give me more credit than that."

"That's... actually not what I'm worried about," he said and left her to go meet everyone. It turned out he knew a couple of the faces, both from the alumni weekends the university team hosted every year and from his old playing days. He wasn't surprised that he was the only one of them still playing competitively. He used the team as part stress relief and part enforced escape from work, but it was a time suck.

For her part, Tess heckled him well, although he noticed her absorbed in one of their phones from time to time. Until she got a little pale and began pacing nervously.

He immediately came off the field. "What's wrong?"

"Shouldn't have trusted me," she said and handed his phone over, open to a text exchange with his mother. She walked away, hugging herself.

Emerson, I just discovered there's a condom delivery service in Port Kenneth. Do you need the number?

Tess had probably laughed at that, Mack thought, because she'd answered *Think they'll have enough in stock?*

Now, Emerson. It's only because I know how hard you and Kelsey were working on having children. I don't want you to be too eager with Tess.

He cocked his head at the text, which Tess hadn't answered.

"Tess?" He followed her over to a water fountain at the edge of the park, his cleats too loud on the asphalt surrounding the fountain.

"It's stupid, I know," she said, waving him off. "Go play. It's what we're here for."

"Not until I know what about that bothered you."

She took a deep breath and looked studiously at what he guessed was a sweat stain on his shirt. "The bit about you and Kelsey and kids. It's... weird to think about, that's all."

"You're not a replacement broodmare."

"That's not it," she said and turned her back on him, rubbing her arms.

"It's the idea of me making love to Kelsey," he said, inspiration striking.

"I told you it was stupid."

"It's not," he said, taking a step closer to her and cupping her elbows. "Right now, it's weird to me, too. We're here and we're having this crazy day and I feel so alive, it's like we've never been apart, and I stop and think about Kelsey and... it feels like some nightmare or something not real. And then we're jolted back into reality and, yeah. I was married. Yeah,

I was hoping we'd make the next generation of Mackenzie kids to take over the company when I'm old and crotchety—but I didn't think I had other options. That was my life, prescribed by Krista."

"I told you it was stupid."

"It's not stupid." He curled forward so he could plant a kiss on the top of her head. "Stop beating yourself up. So I have this history that makes me less amazing and perfect than I used to be."

She shook her head, and when she answered, he knew she was okay. "What is it about Ultimate that magnifies your ego?"

He grinned and kissed the top of her head again. "Just part of why you love me."

"And here I thought it was those legs of yours," she said, her hands coming to rest on his hips.

"Thought you said it was the tights," he said and jogged back to the game, grinning.

Back at her house after dinner with Jamie and her husband and kids, he turned to her. "Can I *finally* shower? Can't believe we went out to dinner with me that sweaty."

He caught the flash in her eyes but she blew a kiss at him and told him to have fun.

Before he did, he paused. "Got more plans for us tonight?"

She met his eyes, searching for something. "I figured you'd want to check in with work."

"And you're going to..."

"Read," she said. "I have a book I want to finish; I think it's due back to the library in a couple of days."

"Just Tess, still reading." He smiled. Of course she still made time to read, and of course she still used the library—probably the same branch she'd worked in during college.

Sure enough, she was on the couch with her book when he got out of the shower, so he brought his laptop to the dining room table and told himself to focus.

Until she got up and got busy in the kitchen, and the next thing he knew, she was sitting down with a bowl of popcorn.

"None for me?" he asked and recognized both her smirk and the sinking feeling in his gut.

She turned to him, all wide-eyed innocence, the smirk gone. "Oh."

He forced a chuckle. "Oh, my ass. You're doing this to mess with me."

"Yeah," she said, and her smile wasn't nearly guilty enough for his liking. "I am. Do you want some for yourself?"

He eyed her. For a long minute, it felt like a standoff of some sort, and then he rubbed his eyes, arching his back to stretch as he did. He might have groaned, too, but he wasn't going to own that so fast. "I really am a pampered little poodle, aren't I?"

"Would you like me to give you the haircut?" she asked, popping a piece of popcorn.

"No. But—" He took a deep breath. This wasn't easy. "I'd like it if you'd help me make my own popcorn."

She blinked in surprise. "Well. That was a hell of a lot more polite and restrained than I was expecting."

"Tess." He pointed to himself. "Dark side, remember?"

"I do," she said gravely and ate another piece of popcorn. "But tell me: do you even *want* popcorn, and if so, is it because you're hungry or because you're feeling left out?"

"It's because I'm a pampered poodle who should have some survival skills the next time no one asks me what I want." He grinned at her, knowing that not only did he have her, it was the truth, too.

THIRTY-FOUR

February 14

After Tess dropped Mack off at the airport, she went home and cleaned, then lucked onto the last bike at her gym's late Sunday ride.

Coming home was horrible. Suddenly, she hated her condo. It was too small. Too trendy. Too sterile.

"Too lacking Mack," she said to its silence.

The condo didn't answer.

She figured that was probably a good thing. She'd had her fill of alligator jokes; she'd have never guessed so many people were tied into the local news or that so many people at the gym even knew who she was.

Then again, with click-bait headlines like *See ya later, Alligator! Look who showed up in a local neighborhood*, Tess could understand why the whole world had seen it. Even her mother had asked about it and if Mack had planted it as an early Valentine's Day gift. Tess had to admit it was something he might have cooked up—except, he hadn't.

The morning meeting at work was full of another round of alligator jokes, but at least Tess could tell them about stopping Mack from jumping in the hole while poor Philip freaked out via text. Everyone dissolved in laughter, Red having to wipe away tears when Tess got to the part about the alligator hissing and scaring Mack.

"Speaking of Mackenzie," Red said when the fun was over, "Tess, you and Charley had a meeting on Friday."

"We did, and the client is happy, our contact at the university is happy. There's one final point we need to come to agreement on, but it should be easy, and then we can turn the entire thing over to the trustees to vote on. Which means we have to wait six weeks, but it sounds like it should be a rubber stamp at this point and we can move on to bidding the contractors. Mack said he'd like to remain involved in that part, since this is his money we'll be playing with, although he's shown me his projected budget and we should be fine."

"Doesn't he trust you with his funds?" Anchey asked, looking a bit confused.

Tess shrugged. "I think he's afraid I'll figure out how to add a couple alligators as line-item additions and have them sent to his office."

Red raised his eyebrows and chuckled.

"Why do I have the feeling you would?" Charley asked as Sanjit nodded his agreement.

"Oh," Tess said, giving them her best faux-innocent look, "because you guys know me." She grinned, then turned thoughtful. "But to do it right, we'd have to recruit his assistant and have them video the whole thing so we don't miss out on the fun. Hmmm." She reached for her organizer and flipped to a clean page. She and Charley made notes and outlined a plan for sending Mack an alligator or two as Red continued to ask about existing projects.

"Okay, so we've got some new projects," Red said, clearing his voice and glancing at Tess and Charley, who closed Tess' organizer for her and sat up a little straighter. Tess just chuckled but paid attention. "We've been approached about a kitty café going in right off the Shadow Avenue area, and Tess, since you just cleared your plate of the field, I'll let you pick from your eager beavers here," he said, waving a hand in the direction of a gaggle of junior people who all suddenly looked hopeful.

"Any idea what's going on over there?" she asked.

"This café?"

"Shadow Avenue. I heard crews were sent there at the end of last week."

"Cornice fell off a building," Sanjit said. "Took a bunch of bricks with it. Did the clean-up crews come from your water main break?"

"I'm not sure," Tess said carefully. Philip hadn't gotten back to her about any of it: the missing crews, the bones, or her water main break. Just the alligator, which had indeed been an illegally owned alligator and not a legal caiman.

"Because I heard that your crews disappeared," Sanjit continued. "Any word on that?"

"All I've gotten is that there are some pretty unhappy people in City Hall this morning," Red said.

"I hope so," Tess said with a glower. She desperately needed to follow up about the bones.

The bones.

She sighed. She also had a call out to the woman at the university's Black Studies department, who could maybe teach her more about what pre-Civil War Port Kenneth had been like. Maybe she knew something about the sheep farm. Maybe she knew something about why bones would have been buried in the utility cavern.

How it all fit together, Tess didn't know. It was entirely possible she was grasping at hunches and hope, but something at the back of her mind kept tickling her, pushing her down these paths.

There was no way that sheep farm really was cursed, or haunted, or whatever. She simply didn't believe it.

After lunch, though, instead of doing anything on her list, she took a minute to check in with Mack and ask how inundated he was with the alligator story.

He texted back a picture of what she assumed was his desk, a stuffed alligator sitting in the middle of it, a pill bottle propped in its mouth.

Fucking Taylor, he added.

I love them.

Forget it. You're mine.

Tess stared at her phone for a long minute, her eyebrows raised and her mouth slightly open, her brain frozen.

Of course, that was when Charley stopped in. "What's with you?"

Tess showed her the texts.

Charley whistled in appreciation. "He's not holding back anymore, is he?"

"No," Tess said softly. She closed her eyes and shook her head, not sure how it felt. "He certainly is not."

"You okay?" Charley cocked her head and studied Tess, who took a deep breath and shook off whatever she was feeling and whatever Mack's comment meant—although knowing him, it was as self-explanatory as it seemed.

"Yes," Tess said, putting more certainty into the word than she felt. In truth, she wanted to scream, to call Jamie, to talk to her mother—even to call Mack and ask what the hell was going on with them. Instead, she took another deep breath and met Charley's eyes. "I spent too many years afraid to admit that was what I wanted to hear."

The other woman nodded. "And now that you did, it's surreal, isn't it? Been there, Tess. You'll be okay."

Tess smiled. "Yeah, I think I will be." Her smile turned into a grin. Maybe there *was* a path forward for her and Mack. Maybe an alligator had unlocked it.

"Hey, can I see the picture of you guys and the alligator again?"

"Sure," Tess said, picking her phone back up and texting Mack a quick *Oh? Really now?* before opening the picture.

"Next time he's in town," Charley said thoughtfully, "have Anchey call the hotel and ask them to put on a set of sheets you'll supply."

"Seriously?"

"Hotels have had weirder requests, believe me. They'll do it."

"Then why do I have to make Anchey ask?"

Charley looked up, smiling. "Because it'll be fun."

"And just what is so special about these sheets I'm asking the hotel to put on his bed?" Tess asked, thankful Charley wasn't immediately assuming Mack would stay with her when he was in town next. It would have been a logical leap after that text.

Charley grabbed her tablet and, in a few taps, turned it to Tess, who gasped, laughed, and decided that yes, to be greeted by a bed covered in alligator-skin-patterned sheets was exactly what Mack needed when he was next in town.

Then she frowned. What if he decided that he wasn't going to sleep on them, so that meant he would invite himself into her bed? Especially after *that* declaration... She wasn't entirely certain she was ready for that. Not yet. Not until they had more logistics worked out between them.

Her phone buzzed. *Next move is yours, but that's where I am.*

"Send me the link," she told Charley, fully intending to buy two sets: one for her bed and one for the guest room.

THIRTY-FIVE

February 25

"So, eight weeks later, your building has water again," Jamie said. It was just the two of them, and Tess had cooked.

"Thankfully. Unfortunately, the area's still as torn up as it was the night the main blew, and everyone at the city is dodging me and Red now. They're not even trying to be subtle about it."

"That stinks."

"I'm worried about what it means." Tess *knew* they'd gotten the results about the bones. The fact that no one would talk about it couldn't possibly be good.

"Probably that it's nothing you have to worry about."

"Then they can do us the courtesy of telling us. And yes, Red has attempted to open that discussion."

"Let it go. There's nothing else you can do."

"I know," she said heavily and decided that Jamie wasn't just right, she was reinforcing what Tess kept telling herself. She and Red had been banging their heads off everything they could. At this point, they couldn't be blamed for anything except trying too hard. "I just worry about what it means for my tenants. They're good people; they don't deserve this."

"I hear they have a good landlord. And let me know if your babysitting place needs anything. Toys the boys outgrew, maybe?"

"Won't you need them for the next kid?"

Jamie took a deep breath. "There won't be a next one. We're done. He's getting snipped next week."

"Jamie!"

"I know. All that talk of a house full of kids, of pumping them out..." She stared out the window. "Hank loves being home, but at the same time, he's still dreaming of his start-up, and I'm horrible if I don't let him follow that dream. So we're stopping with the kids because there's more to life than being a parent." Jamie swirled her wine in her glass and smiled. She took a deep breath and let it out, and Tess could see her tension drain away. She wished she could chase her own problems away so easily.

"Wow. I need some time to process that. In the meantime, I need to show you something." Tess got up from the table and grabbed her tablet from the coffee table by the couch. "I told you about the teenager who's the photographer, right?"

"Yeah. What's up?"

Tess handed her tablet over, cued up and ready to go. "Georgie was having some fun the day we found the alligator. These are all from then."

Jamie scrolled through the pictures silently, slowly. To distract herself, Tess started cleaning up. Cooking for more than just herself had felt like an absolute luxury. She didn't begrudge her mom a boyfriend, especially since it had been so many years since her dad had died, but she missed the time in the kitchen, just the two of them.

"Hey, c'mere!" Jamie called to her.

Her hands full of soap bubbles, Tess took a minute to rinse and dry before turning to Jamie. "What do you think?"

"That kid's got some eye. And you and Mack light it up the way you always did."

"Except now Mack's saying his board is putting pressure on him and he and I have to be beyond discreet until the first anniversary of his wife's death. We're not even a couple! And don't forget that this controlling garbage is the reason I walked away in the first place. I'll do it again, and better to do it *now*, before either of us gets too badly hurt."

Jamie looked up and studied Tess, who turned and went back into the kitchen to finish the rest of the dishes.

The bottle of wine appeared by Tess' right elbow. She looked over her shoulder.

"Which part of all this upsets you? That Mack's board is making demands on you, that he was married, that you're conflicted about whether you want to move things forward, or all of the above?"

Tess wanted to flail, but she also didn't want to knock over the bottle of wine and have to spend the rest of the night scrubbing wine stains off her kitchen. She forced herself to stay calm and choose her words as she finished cleaning up.

Then she picked up the wine bottle and took a healthy swig. "Do I really need to answer that?"

"Yes."

"Fucking shrink," she muttered and led the way to the couch, stopping to grab her wine glass on the way. "All of the above," she said when they were seated.

She missed Mack, missed having him around, missed the way they'd each sit at opposite ends of the couch, their feet overlapping in the middle, looking at each other around their raised knees as they talked. She missed the absolute delight on his face as he'd watched her hold an alligator, then had taken it from her and tapped its taped mouth to the tip of her nose.

"But one aspect of this is worse than the rest."

"Jame, come on. This isn't work. Drink more wine and I'll drive you home."

"Last time we did that, your condo association towed the van."

"So I'll leave you at home with the boys, who ought to be in bed when we get there, and Hank and I will come back so he can bring the van home. Besides, won't he need it tomorrow anyway?"

"Yes. I only took it because..." Jamie closed her eyes and shook her head. "Because I wanted to look in the glove compartment when I stop at lights, and I wanted to dig through the trash in the back for condom wrappers. Or maybe I wanted to pretend I was the one responsible for not cleaning the trash out."

Tess raised her eyebrows and waited. She changed her mind about waiting and refilled Jamie's wine. "Spill."

"My mother is convinced the boys are the right age for a sleepover," Jamie said dubiously. She played with her lower lip, then looked up at Tess. "Do you think they are?"

"I know nothing about kids."

"You become a Mackenzie and you'll have to."

"We're talking about you and Hank. Jame, I know parenting isn't what the media says it is. But how can denying the boys a chance to have fun with their grandparents be wrong?"

"I *know* this, Tess. I do. And I agree. But... it's... what if he agreed to get snipped so he doesn't get his girlfriend pregnant?"

"A girlfriend? This isn't like you. Or him, either. When would he *possibly* have time for a girlfriend if he's busy with the boys all day?"

"I don't know. When they nap? What if he's got someone he's meeting at the park? And what's wrong with me that I'm thinking this way? Logically, I know better. But I can't shake it."

Whatever was going on with her best friend was too much for Tess to handle, at least on the spot like this. She hated to suggest it, but maybe Jamie needed to talk to someone better equipped to handle big issues like this.

"I know," Jamie sighed. "And the worst part is that I know what anyone will tell me: I'm being unreasonable, I need to be more secure, talk to Hank about it, let him be my partner as I work through all this. Maybe the issue is that I'm not comfortable in a non-traditional role. Or that I'm not secure with my post-pregnancy body, more than two years later. Or…" She let out a breath that was so big, she seemed to deflate a couple of inches.

"How about sex?" Tess asked. "Put the boys to bed and jump that man of yours. Let him worship you and fuck your brains out and then tell him all this and let him show you all over again how much he loves you."

Jamie laughed. She actually put her head back and laughed. "Oh, Tess. That just might work. And maybe that's the problem," she said. "Like every other couple I know who has kids, we have no sex life anymore."

"You said your parents were willing to take the boys overnight. Do it."

Jamie picked up her wine glass and clinked it against Tess'. "I think you might have the best solution I could have hoped for."

"I think you were hoping I'd suggest it."

They looked at each other and started to laugh.

THIRTY-SIX

February 28

K rista was right, Mack knew. Not knowing the total history of PharmaSci wasn't a smart idea, especially when it was all there, laid out, waiting for him.

But for crying out loud, it was boring stuff—and yet, cruelly, not so boring that it put him to sleep. And Patrick's handwriting hadn't gotten any better than it had been the first time he'd picked up his great-grandfather's journal.

Still, it beat the alternative.

The last time he'd had lunch with Taylor and Nimisha, he'd complained about his ongoing wars with his bed—but that he'd slept while at Tess'. Nimisha had asked how he'd felt while he'd been there and how it was different than how he felt in the home he'd grown up in and shared with Kelsey.

"I don't have to be Emerson, the CEO of PharmaSci and the widower who should be over it by now," he'd said. "She's been through this, with her dad. She's got my back."

"And do you have hers?" Nimisha asked, and Mack had wondered what it meant that he was actually offended by that question. Of course he would do anything for Tess. She was *Tess*. She was the most capable woman he'd ever met.

The problem, of course, was that he was in Lakeford and she was in Port Kenneth and there were an awful lot of miles between New York and Tennessee. And as natural as it was to have her back in his life, he missed waking up with her, making love with her, being with her. Living with her and living with Kelsey had been two entirely different things—and he'd preferred life with Tess. If an alligator had shown up when Kelsey was around, she'd have run in the opposite direction, dragging him along with her. Tess, though... Tess had walked toward it, had even held it once the game commissioner had taped its jaw shut.

She made him feel like he could accomplish anything.

Which brought him back to the task at hand: learning more about PharmaSci. What was the company's history? Would he violate some huge rule if he moved it?

And for crying out loud, was there such a thing as the Mackenzie treasure? No one seemed to believe there was, but everyone knew of the rumors. He had to admit he liked the idea of it. Something hidden by his forefathers, something worth waiting through the generations to rediscover. Something Kelsey had died trying to learn about.

That probably meant he shouldn't start with Patrick's journal, but should go all the way back to Henry's. Henry Mackenzie, who had founded Pharmaceutical Sciences. The first Mackenzie, as far as the legacy was concerned. And here he was, the seventh—totally disconnected from the men who'd created something, if not specifically for him, then definitely with hopes that the seventh generation would be successful stewards of the company.

And the treasure?

With a sigh, he propped his cheek on his fist and looked at Patrick's handwriting, but his thoughts immediately wandered to what he already knew, thanks to Krista.

PharmaSci had been born of opportunity, not politics, during the Civil War.

He looked out the window, thinking of the war. Why would someone tucked away in upstate New York even care about what was happening so far away, it sounded like a story happening in other peoples' lives? How would they have made that leap to knowing what medicines were needed? Again, why would they care? There was no Internet; news was slow to travel. How could they have pulled all of this off from up here?

Again, he told himself to get out of Patrick's journal and pick up Henry's. The answer was sure to be there—but if Patrick's journal was this hard to read, what was Henry's going to be like? What if the ink had faded and he'd be staring at nothing but blank pages?

He turned the page in Patrick's journal. He was talking about how the house was supposed to be a status symbol, but no one in Lakeford understood how or to what extent the Southern styling was sending a message, not like they did in Tennessee.

He paused.

Was there a chance the Mackenzies had a tie to Port Kenneth beyond his time in college? Was this comment his explanation for why he lived in a Southern plantation-style house up here in the Northeast? Krista had said she thought it was a wink from their

Mackenzie ancestors, but what if she was wrong about the *kind* of wink? Did any of this actually mean anything, or was he so tired, he was delirious?

Why couldn't there be a crash course on what it meant to be a Mackenzie? On the history, the important things, how they'd come to be here in Lakeford in the first place, and why they'd built *this* house?

He took a deep breath and reached for Henry's journal.

Thirty-Seven

March 2

Philip surprised Tess and Red by showing up at their office the following Tuesday. "I had to sneak out to come over here," he told them once they were shut in one of the small conference rooms. "The mayor gave me the okay to do this, but only if we all agree to keep it quiet and agree we never had this conversation, and what I tell you doesn't leave the room."

Tess watched both men. Red looked guarded, expectant. Philip looked nervous.

"Not a problem," she said carefully. Red echoed her.

"We haven't been able to find out anything. Not the how or why of the water line that was hooked up wrong. No one can even pull together a theory; it just doesn't make any sense. Did a contractor cut corners? Was it something else? The root of the problem is that we can't find the records that should be there."

"Why not?" Red asked, folding his arms over his chest. He didn't stay that way long; he unfolded one and grabbed his coffee.

"We don't know. They've just... vanished."

"Come on," Red said, putting his coffee mug down and fixing Philip with one of those looks that made people squirm. "This sort of thing doesn't just vanish. Somewhere in that fancy government building of yours are duplicates of triplicates of things already transferred to obsolete media like microfiche, and then it's been uploaded into some cloud storage somewhere."

"But it *can*," Tess said, "if someone works to make it vanish." She paused a beat, looking from man to man. Philip looked tired. Red was glowering at his coffee. "What does the water line have to do with those bones—other than that the hole the water line runs through was full of bones?"

Philip ran a finger around his collar.

"That bad," Tess said. It wasn't a question.

"We are going to have to rip up more of that plot of land. Just to be safe."

"What have you learned?"

"They're old."

"Are they part of the old sheep farm that used to be nearby? The one that's supposed to be haunted or cursed or otherwise evil?"

"What sheep farm?"

Tess paused. Had those records disappeared, too? How could the mayor's office have all those maps of the city and not have the sheep farm on them?

She asked Red to pull them up. On them, it was simply marked as private land. And it was large: about three hundred acres, if not more, but it was hard to tell because its non-city side butted up against park land. And somehow, it wasn't within the city limits. Right up against them, sure, but not within them.

"Okay, so we've got mystery bones, water lines with missing plans, and now a sheep farm that's conveniently not part of the city. Do we *really* think this isn't all connected?"

"Don't forget," Red said, "you're the one who claimed the land was haunted." He lifted his coffee mug as if to toast her.

"Not me. Well, not only me. Go talk to anyone." She thought back to Harald, his talk of the souls that cried out to be remembered, the spirits who had allowed her to come visit. Were those bones theirs? Not even the historians she'd gotten a hold of had known all that much about the farm, just that yeah, they remembered hearing about a sheep farm on the outskirts of town but it was one of those things that no one talked about and everyone was glad when it closed.

"Tess," Philip asked tentatively, "do you think you can dig around about this so-called sheep farm?"

"I have been," she said. "And it's real. I've been out there twice now."

"Careful," Red said to Philip. "Something like this, with Tess on it, it won't be long before we know the entire history of the place and the names of every person who ever set foot on it—and then she gets busy building her dream house on it."

She closed her eyes. Sadly, he wasn't far off, at least about the farm's history. *If* she could find someone who knew something.

She stood up. "Well, my coffee's empty, so I'm going to go find something that won't keep me awake all night."

"But you have a new project," Red laughed.

"You and I will talk," she told Philip, who nodded weakly and stood up, too, as if deciding to take the exit route she was offering so he could escape from whatever was still on Red's agenda. "We'll solve this," she said.

"I have concerns," Philip said.

She flicked her gaze over to Red, who was watching, his own mug in hand but paused a few inches off the tabletop.

"I think all three of us do," she said. "And I think we all get the ramifications, too. You're leaving this in good hands."

Red's smile, she thought, was paternal, but his nod was appreciated.

THIRTY-EIGHT

March 12

It felt like every time Tess started to get traction with the sheep farm, she was pulled away by something else. This time, it was Mack's field. Before the university trustees gave their final approval at the end of the month, they wanted to hear from him about why he wanted to make this specific gift to the university. He brought along the head of the Port Kenneth Ultimate organization, the coaches of the five university teams, and Tess for moral and technical support. This was one of those things, she told him, that she was glad to have his back for. And, she had to admit when it was over, he spoke eloquently.

"I could make a habit of this," he said when they got back to her office.

"Of what?"

"Working here. With you," he said and set his laptop bag down on the table in her office.

"You are welcome to, at least until something actually happens with your company headquarters," she said and kicked her heels off into the shoe pile behind her door. She flipped her monitor on, woke up her computer, and started to check in and see what she'd missed while she'd been with Mack.

The hallway was unusually noisy, though, with every single person who worked with Tess walking by to check out her visitor. "Is the noise bothering you?" she asked him when she looked over and saw his head was bowed, both hands on top of it and covering his ears.

"Yeah," he said, looking up at her. "Taylor keeps our offices quiet. The doors to the outer office stay closed."

"Watch this," Tess said with a wink and closed her door. The clear glass turned opaque. "What just happened?"

She grinned at him. "Privacy on demand. But expect Red or Anchey in here to make sure our clothes stay on."

He turned serious, his eyes flashing with a darkness that gave her a shiver. "Just Tess, when I take your clothes off for the first time after all these years, it's not going to be here."

"Better not be," she said with a chuckle and a lick of her lips, wondering when she'd agreed to move things between them forward. He'd stated his intent already. Was he really waiting for her? Was he waiting to be over Kelsey? Did his board have that much sway to make him hold back until that anniversary?

And what in the world was *she* waiting on? Other than the two of them in the same city and interested in living the same type of life.

"If you do my new headquarters, can I have this?"

"The glass?" She waited for him to nod. "It's expensive. If you're trying to keep the renovation costs reasonable, you might want to reconsider."

He stretched his legs out, sliding to the edge of the chair and folding his hands on top of his head. Tess tried not to sweep her gaze over him, tried not to let her thoughts go places they shouldn't.

"Yeah, there's that," he was saying. "Is it true that renovation is always more expensive than building? Maybe I should build?"

"First, worry about picking the right city."

"We both know it's here. I haven't confirmed why yet, but there's something about it here. I want to be in Port Kenneth. Even if you weren't here, I'd want to be." He shook his head. "It's stupid, I know, but this city's got a hold on me."

"Not stupid at all," she said. "You're not the first person who's said that about PK. I get it."

He nodded and fell quiet, so Tess got to work, too, and somehow turned the afternoon into a productive one. It helped that Mack was so sunk into whatever he was doing that when she decided to wrap up for the day, she had to call to him repeatedly. When that didn't work, she resorted to the only thing she could think of and closed his laptop, her hand firm on the lid as she eased it shut.

"What the—" He looked up.

"You only called me Taylor twice. I'm impressed."

He slid back in his chair, glancing at the wall. It was transparent again. "It quieted down out there?"

"Red told them to quit coming by to stare at you. Tess showing up in the office with her alligator-loving client who's also her not-boyfriend is apparently quite the newsworthy item." She offered her hand, and he took it. As he stood, she pulled his hand behind her back so that he had to take a step around the table, closer to her, but not quite touching. "Quiet dinner in, right? That was the plan?"

He nodded. "Not-boyfriend, huh?" He put his other hand on her waist.

"What do you want for dinner?"

"Why do you always ask me that?"

"Because it's what *normal* people do. I bet no one's asked you once since the last time I did."

He winced.

"Ha," she said, then frowned. "You know, for someone who is *told* they're important, people don't act like it."

"I think they think they're being respectful. Handling the little details so I can focus on the PharmaSci stuff."

"That's lame," she said. "And I'm not playing along. What do you want for dinner?"

"Ribs," he said, raising his head until he looked at the ceiling. "Barbecued spare ribs." He looked at her again and grinned, all mischief. "I want to lick my fingers and not apologize for it. And maybe some pulled something... brisket or pork. Corn bread. Macaroni and cheese. Slaw. And... Umm... what else?"

"Fries or potato wedges," she said, disengaging from their sort-of embrace and twirling to face her desk. "I have a menu here somewhere..." She opened a couple drawers on her desk, then paused. "Hey, I'm not going to magically have sauce on my face that you just *have* to take care of, am I?"

"Nope. It's an attempt to magically fill your bottomless pit of a not-boyfriend."

"That, I can handle," she said.

They spent a full hour over dinner, Mack chewing the bones clean and licking his fingers with abandon as he sighed with bliss. "This is not better than waking up next to you," he said, "but it's up there."

"No chance to get dirty like this in your elite circles?"

He broke the last piece of cornbread in half and, ignoring her head shake, put it on her plate. He buttered his half and jammed it all in. "No," he said, crumbs flying and his eyes dancing, telling her he'd done this on purpose. "Nothing but the best manners."

"If you spray me with cornbread, you are cleaning my entire condo," she warned, but he shook his head and finished the mouthful, then stood up and stretched.

"Damn, that was good."

"You missed the night of authentic Southern cooking I got a few weeks back," she said and started to tell him about dinner at Serenity's.

After another hour of sitting at the table, talking, Mack returned from the bathroom and plopped himself on the couch. "C'mere," he said, pulling her down between his legs when she got close. "Ever watch movies this way?" he asked, handing her tablet to her.

"Why? I have a perfectly good big screen."

"Try it," he said and rubbed his hands down her arms. His hands on her bare skin felt good and she leaned her head back against him, her eyes closed.

"Don't stop," she said.

"I'm not doing anything."

"Your hands feel good."

"That's because you're cold." His hands stopped idly caressing and rubbed her more vigorously. "Hey," he said, his thumb zeroing in on a spot on the inside of her left arm, barely below her elbow. "What's this?"

She knew what he'd found, of course. You had to look close anymore to see it, but there was still an indent where she'd been speared. "It's what happens when Tess forgets to respect the environment she's in," she said and tried to pull her arm free.

He held tight, his other hand grappling for his phone and turning the flashlight on. He turned her so he could pull her arm closer.

She let him, knowing exactly what he was thinking—and not just because he'd gone pale. Her mother had thought the same thing when she'd seen the bandages, elbow to fingertip, and Jamie hadn't been any better.

"Seriously. It was a really sharp piece of metal, and it sliced me from here," she said, indicating a spot in the middle of her palm, "to here." She tapped the indented scar. "You know that cliché about knives being so sharp, you don't feel the cut at first? That was how it was. I didn't even know it was embedded in there and just started to carry on, but Sanjit noticed the blood. And then it *burned*, and I looked," she said, moving her arm to reenact the moment, "and we noticed that this piece of metal was sticking out of my arm.

Charley was there, too, and she had a scarf on that day, so she wrapped me up real tight and the three of us booked it to the ER, figuring we'd get there faster than an ambulance. Of course, they had to do a whole psych workup because yeah, it looks pretty ominous, but that didn't go anywhere. I mean, Charley and Sanjit had watched it happen. I tripped over some debris and flung my arms out and… Nice and simple, but it needed stitches, especially up here," she said, tapping the scar near her elbow. "It was shallowest down here," she said, indicating the base of her wrist. "Shine the light. You can't see anything there. It's like it skipped from my palm to here," she said, pointing to the spot where the line began.

"You sure? You're for real?"

She turned to face him more fully and cupped his cheek with the hand in question. "I would *not* lie about this to *you*. And save the lectures; Red beat you to them." Of the whole thing, that had been the worst part: letting Red down.

"Red runs a tight ship," Mack said.

"He has a big heart." She smiled. "He helped me find investors for the Woolslayer incubator."

"I know all this," he said and tapped her nose with his index finger, slowly, as if to get her attention and not to be flip. "Trade Creation. He's a silent partner in a unique non-profit designated for business incubation for women and other women-first projects as situations demand. The chief executive and owner is one TC herself, Tess Cartieri, who also happens to be a vested principal or partner in Urban Renewal."

"When you say it like that, it sounds kind of incestuous."

"It does. Know what else it sounds like?"

"You've been digging into me?"

"We said early on that we could Google stalk each other," he reminded her, then deflated. "And come *on*, Tess. Do you think I expected anything less from you?" He gathered her close and pulled her against his chest. She listened to his heartbeat and his voice as he spoke. "You were ambitious back in school. Maybe not to help women like you are, but it's a good look on you. I like it."

"Oh, you do, do you?" She wrinkled her nose, not that he could see it. "Will I make an *appropriate* Mackenzie woman?"

He shrugged. "I don't care about appropriate. I know the board will love you, but they don't get a lot of say in my personal life."

"Which is why they told you to cool things with us."

She could feel his grimace. "That's more of a..." He raised one hand, and now Tess envisioned him running it through his hair, stopping at the back of his head, his elbow out. "Flemming stepped off the board when Kelsey and I married. She'd changed her will at some point and left everything to me, including all her shares of PharmaSci, but Flemming still holds quite a bit. They're trying to placate him by asking me not to move on too quickly."

That made sense, and she told him so.

"It's part of the strategy that Gray and Donovan and Sarah worked up," he said. "I've told you that Tristan and my grandfather, Cullen, didn't do a lot of actual work for PharmaSci. They were the Mackenzie on duty, but they basically handed the running of things over to the board."

Tess pushed up and away from him, then retreated to the far side of the couch, the better to listen.

"So this strategy is to do the easy stuff to keep the board happy. Remind them that I'm capable and trustworthy after the nightmare they had to try to deal with. It's working, for the most part," he admitted. "I mean, some of them still blow up over things—like moving headquarters—but when I hand them hard numbers of the money we'll save, they shut up and admit maybe I know what I'm talking about." He shrugged and looked around the condo, then turned back to Tess. "You know how it is: you play the game the right way and you win. It's that simple."

"I hate the game."

He smiled. "I know. But it's a fact of life, and you have your own fair share of it."

That was true. In fact, she owed Philip an update about the sheep farm, which was that she *still* hadn't learned anything. There had to be some source she hadn't thought to tap yet, but she was damned if she could figure out what it was. It was located on land conveniently between counties, so there was no record there—and, apparently, no taxes paid, although that bothered Tess—so she and Red had to figure out how to approach the state.

"When Mother decided I was ready to take over," Mack said, "I had an awful lot I had to deal with. Here's this upstart kid with zero experience who wants to take over and do more than be the figurehead. I had to present them a vision, one they could get behind and vote for and that wouldn't make us a laughingstock. So I did—well, with the help of Gray and Donovan and Sarah. And Krista, of course. But I was the one who dug up the original company mandate, which wasn't that hard since it had been used in all the marketing stuff until Patrick, Cullen's father and my great-grandfather, changed it."

He planted his feet in the middle of the couch. Tess moved hers on top of his, thinking.

"And you still *seem* to have your soul," she said.

"I think so. At least, I'm not so sure being successful means selling it officially."

Which meant, Tess figured, if she could get to the bottom of the sheep farm and the bones, she could help Red win this latest chapter of the battle with the mayor's office. But... *how*? How do you chase a ghost? And why did she care about what the mayor's office would think of her for meddling where she basically didn't belong?

Well, because of the incubator, of course. Mack was right: She was willing to play the game if it would help her women.

"Tess?"

She shook her head. "Just thinking."

"Better not be beating yourself up about selling out."

"Nope. Just thinking about something Red and I have been working on, related to the building and the water main break."

"Anything new with that?"

"No. They're starting to dig up the land the old firehouse used to be on, but if they've found what they're looking for, no one's telling me or Red." She wrinkled her nose. "It's a bigger mess down there than it was when you were there last, but fortunately Councilwoman Salveggio intervened and got my property cleaned up and put back to rights. I got a tree out of it!"

"Trees are good."

"You should plant some."

"I have more pressing matters. Can't take the time to think about what I want for dinner, remember?"

"Right. And I still say it's crap."

"It's some of both. Nice that people value what I do and try to create space for me to do it. Crap that I'm just a pawn to increase the value of the stock in their portfolio."

"Ever get tired of being a pawn?"

"All the time. You should have seen me when I realized how long Krista had been playing me. Remember all those loopholes I kept finding in the Mackenzie investments back in college, when Tristan would try to bribe the dean to change my schedule?"

Tess remembered. She remembered Mack's rages when it would happen. Despite his size—and he'd been a *lot* more muscular back then, like a bodybuilder instead of a lean, lanky Ultimate player—he had been more funny than scary. What had been scary had been when he'd decided to fight back on Tristan's terms, outsmarting him consistently.

"Krista put all those loopholes in, just to see what I'd do with them. Apparently, I didn't disappoint."

"Were you ever your own man?" she asked after a pause. It had been the most important part of him, the reason he'd stopped being Emerson and started being Mack. It was the reason he'd gone to Kenilworth and studied the Science of Sport and gotten his athletic trainer certification and driven a Jeep and lived in an old but reasonably well-maintained house on the fringes of the off-campus student neighborhoods.

"Krista gave me a lot of room to figure out who I was and what I wanted, so I can live with how it all played out. I mean, Tess, I *could* have moved into the CEO job and spent my days playing Ultimate and working as a trainer. No one would have cared in the least. But somewhere, listening to Tristan go on and on about how his job was just to rubber stamp whatever the board wanted and to do whatever else pleased him so long as he didn't interfere..." He ran a hand through his hair. "That wasn't what I wanted. It only *looked* like freedom, and in the meantime, the company was bloated and out of touch with society's needs and only there to please the board."

"Did you make enemies when you decided to be more involved?"

He nodded. "Enter a gorgeous blonde with ice blue eyes who knew all the right people and all the right wheels to grease, even as she was doing Daddy's bidding to undermine the star-struck boy."

"Except you weren't star-struck."

"You ruined me."

She snorted. "Like Krista didn't have your feet nailed to the ground?"

He smiled. "She did. But at the same time, she was telling me to dream about PharmaSci. What did I want it to be? What did I learn in school—not about the science of sport necessarily, but what people are really like? What do they struggle with? What do they need? And then she taught me how to work the board. She and Kelsey both."

"And you won them over and got to take a more active role in the company." Tess nodded.

Mack pulled his feet out from under hers and put them on top. "So you willing to be part of all this?"

"Maybe?"

"It won't include Trade Creation or anything else you do professionally. In fact, the more you do on that end, the more they'll want to leave you alone."

"So long as it makes the company look good, right?"

He shrugged. "Like that's going to be a concern? Not as far as I can see."

"What about the expectation of what a Mackenzie wife is? I'm still not on board for any of that; in fact, part of why Woolslayer accepts me is because I use chopsticks and love to surround myself with diverse people and don't try to be anyone other than the daughter of a man who worked for the glass factory. I don't want to change that, even if I have to lose you again."

He was quiet for a minute, his blue eyes dark and calm. "If we find room for compromise, will you take it?"

"Depends on what you're thinking," she said slowly, not sure where he was heading with this. She wasn't going to change who she was. She'd just said that.

"Maybe we save your roots for the people who matter and present you the way you come off: community activist, principal at the firm. Successful, powerful in your own expertise. And we save the chopsticks for when we're not being the power couple. Or we throw a sushi party and make everyone use them. Pick our times to conform and our times to rebel." He flashed her a grin. "I kind of like the idea of being a rebel again."

It was the sort of proposal she could stomach, and she was willing to bet he knew it. It was also something that hadn't been an option back then.

"You make a very good rebel," she told him seriously, biting her lower lip.

"I think you bring it out in me." He nodded. "Don't stop."

"Wasn't planning on it."

Thirty-Nine

March 13

"Tess? Tess, wake up. I need you."

She bolted upright. "What's wrong?"

He sat down on the edge of her bed and shuddered, his mouth open, gasping for air, feeling like he was suffocating. He'd been like this since he woke from a nightmare about her, blood covering her arm. He'd been lowering her into a hole next to Kelsey's.

"Mack?" She put a hand on his shoulder. It was warm, soft, but most of all, it was *real*, and that soothed him.

But the words still weren't there.

"I... It's..." He shook his head and she scooted over to him, slipping her left arm between his own arm and his body and holding him. She pressed her cheek to his shoulder and stroked his hair, his right shoulder, his neck, even the side of his face. He turned into her hand and wished he could breathe her in, but his damn nose had stuffed up.

"Talk to me," she said.

"Don't..." He hiccupped and shook his head. "Let go."

She lifted her head. "You want me to let go?"

She started to draw back, but he squeezed his arm against hers, trapping her. "Don't." He shuddered and sobbed once before he managed to say, "Let go. Don't."

"Okay," she said, kissing his shoulder before she set her cheek against it again and pressing herself solidly against him. He forced his attention to her contours, to the way she felt, to the fact that she was there, she was holding him, and that was what he needed.

"I'm right here," she said.

"Yeah. Good." She, quite literally, had his back. Just like she'd promised.

She rubbed small circles on his shoulder as he began to draw in a few deep breaths, shuddering and sobbing at times but mostly beginning to quiet.

"Sorry," he said at last, tracing her left hand, thinking about the wedding band he'd taken off on New Year's, before all the women had chased him into the bathroom. "They... Nimisha warned me I might have times like this. That no matter that I didn't love Kelsey the right way, there's so much wrapped up in it all that it'd come back on me like this. And your scar... I believe you about what happened, but seeing it, going *there*..." He paused and panted slightly, trying to get his breathing back under control, trying to get his thoughts under control. "Sorry. Again. Sorry."

"What do you have to be sorry for?" She ran her nails lightly over his shoulder blade, a signal not to answer. "I remember this. The nights I'd wake up and realize I'd been crying in my sleep. The... *loss* that felt like some giant hole that everything in my life had fallen into and there was no way out and everything going forward was going to be just one long nightmare."

He didn't answer. He *couldn't* answer. Not when she understood so exquisitely.

"And Mack?" She paused. "You loved Kelsey the right way. Don't buy into anyone's idea of what your marriage to her should have been like."

"It wasn't like it is with you."

"It shouldn't be. She's not me. What you and she had was unique to you and her."

He shifted on the bed, pressing on her arm more tightly. "You make it sound like it was enough. That I gave her enough."

"You did."

"Then why did she do it?"

"Because it wasn't about you. Or maybe it was—maybe it was something she had to do because the other choice was to destroy you and she couldn't bear to. We don't know for certain. We don't, and we never will, no matter how long and hard we search for the answers."

He sniffled. "Got tissues?"

"Stretch. They're on the nightstand on this side of the bed."

He did, and she moved with him, still holding him no matter how uncomfortable the movement probably made her. He pulled away slightly, a signal to her to let go. She did, waiting for him while he went through at least half the box.

"My first week back after Kelsey died," he said when he felt a little calmer, "Taylor asked if I'd join a quiet lunch with a college friend of theirs. That's how the little turd got me set up with Nimisha, the grief counselor. She's this super skinny, tall Indian woman in these saris that you'd kill for. All the colors of the peacock: greens and blues and gold. She wore a bindi and took my hand and told me she would be there whenever I needed her. And we had lunch, the three of us, and talked grief. Turns out Taylor's got quite the set of luggage." He winced. "I never knew, but then again, Taylor made it clear I wasn't allowed to ask."

"You *are* the boss."

"Come back," he said, wiping his nose one final time.

She pressed herself against his back again, her arm wrapping under his, her fingers coming up to latch on his collarbone.

He took a deep breath, feeling her against him. She was *solid*. She was Tess, and she was right *there*. "Krista was all over me, wanting me to see some old white guy she knew, and here I had Nimisha who made me feel better just as soon as she walked into my office. Like... I'm part of some club now."

Tess kissed his shoulder again and he knew she understood. As a member, of course she did.

He straightened, lifting her as he did. He took a few breaths. "This is normal, right? To be a mess one minute and perfectly fine the next? Even after this long?"

"Yep." She pulled away from him.

He leaned in and gave her a gentle kiss. "I'm going back now."

"You sure?"

He paused. Part of him thought he had no business being there with her. That he should have been home with Kelsey, that she never should have done it, that he shouldn't have been *free* to be here.

But the other part of him knew he was right where he belonged.

"Yeah," he said. "I have these really cool alligator sheets in there, and it's like I'm getting to live out being a normal little kid, except I'm thirty-one and who'd have ever thought something as stupid as alligator sheets would be cool?"

"I was afraid you'd refuse to sleep on them."

"And what would you have done if I had?" he asked, wondering if that had been her master plan and he'd blown it.

"Pointed you to the couch—which you're not allowed to sleep on here, either. Because the sheets are no better in here." Her voice danced, and he knew the truth of it.

"For real?"

"Of course. I know you, Mac-and-Cheese. You'd take any excuse to wheedle your way in here."

"No. No wheedling. When I'm in your bed, it's because we've agreed. And it's *not* going to be one of those famous *well, shoot, we were watching a movie and just fell asleep* nights like we used to have."

"I can respect that."

"Can you wait?"

"So long as it's not another nine years."

He touched her face and she turned into his hand. "Good night, Just Tess," he said quietly. "Thanks for catching me." He leaned in toward her, kissing her again, every bit as gently as before, and left without saying anything else, her soft *goodnight* echoing in his head as he turned on the light in her guest room and took in the crazy sheets again.

She had her own ways of taking care of him, and dammit, but he needed them.

He felt bad about waking her in the morning, but he needed her car keys. It was his turn to take care of her.

"Why?"

He paused and looked at her. Sure enough, she had the same set of sheets on her bed, her dark hair blending in with them, her face pale against the dark browns and olives. She also hadn't stopped sleeping in t-shirts, he noticed with a rush of relief. Kelsey had loved those frilly things that were supposed to turn him on. They hadn't. "I want to say thanks," he said. "For last night. I found a bakery."

"No. Go to Vera's. Drop my name." She shoved at him, trying to dig deeper into the pillows and sink back into sleep.

He didn't blame her, but he was determined. He was bringing her breakfast, and that was all there was to it.

"Vera's?" he pulled away from her and sat on the edge of her bed.

She whined.

"Oh. One of your Woolslayer friends. That makes sense." He stood up.

She lifted her head out of her pillows, her eyes still closed, her body braced on her forearms. "Park in front of the incubator, in the space marked for me, and walk. No one'll bother the car."

"You be up when I get back?" he asked.

"No."

He left her room, left her to go back to sleep, and paused outside her room, disquieted. It wasn't that it had felt like old times, back when they'd lived together. And it wasn't that as familiar as it felt, it also felt new and mystifying. Something else was wrong.

He snapped his fingers and grinned. She'd gotten him.

He still didn't know where her keys were.

FORTY

March 25

*H*ey, Tess, you love me, right?

Oh, no. It had been two weeks since she'd seen him and their conversations had been light. This, though... this was something else. Something she wasn't braced for. She cautiously glanced at her phone.

And you want an excuse to come spend a weekend in your favorite... what did you call my home? he had asked.

I want to spend a weekend in the Mackenzie Manor? she replied. *And where are you going to be?*

Hopefully right there in you. With you.

She laughed. That had probably been a true mistake; Mack wasn't one for dirty talking. Unless Kelsey had changed him? It seemed unlikely.

Her phone buzzed again. *If I get rid of Krista and Logan for the night, we can spread a blanket on the floor and have some real fun in the ballroom.*

I'm sure generations of rebellious teenage Mackenzies did exactly that. But I doubt they bothered with a blanket.

Which is why we will.

She accepted the video call when it came. "What are you up to?" she asked him, surprised by his surroundings. It was nine o'clock and he was still at the office.

"This women's organization is honoring PharmaSci, along with some other businesses who've been at the forefront of advocating for women's health."

She paused and cocked her head. "This is very interesting, but what's it got to do with *me*?"

He sighed. "I need a date. No. Scratch that. I need Just Tess to have my back."

"No."

"No?" He moved, as if he were sitting forward, carried by the momentum of his surprise. "Tess, I need you! How can you say no?"

"Because, Emerson Mackenzie, you'll recall that I dumped you because this was exactly the sort of thing I don't want to go to. I wasn't kidding about it, and I wasn't putting up a false front, and I most certainly haven't changed my mind—and believe me, Red's tried. I am not the society girl type." If she hadn't been holding her phone, she would have crossed her arms over her chest.

"It's one night."

"You said that about the company holiday party. This makes two."

He scrubbed at his face with his hands. "Okay. I am hearing you. And we have talked about this, and it's not like I want to go back on my word, but I'm stuck. And I could really use *you* at my back. I trust you." He paused and took a breath. "Can you blame me? You're one of the smartest women I know, and you listen when I talk, and you ask questions and you actually *care*, just because it's important to me."

Tess snorted softly. Of course she cared.

"And the work you're doing," he went on, still earnest, "in a lot of ways, it should be you getting that award, not me."

"I'm not doing anything with women's health."

"But you are, indirectly. You're empowering the women who rent space from you to make their lives better. That spills over into a person's overall health. And besides, maybe some of these other people who'll be at this thing will inspire you."

"I'm plenty inspired, Mack." She had more ambitions for the incubator and its occupants than she could act on, although she didn't expect him to know that.

"And you inspire *me*. I mean, I got into this because it seemed like the right thing to do to honor Kelsey, but the more you and I talk and the more I see you in action, the more I know that it's the right thing. That we need to make serious, fundamental changes in how our society approaches and treats women."

"Said by the descendent of generations of white men whose control is explicitly to hold women down."

He narrowed his eyes slightly. "Said by the Mackenzie who's going to help be responsible for that change. Because *you* have convinced me."

"Anything else?"

"Yes."

He was so emphatic that she took notice. He was serious, his eyes flashing, his mouth set. "Maybe I just want to share it with you. Maybe I want you there, beside me, to share it with *me*. I don't want to tell you about it later on. I want you *there*, right there, going through it, watching me try not to blush or stutter or hock a loogie or something when they call me to the podium to say thanks."

"Wow. That... almost sounds like a marriage proposal."

He let out a breath and sat back slightly, some of his fire vanishing. "Almost feels like one, but that's where I am in all this. You. Me. Sharing it all."

Tess paused, a wave of something she couldn't identify washing over her. It was equal parts comforting and begging her to freak out. "That was the last of your arguments? You saved the best for last?" she asked in a small voice.

He flashed her a grin. "Well, you do look pretty hot when you get all dressed up. I never mind seeing that."

Tess closed her eyes. The emotions were coming fast, on top of each other, and she wasn't sure what to think.

"Please, Tess. I'm desperate."

"Why? I mean, other than all that, what prompted the desperation?"

"Alyssa ran up to me at the gym yesterday and told me she was excited about being my date."

"Okay, first off, why do you keep going to the gym? You have a full weight room at the Manor."

"Cardio. I can't run at home. What's next?"

"I assume you've told her to forget it?"

"Multiple times. I'm not the only one, either, but she's Alyssa. Only listens to herself."

"What's wrong with escorting her around for the night?"

He'd had his water bottle at his mouth and he spat water all over the phone. Tess waited for him to clean it off. "Are you *kidding* me? I do that and she's planning the wedding about ten seconds after I say okay. See? I seriously need you, Tess. Even if you forget about Alyssa somehow, there's more like her. They see money, they see a widower, which apparently is something more pathetic than a single man... I'm a sitting duck. We do this, we can cut it off right now and get on with you and me."

Tess passed a hand over her face. Here it was. The kicker. "When?"

He pulled his head into his neck. "Next Saturday?"

"Oh, you."

He straightened. "Since it's short notice, the flight's on me."

"It's not about the money, and you know it."

"And the dress."

She sighed. While she didn't mind making him grovel a bit, he wasn't going about it the right way. "Your dark side is showing."

"Of course it is," he sighed and rubbed at his face. "What's it gonna take?"

"Definitely the dress. There's no way I can get one between now and next Saturday. Not one that's up to Lakeford society standards."

"Krista's already said she'll put her people on it for you."

"You know this isn't how normal people do things, right?"

"Yes. That's why I'm desperate and begging you. What else do you need?"

"I already told you. That ballroom, and *not* while breakfast is cooking."

"Breakfast... Is it okay if I give Marisela the mornings off so we can have breakfast on our own schedule?"

"Oh, so we're sleeping in?"

"Maybe."

Tess paused. He grinned at her and she couldn't help it. She grinned back. Maybe this society thing was just an excuse to get her in town—and, clearly, in his bed.

But if it was, he should have picked a better excuse. Or not used one at all and simply invited her up for the weekend.

"You have to ask Marisela if it's okay if we—and that means you, Macaroni—take over her kitchen."

"She won't mind."

"I do."

"She's never minded before."

"Have you *asked*?"

"No. Why would I?"

"Because that's what you do when you respect someone. Look at it this way: How would you feel about someone coming in your office and using your stuff to do their work?"

"She'll ask what food to stock."

"That's up to you."

He brightened. "One of the things I like best about being around you is that what I want matters."

"Of course it matters—until you're dragging me to more of these awful society things. Just keep groceries reasonable. I'm not taking a side of salmon and smoking it or anything."

He paused, his brow furrowing slightly, his mouth slack. "You know how?" he asked after a minute.

"No, but I know how to Google."

He closed his eyes and smiled, the tense lines in his face easing. "It's late, I'm tired, and I want to get home. Call Taylor about flights. They'll handle it all."

"You don't have to do that."

"I do. I'm a shit for asking you to be here when I know you hate these things."

"You are, and I do."

"But I'm desperate, and even if I weren't, I meant what I said about wanting to share it with you as it happens. Alyssa very well might buy her own engagement ring. I bet it'll be gaudy as fuck. And I know you're going to say that means I'm making the popcorn."

"And helping with breakfast, if it's okay with Marisela, and carrying the blankets into the ballroom"—she caught his intake of breath—"and sleeping in some long-abandoned guest room if you're an ass."

Relief flooded his face. "Just Tess," he said softly, "you have no idea how bad I need you to help with this. She's beyond me."

"Well, you're not hers, and she's just going to have to accept that you and I are..."

"Going to make it work this time," he said, still softly.

"We'd better," she said every bit as softly, feeling how the words felt as she said them. They were equal parts strange and familiar, and she wondered if it really was the right time to jump into bed with him. Although, should she consider it *back* into bed with him?

When she asked Jamie, her friend said exactly what she expected. "Is there a better time to move things forward?"

"When I know for sure he's moving down here?"

"Tess, he can't make it any clearer that you're his priority."

"We'll see. I mean, I'm not about to walk into his house and find boxes packed or anything."

"You sure about that?"

"As sure as I am that Alyssa's not the one winding up in his bed anytime soon."

"Oh, you've *got* to give me the dirt on that woman. I can't believe she's real."

"She sounds kind of pathetic, actually."

"Why? Because she wants Mack?"

"No. Because she refuses to respect him."

"I know you never got over him."

"I set him free. He came back. Isn't that how it works?"

"I'm not sure when it happened, Tess, but I think you've fallen harder for him than you ever had back in school."

"I know," Tess said. She couldn't stop the giggle. "Amazing, isn't it?"

Forty-One

March 29

"How can every single one of those records have been scrubbed?" Tess asked Philip. He'd asked her to meet him at the coffee shop and go back to his office with her, where he'd dropped the latest bomb. "That's... impossible. There's too much, too many."

"Someone's trying to alter history and keep themselves off the hook for those bones."

"Obviously, but *how*?"

Philip gave her a long look.

"Seriously? PK government was *that* corrupt at one point in time?"

"Heck yeah. Clear on up to the nineteen seventies, judging by the state of the records that were kept. I had my people go through them *all*, Tess, clear back to the end of the war. *The* war."

It seemed impossible they were talking the end of the Civil War, but of course they were. What other war could have created such a rich opportunity for a corrupt government? She shook her head. "Were the bones carbon dated?"

"Yes." He looked away.

"Okay, so you know stuff you can't share. Want to know what little I've learned about the history of Woolslayer?"

"The neighborhood was built," he said, "to support this sheep farm that wound up being haunted or cursed or whatever's going on there."

"Do we have the same sources?"

"That much is pretty common knowledge. But no one knows much about this sheep farm, only that the land was finally abandoned for good about forty years ago. There was a big constriction of industry in Port Kenneth at that time and the city went through a serious recession. People left in droves. In some ways, we still haven't recovered."

"I know. We work on a lot of the buildings downtown that were abandoned then. And one thing that's been consistent my whole career is that when there are people who know the stories of a place, they're lost within three or four generations anyway."

They looked at each other for a long minute, Tess feeling like they'd run out of conversation and wondering why.

"Is there *anything* you can tell me about the bones?" she finally asked.

"I'm holding out hope that they wound up here because they were moved out of a small family cemetery—" He held up a hand as she opened her mouth to scoff at that theory. "Let me have my innocence. We are probably looking at something a lot darker, and you know what? I don't want to go there unless we have to."

Tess understood. Of course she did. Port Kenneth had been built at the mouth of the river as a slave market. While it was nicer to think the bones were from a cemetery that had been moved, or some form of kismet piling all those different species together, the reality probably was that any humans had been viewed as every bit as disposable as the wildlife, the sheep, and the dogs.

That thought made her want to hurl.

"Have more bones been found?" she asked cautiously.

"No, and we're going to start on Monday putting everything back together and closing up the original hole."

"At last," she said on a huge breath of relief that was immediately followed by a wave of resentment. To not know how this ended wasn't fair, even though part of her knew that it was the most likely outcome.

"So even if there's an... uglier part to this story," she asked, picking her words carefully, "is it possible the bones were moved from somewhere else?"

"They most likely were," Philip said with a nod. He slid to the edge of his chair, and Tess wondered about the man. What about this had him so excited? "I have some of our historians working on that angle. What was left standing after the war? We know none of the current buildings were built before 1900"—Tess nodded her agreement—"so when *was* everything built? What was here before? What was moved around, and why? And if those *are* bones of slaves, how did they get under a firehall that wasn't built until thirty-five years after slavery ended?"

"I would *love* to know," she said, letting herself dream for a second about having those answers. What sorts of planning had gone into the rebuilding of Port Kenneth—or was it the *building*? How did any of them know that Port Kenneth had been anything other than a slave market... and a sheep farm? How old *was* the sheep farm? How far into the future had the planners of PK been able to dream? What would they think of the current city's layout and how it had evolved? How had the contractions of the 1980s affected it?

"Me, too," Philip said and Tess understood Philip a lot better: The guy was a historian at heart. "We do know that the original sewage lines weren't put in until that building boom of 1900," Philip said. "They've been replaced since, for the most part, including Woolslayer's. The water line that ruptured was actually rebuilt around the 1990s, maybe a little earlier—and again, it's possible the bones were placed in there at that time, too. There's no reason for the water lines to have been done wrong, yet they were. And even though the city rooted out its corruption and started keeping better records after the 1970s, what we do have about Woolslayer before that water main replacement is gone."

"So someone doesn't want us to know something. But what?"

"You mean beyond if this was deliberate, and who did it?"

"Well, yeah. I'm thinking *why*. What sort of secret would someone go to those lengths for? I mean... it just seems *weird*." Tess paused, thinking. "You said the Flaherty family—"

"Don't go there," Philip said quickly. "We are *not* allowed to point fingers at them."

"But if we don't, we're left with a whole lot of weird."

"The whole thing is weird," Philip agreed. "From the bones to the water line, to why that firehall came down in the first place. That was the Woolslayer firehall."

Tess stretched, her arms overhead. "And let me guess," she said after a moment, "the firehall came down around the same time the water lines were rebuilt?"

"Give the brains a gold star," Philip said, pointing his coffee cup at her.

"Nah, that was too easy," she said, pulling her arms back into her lap. "We have bones that are possibly from before or during the war, but they were moved maybe thirty-five years later? Maybe even after that? And we have a piece of ground that's been vacant for about thirty years that no one's ever investigated or done anything about."

"One reason the land was left untouched..." He winced.

"Gotcha. Not white enough, not affluent enough."

"And the community leaders didn't trust government enough to press us to do something with it."

"Well, when we get to the bottom of this, I still want to get some grants together and buy it and use it for the babysitting service. Kids need to get outside."

Philip spent a long minute looking at her. "I remember you saying that before. It's got some teeth to it."

Tess gave him a smile, her eyebrows raised as if to say *yeah, I know*.

"First, we've got to put it back together. Can you get word out that we'll be finishing it up? You can make noise about your playground at that time, too."

"I'm headed out of town for the weekend, but I can ask some of my business owners to help out."

"Out of town?" He raised his mug to his mouth.

"A friend needs me to have his back."

"Wouldn't be any friend of yours that I might have met, would it?"

"Philip—"

"Hey, you know I'm the number one champion of landing that corporate move. See if you can find out what we need to sweeten the deal with."

"More alligators," Tess said with a grin. "Seriously, though. They need a location already."

"There's a couple empty buildings downtown, and I know an architect who specializes in renovations. I'm surprised no one's explored that option."

She held her hands up. "I'm not part of any of that. Other things they want are partnerships with the university. And no social demands."

"Social demands?"

"Yeah, you know: show up, be seen as a big-money donor, have your picture in the gossip or society section of the local news outlets."

"That's a weird one."

Tess shrugged. "Some of us prefer to live quieter lives, under the radar."

Philip all but snorted his coffee at her. "Tess, that is the *opposite* of what you've been doing lately."

"Talking about me is fine, especially when it's for something like Trade Creation and, okay, the alligator was fun. But expecting me in cocktail dresses a couple times a week to promote one cause after another isn't happening—even if you bring me an alligator to play with."

"Wish I could see that."

"I'd gladly send you to this banquet in my place, but man, people would talk, and not in the ways we want them to."

Philip smiled and finished his coffee. "Can't have that."

"At least wait until he moves here," Tess said with a wink. "Some days, I live to torture that man."

"You? No. Not you," Philip said, a smile tugging at his mouth.

Forty-Two

April 2

Mack got to the office early that Friday, the day Tess was due in town. "I don't want to be here today," he told Taylor, who had still managed to get there first. He'd called a mandatory company-wide lunch a few days before. And ten minutes after he'd done that, he'd sent out word that his first-ever round of layoffs would be happening in the morning. Lunch was for the survivors.

"It's not going to be that bad."

Mack gave them a long look. "I thought I said that casual day didn't include pink bunny pajamas."

"These aren't pink bunnies," Taylor said with a sniff, sticking their nose in the air.

Mack leaned in for a closer examination, wrinkling his nose so he wouldn't laugh. "Taylor," he said, straightening up, "tell me you brought other clothes to change into."

"Maybe," Taylor said, arms behind their back. They swung from side to side like a little kid, complete with faux innocent face.

"Tess put you up to this, didn't she." It wasn't a question.

Taylor's mouth opened, then they paused and cocked their head. "I will remember to include her next time, then. But yes, I do have more appropriate clothes, even though everyone I spoke to—which was a grand total of zero, by the way—said you would appreciate being met this morning with some more alligators."

Mack paused to consider, then chuckled. "You know, I do. Thanks."

"Stays between us," Taylor said in a stage whisper as Mack disappeared into his own office, hoping no one was going to come complain to him—about Taylor's outfit or about what was about to happen. Even though he and HR had agreed to keep the layoffs as essential as possible, he still wasn't comfortable with them.

Then again, he wasn't comfortable paying a good salary to the guy who'd been hiding in the back corner of his floor and playing video games from nine to five. Or the woman who'd figured out how to use her work computer to mine cryptocurrency. Legal had been called in to deal with her.

Despite the shedding of the deadweight—and it pained him that there had even *been* deadweight, but then again, that's what at least the two Mackenzies before him had been—it was a surprisingly good day, and he headed out of the office early, eager to see Tess and hear what she was up to.

He wasn't expecting to find her in his home office, and he wanted to kick himself when he saw what she'd found. The stack of diaries from the Mackenzie men who'd come before him were supposed to be sacred, shared only with the heir. And he'd left them on his desk, in plain view.

She looked up at him, pain etched across her face, and his stomach sank into the floor and halfway through the ground. Her eyes were red and puffy. "What's wrong?"

She shook her head and closed her eyes, covering them with her hand. "I can't lose you again, but I don't know how to process this."

"Tess?" He came around the side of the desk and knelt beside her.

She pulled her knees to her chest and rested her forehead on them.

"Why are you afraid of losing me?" he asked softly. Some sort of ball or lump had formed at the bottom of his throat, making it impossible to swallow and hard to talk.

She waved her hand at the journals. "Have you read these?"

"Not cover to cover," he said heavily. "I know I was supposed to, but I couldn't stand to see Tristan's, and the old ones are really hard to decipher. I've been trying, but I think you found something I've missed."

She raised her head and looked at him. Her eyes were full of tears again.

"What did you find?" he asked softly, the ball of whatever was in his throat dropping into his gut. It was so heavy, he felt pinned to the floor. And worst of all, another ball had shown up to take the place of the first one.

Okay, he thought, maybe that wasn't the worst part. Now he was having trouble breathing.

And he still didn't know why.

"Remember I told you about that piece of land near the incubator? The haunted sheep farm?"

He glanced at the stack of journals, then back at her. "Yeah. So?"

"It's Mackenzie land. The *original* Mackenzie land, at least as far as PharmaSci is concerned."

He sat back on his heels, a sense of awe washing over him. No wonder he felt a pull to Port Kenneth. And it answered his questions about how Henry Mackenzie had known how to launch a pharmaceutical company in the middle of a war he hadn't been anywhere near—he'd actually been almost in the middle of it.

But it also raised new questions, especially about why Tess was crying again.

"There's a piece of all this that I'm missing," he said gently, wiping a tear off her cheek.

"The farm." She shook her head, squeezing her eyes closed, and swiveled the chair, turning her back to him.

He got up and walked around the desk, then resumed kneeling in front of her. This time, he took her hands. "Tess. Tell me."

She took a deep breath. "Slaves, Mack. Mackenzies were slavers."

As she started crying yet again, he pulled her into his arms, adjusting awkwardly so he was sitting flat on the floor, his back against his desk, one of the overly ornate drawer pulls digging into his back. It was better to think about the pain from the drawer pull instead of what she'd said.

A million rationalizations ran through his mind. Port Kenneth was south of the Mason-Dixon line; of course they'd owned slaves. It was what they did. It didn't mean they were horrible slave owners. Maybe they were that rare breed of kind slave owner, the kind he'd grown up hearing stories about, although he had to admit that reality didn't seem to match the myth.

"Okay," he said slowly as Tess began to calm. He shifted slightly, trying to get rid of the drawer pull. "C'mon. Let's sit on the couch and talk this through."

"What's to talk through?"

He felt a faint smile ghost across his face. "How you found out, how to reconcile the fact that this is Mackenzie history but I'm certainly not the type who could stomach treating another human being *that* way."

"You could if you were raised with it and didn't know any better."

"I was raised with Tristan and I know better," he pointed out, shifting her in his arms. "C'mon. To the couch."

She got up and, holding his hand, led the way. Not that it was far; about six steps. He sank into it, its contours familiar. He'd spent most of his sleepless nights after Kelsey's death here and he hoped he wasn't conditioned to fall asleep immediately on it.

Then again, if you were conditioned to do a thing, didn't that mean it happened? He wasn't sure he'd slept at all those first few months, but Krista and Logan insisted he had, at least a little bit.

"What happened then, who they were," he said, shaking himself out of his thoughts and telling himself to stop avoiding the subject at hand, "doesn't mean that's who I am. And you *know* that, Tess."

She nodded, not looking at him, her chin raised as if she were trying to stop more tears.

"Tell me what the journals say," he said, wincing as he did. He should know. Nothing she was about to say should have been news to him.

"It was in Cullen's."

"Cullen's? But I read that one." Mostly. He hadn't cared about the jerk's personal life and had skipped a lot of those ramblings.

She studied him for a long minute. "Know what happened after his daughter died?"

"No," he admitted, feeling not just sheepish but stupid, too.

"His wife kicked him out of her bed—"

Mack groaned. It seemed to be an unpleasant trend among Mackenzie wives.

"We're talking about them, not us. For now."

"Tell me there's more to this."

"There is. Cullen fell in love with a woman named Rachel. She was a chemist at PharmaSci, in case you were wondering—"

He frowned, trying to remember if he'd caught that in his skimming.

"And," Tess went on, "they had three kids together. It sounds like he was a relatively involved father, too, spending time with them whenever he could, until someone figured it out. The scandal broke and so Cullen arranged for Rachel to retire from research and go teach chemistry at…" Her eyes had brightened as she'd told the story and she'd turned more fully to look at him. Now, she held her hands up as if to invite him to guess.

"Kenilworth?" he asked, feeling like it was too coincidental to believe. Life didn't really work like this. Did it?

"Yes! And there's a line in Cullen's journal, about closing the farm entirely at last, too. Something about his wife wanting to be rid of it so there were no more ties to Port Kenneth, no reason for him to lie about visiting Rachel. PharmaSci headquarters had already been moved to Lakeford, but for whatever reason, the sheep farm was still... sheeping?" She shook her head. "It was active. You know what I mean."

Mack scrubbed at his face. "I should know all this."

Tess shrugged and pulled at his forearm until he was looking at her. "But you do *now*, and it's what we do from *here* that matters."

It was the opposite to the song she'd been singing through her tears, but Tess had a resiliency to her that he couldn't get enough of. It was in part why her tears had been such a surprise.

"So I double-checked. I mean, the land around PK isn't good for much in terms of farming. And sure enough, Robert's journal talks about establishing the Woolslayer business district as the last thing before moving PharmaSci, to help give his farm workers more income. He helped set up that stretch of street the incubator's on. Staffed the butchery from his farm employees, helped establish a grocery... helped the people as much as he could before he yanked PharmaSci out of the area, but he hid what he did for them. Silent benefactor and all that." She took a deep breath and gave him a cautious look. "Apparently, he says, it's a Mackenzie thing. Good deeds done anonymously."

"But why?"

"Because no one in PK *liked* the Mackenzies much. Remember, even now, it's widely believed that the land is cursed... by the enslaved who lived on it."

Mack frowned and rubbed the back of his neck. "Tess... How do we know the Mackenzies didn't buy the farm *after* slavery ended?"

She got off the couch and picked up the bottom journal. Mack guessed it was Henry's. "Because it's where PharmaSci began. On the family sheep farm outside of Port Kenneth." She set the journal down and returned to him, straddling his lap.

He liked that. He put his hands on her waist and looked her over. Other than the red eyes, she looked cute, wearing a thick grey hoodie that, as he looked at it, might have been his. Her hair fell over the folds of the hood, somehow smooth and haphazard, all at the same time.

"I'm sorry I'm being a downer," she said.

"Why'd this hit you so hard?"

"Because," she said, looking up at the ceiling, a hint of exasperation entering her voice, "who are the women I fight for? The descendants of the enslaved. Refugees. Hell, just the fact that they're women means they're marginalized. And here's the man I've always loved, a descendant of the quintessential oppressors." She waved an arm around but he caught it, folding it into the space between them.

"I know," he sighed, "and we're sitting in a house with a front that most people equate with that oppression. Okay. I get it."

"It feels like loving you makes me a hypocrite."

"Maybe just like me a lot?"

She smiled. "That doesn't solve the problem."

"But you do, right?"

"Mack—"

He leaned his head back against the couch, moving his hands onto her thighs. "When I invited you up here," he said slowly, trying to think of the best way to phrase this, "it was partly because of Alyssa, but she's really an excuse. It's that when I think of taking a stand for women, it's you I think about. How strong you are. How fierce. And *smart*," he said, tapping her legs gently for emphasis. "You know that the sins of my ancestors aren't mine."

"Who else can set things right?"

He paused, thinking that over. Was it his responsibility, or was that too simplistic a response? Did they even know the full story? What even needed to be set right after this amount of time? "Can we put this aside for the weekend, get on with our plans"—and he pulled at a fold of her sweatshirt—"and I'll talk this through with Krista during the week? Really give it the consideration it's due?"

"Do I have a choice?"

"Well, yeah. You could tell me to make up a guest room for you."

She wrinkled her nose. "But what if I want to sleep on the famous couch?" But her hands were on his chest as she said that, and he was all too aware suddenly that his shirt was lightweight and her hands were hot.

"I don't know if we'd both fit that well. Not for a full night's sleep." He wanted to kiss her, wondered if she'd let him.

"You need a full night's sleep." She nipped at the tip of his nose.

"I do," he said, raising his chin and hoping she'd accept his invitation. "But I'd be fine with a partial night's sleep and the most incredible woman I've ever known in my bed with me."

"Need someone to make it stop torturing you?"

He let out his breath in one quick, surprised exhale. "That too."

She shook her head, her eyes closed. "Mack. I just told you that your ancestors were slavers. Doesn't it bother you?"

"It will once I let myself think about it. Right now, I want to think about you." He moved his hands to her calves, to her hips, her upper arms, her shoulders, and then cupped her face. She leaned into the caress, her eyes closed.

"I..." He felt her relax. "I would like to be thought about." As his thumb found her lips, she ran her own hand up his neck. "And I would like to think about you."

FORTY-THREE

It didn't seem to matter how badly they wanted to think only about each other, Tess thought as they came apart by some sort of mutual accord. Mack's eyes as he opened them were dilated and dark with desire, but also haunted.

What she had told him was sinking in. She could see it.

"I know," she said and briefly cupped his cheek.

He took one of those deep, shuddering breaths that she knew meant he was pulling himself back under control. "There is an absolute cruelty to wanting you this much, to having you right here, and..." He shook his head, then wiped a hand across his face.

"We need more answers."

"We do."

She looked over her shoulder at the journals, willing them to magically rise up and float across the room and join them on the couch.

He must have followed her gaze because he said, "Will you read Tristan's?"

"Of course," she said, although she wanted to read any comments about young Emerson about as much as he did.

They weren't complimentary, as she'd expected. But when she got to the part where he made choices about Rachel and his half-siblings, she gasped out loud and grabbed Mack's arm, propped on the desk beside hers.

"What?" he asked, an undercurrent of panic cutting through his voice.

"This. This is the most..." she paused, licking her lips. "I can't even. Here, let me read it to you."

And she did. About how Tristan had learned that his oldest half-brother had lung cancer. Tristan had known what would happen if he pushed SH-34, the cancer drug her dad had taken, into human trials. But he'd wanted there to be no doubt who the Mackenzie heir was. The other six people he'd given the drug to—including her father—had merely been to hide his homicide.

Anger filled her, but it was Mack who pushed away from his desk, stormed across his office, ripped the door open, and bellowed for his mother.

She and Logan arrived together, eyes wide. "Emerson?"

"Read it, Tess."

She shook her head. "I can't. Not again." But she held the journal up, offering it to Krista.

"Did you know?" Mack asked through gritted teeth as his mother read.

Given how pale she, too, turned, Tess figured she hadn't.

"Tess," she said when she was done, "I am so sorry. Whatever your family received in compensation wasn't nearly enough."

It was the last thing Tess had expected to hear.

Krista pulled Logan into a corner, where they had a heated discussion. Tess glanced at Mack, who was watching carefully, and she wondered if he was able to make anything out. All she caught was Krista insisting she hadn't agreed to something of this magnitude.

After a minute, Logan and Krista rejoined them, and they read on.

Tristan had passive-aggressively pushed Mack to school at Kenilworth in the hopes that he'd run into Rachel's kids and hand PharmaSci over to them, although an ugly confrontation that would paint Mack as too hot-headed to handle PharmaSci would have been good, too.

"He was so threatened by you," Krista said, shaking her head. "As he should have been, given what you've accomplished so far. And remember, Cullen was threatened by Tristan, Robert by Cullen... It's how the Mackenzies are, damaging each other for generations." She pierced Mack with her gaze. Tess also felt pasted to her chair. "It's time for the past to stop repeating and for *you* to be the new model of what a Mackenzie is supposed to be."

Just in case she'd forgotten, Tess reminded herself that Krista was a formidable woman.

Mack was nodding. "I'm the rebel, huh? The one with a conscience." He flicked a look at Tess.

"It's who I raised you to be," Krista said.

"But you and me, Mack," Tess said thoughtfully. "Why does it feel now like maybe our meeting wasn't left to chance?"

"Go on," Krista said carefully.

"Well, Tristan was hoping for an encounter between Rachel's kids and Mack. So why not the two of us? Family of the victim and the heir. I mean, he meddled in Mack's course load every semester. Why *not* try to push us together? Except, we did it on our own the day I cut through the stadium and you threw a disc at me."

"And you tell me to quit the team," Mack told Krista, who was thoughtful, her eyes narrowed, her mouth pursed.

"You could be right," she said. "He can be a vengeful bastard. As you've seen," she added, nodding at the journal.

"But this," Mack said, gesturing between himself and Tess, "isn't revenge."

"That's because Dad died when I was thirteen. I had years to make peace with it before we met." She reminded herself that they'd gotten past their strange connection to each other. They could do it again.

But the slavery issue was a heck of a lot bigger than SH-34 had been. Wasn't it? One was certainly closer to home than the other, but which was *bigger*?

Krista pinned her searching look on Tess, who raised her chin and, behind the desk, wove her fingers through Mack's. "So the idea of pushing you two together backfired on him."

"Yes," Tess said, squeezing Mack's hand. "Tristan failed, Krista. He failed you, he failed Mack, he failed the company, he failed... everything. No wonder he tucked tail and ran to Bora Bora or wherever he is."

"Dinner's ready," Logan said softly, leaning in from behind Krista. "Why don't we take a break from this and clear our heads?"

They did, Tess not sure what to expect. Would Marisela, the housekeeper, serve them? Would a plate full of food be put in front of her? Was she dressed okay for the formal dining room?

But Marisela served a family-style feast, and in the kitchen, too. Apparently, a family dinner meant making the recipes she'd grown up eating, and Tess couldn't have been happier with the fried plantains, the *gallo pinto*, and the chicken dish with a name she hadn't caught. *Pollo* something, of course. And fresh, homemade tortillas.

It was the exact antithesis of what she'd expected.

So was the conversation, staying away from the discoveries in the journals and only delving into PharmaSci business for a short time. Best of all, it never swirled into an interrogation of Tess.

As the meal wound down, Mack leaned over and kissed her forehead. "On that note," he said. "We've been sitting too long. If you two will excuse us," he said to Krista and Logan, "I'd like to take a walk."

"It's cold out," Tess said.

He leaned over, a grin plastered on his face. "Baby, I'll keep you warm."

She groaned but stood up anyway. He winked at her and nodded to his mother and Logan before leading her to get their coats.

Outside, they strolled the property. "It's ten acres," he said, "which is small for up here. I never understood why."

Tess needed to think for a minute. "Because initially this was the summer home," she said. "Even though we're in the mountains, PK gets awfully humid in the summers. Remember?"

"Yeah." He faked a shudder. "Maybe we should talk about doing that, ourselves? That first summer I stayed in town... It was brutal. I don't know how you do it."

Tess shrugged. "You'll adapt."

"Or we can have a summer home and a winter home."

Tess chuckled. It sounded crazily luxurious—and impossible. "We'll see," she said. "I might be able to work from here, but I don't know if I could take care of the incubator."

"One more thing to work out," he said heavily.

"But we're figuring out what we have to work out. It's progress."

He shook his head and didn't say anything.

She squeezed his hand. "So tell me about how the company meeting went. Was it awful?"

He sighed heavily. "It got off to a rough start."

"I can imagine," she said.

He didn't answer at first, and Tess realized how deeply he was feeling it all. Then again, the fact that he was successful at making positive changes was pretty extraordinary.

"Follow that path," he said.

They followed it around a corner and stopped at a pond. It looked black in the night, which was both kind of romantic and definitely creepy—which made Tess think about the sheep farm all over again. Until Mack pulled her into his arms and kissed the tip of her nose. "Where you sleeping tonight?"

"I thought the plan was with you."

"I'm nervous. You nervous?"

She laughed. "About what?"

"You. Me. Being with you again. It's been awhile."

"It has," she agreed gravely although she just wanted to laugh. At him. At how he was overthinking everything. At the sheer pleasure of being in his arms and not having to face the very big, very real obstacles still in front of them. "But I think we'll remember what we're doing."

He chuckled softly and raised his head, so he was looking over hers. "You think?"

"I do." She slipped her hand around his neck, stretching up to meet his lips and prove it.

Forty-Four

"Why are we taking the long way?" Tess asked when it was either take their clothes off right there, by the pond, or go back inside and do it properly. Ordinarily, the idea of making love by the pond might have been romantic, or at least daring—if they had a blanket or three—but early April in Lakeford, New York was a lot colder than early April in Port Kenneth, Tennessee. And as warm as Mack was, he wasn't warm enough to keep her from feeling like it was still winter.

"We're not taking the long way," Mack said.

Tess stopped walking. Since he had tucked her under his arm, he stumbled to a stop, too. "Macintosh, I work with space for a living. Do you really think I don't know the house is behind us?"

He pressed her more firmly against himself. "I just don't want to go in yet. I know you're cold, but humor me?"

She pulled her hand out of her coat pocket and touched his cheek. "It's going to be just fine tonight. Quite good, if I remember right. Probably even better than that, although I sort of hope mind-blowing isn't happening. Not tonight. That's always a hard act to follow."

He gave her a half-chuckle and nuzzled the top of her head, pulling her against him.

"Memories of Kelsey?" she asked softly into his chest.

"Yeah," he said and lifted his face to the sky. "I don't know."

"Could you be overthinking this?" Tess stamped her feet. That seemed to wake something in him because he tucked her back under his arm and actually started toward the house this time.

"Yes. But c'mon. This is the point of no return, and if you dump me again, I think I'm done for."

"Drama king," Tess muttered and, when he turned to her, mouth half-open in surprise, she kissed him. It wasn't one of her better ideas, she decided quickly, because that meant they stopped walking, which meant she got colder, which meant the only way to get warm was to get closer to him, which made the kiss longer and hotter, but her fingers were starting to turn into ice cubes.

She slid them around the back of Mack's neck, simply for the shock value.

It worked. "Let's get you inside."

"Finally."

"Go easy, Tess. Two of my favorite things are being out here and you. Can't blame me if I want to linger."

"I can when I'm frozen solid!"

He grabbed her hands and held them tightly in his, then pressed his lips against them—Tess noticed they were cold, too—and let go of her right hand, which she slipped back into her pocket. "Let's go in," he said and started off toward the house before she could say anything.

Once inside, she let him take her coat while she beelined for the kitchen. Tess felt like she was snooping, but she also knew there was no way Marisela wouldn't have cocoa powder in her pantry.

She was right, and as she opened cabinets to find a saucepan, she appreciated Marisela's organization.

Mack wandered in and sat at one of the counter stools.

"I may have to reorganize my kitchen when I get home," Tess said to him, saucepan in hand.

"Not what I was expecting you to take home from the weekend," he said and turned as Tess did, alerted to the sound of approaching footsteps.

"Oh, Tess, cocoa. What a treat. Can you make enough for all of us?" Krista asked.

"Mother," Mack groaned.

"Of course," Tess said and paused in pouring the milk. "Need a bigger pot, though."

"Is it legal for anyone associated with this family to know their way around a kitchen?" Logan asked but moved to the far side of the island and showed Tess where the bigger pots were. Once she'd emptied the first into the second, he carried the newly empty pot over to the sink and washed it out.

"Logan," Mack chuckled. "Revealing hidden skills."

"We don't have Marisela at the townhouse," Logan said. "It was learn something or die of starvation."

"Are you two going to move back in?" Mack asked. "I mean, you were supposed to be here for what, three days?"

"You've needed us around," Krista said, brushing at something on his shoulder.

"The company has been nice." Tess glanced at Mack as he spoke. Not a hint of sheepishness; he'd truly needed Krista and Logan around. Mack was, at heart, social. Dealing with his grief while totally alone would *not* have gone well.

"We should talk about what to do with this house once you move in with Tess," Krista said.

Mack groaned. "One night. Can we have *one night* where we're not talking about mysteries and business and family heritage and plans?"

"No," Tess said and crossed to the pantry. The vanilla wasn't hard to find. She stirred it in and returned it, then took a taste. Not bad; it needed a bit more... She went back to the pantry and looked behind the cocoa. Sure enough, Marisela had a container of dark chocolate cocoa powder. Perfect.

"Ten minutes?" he asked. She turned to him, raising an eyebrow. He was uncharacteristically crabby and had crossed his arms over his chest.

"So talk about something else," she told him while his mother purred a reprimand at him.

"Like what?" he asked. "I can't talk to you the way I *want* to with an audience."

She turned back to the stove, hoping that doing so would keep her from getting called out for blushing.

"Emerson, really," his mother said, and without turning around, Tess could feel Krista's displeasure. "You are pushing the bounds of propriety tonight."

"Krista," Logan said, "he's fine."

"This is *not* Mackenzie behavior. Even in private."

At the stove, Tess kept stirring, not that she needed to.

Logan continued. "You've said it yourself. Emerson is a Mackenzie through and through. Kid's pushed your boundaries since he was five and he'd ignore you when you would try to threaten him into staying clean when he went outside to play. You just got lucky that he adored you despite the fact that you're his parent—"

Tess glanced up from the stove. Mack was watching, slack-jawed. Krista was angry, and Logan was relaxed, leaning against the island, his arms crossed over his chest, his feet crossed at the ankle.

"I liked her because she was as angry about SH-34 as I was," Mack recovered enough to say.

"And that!" Logan continued, gesturing at Mack. "*That* was a watershed moment for our boy! I knew right then—and so did you, Krista, so don't you try to deny it—that he was going to be the caretaker for PharmaSci that we'd been missing for generations. That we *finally* had the right person, the right *Mackenzie,* to save this company. So don't get angry that he's coming into his own and finding his way. This is what we raised him to do. This is who we raised him to be."

Tess watched as Krista looked from Logan to Mack and back again. She let out a breath and, Tess thought, she shrunk.

"Mother," Mack said gently, "I still need you. Even with Tess here, I'll need you tomorrow night, and you know it without me needing to say it."

"Emerson—"

"Alyssa's going to be there tomorrow, and she's not going to be glad to see Tess with me. Have I told you the latest? She's started calling me *Emmie*, Mother." He cleared his throat before he said in falsetto, "Oh, Emmie! Emmie!" He glowered at her and Logan and Tess told herself not to laugh.

"And then she turns to whoever's around us and starts talking about her plans for our life together. *She's* going to be the first Mackenzie woman to be hands-on with her kids—"

Tess turned in time to see Krista arch one eyebrow. Her mouth was still tight, the tension deep at her eyes.

"*Her* kids, mind you. Like I'm some stallion at stud."

Tess wasn't sure how she kept herself from snorting at that, but apparently Krista couldn't. Logan had started to chuckle.

"And *then* she says I'm going to retire at forty-five and we're going to travel the world." He cleared his throat, and it was back into his falsetto. "*Emmie's going to take me to every last inch of this planet and we're going to do good works for the poor, indigenous people who aren't as lucky to have what we have. So we're going to spread our wealth to them and lift them up.*"

"You're lucky she didn't get all religious on you," Logan said, one hand held to his mouth and nose as if he could stuff the laughter back in.

Tess wasn't having much more success.

"Oh, she's asked me more than once why I won't come to church with her." Mack glowered again. "So I asked her if she went to church because of her faith in God or her faith in society seeing her and talking about what she was wearing."

That did it. Tess dissolved into laughter.

"Tess. This isn't funny."

She nodded. Yes, it was.

"And so," Mack went on, "know what she said? She asked me who cared. I don't know, but maybe people with actual *faith* would care?"

"Oh, no," Logan said through his laughter, although Tess found herself a little calmer. The girl's priorities were seriously off. "How did she react to that?"

"She actually fucking *touched* me. Put a hand on my face and said *Oh, Emmie. You're so cute, thinking people actually have faith in a higher being.*"

"Wow," Tess said, feeling her eyes were big, but Mack *still* wasn't done.

"So I told her to get the hell away from me until she'd hung around actual, you know, human beings and learned a little bit about what it meant to be one, and she stomped her foot—she fucking *stomped her foot*—and told me I was the one who needed lessons in compassion and how to treat a lady—and she'd be glad to give them to me." He paused and Tess braced herself for another round of Alyssa voice. "*We can even make it fun, Emmie. I'll give you a BJ for every lesson you get right.*"

Nothing could have prepared Tess for that. She and Logan both burst out into fresh laughter and even Krista was smiling and shaking her head. Of all the performances Mack had given over the years, this might be the best.

He stood up and leaned toward Krista. Tess squeezed her eyes and lips closed, willing herself not to explode.

"Do you know that when she gets near me, parts of me shrivel up and *die*? *Die*, Mother. All those grandkids you dream of? *Dead*."

Tess reached for Mack and let him hold her up as she shook with not-silent-at-all laughter, the tears streaming down her face anew.

"Breathe," he told her, his hand on her waist. "Tess, seriously. You're turning purple."

She shook her head, her mouth open, laughing too hard to make noise. She also couldn't breathe, so she held up a hand and focused on fixing that.

Thankfully, Mack stayed quiet, still holding her.

"Glad you picked a woman who appreciates you," Logan said, "and takes you seriously."

Tess shook her head, broke into a fresh peal of laughter, and wiped at her eyes.

Mack pulled her close. "Now look what you've done," he said. "You've made her hysterical. *Again*. Logan, go to your room!"

Logan's laughter deepened. Tess, her face pressed against Mack's chest, closed her eyes and tried to resume focusing on her breathing because she was right back at that spot of laughing too hard to inhale. His racing heart didn't help.

"Maybe the cocoa is ready?" Krista asked in the coldest voice Tess had ever heard. It sobered both her and Logan immediately, and even Mack stiffened.

Tess started to turn, but Logan waved her off. "I've got it." He produced a ladle and four mugs.

As Logan set a mug for Mack on the island in front of him, Tess thought she could still feel smoke coming out of his nose. "I'll handle Alyssa if you need me to," she said. "No worries. Your days of being *Emmie*"—and she tried to pitch her voice to match his—"are over." She cocked an eyebrow at him. *Emmie*. Of all the things that didn't fit the man...

"You haven't met her."

"I've had to deal with all sorts of personalities, between the firm and the incubator. Women who like to tear others down are actually pretty easy to handle." She took a sip of the chocolate. It was hotter than she'd intended.

"Your incubator," Krista said, and Tess wondered if it was an attempt to salvage her dignity. "Would you do it full-time?"

Logan emerged from the pantry with a bag of mini marshmallows, which he opened and set on the counter. Tess carelessly dropped a handful in. Mack popped a few directly into his mouth before adding a second handful to his mug. Krista carefully picked six and put each in her cocoa, one at a time, deliberately.

"No," Tess said at last, thinking of the quick exchange she and Mack had had about spending summers in Lakeford. There was no way she could do both. "I love architecture too much." She yawned. "Sorry. Long day."

Mack caught her eye and motioned toward his room. She nodded and picked up her mug, her hands cradling it again. It was warm, and despite the warm kitchen and the laughing jag that had landed her in Mack's very warm arms, she still was not.

"If you don't mind," she said, yawning again, "I'm going to put on about three layers of sweats and fleece and crawl into a bed that's buried under five blankets until I warm up. Good night." Grabbing her hot chocolate, she left the kitchen, hoping Mack would linger some more.

He did, not coming into his room until she was, as promised, buried in his bed, a book propped against her raised knees, the cocoa on the nightstand beside her, less than half remaining.

"You're on my side of the bed," Mack said, standing by the edge of the bed closest to the door and looking confused.

"No," she said. "This is *always* my side when we share a bed."

"You sure?"

"*Always* means every time. It's hard not to be sure about every time." She watched him, but he still looked lost and a little confused. "It is a big bed," she added, softening. "You were right about that."

"I told you."

"You did."

He stretched out on the bed beside her, propped on his elbows. "Tess," he said. "Just Tess. I'm not going to get you out of those clothes so fast, am I?"

"I told you I was cold," she said and motioned to him to give her his hand, which she slipped under the covers and then under her shirt. She put his hand on her stomach.

"Wow," he said, his fingers splayed and so, so warm. She wanted to leave it there, but she also had more to show him.

"And that was covered by my coat." She motioned again with her fingers. He sat up at the command and followed her instructions, this time slipping his hand down the pair of his fleece pants that she'd appropriated. He ran his hand over her rear and down her legs.

"You are an ice cube."

"I kept telling you I was cold."

"Yeah, well," he said, pulling his hand free and smoothing the covers over her, "I should have listened. Or made you wear Krista's fur. Forgive me?"

She shoved at him and his puppy dog eyes, then closed her book and set it on the nightstand beside the mug. "It was nice to be out there. The air was super crisp. But," she added when he started to beam, "it was still cold and now I'm like an ice cube and that's hardly sexy."

"Oh," he said, sitting on the edge of the bed and putting an ankle on the opposite knee to pull his shoe and sock off, "but that's where it *starts* to get fun. Warming Tess back up."

"What happened to not getting my clothes off anytime soon? Mack, I'm *cold*."

His other shoe and sock landed on the floor. He stood up and dropped his pants, then pulled his shirt over his head.

Tess could imagine the clothes pile he'd just made. Then again, she'd seen enough of them. Besides, it was more fun to look at him. It had been a long time since she'd been able to. Like her, he'd changed. He wasn't as over-muscled as he had been, but he was still toned, his belly still flat. He actually looked better than he had back in college.

He crawled under the covers and said, "C'mere. Like I said, warming you up should be fun."

She slipped onto her side with an exaggerated sigh but snuggled up against him. "You feel good."

He caressed her cheek. "Just wait, Just Tess. Once you're good and warm, we're doing this."

"You're the idiot who wanted to go outside," she reminded him. He gave off a lot of warmth and having him there, pressed against her back, gave her a sense of security she hadn't felt in a long time. Something inside her relaxed. She hadn't even known it was tense.

"I am the idiot who wanted to go outside. And now I'm the idiot who gets to hold his girl until she warms up."

"So long as we're clear on who's playing what role," she said.

"We are. The part of the idiot is played by Emerson."

"Emerson? Not Mack?" She tried to turn her head to see him, but to do that, she'd have to turn onto her back, which meant losing the warmth against her icy backside and legs. In a sense, she couldn't believe he was willing to hold himself against that much cold.

He shrugged. "I think they've kind of merged and become one. But I like being Mack to you. It reminds me we can figure all this out."

"Do you really think we can?"

"Why not? We got past the whole *my dad murdered your dad* bit. This can't be much different."

She stiffened.

"Sorry," he said and rubbed her arm. "I guess it was a lot easier to joke about when we didn't know how deliberate it was."

"I can't believe he'll get away with it."

"I'm not sure Krista will let him. Give her time and space, and when you least expect it, she'll handle it, either through the legal system or she'll get something out of him that he'll hate to give up. We can, too, you know."

"Ahh, yes. Blackmailing one's father. Always a fun time."

He snorted softly. "My dark side's showing?"

"Yes. And honestly, Mack, it can't. Not with this Mackenzie history thing. It's just too big. People are too angry still."

"Still? Tess, it's been over a century and a half."

"I know. But the more you hang out in PK, the more you'll see it. There's a lot of anger, and in a lot of cases, it's warranted. Skin color holds people back."

"Maybe that is something PharmaSci can help address."

"Good luck. It's a loop. People can't get good jobs because they don't have the education because schools aren't funded equally." She took a deep breath. "Red pulled a secret benefactor and bought the sixth-grade social studies textbooks this year."

"So we'll do it too. They'll have a couple of secret benefactors."

"You make it sound so easy."

"Easier than warming you up, I think. You're radiating so much cold," he said and shifted his hips away from her, "we might both wind up frozen."

She turned so she could look at him, wiggling in his arms. He was watching her, desire and concern flickering in his eyes.

"Oh, so I get to warm *you* up now?" she asked.

"Please?" he said and lowered his mouth to hers.

FORTY-FIVE

It was 4:48 before Tess warmed up enough to take her fleece pants off. Mack wasn't even sure she was awake when she did it, given how much she—whose movements were usually economical—thrashed around as she did it. Then again, given that their legs were a tangle, he wasn't sure she'd had an option.

At least her movement woke him enough to help. He ran his hands over her, pleased she wasn't cold anymore, although there had been something really erotic about the silky skin of her upper body and the contrast of the fleece pants.

"Don't stop," she said when he stilled. "Mack," she said when he didn't answer. She squirmed in his arms until she'd turned to face him. "After all this waiting, you're going to fall back to sleep *now*?"

"No," he said and shoved the covers down, out of their way. "Too cold?" It had been earlier, leaving him feeling like an inexperienced, bumbling kid afraid to let the covers fall away.

"Nope," she said, and he could feel her grin, her good nature even as she pushed up against him and nipped at whatever skin she could reach.

He cupped her breast, closing his eyes and savoring the feel of her. "Tess," he said, "no matter what happens, no matter how scared we get, there's no going back now."

"Macaroon, please. There's been no going back for a long time now."

"Then why were you crying and talking about breaking up earlier?"

"Because I'm terrified of how this is going to play out." She put her hand on his, but he hadn't needed her signal to know how serious she was being. "It's one thing to keep SH-34 between us. It's another to try to hide your heritage from the world."

"We'll figure it out. Krista will help, and we've got allies on the board."

"This isn't a PharmaSci thing."

"No, but these are people who will have life experience and who we can network through to find the best answers." He shifted, propping himself up more fully and looking down at her. He slipped his hand from her breast to her belly, her hand on his moving with him. "Look. We're not alone in dealing with this. Not like we were back in college. We'll find the solutions that work best for us as a couple, and us as Mackenzies who have a complicated history."

She nodded, but she bit her lower lip. In the dark of the room, it was hard to make out, but he didn't need to see her to know her. He bent to kiss her, stealing her lip from between her teeth.

She buried one hand in his hair and cupped his cheek with the other and if he'd had any further worries that he'd keep dwelling on Kelsey, they vanished when she slipped her hand between them and around his cock, just like she'd used to.

He'd waited a long time for his Tess to come back to him.

Forty-Six

They didn't sleep much after that, not that Tess minded—or had expected to. They had a lot to make up for, but that didn't mean that old habits, established years ago when they were in college, didn't return as naturally as if there hadn't been years, and a wife, and such divergent lives between them.

They stayed in bed the next morning until eleven, which Mack said was going to scandalize Krista, but Tess disagreed. She thought it was likely Krista would ask why they were up and about at all, but of course, Mack was hungry. So was she, but her stomach wasn't growling nearly as loudly as his.

Pulling on clothes felt like a surrender somehow, although Tess wasn't sure what she was surrendering to. Propriety and expectation, maybe. Committing to being a Mackenzie, perhaps. But it didn't stop Mack from lifting her onto the kitchen counter and stepping close, entirely too close, as they shared fruit and toast—and long, slow kisses.

She didn't even realize she'd wrapped her legs around him and was holding him closer until she heard the shocked, "Emerson! Tess!" coming from the doorway.

Mack waved his mother off and cupped Tess' face in his hands, searching her face for something. Tess wasn't sure what.

"While I'm glad to see you two finally together like you should be," Krista went on, "the kitchen counter is so far beyond any sense of what's proper, I can't allow this."

Tess winced and started to unwrap her legs, but Mack caught her eye until she stopped.

"Good morning, Mother," he said, still searching Tess' face. "You and Logan should try this. Might like it." He kissed her again, his eyes open and watching her.

"Tess, I hope his tattoo isn't terrible."

She gave Mack a look, and he winked. "They're sexy as hell," she said, wondering if she had missed something.

"He has two?" Krista sounded less scandalized and more mournful.

"Three," Mack said. He let go of Tess and hooked a thumb in the waistband of his lounge pants. "Want to see?"

"Emerson!"

Tess bit her lips and bent her head, propping her forehead on his shoulder as he said, "Guess that's a no?" He wrapped his arms around her, one hand wandering up the back of her shirt. She let him, figuring that Krista already thought the worst; there was no real reason to hold back now.

"I am going out," she said, her voice falling into her usual cultured, proper cadence and tones. "Logan had an early tee time and should be home around four. I won't be back much before that, so if you decide to"—she sniffed, which made Tess bite her lip to keep from giggling—"*christen* other parts of the house, please have them all cleaned and sanitized before we return. We are leaving here promptly at six-thirty for the banquet."

How they were able to wait until the door closed behind them, Tess didn't know, but they dissolved into laughter as soon as the door was shut.

"What is this with you and tats?" Granted, even once it had been daylight, Mack's room hadn't been very bright, but she was fairly certain he didn't have any.

"She's convinced I've got one on my hip or thigh, and that's why I always wear tights when I go play."

Tess snickered but Mack tapped her thighs, a sign she should let go so he could round up more food. As he rummaged in the fridge, Tess slipped down off the counter and shook out her shorts. He had shoved them up pretty high; she had no doubt Krista had walked in on something that looked a lot more graphic than it actually was.

He emerged from the fridge with a container of cottage cheese, some yogurt, more grapes, and a half gallon of orange juice. He set them down beside Tess, sliding her coffee out of the way to do so, and leaned in to kiss her again.

"How did I ever get enough of you when we were younger?"

"We lived together," she said, twisting to pick up her coffee before it got lost in the mess as Mack pulled English muffins out of a bread box, followed by bagels and the rest of the loaf of sourdough that they'd used for the toast.

"Shouldn't have stopped."

"Mack—"

"I know," he said, holding up a hand in surrender. "Besides, even more than me needing to be apart from you, let's face it, Just Tess. You wouldn't be half the woman you are if you'd stayed with me and played the good, dutiful wife. I mean, I'd have made sure you worked, but you'd have probably wound up in some stuffy architectural firm, doing boring, safe designs, instead of this cutting-edge, environmentally friendly stuff you're doing. And Trade Creation? Never would have happened."

"I was actually working at a stuffy firm when Red found me," she said, swirling her finger along the back waistband of his lounge pants. "Hated it and was thinking about leaving the industry entirely."

"And instead," he said, twisting around to give her a long, lingering kiss, "you went with Red and turned into this confident, competent woman who's hotter than she ever was."

Tess patted his cheek, then gave him a shove in whatever direction he'd been heading when he'd stopped to kiss her. "You're still full of it, though."

He pulled jelly out of the fridge and grabbed peanut butter from the pantry, then a butter dish that had been left near the stove and put them all beside the variety of bread products. "Not this time. Seeing you at work?" He shook his head and put his hand on her waist, leaning in to kiss her some more. "What do they call it? Competence porn? Yeah. I'll be in your office for that whenever you let me in."

"You'll get me fired."

He pulled back, opening a drawer and pulling out handfuls of knives, forks, and even a couple spoons. They clattered to the counter beside all the food. "Red doesn't have the balls to fire you, and we both know it. And it's not just the balls. It's the *sense*. He knows what you bring the company." He paused, having grabbed the peanut butter and a knife. "Besides, aren't you a vested principal? He can't fire you; he'd have to buy you out."

Tess picked up a spoon and pointed it at him. "True, but I'm not risking anything. He may push me hard, but I love my life."

Mack raised his eyebrows and stuck the knife in the peanut butter. "Got room for me?"

"Dumbass," Tess said as one of their phones, left on the kitchen table, went off, saving her from admitting it was a valid question—for both of them. She would make room for him, of course, within reason. She wasn't going to magically morph into a proper Mackenzie woman.

Then again, she considered as he set down the peanut butter to check whose phone it was, hadn't Logan said that Mack was a new Mackenzie man? Maybe that meant she had some wiggle room, too.

He was frowning at his phone. "It's me. Taylor." He motioned and wandered out of the room, eyes locked on the screen.

Taking her coffee, she slid into a seat at the table and checked her own phone.

Jamie had texted her, wanting to know how the weekend was going. Red had checked in, as well. She answered them both that things were fine.

Jamie replied almost immediately, and Tess spent a few minutes trying to feed her friend details without giving her anything that was best saved for in-person discussion. It wasn't so easy.

Her phone buzzed again. *Don't eat all that food. I'll be right back.*

You seriously just texted me from the next room?

It's a big house. Lots of distance between rooms.

I'm exploring. Come find me, Tess told him and stood up, coffee in one hand and phone in the other, and started with Mack's rooms. He had said the master suite had at one time been almost three times the size it was now, and Tess wanted to turn her architect's eye to the renovations. She was curious if she could find the original footprint, so she went carefully around his bedroom and bathroom, including the closets and dressing area, but whoever had done the work had been quite good. Tess wondered if the space had been completely gutted, and wandered down the stairs in the two-floor master's suite and turned into Mack's home gym. Surely there had to be a sign in here; if you were going to cut corners, the place to do it was in the room that was the least visible to outsiders.

She found a metal ring behind the door. It was down at the rubber matting on the floor, sticking up and actually set into the drywall. Clearly, it predated the home gym.

Tess got down on the floor, setting her coffee down and exploring with her hands, doubtful she'd discover anything. But she did: the bottom part of the ring was embedded in the floor, like there were layers of flooring. She bent closer, using the flashlight on her phone, trying to figure out what was going on. It was buried, but not. Like it wasn't supposed to be used, but it was important somehow.

She didn't understand.

"Interesting way of working out," Mack said.

She looked over her shoulder at him. His eyes were fixed on her ass, of course, and he held a plate with halved bagels on it. He took a bite of the one in his hand.

"You handle what you needed to?" she asked him.

"Yeah. These people have me glad I didn't go into politics."

"What people?" she asked, pushing back to her knees and reaching for her coffee. She took a sip, watching him over the rim.

"Senator Coles. He wants to meet to talk about drug prices and my *vision* of universal health care." He shook his head. "Wish I'd kept quiet. Taylor thinks he's going to rake me over the coals for stirring the pot. They're probably right, but Gray and Krista aren't so sure. They think the senator wants to take the credit for my ideas." He shrugged. "All I know is he wants *me,* and now he's apparently putting pressure on Taylor on weekends because we've been stonewalling."

"Is it wise to stonewall a senator?" Tess stood. Mack held out the bagels. She took one that had been toasted and buttered; he'd remembered.

"I keep asking Krista that."

"And?" She gestured at him.

He shrugged. "She's been right up to now."

"Maybe you should go rogue on this one, see how soon you can invite everyone over for dinner here at the Manor. Quiet, intimate... you and Gray and Krista and the government types, and make it seem like a social call."

Mack set the plate down so he could pull out his phone and start texting. After a minute, he looked up. "Taylor's on it, and they agree with you." His phone buzzed again and he read the message, then frowned. "They asked if the idea came from you because there's no way I'm this smart."

"I can't wait to meet them," Tess said, raising up on her toes to kiss his nose. He put a hand on her waist and pulled her against him. She paused for a minute, savoring the embrace, then said, "Tell me about this." She tapped the wall above the iron ring.

"I don't know what it is. I remember seeing it when I was a kid and these were Tristan's rooms. The ring was flush against the floor, and I used to dream that maybe it was the key to the missing Mackenzie treasure. Tristan, of course, told me to stop being an ass and there was no treasure."

"I think the real treasure is those old journals." Tess took another bite of bagel, leaning away from him so she could. "Speaking of which, I'd like to read through them some more before I leave, if you don't mind."

"But if you do," he said, adjusting his hold on her, and Tess braced herself for what she knew was coming, "I can't have you naked in my bed."

She kissed his lips this time, just a peck. "We have, what? Four hours until your mother gets back? What's she going to be more tolerant of? Us in bed, or us barricaded in your office?"

"In bed, definitely."

"Then journals first."

"I thought we went through them."

"We did—the recent ones. Now I'm curious if we can go back far enough to learn more about this ring." She didn't add that she was curious to find out if there was anything about what sort of slave owners they'd been, too.

"Tess," Mack groaned, turning his face to the ceiling. "You're not even supposed to *know* about the journals, let alone read them."

She took a step closer, wishing he had a shirt on so she could tug on it. Instead, she poked him below the ribs, smiling as he flinched. "But I do, and what's in them is going to directly affect our life, especially if you do manage to move PharmaSci back home."

"No ifs about that, Just Tess. PharmaSci's relocating. Everyone knows it's on the radar." He grimaced and rubbed the back of his neck. "I just wish we had a timetable."

"If only you knew someone who can help with that."

Mack grabbed her around the waist and pushed her up against the wall. "If only," he said in a half-growl.

"You should try talking to that someone," she said, reaching for his hips.

He took a step closer, pressing her against the wall. "No."

"No? Then you can't—"

He cut her off with a kiss that she had to break off. "Journals," she said, panting slightly. So was he, she noticed.

"You have a one-track mind, Just Tess."

"You'll be thanking me for that later."

"Why don't we go the long way and walk past the bed to get to my office? Maybe we should stop and make sure it's still working right?"

"It's a bed, Mack. It works just fine."

"But..."

"Journals first."

"Tess..."

"Journals, Macaron." She put as much of a French accent onto the word as she could, then patted his cheek. "Grab the food. We're going to be awhile."

FORTY-SEVEN

A fter an hour and a half, Tess sat up and stretched, her arms overhead. "This makes no sense," she said.

Mack, who had stretched out on the couch and who may or may not have been asleep for parts of the past ninety minutes, said, "Let's hear it."

"*I remain convinced that every human being has rights to liberty, freedom, and pursuits of happiness.* It's... an odd thing for a slave owner to say. It has zero context." She scanned the page again, then the page before it, then the one after, but found nothing. Then again, this old dead guy's handwriting wasn't easy to read. Mack had been right about that.

"Who knows?" he asked and rolled off the couch, coming to his knees on the floor with a groan. "If I promise not to freeze you this time, want to take a walk?"

"No," Tess said. "I believe the plan was to be gloriously naked, in bed, and wrapped around each other when Krista and Logan got back."

"With all the furniture clean," Mack said and hauled himself to his feet. He turned to Tess, taking the journal from her hand and picking up the other two she'd been looking through, returning them to their safe behind his desk.

"Makes me want to leave something dirty, just to mess with her."

He gave her a sharp look. "That's not the sort of messing with Krista that she'd appreciate. She'll roll with a few verbal jabs, but that's the extent of it. I can't imagine what she'd have done if we really *had* been making love on the counter this morning."

She nodded.

He held out a hand to her, waiting until she took it, then pulling it behind his back, twining his fingers through hers. She leaned into him, putting her head on his chest, savoring the feel of his warm, soft skin and the tease of his chest hair.

"So you approve of Emerson?" he asked softly, stroking her hair.

"Very much," she said. "I could grow old with him, although I'd miss Mack. He could be... outrageous on a more regular basis. But Emerson? He's got the best of Mack and at the same time, he's more... I don't know. Polished? Grown up? Settled?"

She lifted her head off his chest and looked up at him, waiting for him to bend and kiss her, but he continued to stare off over her head.

"Mack?"

"I tell you that watching you work makes me hard and you answer that by pointing out I'm now a grownup," he sighed, letting go of the hand behind his back and instead wrapping his arm around her waist, pulling her as tightly against him as she thought she could get while they had clothes on.

"Yeah, there does seem to be an imbalance there. Maybe we need to go to your room and explore it more thoroughly."

"Yeah?"

"Yeah. Maybe I'll even work and let you watch."

He chuckled and, with the hand that had been stroking her hair, caressed her cheek. "You'd do that?"

"For you? Of course."

He kissed her, then held her close and sighed. "So let me ask my friendly someone. Let's say I have a building," he said, tightening his hands on her. "To have it renovated... we're looking at what? A year?"

"Most likely more. As you've seen with your field, it *all* moves slow."

"What do we do in the meantime?"

"The same thing other long-distance couples have done."

"I'm drawing the line at phone sex."

Tess smiled. That should have been her line. "Then why are we standing *here*?"

"You mean when we could be on the couch?" He jerked his head at it.

"Your mother..."

"Yeah." He rubbed the back of his neck. Tess watched. "Technically, it's still her property. And she doesn't ask me for much, so... seems like no matter how handy the couch is, I just have to keep on being boring, vanilla, unimaginative Emerson."

"Only when we're here," Tess said, picking at the drawstring on his pants.

He covered her hand with his. "Don't tease."

"Should I tell you that I've been given the wonderful gift of waterproof sheets and blankets specifically for sexy times?"

He groaned. "No, but bring them with you next time."

She chuckled and let him lead the way to his bedroom. They were still there when Krista knocked.

"Emerson?" she called through the door.

"Now, Mother?"

"If you're not busy."

Tess couldn't hold in the peal of laughter. Not busy. Mack was, in fact, quite busy. Or, he had been. As she laughed, he was untangling himself from her and muttering about respect and boundaries. He pulled on the same pair of lounge pants he'd been wearing earlier and slipped through the door.

Tess tried to listen, but only heard voices, not any distinct words. Not that it would have mattered one way or the other, but she was curious to know if Mack was expressing unhappiness that the conversation couldn't wait.

He slipped back into the room. "Coordinating schedules for tonight. She seems to think that you might need help getting ready to leave on time. I suspect she wants stories of her son the lover."

"Eww."

He flashed her a grin. "I'm counting on your imagination to make me sound good."

"Oh, you sound *very* good at times." Tess sat up as he blinked in surprise. "C'mon. Shower."

"Are you going to be able to be ready? Kelsey would have made some pretty impressive threats if I'd only given her two hours."

She leaned forward, beckoning him close with a finger. When he leaned in, she framed his cheeks with her hands. "It depends on how long we take in the shower. Because last I checked, it's pretty self-cleaning."

His breath caught. "I... should have thought of that earlier."

"Stop beating yourself up and get in there. You still need to shave."

"Do you mind?" He rubbed at his stubble.

"If I did, I'd have asked you to do it earlier."

He grinned, shook his head, and said, "What did I do to deserve you?" then headed for his bathroom.

Tess waited a beat and then unwound from the sheets and followed.

The water was warm, Mack was hot, and for a few minutes, Tess wasn't sure she could stand. He eased her onto the built-in seat in the shower and knelt in front of her, and when he was done, she was positive she couldn't stand.

"I didn't *quite* mean to do that to you," he said once she'd recovered and they'd gotten out. She was combing out her hair; he was slathering his face and throat with shaving cream.

"I am not complaining."

"Just puts us short on time."

Tess pulled herself up on the counter, between the sink he wasn't using and the wall, and hugged her knees to her chest, making sure the towel she wore wasn't revealing anything that would delay them further. She should have started on her makeup, she knew, but it had been so long since she'd watched any man shave, let alone him…

When he was done, his face rinsed off, he turned to her, but she held a hand up. "Rinse that sink out, you ungrateful, pampered poodle."

"Marisela asks me not to. Apparently if I do, the pipes clog."

Tess frowned. That didn't sound right, especially since they were on the second story. "Why doesn't someone fix that?"

He shrugged. "I think they've tried, but I'll talk to Juan about it again."

"Do," she said. "That shouldn't be happening. Not from shaving. Shearing a beard, sure."

"Later. Right now, we have to get moving." He held out a hand and she slipped off the counter, smiling and moving into his arms for one last embrace before they dressed.

"Why do you just feel *right*?" he asked. "It never felt like this with Kelsey."

"Maybe because this is what's right." She paused to kiss him, then left the bathroom to get dressed.

A fresh set of sheets was sitting on his bed. Tess laughed and shook her head. "Hey," she called to him. "Who would have done this?"

He stuck his head in the room. She pointed and he shrugged. "Could have been my mother, could have been Marisela."

"I thought you'd given her the day off."

"We did, but the idea of Krista coming in here while we were in the shower makes my skin crawl."

Tess chuckled and got busy with her makeup.

When Mack emerged from his closet in a tux with a sapphire blue bowtie, he fingered a lock of Tess' hair. "Shouldn't leave this wet."

"I forgot a hairdryer."

"Let's go get Krista's. Depending on how ready she is, she might get all excited and dry it for you."

Tess eyed him, unsure of how to take that.

"She's your biggest cheerleader," he told her.

"I thought you were."

"Nah. I'm just a mackerel. A macaroni, a macaroon..."

"You've got that right." She kissed him and lowered off her toes. At least she'd be wearing heels to the event, cutting some of their height difference. "Oh, I wish we could stay in. I really hate these things."

"I know. And I'm grateful as hell that you're willing to be my buffer against Alyssa." He brushed her wet hair off her neck and started to kiss her, then stopped, lifting all of her hair for a full view. "How did I not notice this earlier?"

"You weren't looking. It's my tribute to my dad." She shrugged and held still as Mack traced the tattooed phoenix with his fingers.

"He told me," she said as he bent and pressed his mouth to it, "that I was supposed to rise from the ashes of his death, like a phoenix, and be something bigger, better than he ever could have been."

"You've done that."

She turned to him. "I'm trying. And hopefully, there's more to come."

"I've got your back," he said. "But first, we have to get your hair dry."

FORTY-EIGHT

Mack didn't even care when Alyssa was waiting for them to arrive at the awards banquet. He'd talked to Nimisha briefly while Tess had been drying her hair, but he hadn't needed to. Things had shifted. It was like part of what had been eating at him about Kelsey was how wrong it had been. He'd known it. She'd known it. And they'd gone ahead with it anyway, nothing but pawns—and they'd gotten the ending they'd probably deserved.

But making commitments to Tess made it feel like the past nine years had been erased. That the mistakes he'd made didn't matter anymore. She'd accepted them, and it was time for him to do the same thing.

Kelsey could finally sleep.

He thought about Tess' tattoo. A phoenix. It almost felt like that's what they both were, rising out of the ashes of their own college selves, better, stronger, and ready for what was ahead.

"Oh, really?" Tess breathed as Alyssa waved at them, her plastered-on smile faltering and betraying her feelings.

"Knock yourself out," he answered softly, trying to keep his lips from moving. This might not have been a society event, but the local gossips were out in force and it felt like every eye had turned to them the minute they'd walked through the doors. Every eye except Alyssa's, he noticed. She'd just slipped away.

"Can we?" he asked Tess, jerking his head at one of the media women.

She stiffened, but he patted her hand, which was tucked in his elbow. "I've got you," he told her and led her to Debbie Sanders. Word about Tess would be out within the next five minutes, so he told himself to make it good.

"Remember that alligator?" he started with, and thankfully Tess laughed.

They made their escape from the whole affair as soon as they could, leaving Krista and Logan behind to network. "Are we going to sleep tonight?" he asked, slipping his hand in the thigh-high slit in her dusky pink dress. It had driven him crazy all night, the color of that dress that so closely matched parts of her that only he got to see. He didn't know how he had kept from finding a private spot for a quickie.

No, he did know. Fear of what Krista would do when she found out.

"Maybe?" she said, turning to him, then pulling back slightly.

He frowned.

"If I touch you before we get home," she said, "Juan's going to be either very discreet or very sorry we're not in a proper limo with a privacy panel."

He chuckled. "Probably both." But she was right, and he knew it. "Isn't anticipation supposed to be healthy?"

"Not like this," she said and fanned herself, grinning at him as she did.

He leaned over and gave her a gentle kiss, pulling away to keep himself under control, but unfortunately he couldn't help but look down, at her knees. Both were poking out and threatening to undo him. "Mack, up here," she said, touching the underside of his chin.

He licked his lips and met her eyes. "Not sorry," he said. "Very sorry we're not home yet."

"I know. By the way, I ran into Alyssa in the bathroom. What *is* it with so many of these women? All this money and the power it gives them, and the only one who's making use of it is your mother. Everyone else just seems so *helpless*. It's gross."

"Mackenzies are rebels," he said with a quick tilt of his head.

"Apparently you marry them, too."

He caught his breath. Was she saying? No, he decided. She wasn't thinking that far ahead. Not yet. Not until they'd worked out what he was going to do with moving PharmaSci—and these damn social events.

"I got an earful about Kelsey," Tess went on. "How she was never the right woman for you, how Alyssa hadn't slept with you in high school because she was waiting for the right time to be with you and I've ruined that for her and why can't I go back to wherever I came from and let her have you?"

Mack closed his eyes, searching for patience buried somewhere deep within himself. "What did you tell her?"

"That you make your own decisions about who you're with. I... don't think she got it."

He snorted softly. "She probably didn't." He let his fingers play over her knees, but he turned to look out the window as he did. If he watched his hand slip under the edge of her dress, trouble would follow. "But it's not my responsibility to make sure she does," he said, turning back to her as she gently extracted his hand and wrapped it between both of hers.

"You don't think by choosing me, by relocating to PK, you're not making a statement to that effect?"

"But it's not my *responsibility*," he said, pulling his hand free. "My responsibilities are to PharmaSci, to the Mackenzies, and to you. Not in that order," he added quickly, but she gave him one of those gentle, close-lipped smiles, her eyes soft, and he knew she understood that all three were equals and were completely and utterly intertwined.

Juan pulled the car into the drive and Mack gave the biggest sigh of relief he could manage.

"Glad to be home?" Tess asked, amused.

"That much closer to getting you naked and where we belong," he said, letting himself nuzzle her neck, if only so he could speak quietly, without Juan hearing. "You make one play to get that dress off by yourself and I'll never forgive you."

"Oh. Well. I guess I need some help, don't I?"

Forty-Nine

A round two, Mack raised his head. "I'm hungry."

"You're always hungry."

"Not true anymore," he said and touched the tip of her nose, then shifted so he could kiss it, then her lips. "Unless we're talking about you. But right now, we're not. C'mon. Let's go see what's in the fridge."

"What are you hoping to find?" she asked as he swung his legs over the edge of the bed, his back to her, then went in pursuit of, Tess assumed, clothes.

She figured she needed to do the same.

Hand in hand, they headed for the kitchen. Tess pulled herself up onto the counter and waited as he rummaged in the fridge. "Hey, there's tuna salad. And egg salad." He straightened and pursed his lips slightly, the way he did when he was thinking, then shook his head. "If it's here, it's fair game. Marisela's told me that more than once. Grab forks," he said and carried the bowls over to Tess, who was opening the drawer to her right and reaching for the silverware. She handed Mack a fork and shook her head, her nose wrinkled, when he offered her the bowls.

He'd gotten the first mouthful in when Krista and Logan arrived. They were still in their dress clothes; Tess guessed they were just now getting back from the banquet. "Oh, Emerson, really? That's for breakfast."

"It's morning. Time for breakfast."

"Thomas is coming at eight. He says he has some things he wants to talk to you about."

Mack shoved the fork in his mouth and used the hand he'd just freed to cover the food, which he shoved back in the fridge. "What sorts of things?" he asked around the fork, then removed it and repeated the question.

"He didn't say. Just that it was important. I asked him to come for dinner so we have some time to sleep in and get Tess off, but he said no. He's coming at eight." She yawned, turning away to do so. "We hadn't meant to stay out so late, but there were some very interesting people at that banquet. You and I will talk about that later; it was interesting, not important."

"Alyssa?" Mack asked.

"Her too," Krista said smoothly. "Logan, since the kids are up…"

He nodded and reached for the bread box beside Tess, producing four hoagie-style sandwich rolls. "Toasted?" he asked Tess, who frowned but nodded and watched as he opened the rolls and put them face up on a baking sheet. "Emerson," Logan said, and Mack turned to the fridge and opened a drawer, then started pulling out meats and cheeses.

This, Tess thought, had the feel of a familiar ritual.

The rolls went under the broiler. Logan and Mack sorted the bags of meat and cheeses. Mack held a hand out to Tess, an invitation to slip off the counter and join him. There were two kinds of sliced cheese—Swiss and provolone—and sliced smoked turkey, ham—regular and honey roasted—salami, capicola, and roast beef.

"Are any of us going to be awake enough to hear what Thomas has to say?" Mack asked as Logan pulled the rolls out from under the broiler and set them on four individual plates, which he distributed.

Tess figured that was a good question.

"Yes," Krista said with a firmness that put that question to bed.

They got quiet for a few minutes, opening packages of meat and cheese, passing them around in a circle and adding shredded lettuce and other vegetables that Krista had produced, along with various mustards, a jar of mayo, and two kinds of Italian dressing.

It was, Tess decided, the most family-like and homey she'd felt yet from Mack's mother and her lover, as they all stood around the kitchen island and ate deli sandwiches at two in the morning and chatted about the banquet. It was also one of the most bizarre things she'd ever done, in that it was two in the morning and they were effectively eating lunch.

"Remember," Krista said as Logan gathered the plates and any knives they'd used for condiments—and the fork Mack had been using to raid the salad—and set them all in the sink. "Thomas will be here at eight and he's never late. Never early, thankfully," she said, closing her eyes briefly. "I expect you two will be ready."

"I expect you two will be ready," Mack told her as gravely as she had just spoken.

"Emerson—"

He grinned and gave her a rough hug, which actually produced a squeal from her. "Love you, Mother. You, too, Logan. And you," he said, turning to Tess and holding out a hand. "You, I can show. C'mon."

She took his hand. "Why do I get the feeling that was some Mackenzie family ritual I just took part in?" she asked when they were back in his room.

"It was," he agreed. "Best part of these nights out, since it's not the food." He flopped on his back on the bed and held up a hand, index finger raised.

Tess knew what was coming.

He burped and tapped his chest as if to excuse himself. "We got lucky, being up when they came in. Man, they were out late," he said, shaking his head. "That's not like Mother, so something's definitely up, and I bet it's related to this early breakfast with Thomas." His face grew more serious, his top lip pursing slightly. "I'm not sure I like it." He covered his face with a hand, which he then held out to her, inviting her to snuggle up against him, her head on his shoulder. "But back to the question, yes. If we don't eat beforehand, we do this when we get home—and I like these back-end times best of all, comparing notes and wrapping up the night."

"I think that's the most relaxed I've ever seen your mother."

"She's starting to loosen up around you. You're lucky; it took her a good twenty-five years with me, and she never did with Kelsey." He stroked her back, then lifted her shirt and stroked her again. Tess purred.

"We should get some sleep," he said, "but I don't want to."

"This is why coffee exists," Tess said and let him, once again, undress her.

Fifty

Tess started awake when the knock came at the door. "Tess. Emerson. One hour."

Mack groaned and held her closer. They'd started out spooned, but she had half-rolled onto her stomach, propped up by one of the million pillows on his bed, and he had mostly moved with her.

"Am I crushing you?" he asked, tightening his arm around her waist, his voice half-muffled by the pillow she bet his face was pressed into.

"Don't move."

"So that's a no?"

"That's a *don't move.*"

"Don't think I can," he said, and neither of them tried until the knock came again.

"Tess. Emerson. Forty-five minutes. Krista's threatening to walk in."

Mack lifted his head. "She's seen my bare ass before."

"That's between you two," Logan called back, but Tess could hear the chuckle lacing his voice.

They both whined a little as they moved apart. "I am beyond tired," Tess said and looked at Mack. His eyes and lips were equally swollen and barely open and he rolled onto his back, an arm coming up to rest on his forehead. It looked like it took him a lot of effort to move it.

"Worth it?" he asked as she, in slow motion, kicked away the mess of sheets and blankets.

"Always." Leaning over to kiss him, one hand on his chest, she pushed herself up and over him, climbing out of bed that way. He whined again but joined her in the shower.

She dressed and packed as quickly as she could, frowning when Mack told her to leave the dress in what used to be Kelsey's closet.

"I have to return it to Krista," she said and told him about the designer who'd contacted her, wanting an entire floor of the incubator, which was space she didn't have.

"Marisela will look for it in there," he said and asked if she was going to find space.

They were discussing the idea of expanding into a second incubator building as they got to the dining room, Krista and Logan looking equally as tired as Tess felt.

"What's this, dear?" Krista asked as she waved Tess in for morning air kisses.

Tess explained, Mack served the coffee, and they were talking about the ramifications of a possible expansion when Thomas arrived, surprising them all by having fellow board member—and frequent source of opposing views—Gray Stein in tow.

"You know," Thomas said after he had greeted everyone at the table—including a set of air kisses for both Krista and Tess—and seated himself, nodding to Marisela to begin serving as she finished setting out plates for Gray, "that I have not been a fan of relocating PharmaSci. After watching the two of you last night, I realize it's time to tell you secrets that I thought would go to the grave with me." He looked around the table, holding the gaze of everyone but Gray for a moment. "I'm glad they don't have to."

"What do Tess and I have to do with anything?" Mack asked. His voice was tired and he rubbed at his eyes with a thumb and index finger. He was also on his second cup of coffee. Tess wasn't far behind.

"The sheep farm," she said, breathless and suddenly strangely awake. "You know who's been taking care of it—because someone has been."

"I do. It was part of the deal when I counseled Cullen to close it as a way to distance himself from Rachel. I assume the caretaker has been doing his job? All the fencing is intact? The cemeteries are tended?"

"From what I've seen," she said, then paused. "Well, there's a gap in the fence that I used the day I found what must be the cemetery. It looked intentional—the gap. But there's more than one cemetery? I only saw one, although there's an overgrown area right up against it."

"You've been there?" Mack asked. "To the cemeteries?"

"Well, the one," Tess said and turned to Thomas, waiting for an explanation.

"The two are attached. If you saw the one, the other should be right there." He paused, frowning. "I will not be surprised if care of the family plot had to be suspended. I understand there is still quite a deal of animosity toward the family."

"*My* family?" Mack asked, eyebrows raised. He looked from Tess to Thomas and back again. "Maybe you should fill me on what I'm missing."

"Remember Friday?" Tess asked him. "That wasn't drama. I don't know how much people remember, but they remember there were slaves on that land."

He nodded, his blue eyes darker than usual, his mouth tense. "But," he started, "we're not going to put the company on the land."

"The Mackenzies *are* PharmaSci," Thomas said. "And I guarantee someone will remember that and cause problems," Thomas said, looking from Mack to Krista, and then to Gray. "So I ask again, is moving such a wise idea?"

"Yes," Mack said immediately, but Krista motioned him quiet.

"It makes the situation more difficult," she said carefully. She picked up her teaspoon and swirled it through her coffee. "But handled properly"—she glanced at Mack, who nodded and swallowed—"it can actually benefit both the company and the city. In many ways. Emerson, the first would be a commitment to hire locally, and among minorities when possible, and not for menial jobs."

"We do that now, Mother."

It was, Tess noticed, more of a reminder than a protest.

Krista set the teaspoon down on the saucer her cup rested on. It made a thin, tinkling clink that Tess figured probably meant this was the super good china, the stuff that only came out for special occasions—or important meetings. "This is not insurmountable." She raised her chin and speared Thomas with a look. "You and I will discuss this matter of Cullen and Rachel in more depth, including Tristan's response to it."

Thomas merely nodded.

"What happened to Cullen?" Mack asked abruptly. "I don't think I ever met him. How'd he die?"

"He was a drunk," Krista spat.

"Now," Thomas went on before anyone could respond, patting his lips with his napkin and giving Krista a look Tess wasn't sure about, "I have a question for you, Emerson. I understand you renovated the heir's suite. I assume this isn't a good time to see what you've done with it, so I'll have to satisfy myself with asking about the iron ring. Did you have it removed?"

"No," he said, giving Tess another uneasy look. "I had it... Don't laugh, okay? I lifted it off the floor and had it built into the wall over where it had been. Why? What is it?"

"Interesting thing to do with it," Thomas said, fingering his coffee cup. "What possessed you to do that?"

Mack shrugged. "It just seemed wrong to remove it."

"Ahh, it would have been. It leads to an underground vault you may want to explore."

"It's buried under more than a couple layers of floor," Tess said. "What was it used for?"

"That, you'll have to discover yourself. I am afraid I only have some of the answers."

"You only have some," she countered despite Mack's warning nudge under the table, "or you're not willing to share?"

Thomas spent a long minute looking at her, his green eyes piercing. "I only know there's a vault and that the Mackenzie treasure is not what Kelsey and Flemming thought it was."

"So there *is* a treasure?" Mack asked, leaning forward.

"Tristan and Cullen both believed that there was, and that it was hidden in that vault." He held up a hand as Mack drew a breath. "But they were both given to understand it was not of the sort that would increase the family investment portfolio," he said, giving both Krista and Mack a stern look, "and neither was inclined to go to the effort of excavation for something they couldn't easily profit from. Emerson, you can decide for yourself what to do with it."

"If it's not a financial treasure," Mack said slowly, rubbing the back of his neck, "what other sort of treasure could it be?"

"I'm almost more curious now," Krista said.

Tess took her in: her back straight, not touching the back of her chair, her hands folded in her lap, her hair done in its chignon, small earrings dancing as she spoke. And, as always, she gave no clue to what she was thinking.

"If you decide to open it, I'd ask if you'd do me the honor of being there when you do," Thomas said. "I have carried some of these secrets for many years, since I was very young. I would request you allow me closure."

"Of course," Mack said.

"May I ask," Gray said, "why you brought me along today, Thomas?"

The two older men shared a look.

"Because you have been a steady influence on Emerson. Both of you," he said, nodding to Krista, then Logan. "I wanted you to hear this when they did. But now, I understand you need to be taking Tess to the airport shortly, Emerson?"

He checked his phone. "We still have time, if there's more to tell."

"Emerson, don't risk a speeding ticket," Krista said in her soft purr of a reprimand. "You'll miss Tess' flight."

"It'll be fine, Mother. We have time."

"There is one last thing I can share," Thomas said. "As you all know, PharmaSci was originally founded in Port Kenneth. As the family had ties both here and more deeply there, so did the company. Emerson, as I said before, I have not supported this move, but since it's clear that you are going to go ahead with it, may I drop the pretense of ignorance and make a suggestion that I suspect will help greatly?"

"Please," Mack said tightly. He grabbed Tess' hand under the table.

"First, know not only the family history you are going to be grappling with, but the city history as well, although it seems that Tess can teach you that. I suggest you listen to her. Carefully, including any silences. Second, you may want to investigate this." He opened the folio he had brought with him and removed something, which he slid across the table.

Tess gasped as she looked at it. "That's the Piston Building! I *love* that building. It's been empty since before I was born." She wondered if the citywide contraction Philip had spoken of was related to its abandonment.

"Piston?"

"That's what we've always called it. All that's left on the signage is the P, the S, and the T. Oh." She felt the flare in her eyes as it clicked into place. "*Oh.* Is this... was this..."

"The original high-rise headquarters, built in the late 1960s for a move returning the company to Port Kenneth, but never occupied." Thomas nodded.

Mack sat back, face glazed, but she grabbed her phone and sent a text to Red: *THE PISTON BUILDING IS MINE*

Her phone buzzed back almost immediately. *Brain won't be on until noon. Bother me then.*

She sent him a string of poop emojis.

He returned them. Tess laughed and shook her head, tucking her phone under the rim of her plate, ignoring the look from Krista. Phones weren't allowed at her table.

Tess opened her mouth to ask more, her brain whirling. Did Thomas' knowledge include who currently owned the building? She or Red could easily access that information, but how much did the old man know? How involved in all of this—the Piston Building, the farm, maybe even the sabotaged water line and the bones—was he?

"If there's more," Mack said, letting go of Tess' hand to remove his napkin from his lap, "it needs to wait. I need to process all of this." He set his napkin down on his plate, but signaled to Marisela to stay where she was. "Right now, I'd like to take a *leisurely* drive to the airport"—he glared at his mother, who glared back—"and take care of my girl. Tess, when you're ready. I'm going to get my keys and take your bags out to the car. Meet me there?"

"Yes," she said and stood up to say her goodbyes.

Krista hugged her more tightly than she had expected. "Come visit soon. Say hello to your mother."

Tess was still smiling when she met Mack at his car. He looked tired and moody.

"Can we not talk?" he asked. "I need to think all this through."

"Sure, if you tell me why it hit you so hard. It sounded like all good news to me." Although, she thought, there was that whole thing with Kelsey having done everything she could to find the Mackenzie treasure, and it apparently had been right there, all but under her own bed, probably worth nothing in her eyes.

"Finding that I suspect I own a building in the city I want to move to sure is," he said. "But there's this treasure issue, and if I'm reading the situation right, it doesn't mean everyone in town is going to be glad to welcome us—*me*—home." He glanced at her. "Will you go see if you can find that other cemetery?"

"Of course," she said, strangely eager to do so.

Fifty-One

Mack felt bad about asking Tess not to talk, but when he hit the highway and lifted his hand off the gear shift, inviting her to twine her fingers through his, he felt better when she did. If only it was so easy to make sense of all the rest of it.

"Patricia and Ebony," she said at last.

"What?"

"Patricia and Ebony," she said again. "They planned the New Year's party and have been talking about formally going into event planning. I should see if they want the last space in the incubator. They're the perfect fit."

And just like that, the woman who'd been a bulldog about finding answers to his family secrets was equally as insistent that they just *talk*. About what would be waiting for them at their offices in the morning, about progress on his field, about his team and their springtime workouts.

By the time they approached the airport, he was feeling better. "Should I park and get a gate pass?"

"On what grounds are they going to give you a gate pass? Because you're *Emerson Mackenzie* and you want to hold onto your girlfriend until the last second possible?"

"No to the first and I guess you're right about the second. Drop you at the curb, then?"

She gave him a bright, fake grin. "Thanks, love. I've always wanted to be kicked to the curb."

He smiled and shook his head.

"You should get home and take a nap," she said softly.

"In our bed."

"Which you can sleep in again," she said and removed her hand while he worked the gears. She put it back almost immediately.

"Yeah," he said and followed the signs to the drop-off area. "Look. When Krista pulled me back into PharmaSci, the first thing she told me was that to be successful, I'd need the best people around me. That was the key." He slowed, trying to take in the colorful signs for all the various airlines. Usually, when he was here, Juan was driving.

"That's why I hired Taylor. HR was hesitant, worried about lawsuits and such over the whole nonbinary thing, but I had final say over my assistant, and when they showed up for that interview with me and started anticipating what I was thinking, that fast, I knew."

"Okay," Tess said slowly. Mack thought she looked confused, her tongue sticking between her lips, her brow furrowed.

He wove through traffic, headed to her airline.

"I've always known about you," he said simply. "When you left me, I figured maybe one day, but then Kelsey and," he paused, remembering. "Well, she knew I still loved you."

Tess cocked her head but didn't say anything.

He sighed. "I might have called her Tess... once... twice... okay, more often than I should have. And at times when I really shouldn't have." He grimaced, remembering how hurt she had looked every time he'd done it. He'd never *meant* to...

Tess bit her lip and turned her face away, but not before he caught her emotion. It was as complex as he'd expected. She had to know he hadn't purposely held on to the idea they'd be together. It was just that something deep inside him couldn't let go.

He pulled up to the curb and put the car in park. "Krista knew, too. She knew perfectly well what she was doing when she told me it was time to get my name on that field. Maybe she knew better than she realized," he said, "given what we've learned, but that just makes it feel more *right*, you know? Another Mackenzie stamp on the city."

Tess turned to him. "But Mack... Mackenzies *owned* human beings, the way you own the Manor or this car. That's... it's not *moral*."

"It's not," he agreed gravely. "And don't think I haven't heard the calls for reparations and restoration and all the rest. Like Krista said, we have a new obstacle, but it's one we can overcome with some creative Emerson thinking." Ideas were already spinning through his head, policies he could institute both publicly and privately, through Krista's various charitable networks. If he could convince her to refocus even one of them, they could accomplish a lot of good in the world.

He got out of the car, Tess following and meeting him at the trunk, where he'd put her bags. "I need time to explore all of this. Lots of meetings with experts," he added with a grimace, then handed her the bags, pouring the handles into her hand as if he were afraid to touch her. In a sense, he was. If he did, he might not let her leave.

She leaned in to kiss him. "Be prepared for a *lot* of hate, anger, and resentment."

He nodded, Thomas' reminder to listen to her jabbing at him. This wasn't what he wanted to hear, but he needed to.

He leaned down for another kiss, then another. "Text me when you get in."

"As soon as we land."

He couldn't help himself and he grabbed her around the waist, pulling her close and kissing her the way he ached to. A cop finally broke them up. "You've been here long enough. Gotta get moving or get a ticket. You choose."

Tess met his eyes, a smile playing around her lips. "I love you," she said at the same time he did.

The cop chuckled and clapped Mack on the back. "Seriously. Move your car now or I'm ticketing you."

FIFTY-TWO

April 5

T ess had originally planned to take the following Monday morning off to get some sleep, but she needed to know more about the Piston Building. When Red ended the morning meeting, he caught Tess' eye and raised his hand over his head, pointing at his office. "Tess. Now."

She was grateful. All she wanted to do was go home and sleep.

"Piston Building," Red said as they got into his office.

"I need to know who owns it. I've heard a rumor."

"Oh?" But he was already busy, tapping into the database. "You know, you can do this yourself."

"I never remember the password. Besides, I like involving you in my harebrained projects."

He eyed her. "How harebrained is this going to be?"

"If the answer's what I think it is, there are some corporate real estate people with a lot of explaining to do."

He raised his eyebrows, blinked a number of times, took a sip of his coffee, and sat back. "Hunh. It just says it's owned by PST Holdings and isn't open for inquiries."

"Do they own other properties?"

Red stared at his screen, his mouth slack the way it got when he was looking for something. "If they do," he said at last, "I can't tell."

"That's convenient," Tess said and reached for her phone.

"Hi, Tess," Taylor chirped when they answered.

"Can I borrow your sleuthing skills?"

"You know I work for Emerson."

"Like this isn't for him?"

Taylor sighed, long and put upon. "Let's hear it."

"PST Holdings. What do your highest-executive-in-the-room privileges grant you?"

"You know, Krista's assistant was asking me about them not more than ten minutes ago. I need to clear this information with Emerson before I talk to either of you."

Tess and Red exchanged looks. "He's not ready," Tess said.

"I noticed." Taylor's voice was chagrined.

"Do I have to yell at him for yelling at you?"

"While I would appreciate it, that's not your job, and I did quite a good job of it on my own, if I do say so myself."

"Oof. Should I check on him?"

"Maybe later today. Now, is there anything I can truly help you with? Some merriment we need to plan in tandem?"

"We'll have to come up with something, definitely, and thanks for what you *could* tell me. It helped." As she disconnected the call, she sat back and gave Red a raised eyebrow. "So who do you think PST Holdings is?"

"If it's who you're hinting, why would the guy hire someone in the first place to find a site?"

"Because I bet you anything that until ten minutes ago, he didn't know there *was* a PST Holdings. And until yesterday, he didn't know that the Piston Building was built to be PharmaSci's headquarters in Port Kenneth, and one thing he *still* doesn't know is that you and I aren't going to let him hire another firm."

"Hmm." He frowned, one hand tapping a pen on his desk and the other playing with his coffee cup. After a minute, he asked, "Someone's trying to keep this from him?"

"Possibly, but I think," Tess said slowly, feeling the idea out as she spoke it, "I wonder if it was more of a test, to see how much he was willing to dig into the family legacy on his own." She tapped her index finger on the top of Red's desk, then sat back in frustration. "Typical Mack. Knowing he needs to know his history but refusing to learn it on his own. I spent too much of the weekend leading him down some pretty dark history."

"This is starting to sound a little too personal and not enough architectural," Red said.

Tess waved him off. "Of course it is." She stood up, wondering if there were any literal skeletons—or just random bones—involved in any of this, as well. "Thanks, Red. I'm probably going to take the afternoon. Not a lot of sleep this weekend."

"I warned you about him."

"You did," Tess agreed. "And, yes, Dad, you were right about him."

FIFTY-THREE

After an early lunch with Charley and Sanjit, Tess made good on her promise and went home. A three-hour nap was just what she needed, she realized when she woke up from it.

Funny how easy it is to stay up all night and have sex when you're twenty, and how hard it's gotten now that I'm thirty, she texted to Jamie, wincing at all the puns. *Staying up, I mean.*

Jamie got back to her between clients. *Right? First sleepover with Grandma was a success. I'm an idiot for doubting Hank, and I'm jealous that you can take the afternoon off. When are you free so we can compare notes?*

When her phone buzzed again, Tess figured it was more from Jamie, or that it was late enough in the day that it could have been Mack, but it was Serenity. *I learned something from Harald. Can you come down?*

Tess glanced at the time. She had to be at her mother's at six. *I have about an hour.*

You will find me in my office.

Serenity was actually waiting outside, bundled up against the chilly spring day, when Tess pulled up. "Harald asked me to pass some information to you," she said and led the way to her office. "That sheep farm's history is worse than even I knew," Serenity said when they were settled.

Tess' stomach took a nosedive to her toes. "When you say worse, what do you mean?"

Serenity gave her a long look. "The people who owned that farm were evil men. They bought more enslaved people than anyone else in the county. They bought so many, people doubted there were sheep on that farm and concluded it was just a place of human misery. And it might have been; just like today, the entire place was surrounded by trees and, Harald says, guarded so no one could get near. No one knew if those sheep were real or not." She laid poor copies of ancient pictures on her desk. Pictures of thick trees, like a forest.

It did look like the most effective privacy fence she'd ever seen.

"And word got around. They were buying so many, the only explanation was genocide. Working them to death. Just outright executing them. No one knew, but it wasn't a plantation. They didn't need help picking cotton. What could they be doing with all those people? Once someone wound up in their possession, they were never heard from again. But that's not the bottom of this nightmare. The bottom is the children. If there were children on the auction blocks, they'd bid as high as they had to in order to win. Children!" Serenity pressed her lips together and shook her head. "But no one knows where their bodies lie. Harald said you saw for yourself that the cemetery isn't big enough to hold that many people. There are headstones for twenty, most with names that you can read to this day. They've been protected, cared for. But where are the rest of those people? Over the years, people have asked for a search for a mass burial, but there's never been enough evidence to make it worth the fight. It appears that it is still private property."

"Let me guess. The records of who owns it have been lost."

Serenity gave Tess a sharp look. "You know things."

"More than I'd like to, and I'm wondering if it's tied into our water main break. Among other things," she added, thinking of Mack, unsure of how he was going to react to this news. *Hi, honey. I love you but those ancestors we talked about? They were more like Tristan and Cullen than we'd realized. They murdered their property at whim and I know you're worried about how to redeem the Mackenzie name, but this maybe isn't something there can be redemption from.*

Yeah, that would go over well.

"I would like to see the cemetery again," Tess said softly, wondering if it was yet another piece to this puzzle—and why, if the land was so cursed and creepy, people went to the cemetery and knew about it.

Besides, she had promised Mack she'd look for the family plot up the hill.

"People have always avoided that place, as if the land itself is contagious, although whenever the butcher had local lamb, we all knew where it was from but bought it anyway." Serenity made a noise in the back of her throat, like she was now second-guessing those actions. "So at least at the end of its life, it was a sheep farm. That, I can attest to."

Tess thought about all of that. "We're still missing an awful lot of pieces."

"Somewhere, there should be a registry of all the people who crossed over onto that devil's farm."

"I'll find it."

Serenity eyed her. "Why you?"

Tess paused. There were layers of truth that she could share, and she wasn't sure she wanted to tell Serenity that this was Mack's history, and if she wasn't letting go of him so fast or easily this time, that meant she had to know what they were going to have to deal with. Not to protect him or be a buffer against it, she told herself. Not like everyone else in his world.

No. She needed to know so she could make sure he owned it properly. If she'd thought it was going to be hard before, it had just gotten ten times worse. Despite the family history, Mack wasn't from Port Kenneth. He was, without a doubt, from Lakeford. Lakeford society, to be precise. The city wasn't going to embrace him as a long-lost community member.

She needed to get over to her mother's, but as she stood, she had to catch herself on Serenity's desk. The news had made her lightheaded. Mackenzies... definitely not the mythical good type of slavers. Their house in Lakeford probably was a tribute to the horrors that had happened on their property here in PK. Had they buried the bodies in mass graves? If so, where?

She flashed to the bunch of bones that had been found under the old firehall. People, dogs, sheep... and wildlife. Like none of it mattered. Like *life* didn't matter.

She sat down and shoved her head between her knees.

"Tess?"

"No," she said. "I am *not* okay. Just... give me a minute."

"Why is this hitting you so hard?"

She lifted her head slowly. "My boyfriend? His people owned that sheep farm."

Serenity pushed Tess' head back between her knees. "You stay that way for another minute, child."

"I have to get to dinner," Tess said without moving. It felt like she was talking to her pant legs, and she rubbed at some dust on her shoe. She'd worn ballet flats, and as she looked at them, she wondered if she'd picked them that morning because part of her had known she'd have this strong urge to run.

Of course, there was no outrunning this.

"You just rest a minute. Adjust to this. His people can't be as good as you think they are. They simply can't be."

Tess sat up slowly. Serenity was sitting in her chair, her legs together, her hands on her lap, her shoulders back and square, her expression fierce. In a way, she reminded Tess of Krista.

She took a deep breath and let it out slowly, then did it again. "Please tell Harald I'd like to meet him and see that cemetery again."

FIFTY-FOUR

April 7

T homas had summoned Mack to meet him in one of those old-style restaurants he'd spent entirely too much time in when Tristan had been teaching him the ropes of PharmaSci. It felt like stepping back in time, to a lifestyle he'd tried hard to yank the company away from. He hoped the meeting wouldn't be the same.

A waiter was putting food on the table as Mack was led to it. Thomas sat alone, although the table had been set for three.

"Who are we expecting?" Mack asked after he'd greeted Thomas and asked for coffee.

"Gray will be here in forty-five minutes. Sit, sit, and help yourself." Thomas extended a hand across the spread.

"I had a lunch meeting," Mack said, trying not to sigh. He *always* had lunch meetings; he suspected Taylor booked his day that way on purpose. "But you go ahead."

Thomas nodded once and began helping himself. Oysters on the half shell, baked brie, some pâté; it was the sort of food Mack had seen at entirely too many society events.

But then, it was also what he expected from Thomas. The man was old-school.

Mack's coffee arrived and he took his time adding sugar and cream, both dreading what Thomas wanted to talk about and trying to control his curiosity.

"I wanted to meet you here," Thomas said as he helped himself, carefully picking over a column of strawberries on a white platter. "How many of the journals have you read by now?"

Mack had just taken a mouthful of coffee and it was all he could do to keep from either spewing it across the table or snorting it onto the place setting in front of him. Setting the coffee cup down, he reached for his napkin and held it to his mouth and nose as he tried to regain his composure.

"Does everyone know about these things?" he asked at last. Thomas, he noticed, was smiling and his eyes were dancing.

Apparently, Mack's coffee issues were amusing.

"Who else knows of them?" Thomas asked.

"Well, Krista, for one. Probably Logan, too," he added with a frown, recalling the morning in his office when he and Tess had discovered Tristan's and the truth about SH-34.

Thomas was nodding. "I'd expect Krista would. Just as Tess will, I'm sure. Did Kelsey?"

Mack shook his head.

"Probably just as well. That means Flemming may not know." He scooped an oyster out of the shell and paused to suck it down. "I only know because I walked into Cullen's office unannounced one day just as he threw them in his trash can and was about to set a match to them."

Mack just stared, not caring that his mouth had fallen open slightly. He could hear his mother's reprimand in the back of his head, but he didn't care about that, either.

"I stopped him, if only to keep the fire department from responding to a call at the office, and rescued them. They remained in my possession until your father came of age. Unfortunately, he stuck them in the safe in your rooms at the Manor, most likely unread. I assume they are still there?"

"Yes," Mack said, nodding and playing with his coffee cup, twirling it on its saucer. "Tristan did keep his. So did Cullen. I've read them both." It had been brutal, especially Tristan's. He'd gone to Krista when he'd finished that one and asked her why she'd let him live when she'd had the opportunity to wipe the earth clean of him.

Thomas paused.

"You're wondering how much I know," Mack said after the silence had stretched.

"PST Holdings."

Mack shook his head. "They own the building in Port Kenneth, the one that PharmaSci had built to be their headquarters."

"Let's focus on PST Holdings and what it means for your future," Thomas said and pushed his plate aside. He leaned forward and began to speak.

Fifty-Five

April 12

"Another day, another summons to the mayor's office," Red said to Tess as they left the office at the end of the morning meeting. He pulled a ball cap out of his pocket and settled it on his head, using both hands to adjust it precisely.

"Maybe we'll get answers and not more runaround."

He arched an eyebrow at her but didn't say anything. Instead, he folded his hands inside his coat pockets and hunched his shoulders.

Tess wasn't sure why. It was a beautiful day. The air had a new warmth to it and she honestly wanted to run instead of stroll, just to feel its tender touch filling her lungs. She bet it would make her feel amazingly alive. Spring was often her favorite season.

Philip was waiting for them in the main lobby once they'd cleared the metal detectors. "Come on in. Before we get to what I need to talk to you about, I wanted to let you know, Tess, that Pharmaceutical Sciences Technologies has reached out to the mayor about a relocation. That was yesterday, and already they're deep in conversation about incentives to move here."

Tess felt a flash of excitement about it all over again. Maybe dreams could come true. Maybe she and Mack could be together yet.

"I don't have all the details, but there seems to be a tie to that sheep farm you're so obsessed with?"

She felt Red's eyes boring into her. "Seems to be," she said, trying for nonchalance. "But you should talk to them about it, not me. What do you have for us?"

"More about the sheep farm—sort of," he said as he led them to his office. Tess tossed Red a surprised look. His office? That was new territory for them. They usually barely rated a meeting room.

Once their coats had been left draped over a chair, Red's baseball cap perched on top, they sat down in front of Philip's desk while he took his seat behind it. "So this is what we're thinking right now," Philip said. "The bones are a plant. Someone put them there to make us think that the sabotage of the water lines is related to the sheep farm."

Tess didn't try to hide her surprise. That wasn't a leap she'd expected anyone to make—but it was one she'd been hoping for.

"There was a lot of bad will associated with the people who owned that farm and the company. The company had moved out of town in the nineteen-thirties and built the Piston Building in the late sixties, hoping it had blown over. But it hadn't. The building was used until the contraction of the nineteen eighties and has stood empty ever since."

"What sort of bad will?" Tess asked, after getting a small nod from Red to go ahead with the question.

"Well..."

"It's all going to come out by the time they relocate," she warned.

"Anyway, your friend's off the hook on the water line issue; they were long gone when that line was rebuilt," Philip said. He sat back in his chair, tipping it backward slightly, as if he were bouncing off his toes. "But there seems to be a *lot* of ill will toward them still."

Red nodded. "They seemed to have a lot of fingers in town. The sheep farm, the Piston Building, even establishing Woolslayer as a neighborhood." He paused.

"The family put Port Kenneth on the map," Philip said heavily, like that wasn't a good thing. But then again, Tess figured, in Philip's eyes, it probably wasn't. No moral person could excuse it—which was something she was still struggling with.

Philip opened his mouth to say something but closed it, giving his head a small shake, his eyes closing for the briefest of seconds.

"Changing directions," Tess said, "Why isn't the sheep farm part of the city limits?"

Philip raised his eyebrows. "It is... sort of. I had to send a couple of our archivists deep into our records, but we found it. They've paid taxes on that property to the city, the county, and the state. It's all up to date. It's just carefully hidden to make it look like they are outside it all."

Tess cocked her head and thought about that. Then she started to laugh.

"Tess?" Red asked.

"If you're angry they're above the law, you're not looking at what they're actually doing." She didn't know the whole story, but that fit with what little she knew so far.

"What else is going on?" Philip asked.

"I'm not sure," Tess said, "but all signs point to it being something wonderful."

"If you tell me it's another alligator someone tossed in a hole... Or bones. I'm done with bones," Philip said, eyeing her warily.

Fifty-Six

Tess was folding laundry that night when Mack video chatted her. "Maybe I should have been a figurehead like Tristan and Cullen."

"That bad?"

He scrubbed at his face with both hands. "Worse. I'm trying to deal with the relocation issues, and that includes streamlining the company, making it more efficient, and I had three different people in my face today, trying to convince me to buy this smaller company that makes an antibiotic that's sorta like what we already make, but no one's using it; they're using ours because it's better and cheaper and has a longer track record. So this start-up's going under; they'll be cheap and we should buy them! But what's the point of buying them if theirs doesn't quite do what ours does—and no one's using it? Will we gain some really good researchers? And you know what the answer is?"

Tess had a feeling she knew, but she tilted her head, a sign to keep talking.

"We need it so no one else can buy it and compete with us." He narrowed his eyes and Tess had a feeling that whoever had been the third person to propose this hadn't been met terribly graciously. "That's what they told me. Like the people aren't important? They're the ones doing the work, coming up with ideas. The people are what makes it worthwhile." This time, he used the heels of his hands to scrub at his face. Tess wanted to grab him and make him stop.

"So I said to them," he continued, his face starting to get red, "that I wanted to know why I should be throwing money at something that's not going to *make* us money. And do you know what the answer was?"

"Tell me," Tess said, making note that he'd put a value on the human beings involved in all this. But of course he had. He was Mack and he'd done that as long as she'd known him. When they'd been in school, he'd taken care of the next-door neighbors, an elderly couple most of the other students in the neighborhood had ignored.

"The answer was *well, it won't make your competitors money*. Like I care about that? I mean, yeah, to a degree, but if no one's using the damn antibiotic in the first place, no one's making money. Me or them, and I still don't know if the researchers who had the initial idea are worth bringing on board here."

He was, Tess thought, awfully worked up.

"And then, then," he went on, and he leaned forward, as if trying to look through the phone at her. His eyes mirrored his emotion: They were almost black. "I met with Thomas about PST Holdings and you're not going to believe *this*, either."

"Go."

"Your Piston Building, or whatever you call it, is only one of *seven*. They're all across the country, and all in secondary cities: Milwaukee, Tempe, Louisville, Port Kenneth... I can't remember the other three, but there's seven of them."

"Seven."

"Seven!" He flung one hand into the air. "They've all been shut down but not sold, and we've been paying taxes and upkeep on empty buildings, which is exactly how a business increases profits. Yep. Sure is." His nostrils flared as he took a breath. "The only good news in this is that when I talked about taking PharmaSci home, I didn't know how right I was." He paused and flashed a half-smile, half-glower.

"So the question becomes," he went on, "how much space do we need and what do we do with the other floors? I'm leaning toward opening *all* the buildings and renting them out. May as well make some money."

"Can I make a suggestion?" she asked.

"Always," he said and his glower faded.

"Put in a day care center in every one of those seven buildings, and let employees have first dibs to enroll their kids—at as much of a discount as you can afford. It makes life so much easier for everyone. And if you can afford to pay the staff above minimum wage, you'll keep them around longer and foster an even better environment for everyone."

He nodded, then licked his lips and pressed them inward, the way he did when he was thinking. "That makes sense. Is this your experience or your brilliance at work?"

"Both."

"Good. I'm going to need it, you know. I found out today that I will own seven empty buildings—and a sheep farm. And Tess? I run a *pharmaceutical* company. But in the span of about thirty seconds, we turned me into a multi-property landlord who runs day cares. Or we will when Thomas hands it all over to me. Got ideas what else I can do with them?"

"You need to discuss that with Red, not me. I'm just the hired help."

He paused, studying her. "You don't give yourself enough credit."

"Red makes the decisions about the projects we work on. You know that."

"Know what else I know?"

"Hmm?" She raised her eyebrows and waited, mouth slightly pursed.

"I know how to get my hands on the keys."

"And?" She licked her lips, smiling as his eyes locked on them.

"And I miss you like crazy."

"What's that got to do with keys?" She made her eyes big, pretending an innocence that bordered on making her gag. His dilated and she knew she had him.

"How soon you want to go through it?" he asked.

"Tonight. Tomorrow."

He shook his head, his eyes closing briefly.

"You could overnight me the keys."

"I thought you had to talk to Red because you're only the hired help."

"Well, yeah. But that has nothing to do with what I *want*. Which, right now, is to go through that building. Mack, I have *dreamed* of being able to set foot in there."

"Why?"

"Why?" she echoed, unable to believe he'd asked. "Have you *seen* it? The Piston Building is one of the gems of the PK skyline. It's... it's iconic. It's amazing. It's what made me want to be an architect. To create something like *that*..." She broke off, breathless. Mack was watching her, his eyes wide and a little concerned.

"You don't get this passionate often," he said. "Just with me. And even when you do, it's... different."

"That should tell you something."

"It does, Just Tess," he said gravely. She gave him a funny look. "What?" he asked.

"I'm... a little concerned about what you're thinking right now."

His smile was slow and seductive. "That I've got to bring a couple blankets and hope there's a lot of interior rooms and no one to miss us for a couple hours?"

"Who needs interior rooms? I mean, no one's going to know to look..."

He laughed. "You want me to go through Red?"

"Probably should," she said heavily. "It'll make him happy, at least."

"And neither of us want to appear like I'm calling in favors."

"No, this would be straight taking advantage."

He laughed, and Tess watched over her phone as his stress finally melted away. She smiled, satisfied that she'd done it but sorry it had taken so long. Then again, he had a lot to be stressed about, it seemed.

"I've been meaning to thank you for the presents you left me when you were here," he said.

"Oh, you found them? Be good to the one; it was expensive." The other was, of course, a chocolate alligator that she'd left on their pillows.

"Why you women pay so much for a little bit of lace, I'll never understand."

"Why? Because what choice do we have?"

"You could go without..."

"Yeah, no."

He chuckled again, and finally, his smile reached his eyes. She wanted to be there, to smooth his laugh lines, to egg him on as she slid her hands around him, then her legs, then...

She shook her head.

"Tess?"

"Just thinking the sorts of things I shouldn't be thinking when you're there and I'm here."

"I wish you were here," he said softly.

"Now there you go," Tess said, not wanting to get caught in a cycle of missing each other, "like a typical guy. Give up your life. Come here. Be with me. Assimilate into my world." She threw her hands in the air and let out a puffy breath, hoping he saw through her act.

"I meant here," he said, gesturing, but it was out of view of his phone. "Right here. Next to me. I don't care if it's here or there. Well, I'd rather be there so I can hide from... Mother! Were you just sitting out there, listening, waiting for the perfect moment to interrupt, or what?"

"Emerson, really. The things you get in your head," Tess heard.

Mack swung the phone around. "Say hello."

"Hi, Krista," Tess called. She got a watery smile in return.

Tess wondered what was up. "Call back when you can," she told Mack. "Yeah," he said, frowning. And then the phone went dead.

FIFTY-SEVEN

"It's been quite a day," Krista said. "Join me in the other room?"

It wasn't a question, and Mack knew it. He got off his bed and followed her into the first-floor sitting room.

"Do we have to talk business?" he asked.

She looked up at him, her eyes wide. "What else would we discuss?"

"Oh, I don't know. Umm..." He froze as he realized he truly didn't know.

"Just this one thing," she said, putting her hands in her lap. "And that's a question I know you were too busy today to dwell on."

"What is it?" He rubbed at his face with both hands, really not wanting to hear this.

"Why did we hire a real estate agent who did not know that every city they were suggesting had a PST Holdings building in it?"

Mack paused, wondering how much she knew. "Mother, maybe PharmaSci and the Mackenzies, collectively or separately, need to stop and inventory every last piece of our holdings, even beyond what Thomas is in charge of. I have a feeling they've gotten a little out of hand."

"You do me proud," Krista said.

He lay his head on the back of the chair he'd sat in, splaying his legs in front of him. She wouldn't approve—she'd probably loudly disapprove—but he was too tired to care. "Do you think we can ever be *normal* people?"

"No," she said immediately, without needing to stop and think about it, or even consider what he was getting at.

294   SUSAN HELENE GOTTFRIED

"How about being normal enough to fold laundry," he said and covered his face with his hands, thinking of Tess and the way she'd swayed with the gentle motions of the chore.

"Why would you want to do *that*?"

He lifted one hand off his face and waved it vaguely at her. "Okay, fine. Maybe I want to be normal enough to actually do all the things a CEO is supposed to do, without the microscope you guys keep me under."

"Give *that* time," Krista said, and her voice softened, as if she understood his frustration. "You're ahead of schedule and expectation."

He shrugged. He didn't really care.

"Emerson," she said in that same soft tone, "you are very young to have so much power. And you are very inexperienced, too. By taking it slowly, as you have been, you have consistently proven that you are growing into the sort of leader we need at PharmaSci."

"Despite my desire to move away from Lakeford."

"Well, there is that, but I understand where it's coming from. And now that it seems like it's about more than a woman, it makes it easier to support. Which brings me to the other thing we need to discuss tonight. There's apparently a vault hidden in this house. In your set of rooms, in fact."

"Thanks, Mother. I *am* not allowed to sleep on couches anymore."

"I would think the vault would be added incentive to sleep in your own room, an entire floor away from whatever it holds."

He raised his head and then an eyebrow. "What are you getting at?"

"One of us needs to find what's inside."

"And you don't want to deal with the dead bodies." He bit back a smile, wondering if he'd find another alligator inside—and how it would feel if he did.

"I would prefer that." She pressed her lips together and grabbed her hands, tucked into her lap.

"Mother?" he asked softly.

"No one said being a Mackenzie is easy."

"I don't want *easy*," he said. "I just want something resembling *sane*, if I can't have normal."

She leaned forward and gave his leg a pat. "We all have things we want, Emerson. Of it all, what do you want the most?"

"Tess. PharmaSci. Family. It's all one."

"Does Tess know that? I seem to recall at one time, she wasn't on board with that."

"She does. And we were right to call it off back then." He grimaced, remembering the weeks of conversations, the dead ends they'd kept bumping into, the pain of finally agreeing they had no choices.

Krista raised her eyebrows. "I'm glad you recognize that. She's become an influential woman in her own right."

"The opposite of Kelsey," he said heavily.

She waved him off. "Kelsey brought out different things in you than Tess does. Remember who she needed you to be, and don't stop being that man. Be *more* with Tess, Emerson."

He nodded.

"Okay," Krista said, patting his leg again and standing up, then smoothing out her skirt. "It's getting late. We have our assignments." She bent down and actually kissed him on the cheek. He tried not to jump in shock.

After she'd left the room, he picked up his phone to continue his discussion with Tess, but she'd left him a text.

She'd gone to bed.

Alone. Without him.

It was just him and the vault.

Fifty-Eight

April 13

Tess walked into the morning meeting the next day fully expecting to hear Red talk about the Piston Building. When he didn't bring it up, she had to wait until after the meeting to ask him why.

"Nothing to tell. If Mackenzie was supposed to call me, he didn't."

Tess frowned and made a mental note to ask about that. "Okay," she said slowly, trying to get her thoughts in order. "I need your help with something else that's Mackenzie-related."

Red frowned. "You're in deep. Too deep?"

It was a valid question—if you didn't know the history. "I don't think so," she said. "But this thing with the bones... I wonder if the mayor's office is writing it off too fast."

"They know things they're not sharing. Let it go," Red said and lifted his coffee mug to his mouth but made a face. Tess guessed it was empty, which she confirmed when Red set it aside, untasted.

"It's just that... I'm second-guessing... well, everything. I mean, they started a pharmaceutical company during the Civil War. And they bought a lot of slaves. Like, a *lot*. What if... what if..." She swallowed, unable to continue. *What if Tristan was just acting like his forefathers* was one of the questions that had bugged her all night. The other ones, of course, were *What if Mack turns out to be like them? What are the chances he's the true Mackenzie rebel and is nothing like these bloodthirsty fools his family tree is apparently full of? And how do we square this with the city so they don't run him out again?*

Red cocked an eyebrow at her, and she didn't know if he followed her thoughts until he spoke. "From what we've seen so far, and from what you've said, these present-day Mackenzies have big hearts to go with those big bank accounts of theirs. I haven't seen as much as you have, and I trust your judgement, but overall, I'd say it's hard to hold a grudge against them."

That was true. She hoped.

"Need anything else?" Red asked.

"Yes." She outlined the issue with the vault.

Red frowned. "Did you get pictures?"

"No. I didn't have time." She envisioned herself, ass in the air and cheek on the rubber matting that made up the floor, examining the iron ring when Mack had come in the weight room, holding a plate with bagels and not expecting anything out of the ordinary. Poor Mack. He had never expected any of this.

She let out a breath. Not all the alligators hanging out in holes were welcome.

"We need more to go on," Red said.

"I know. And I have the name of the firm who's done a lot of work on the house, but..." She paused, half-hoping he would say what she was counting on him to say.

"If I got a phone call like you're thinking I should make, I wouldn't exactly welcome it. How far back does this other firm go with the client?"

"Far," Tess said in a small voice, ducking her head into her shoulders.

He cocked an eyebrow and looked down at his tablet again. "I'm not comfortable. Have Mackenzie call me directly to discuss this."

As she started to reach for her phone, Red stared her down. "You have other projects that are waiting."

"I know," she half-snapped. "Don't even question my loyalty."

"I don't. Bring in Yvette or Carter for the Grant Street building, and how's the kitty team?"

They talked about its status in more depth than the morning meeting had given it for the past few days, and finally Red nodded and sat back, absently lifting his coffee cup to his lips and giving it a frustrated look as he set it back down. "I like how you're working with the junior people."

"Thanks. I like working with them and hearing their perspectives and ideas. And... I can't get lost in my head like I can when I'm working on something solo." She took a deep breath. "I can't get out from under the whole slavery thing, Red. It makes me want to throw up."

"I understand."

"Spoken by a man not worried he's about to marry into a family of slavers."

Red paused and looked at her, his hands still on his mug.

"What?"

"It's no secret I've got slave blood in me."

Tess groaned. "We are *not* on opposite sides of the issue. I swear it. I just... I set him free, Red. He came back, all new and improved, but still perfectly familiar." She paused, envisioning the older, better, present-day Mack. "Just tell me one thing?"

"What?"

"Your ancestors didn't have anything to do with the sheep farm, did they?"

He smiled. "I don't think so. My people were from farther south. And remember: It doesn't *all* come back to the Mackenzies. Don't lose yourself to them."

It was good advice.

"Thanks, Dad."

"Dad? I'm five years older than you."

"So? You've always been my dad. You just hate to admit it."

"Maybe." He gave her a half-smile. "Go get to work. Grab Yvette or Carter now, before they get any busier. One of them's bound to have more time than the other."

"Any issues with letting them work together? Their styles are so different and the client's been so picky, it might not be a bad idea to let them both run with ideas independently and then bring it all together."

Red stared at the ceiling, stroking his throat. "Good thinking." He shook his head and gave Tess an admiring smile. "See? I unload your stress and you come through."

"Only if the client likes what we come up with."

"They will. May take a bit, but they will."

Tess went to find Yvette and Carter instead of going to back to her office. She and Mack tried to give each other space to focus on what they had to during their days; it was an unspoken agreement they'd settled into. But still, if he had to talk to Red about the vault, that needed to happen during the business day.

Sending a text shouldn't have taken too terribly long. But it felt like every time she tried, someone else needed her or something called her attention away from her phone, and it was late by the time she sent Mack a quick text: *Red wants you to call him re: Vault.*

It was even later when he answered. *Love you.*

Fifty-Nine

I t took a full week for Red to get the go-ahead from the firm the Mackenzies had traditionally used for renovations at the Manor. Tess wasn't sure if she or Red were more surprised when a package arrived via overnight delivery, full of blueprints—some so old, they truly were blue. And a little fragile, too.

Red instructed they be spread out on the table in the big conference room and let Tess, Sanjit, and Charley have the first look at them.

"This place is amazing," Sanjit said, leaning over the table and peering at the oldest set of blueprints, tracing rooms and hallways with the capped tip of his favorite pen.

"It's a plantation house," Red agreed. "Built in upstate New York."

"Right?" Tess asked, meeting his gaze. "Do you get it better now?"

"It's definitely strange."

"What is?" Sanjit asked, raising his head and blinking a few times behind his glasses.

Charley swept into the office. "I can't believe you guys didn't wait. Is this them?" Tess stepped back to let her in. "Oh, I see why you couldn't wait. Holy cow. Is this real?" She turned to Tess, her mouth slack, her eyes shining.

Tess shared her enthusiasm. The original house had been a treasure. What they'd done to it was simply terrible.

"Tess, what are we supposed to be focusing on?" Sanjit asked. He motioned to Charley, who moved around the table to stand beside him and bend over the fragile paper.

"Right here," Tess said, pulling the plans for Mack's rooms up on her tablet. It had been jarring to see them; they'd been the complete set, from the original renderings to pictures of the finished product. Kelsey, it seemed, had made a number of changes, and

Tess wasn't sure how to feel about the loss of the shower's multiple body jets and the rainfall showerhead. But she had a pretty good idea what Mack would say about it—and the puppy dog eyes he would give her before she would admit she'd like to have them, too.

"This is the iron ring in the floor," she said, zooming in on it. "Supposedly, it signals the entrance to a vault of some sort. But I don't know," she said, holding her tablet so Sanjit and Charley could see it better. "It makes as much sense to me now as it did when I was looking at the actual thing. Who would build a vault in their personal suite of rooms? Sanjit? Help?"

He nodded and motioned for her tablet. She slid it across the conference table to him.

"And a word to the wise," she said into the silence that fell as he studied. "Mack's convinced there are skeletons in there and he's threatening to rip up the floor himself if we don't get moving."

"Rein him in," Red said.

"Trying," Tess said and shot him a look over her shoulder. He was standing, his arms crossed over his chest, his legs wide, a frown crossing his entire face. One of the overhead lights reflected off his head, showing which parts he still had to shave and which had given up trying to grow.

"We'll get moving," Sanjit said. "Wait. Am I seeing this right? They just kept laying new floor over the old? What's wrong with these people?"

"If you're going to bury something," Red said, watching Tess, "bury it deep."

"Then why keep the ring out?" she asked. "It's like it's a tease of some sort. Here's your history, but you can't get to it."

"Something sadistic in there," Charley said.

Tess had to consider that, especially in light of everything they knew so far. There was no way Mack could turn into that. It just wasn't *him*. She frowned and wished, again, that they were able to see each other in person. Long video chats were good but not the same, and the deeper she got into this whole thing, the scarier it was becoming.

Sanjit was frowning and thumbing through various digitized plans for the manor. Tess was aching to properly look through them. Later, she promised herself. At home, with no one to interrupt.

"A ballroom?" Charley asked, turning to Tess, her eyes wide.

"It's pretty cool," Tess said and, with a grin, winked at her.

"You didn't."

"Not yet, but it's been discussed."

Red cleared his throat and turned his back. Sanjit clapped his hands over his ears.

"All those windows!" Charley went on.

"In the middle of ten private acres."

"Ten?" Red asked, turning back as Sanjit started to sing. "That's small for that area."

"I know," Tess told him. "That's one of the reasons I think it's the summer home, and the full-time property was the *other* one."

Sanjit stopped singing and lifted his head. "Another one?"

"Just focus on this one for now," Tess told him.

"How much demolition, do you know, is he willing to put up with?" Sanjit asked, turning back to the various design materials. "From the look of this newest plan, we need to get under the weight room floor, and this storage closet here." He pointed. "Oh, and this wall's definitely got to come down. If the ring's buried in it, it's definitely in the way."

Tess's quick first look had told her the same. "What about the plumbing? Mack says it stops up routinely, even on the second floor."

"Look here," he said, tapping a spot. "These lines run slightly more horizontal than I'd advise, so if he has drainage or backup issues, that's why." He turned his head so far to the side, his whole body twisted. "And don't tell me you're surprised to hear that I think the lines run near or through this mystery vault."

"Don't... most people get concerned when their plumbing backs up or is slow?" Charley asked, giving Tess a strange look.

"*Most* people, yes. But the Mackenzies? They... well, they have a very interesting lifestyle."

Charley gave Tess a long look that either meant Tess was supposed to spill it all right then, or maybe they'd spare Sanjit and Red and wait for lunch.

Sanjit started shaking his head, looking back over the various plans and renovations that each Mackenzie man had done on the set of rooms. "Tess, tell your boy to stand down on the demolition. We need to get a crew in there and do it right. He's probably not the only one who's moved walls around. The smart move might be to return it to its original state, although we'll have to see how many beams have wound up in that ceiling."

"I did," Tess sighed. "And he will, if only because I'm not sure he'd know which end of a crowbar to use." She gave them a saucy grin as they gave her bewildered looks, although Red was chuckling. "But if I go up there for the weekend, you know he's going to make me do it."

"Like you're a demolition expert?" Charley asked.

"Poor impulse control."

"Yeah," Charley said with an exaggerated sigh. "He did jump into a hole in the ground when it was full of alligator."

"No, he backed off."

"Oh?" Charley raised her eyebrows. "For real?"

Tess chuckled. "Yeah. It hissed at him and he decided he'd gotten close enough."

"You chose him, Tess," Red said.

"I tried to get rid of him! And we should focus on the issue at hand. Do we have contact with any crews we trust up in Lakeford? How soon can we get them in there?"

"One-track mind," Red said, and his smile turned into one of approval that made Tess glow.

She swallowed it and shot him a glare, just to be contrary.

"I like you when you're focused like this."

"Do we have contact with any crews we trust up in Lakeford?"

"I'll check," Red said and left the conference room.

"What was that about?" Charley asked.

Tess shook her head. "He asks why I call him Dad."

"He's worried about you. None of us have ever seen you this intense with a guy before."

"Intense? How can it be intense when I'm here and he's there?"

"Because he's so deep in your head that we're *all* a little worried. Tess, this isn't you."

"No," she said. "It's Mack. He's always been there, even when I knew there was zero chance for us and I thought I was okay with that." She closed her eyes, trying to sort the emotion out of her thoughts. "If he ever gets down here, you'll see what I mean."

"If?"

Tess shrugged. "I'm allowed to have doubts. We both have consuming jobs and big lives. And his Ultimate team kicks back into gear soon, so we'll have weekend tournaments to deal with on top of everything else because I am *not* going to let him skip team events to be with me. This location thing has been..." She paused and looked from Charley to Sanjit, who was pretending to stare at the blueprint again. "It's been hard."

Charley gave her arm a squeeze. "Not to be harsh, but you'll either work it out or you won't."

"I know."

"I vote for working it out," Sanjit said. "Since he's come around, you've been more fun. Like you were when we started this whole thing." He waved vaguely at the room they were in, and Tess understood. She also noticed the second when he blinked and engaged with the blueprint more fully.

"What did you find?" she asked.

"Here," he said, pointing. "Here's your vault. It was in the original plans, from"—he checked the date on the print—"1855." He shook his head. "I'd bet this is a copy of the original. No way it could have survived almost two hundred years."

"You might be surprised," Tess said. "Did they include the vault in it?"

"Right here," Sanjit said. "You have to look really closely because it's super faded, or maybe it was never meant to be anything more than a shadow, something you'd ignore unless you knew to look for it. It's even taken me half an hour to see it."

"But you see it."

"Assuming this is correct. It may not be. From what you've said, there's been enough obfuscation that I wouldn't be surprised if this isn't entirely accurate."

Tess thought about that, her fingers playing at her lips as she did. "Well, only one thing to do, and that's get in there and see for ourselves."

Sixty

May 4

Two weeks later, Mack stood in the doorway of what had been the first floor of his suite of rooms. His weights and benches were currently sitting on salvaged rubber matting in the ballroom, and he'd been putting them to heavy use. So much so that Logan and Krista were worried. But it was how he dealt with this sort of stress, so he told them to get used to it. It wasn't like Tess had been able to come and supervise the demolition.

He hadn't really wanted to ask her to sleep in the mess, anyway, let alone get sweaty in it. With all that dust—even though his bedroom was on the second floor and despite plastic sheeting closing off the room, along with heroic efforts by Marisela, which he'd even helped with—he could only imagine that their lovemaking would result in some pretty gross aftereffects.

He shuddered, telling himself not to go there.

"You ready?" Logan asked, coming up behind him and putting a hand on his shoulder.

"I think," Mack said. "Where's Mother?"

"She'll be here."

"Is she seriously going to wear a dust mask?"

"I told her she didn't have to," Logan said, "but I don't think she believed me. I've got to say that you've been a better sport about the mess than she has."

Mack shrugged. "Tess is right. We need to know what's in there. *I* need to know if I've been working out with skeletons."

"I doubt that. Maybe some gold coins, though."

"Wouldn't complain about that."

Logan gave a bark of laughter that echoed in the half-demolished space. "Don't you have enough?"

"Nah," Mack said easily. "No such thing as enough." He caught Logan's eye and they exchanged a look. They both knew the worth of the Mackenzie estate, although the addition of the PST Holdings properties would only swell it further.

Frankly, it was a bit embarrassing. More than a bit, actually.

"Emerson?" the foreman of the work crew asked. "If you're ready, so are we."

He took a deep breath and rubbed his hands on his pants. For the millionth time, he wished Tess were here. No one from her firm was, although he'd done his best to change that. They had other clients, other projects. He understood that. Maybe if he'd been local, it would have been worth the time to be here in person.

He video called Tess, and when she answered, he laughed. She'd gathered the gang in the conference room for the big reveal. He should have expected her to do exactly that.

The foreman pried open the lid of the vault. The iron ring, it turned out, was decorative, there to remind them all that something had been buried.

Mack hoped that whatever it was, it wasn't nothing. Well, he'd take nothing over skeletons.

"Papers," he said, accepting the first handful the foreman handed him.

Krista and her dust mask showed up then. "Papers?" she asked, reaching for them. He handed them over.

"Papers?" Tess asked over the connection. "What *sort* of papers?"

Mack took the second handful from the foreman and looked them over. "Names, and... cities? The writing's faded." He turned to his phone. "I bet I have a match in my office," he said, trusting Tess to understand and wishing Thomas had been there, after all. He'd begged off, worried about the dust.

She cocked her head. "You think?"

He looked at the top page more closely. "Yeah. I think."

"Would you FedEx me a couple pages?" she asked, "or take pictures, but be careful with the flash."

Her thoughtfulness made him pause. She knew more than she was letting on. "Should we be passing these around before we know what they are?"

"I'm not going to share them," she said. "I just want to see them for myself."

"Just Tess—"

"Emerson," the foreman said, and Mack turned to receive another armful of papers. Logan jumped to start to stack them.

"Let's see if we can keep them in some sort of order," Logan said. "Krista, can you take Emerson's phone so Tess and the crew can keep watching?"

They heaved papers until Logan was breathless. Mack held himself back from reminding the other man that there was a good set of weights in the ballroom and ten acres of land that was good for walking across.

"Now we've got notebooks," the foreman said and lifted some out.

Mack glanced at his phone, wondering if all of Tess' crew was still there. They were, but they weren't watching as avidly as they had been at first. Idly, he wished he'd put a toy alligator in his pocket. Something to liven this up. Papers weren't terribly exciting.

How could a bunch of papers be the Mackenzie treasure, anyway?

"Emerson," the foreman said again and Mack turned. They'd gotten to the last of the notebooks and Mack looked into the vault. What he saw chilled him to the core.

"Tess," he said, looking up. "Mother, point the phone here. No, give it—" Krista handed it over, her eyes wide. "Am I seeing what I think I am?" he asked, only to be met with gasps from the phone.

It was a crude, beat-up stuffed rabbit. And some clothes.

He scanned the vault. It was a lot of clothes.

"How was all of this preserved?" Sanjit asked.

"Is any of it crumbling? Does it feel ready to turn to dust? We may need to get a conservator in there before you touch anything else," Charley was saying.

"Whose was all this?" Mack asked. He looked up at the phone. Where before he'd been able to see Tess, now it looked like she'd ducked out of view.

"Tess?" Charley asked. She, too, moved out of view, and Mack could make out the soft sounds of the women talking. Charley came back on the screen. "Emerson, listen. If this is what Tess is hoping it is, what you've found is significant. I'm going to make some calls and get some experts on this for you." She glanced off screen. "I *know*, Tess, but I think this time, they'll listen. We'll show up in their offices if we have to."

"You *must* be discreet," Krista commanded, her voice muffled behind her dust mask. "This could be one of those significant findings that the press loves. Am I clear?"

Mack shot his mother an annoyed look. By the time he turned back to his phone, Charley was gone and he was staring at a blank wall. He could hear raised voices on the other end and could make out snippets, then Red's voice obscured it.

"Just Tess?" he asked when it seemed they'd hit a lull.

She moved into camera range. "Give us a few? We're... we're actually having an argument. Someone write the date down," she added, raising her voice, her attention on the off-camera group. "This doesn't happen with us," she said, looking at him again and for a second, he felt her concern.

"Go take care of it."

"Of course, but to be honest, part of me wants to make some popcorn and watch." She winked, and the connection ended.

He looked up at his mother and Logan, then the foreman, who was looking awkward. "Is there anything more you can do right now?" he asked the man, who shook his head.

Mack told him to take the rest of the day off. Krista offered to walk him out, and Mack figured that meant she was going to give him the *don't talk about this* lecture on the way.

He glanced at Logan, who was looking out the window, his back to Mack.

"You know her better than anyone," Mack said. "What's the smart thing to do right now?"

Logan turned and, maybe it was because he was backlit, but Mack realized he'd never taken a real *look* at the man who really was, like his mother had said, his father. Logan was slight. He'd been a sandy blond before he'd gone grey. His face was slender but not long; his chin protruded slightly. And he had the same blue eyes that Krista did. "If I were you, I'd go move those journals. Put them upstairs in your room. And keep the door locked for the time being."

Mack nodded. "What about this?"

"Leave it for her. And whatever Tess and her team decides, let them."

"Just walk away from all this?" He gestured to the vault, the hole in the floor of what should have been part of his weight room and part of a room that he'd simply walled off, figuring that it would eventually be forgotten space.

That hadn't been such a smart move, he realized. Not when there were Mackenzies involved. He had to open things up, not close them off.

He turned and looked thoughtfully at where the rest of the house would be if it weren't hidden behind a wall. Maybe Tess was about to have another restoration project on her hands.

"No," Logan said. "You're going to delegate this out and keep focused on business, as hard as it's going to be. If Krista is going to be focused on this, we can't leave the business unattended."

Mack let out a breath. He'd have rather been involved in this mystery, but Logan was right. He was the CEO. Krista, for all her involvement, wasn't.

He knelt by the open vault, wanting to touch the clothing, wanting to ruffle through it and see what else was in there. Why keep it? What did it all mean?

"Emerson," Logan said. "I wouldn't dawdle."

With a nod, he pulled himself back to his feet and left the remnants of his weight room, intent on saving the journals—and maybe finally learning the rest of their secrets.

Sixty-One

May 5

An overnight box arrived at the office the next day, surprising Tess. The note inside was from Krista, asking for Tess' absolute discretion, suggesting a nondisclosure might be necessary for anyone who wasn't family, and saying she was going to be in charge of this while Mack focused on PharmaSci.

"I'm surprised she sent it," he said when he and Tess talked that night.

"So was I. And, of course, everyone wanted to know what it was."

"I can imagine."

"In case you were wondering, I'm now on fertility drugs."

He chuckled, then did a double-take. "Tess?"

"The box came direct from PharmaSci, Mack. What was I supposed to say? If I told them the truth, they'd have yanked the pages out of my hands."

He was quiet for a long minute, and Tess wondered what had hit a nerve.

"They didn't buy it," she said. "But at least they backed off and respected me when I told them Krista asked me not to share. Oh, that was the other thing I wanted to tell you."

"Hmm?" He raised an eyebrow but still, Tess thought, looked vacant.

"Krista's note. Said it was okay to share with the family. I guess I've made the cut."

"I keep telling you..."

"You do, and I should listen to you more."

He smiled. "Have you learned anything yet?"

"I have too many projects at work and Patricia and Ebony, the party planners, are in at the incubator, and the fashion designer and I have a meeting to talk about how Trade Creation can expand to help her."

"So that means in terms of the Mackenzie treasure, no." He grimaced. "Me, either. Logan suggested I hide the journals from Krista, so I had to get them off the property entirely. You're not going to believe where I hid them."

"If you tell me Alyssa's got them—"

"No. Absolutely not." He glared at her, but softened when she giggled. "Taylor does."

"Ooh, smart thinking."

"Only until I get a locksmith in here to deal with the safe."

"Why exactly do you need to hide them from her?"

Mack paused, and Tess had a feeling he hadn't thought about the reason behind the suggestion. "Logan's feeling," he said slowly, pretty well confirming Tess' suspicion, "was that I should focus on PharmaSci and let Krista worry about what's in the vault. But at the same time, when he told me to get them somewhere safe, I got the feeling he was telling me to make the time to finish reading them already."

"I can't wait to hear what they say."

"Me, either, but between Krista watching me like a hawk—probably to get her hands on them and read them before I can—while I'm here and then being busy at the office, I don't know when I'll be able to make the time."

"Come down for the weekend?"

He smiled. "Best idea I've heard in awhile. Let me see what I can do."

Two weeks later, the conversations hadn't changed much. With Krista's permission, Tess had contacted someone in Knoxville about the papers. The Mackenzie matriarch, it seemed, wasn't making much progress figuring out what exactly they were, either. It didn't help that things at PharmaSci had gotten busy, trying to set up time with the senator and issues with the board including the pending move and the renovation of the Piston Building—which even they were now calling it, apparently—only two of the more pressing problems Mack was trying to juggle and Krista was trying to oversee.

"Have you gotten out to the sheep farm again?" Mack asked on the night he told Tess he wasn't coming to visit yet again.

"No," Tess said. "I was hoping we'd do it together."

He gave her a sour smile. "You probably shouldn't wait on me."

"It's starting to sound like it. I'll go this weekend."

"Video with me?"

"Have you seen maps?" she asked. "That land is squished between Woolslayer and state wilderness. Service isn't going to be great much beyond the cemeteries; everything else is too far from town."

He shook his head. It figured.

"I did hear back from the people in Knoxville," she said. "Those papers are interesting, Mack. Near as we can tell, they're the Mackenzie registry of all the"—she paused, licking her lips—"*people* your ancestors bought. But then there's other notes about them, and that's where it gets *fascinating*."

"Does it line up with what I've managed to decipher so far from Henry's journal?"

"I don't know. Oh, I *can* tell you there's more than one person keeping these ledgers. Both are probably male." She paused again. "Should I keep going and you tell me where things line up or deviate from what you've learned?"

"Please."

"The rumors and stories seem to be quite true that your Mackenzie ancestors did buy as many children and teens as they could. But if we're reading the records right, very few of them died on the sheep farm. It looks like they were moved from here to various other places around the country, but it's not always clear what happened to them after that. It looks like the second handwriting did a number of the updates. On these few pages, we've got a couple updates of marriages and kids and even some winding up at Lincoln College? I've never heard of it."

"Me, either," he said and gave her a nod. It was his turn. "Henry's journal is the only one I've been trying to get through so far, but he lays out his plans. He relocated almost everyone he bought. He also had Mackenzie friends and relatives across the country, in cities where slavery was technically outlawed, and they'd take in people who were freed by Henry and try to help them find jobs and establish new lives."

"They freed them?" Tess blinked.

"They tried. Make note that I said they went to places where slavery was *technically* outlawed. Turns out that even in cities where the laws outlawed slavery, racism was still embedded pretty deeply and expectations ran deep. Henry writes about his frustration with some of the attitudes in cities he's heard are welcoming to freed slaves."

"Changing the law doesn't change minds," Tess said. They ran into that frequently at work, the push-pull of which buildings to designate as historic and which to demolish and build something new.

"Sure doesn't, especially when it means elevating a person to your own personal status, and Henry's life was threatened more a few times. Abolitionists weren't popular people."

"Was it him with that line I found?"

"The one about every human having basic rights, regardless?"

"Yeah."

"Yep. Guy was a progressive before they were a thing. He cultivated that nasty reputation on the sheep farm, too, you know. It was the perfect smokescreen because if people thought they were treating the slaves like everyone else did—or worse—no one looked too closely at what was really happening, and no one had any reason to think there were abolitionists right there in their community—which was good. They'd have killed him for it."

"So..." Tess said after neither of them had said anything for a long minute, "maybe Tristan and Cullen *weren't* typical Mackenzies?"

"I can sleep a lot better with that mindset, that's for sure."

"Maybe I should go out to the cemeteries tomorrow. I have time off I can use."

"What'll Red say?"

Tess waved him off. "My paid time off is mine to do what I want with. He's not allowed to ask."

"It can wait for the weekend. Didn't you say you've been busy at work?"

"Well, yeah, but..."

"Just Tess. It can wait."

She cocked her head and looked at him. He looked calm, in a way. "Maybe I need this for me," she said. "I'd hoped there was some happier ending to the story than everyone here was saying, but what were the odds?"

"About zero, but it looks like it happened. I'm going to keep reading, but really. The cemetery can wait for the weekend. I'll push harder to at least tour the Piston Building, too, and see what else I can get out of Krista about this mess."

"It's not really a mess. Not anymore."

"It is. How do you deal with the demand for reparations when it looks like they were made generations ago? Do you really owe reparations to someone whose ancestor you've freed and whose life you protected and bettered? And is there a better way for these reparations than handing cash to descendants? What if the Mackenzies invest more heavily in communities instead of specific individuals, like you're doing? What's wrong with lifting *everyone*?"

Tess shook her head, her eyes closed. "I'm a little overwhelmed by all this. I need to process it."

"So do I," he admitted, the passion that had crept into his voice gone and replaced with a sheepishness. "I feel like a fucking teeter-totter. On one hand, I'm related to this American Oskar Schindler. If we can track these families down and see who they are, what they've turned into... but on the other hand, I feel like the more we dig, the bigger our responsibilities get. And you and Krista and Logan have to be the center of family, at least for the time being. PharmaSci's the center of the work day. Without PharmaSci, we've got nothing."

"You've got a family bank account that could fuel a small country."

"Only if done carefully. And Logan's on that, by the way. He still handles the Mackenzie money, and our needs just changed pretty drastically."

"Everything just changed pretty drastically."

"Not you and me, I hope."

Tess smiled at him. "Not you and me."

Sixty-Two

May 27

Before Tess could get out to the cemeteries, Mack arranged a formal site visit for the Piston Building—and the rest of the weekend so he and Tess could investigate the sheep farm. The trade-off was that they had to wait yet another week.

It was doubtful he'd be moving before the autumn, so Mack had to prepare to spend the summer with his Lakeford Ultimate team. That meant fewer weekends that he'd be around, but it also, he told Tess, gave her a reason to log some travel miles, herself.

The idea of warm, sunny days on a field, watching her man in his tights, was strangely appealing.

But first, they had to learn more about the Mackenzie history, and just what this treasure was. Could it really be the however many people Henry had freed? Was it that simple?

She could hardly wait to hear what else Mack had learned. She could hardly wait to see him, either. Which, of course, was why she was waiting for him to get to her condo, rather than picking him up at the airport.

Oh, she understood. He and Taylor were flying in together, and he'd said that was awkward enough without having to brush off his assistant because Tess drove a two-seater. But she'd have been willing to put up with any awkwardness if she didn't have to wait like this.

At least she could make chocolate chip cookie dough as she waited. She debated baking it, but didn't want cookies in the oven when he showed up; that had too much potential to turn into little charcoal briquettes after he walked through the door and they got lost in greeting each other.

Besides, he might appreciate it if she smeared the dough over him and licked it off. She grinned at the mental image. He'd probably love it, just because that meant she'd have to go slow.

The buzz of her phone when he got into the lobby startled her, making her jump. She was waiting at her own front door when he got off the elevator, looking tired and harried but smiling as soon as he saw her.

She put a hand out to him, grabbed him by the front of the shirt, and pulled him inside. As soon as she shut the door behind him, she stretched to kiss him, then decided there was no reason to hold back. Jumping up, she wrapped her legs around his waist and kissed him for all she was worth.

He staggered back a step, coming to rest with his back against the door, her legs pinned, as he responded. His bags fell with a thud and he grabbed her thighs, holding her in place.

"Hi," she said when she finally decided to come up for air.

"Damn," he said, breathing hard. "That's some welcome."

"You've been missed," she said and leaned away until he freed her legs so she could jump down.

"Good thing I showed up alone." He bent to grab his bags.

"Did you get Taylor settled in their hotel?" They were, she recalled Mack saying, staying at the Hotel Monaco that had just opened. Taylor, it seemed, travelled in style.

"They wouldn't let me. I wanted to see the place, too." He led the way to her bedroom. "I bet your walls are thicker. Aren't they?" he asked over his shoulder.

"Hope so," she said. "I know you're tired and probably hungry, but frankly, Mack, if you don't let me take your clothes off, Taylor's got a roommate."

He simply held his arms out, giving her full access.

She wasn't sure what time it was when they decided to go in search of food. Mack was happy with the cookie dough, even though she'd left it on the counter when he'd shown up. He carried the bowl and a couple of spoons over to the couch and jerked his head, inviting her to join him.

"Do you want *real* food?" she asked from the far side of the couch.

"Wouldn't mind," he said around the spoon in his mouth. "Whatcha got?"

"Oh, no. You're helping cook." She dipped her own spoon into the dough.

He shook his head and forcefully pulled his spoon free. "You keep trying to make me normal."

"There's *nothing* normal about you. Stop wishing for it."

He chuckled. Tess peeked at the clock. While cooking a full dinner at nine at night wasn't nearly as strange as hoagies at two in the morning, it still wasn't something she wanted to get into the habit of doing. By the time they'd eaten and cleaned up—complete with a heavy make-out session as dinner cooked—it was time to go back to bed.

"Work in the morning," he sighed and scrubbed at his face with the heels of his hands. "How much vacation do you have? Let's go somewhere and spend days in bed."

She tapped the tip of his nose. "Tempting, but all that does it leave us both hungry and sleep deprived, and it doesn't accomplish anything about any of this Mackenzie stuff."

"You excited to see the building tomorrow?"

"Beyond," she said, widening her eyes slightly.

He nodded, yawning. "Good. So'm I."

"Do I need to tuck you in?" she asked, taking his hand and leading him to the bed. He followed, his eyes already half shut. In fact, so much tension had left his face, Tess was willing to bet he was all but asleep.

"Yes," he said, putting a knee on the bed. "How late can we sleep?"

"Well," she said, wincing.

He paused, half on the bed, and opened one eye.

"Unless you have something I don't know about, you can sleep and meet us at the building at eleven. I have to be at the office before nine. I won't wake you."

He nodded and motioned for her to make room for him. As soon as she did, he grabbed her around the waist and pulled her against him. "You know," he said as she snuggled close, "if Kelsey had given me half of what you do, I probably wouldn't have let Krista talk me into renovating that field."

"I'll take you over to see it this weekend if you want," she said, not sure what else to say.

"I want. But just think, Tess. If it weren't for that field, no one would know about what we've learned."

"The good and the bad."

"Yeah," he said, nodding and yawned again. "Lots to say, but later."

She was only a little surprised when he fell asleep that quickly, and even less so when, in the morning, he didn't even stir when she got up, showered, and left for the office. When she got in, she texted him instructions on where to meet her, Red, and Georgie.

They were going to be a motley crew, she thought as Red drove over to Woolslayer to pick up Georgie and his camera.

He was waiting for them on the steps of the school and after he'd slid into the backseat of Red's car, he handed her a piece of paper. "Look, Miss Tess. I did it. All B grades except for math, and that's a C."

She grinned. "I owe you a mentor, don't I?"

"Yes please. And, if it's not too much to ask, would you ask Miss Serenity to have a chat with my ma? She still thinks school's a waste."

"Do you?"

"No! I mean, I don't like it, but Mr. Jones talked to me and he suggested I take accounting next year and maybe join the business club, so I can start to learn what to do if I want to be my own man."

Tess turned to look at him. His eyes were serious, his mouth set.

"Do you think you want to work for yourself?"

"Why not? All the women in your building do. Vera does, in her café. Reggie does with his plumbing business. Lots more people do. And if I do, that means I can take pictures of what I want and sell them where I want, and I only answer to me."

"It also means a paycheck may not come every week."

Georgie fell quiet. Tess watched his mouth work as he thought about that. "Can you find me a mentor who works by himself?"

"I actually did," she said thoughtfully, just now realizing that detail. She watched as he nodded and settled back in the seat. His thought process was impressive.

The ride wasn't long and they had just passed the building when Tess' phone buzzed.

LMK when you're here

Looking for parking, she responded, glad he hadn't overslept.

"Mackenzie?" Red asked.

"Here and ready to go," Tess said. She glanced out the window and smiled. "This is like a dream come true, you know that? To get inside the Piston Building. Oh, by the way, I ran into Philip at the coffee shop this morning, so his office knows what we're up to. He said he'd keep it away from the media but would let the cops know we'll be here."

"Good thinking."

"Tell Philip. I bet he'll be glad to hear he's done something right for once."

Red found parking behind the building. "You ready, Tess? It's showtime."

She took a deep breath and looked up at the building again, the riveted iron and steel exterior making her heart beat faster. The building was a classic, a representative of an iconic architecture style. With the electric off, she doubted they'd go the whole way up to the top, but hoped whatever they did see would be as amazing as she'd always dreamed it would be.

Sixty-Three

Ever since he'd gotten to the Piston Building, Mack had been walking around it, trying to get a feel for it. It was tall, all right, thirty floors. He couldn't imagine PharmaSci needing that much space. Maybe, he reasoned, that was part of why they hadn't already relocated from Lakeford—although really, they got bit by that lousy reputation his forefathers had cultivated. They'd been all but run out of town, if the journals were accurate. No wonder even this fancy building hadn't been enough to change public opinion about them.

He grimaced. Changing that attitude wasn't going to be fun.

His phone buzzed. *Where you? We're all out front.*

At the doors. He looked around, surprised to see his wanderings had brought him under the overhang that protected the entry from weather, but what hid him from view was the landscaping. It was rather neglected and out of control.

Tess led everyone to him, and he paused to appreciate the view all over again. She wore jeans and hiking boots, and a gauzy long-sleeved shirt that flowed to her hips. The neckline didn't reveal too much, but the shirt fit over her breasts just right and he had to look beyond her, to his mother and Logan and Taylor, and then to Red and the photographer kid who'd shown them the alligator. And bringing up the rear were Gray and Thomas.

Mack paused and shook his head. Since Krista and Logan had brought the PharmaSci jet, it looked like Thomas and Gray had hopped a ride.

He didn't blame them, but it was more of an entourage than he'd wanted.

"Emerson," his mother said as he leaned in to give her air kisses. "You look well rested."

"Sarcasm's never been a good look on you, Mother." He flinched as Tess smacked his arm.

"Friend of Miss Tess!" the photographer kid said, raising his hand in that way teenage boys did when they were tired of waiting to be noticed. "Nice to see you again."

He ignored his mother's look and took a step toward the kid and introduced himself—as Emerson, as he was sure Tess noticed. The kid's name was Georgie, and he was full of thanks for giving him both a paid gig and a legitimate reason to skip one of the last days of school. Immediately, he started taking pictures. Of what, Mack wasn't certain, but after seeing the pictures of him and Tess on the day of the alligator, he was pretty confident they'd be good. He'd put a couple on his phone.

"Ready?" Tess asked, her eyes sparkling. Mack hoped she wouldn't be disappointed by whatever they found inside.

With the keys in hand, Mack took a deep breath and turned the lock. It gave with a snap and he blinked in surprise. "Did I break it?"

"Nope," Tess said, slipping her hand under his in a request that he relinquish the key so she could pull it out of the lock to show him. "It's old and hasn't been used. Wait. What? Red, someone's been in here," she said over her shoulder, slipping past Mack and through the double doors, into the foyer.

Red came up behind Mack and put a hand on his shoulder, propelling him forward, but before he could say anything, Thomas joined them. "I requested that the electric be turned on, the elevators tested for safety, and the floor in the foyer be mopped so we wouldn't leave footprints in the dust, and so that any allergies would be minimized."

"I still want to know why our real estate team wasn't told about PST Holdings."

"The building wasn't open to inquiries," Tess said.

Thomas didn't add anything to that explanation.

Mack glanced at Tess, who was studiously looking at the floor, brushing her toe across it like she was trying to determine what it was made out of.

"May I join?" Gray asked.

Thomas grunted. "Figured you would. Curious old coot."

"Thomas," Krista chided, and Mack was glad to see her using that tone of voice on someone other than him for once, "aren't you ten years older?"

"Details," Thomas said, waving a hand in front of him in what could only be an old man's attempt to wave off the truth.

Mack turned to Tess, but she and Red were exploring the lobby, talking, pointing to things. She grabbed Red's arm and gave it a little shake, raising slightly onto her toes, grinning at him. He knew that look, and it made him smile to see it. She was in her element. In *his* building.

He raised his face to the ceiling. It was vast in this part of the lobby, completely open from the doors to the elevator banks, and a couple stories high. The walls were all glass but the metal framework on the outside defined and framed the view.

More than that, though, he thought as he took a deep breath, smelling the stale air, this was it. Even though it had never been occupied, this was home.

Something within him shifted, but he wasn't sure if it was wishful thinking, if it was something real and primal calling to the Mackenzie part of him, or just his own satisfaction that they were here and he understood so much more about what it meant to be a Mackenzie.

He really should have read those journals sooner.

Tess came back to him. Her eyes danced, but not in their usual playful way. This was anticipation, the thrill of the chase—and it was hot. "Ready to risk the elevators?" she asked. "What floor was the executive suite supposed to be on?"

"I know nothing about this place."

"Eight," Thomas said, leaning out of a conversation with Gray and Krista to answer.

Tess held out her hand. "Well, I can't think of a better group to be trapped in an elevator with."

"I may take the stairs," Taylor said, shifting their weight from foot to foot.

Mack wasn't sure he blamed them and for a second, he thought about challenging them to a race up the stairs. Krista was waiting for him, though, her arms folded over her chest and her gaze steady on him, as if she knew what he was thinking.

"It'll be fine," Tess said and shrugged. "Besides, the cops know we're here, so if there are any problems, we'll call them in and pretend they are the cavalry."

"We've done this before," Red told Taylor, his gaze sweeping across Mack, too.

He opened his mouth to protest that he wasn't worried about getting stuck. He wanted to see if he could run up eight flights of steps without getting winded.

The nine of them piled into the elevator, Taylor a little pale. It was a quiet, tense ride up and Mack smiled when Tess slipped her hand into his and gave him a squeeze.

As soon as they opened the door to the eighth floor, Mack froze. Tess stopped halfway out of the elevator, her back holding the doors open, and turned to him. "What? You're holding everyone up."

"Even if I hadn't known this was it, I'd know," he said, wondering if that made any sense at all. Something deep in his bones was responding to being here. He let it lead him to the executive suite, Tess and Taylor both keeping pace with him, the sound of Georgie's camera following.

It was locked.

"Here," Taylor said, and Mack, expecting them to have taken the keys from Thomas, stepped aside.

Taylor picked the lock.

"I don't want to know," Mack said, shaking his head and grinning.

"One of my many skills."

"Not arguing with you on that one." He took a deep breath and walked through the door.

The assistant's station was built-in, large and roomy but too far away from the door to what Mack was willing to bet was the specific domain in this building that would soon be his.

Taylor walked behind the heavy wooden counter and held a hand over an imaginary phone. With thumb and index finger, they pantomimed picking up the phone.

"Emerson Mackenzie's office. This is Taylor," they said and struck a pose for Georgie.

Mack grabbed Tess and engulfed her in a hug. This. This was PharmaSci's home.

Sixty-Four

A fter the discovery of the executive suite and Mack's approval of the view, they left the building. Tess and Red would come back with some of the juniors and do a full survey, figuring out what needed to be upgraded and what could be greened up. They'd seen enough to get a rough idea of what they had to work with.

Taylor was trying to figure out how many floors they would need.

At lunch, Tess dropped the next bombshell: She had arranged for Harald to meet them for a visit to the cemeteries.

This, even more than the Piston Building, was what she had hired Georgie for.

They had to pass the barricades by the water main break. Although Philip had told Tess they were going to finally close up the hole, the city was, once again, dragging its heels, and the fencing and Jersey barriers remained. It was going on six months.

Mack tried to climb the fence, calling for the alligator. Taylor looked confused for a minute, opened their mouth into an O of understanding, and climbed up beside their boss. "So this is alligator habitat?" they asked. "I always thought it would be swampier."

Red, who was still with them, shook his head and chuckled. "I'm starting to worry about you, Tess."

"That makes two of us," she said, risking a glance at Krista and Logan. He looked amused, but what surprised Tess was the smile tugging at Krista's lips, almost as if she *liked* seeing her grown son hanging off a fence.

"Are you two fools going to stay there, or are you here for something else?" Thomas called to them.

Mack jumped down but Taylor climbed down a few steps before jumping. "Hey, you never know what you'll find in a hole in the ground," Mack told Thomas.

Tess and Red exchanged a look, Tess thinking Mack had no idea how true that was.

They followed the trail, past the spot where Tess had met Harald the first time. They kept going, past it, the woods on their left deepening and the grasses on their right, in that creepy former pasture, a bright, vibrant green with the new season.

"This," Tess said, loudly enough for Krista and Logan to hear, "reminds me of the Manor. It's close to town but in an area so heavily wooded, it's shut off from it all by a thick barrier of trees."

Krista cocked her head, then nodded once. No one else responded, but Mack, Tess noted, looked thoughtful.

"Are we there yet?" Taylor called.

"Almost," Tess said. She tossed a look over her shoulder at Mack's assistant. They didn't look out of place. Maybe that had been playful? "Not a fan of the outdoors?"

"I spend most weekends backpacking," Taylor said, zero inflection in their voice. "The difference between then and now is that then, I'm prepared and I know where I'm going, and now, I'm not and I don't."

They reached the hole in the fence, and there it was. Surrounded by a wrought-iron fence that was still in good shape, the lower cemetery was once again mowed and obviously tended. "Here we are," Tess said. She glanced at Thomas and Gray, worried she'd walked too fast for two senior citizens, worried they physically weren't up to the short hike, but they both looked interested.

Honestly, Tess was surprised everyone had come, even Red. She'd expected it to be her, Mack, and Georgie. But they fanned out across the cemetery, pausing so Tess could make the introductions to Harald, who remained gracious, if a bit cautious and defensive.

"These are the markers of the spirits who are here," Harald said, taking his fedora off his head and holding it against his chest.

Thomas motioned to him to put it back on. "You don't want a sunburn on your scalp. It's bad enough the two of us didn't know to bring hats."

"I didn't think you'd want to come out here," Tess said.

"And miss seeing this? Tess, I have been this property's caretaker for more than forty years and this is the first time I've gotten to set foot on the property." He looked around, then turned to Harald. "Who are these people who've gotten the first-rate care?"

Harald repeated his line about the markers representing the spirits, but Thomas led the way to one and paused. "Maybe," he said, "but these were also people who were important somehow or they wouldn't have markers."

"They don't have last names," Mack pointed out, leaning forward to rub at a smudge of something on the one they had gathered around.

Tess was suddenly aware of the click of Georgie's shutter. "Where's the other plot?" she asked Harald and Thomas both. "All you told me, Thomas, was *uphill*." She gestured. The only thing uphill that she could see between where she stood and some trees were more tall grasses. They were brown, so Tess figured they were last year's growth.

"There's a break in the fence at the top left corner," Harald said. "I've never gone beyond it. Are you telling me—"

"That the Mackenzies are in that one," Tess said, giving him a stern look.

He nodded and motioned to her to lead the way to the open corner in the fence. When she got up there, she paused. As it had seemed from below, the Mackenzie plot hadn't been taken care of. The grasses were overgrown, the stones mostly hidden. Some in the far corner looked like they'd been knocked or had fallen over.

"This speaks volumes," Mack said, disdain, frustration, and anger dripping from his words.

Tess agreed. It did, although not the way Mack was probably thinking. It wasn't only that the neglect had tried to erase the Mackenzies so much as Thomas believed that both cemeteries had been maintained in order to honor everyone buried here.

That was important, too.

But so were the Mackenzies. PharmaSci aside, they now had the paperwork to show that Henry and Patrick had saved lives and given human beings the chance to live lives free of slavery, hopefully with dignity and education of all sorts and a chance to better themselves.

Their story deserved to be told—the stories of Henry and his son Everett, and the people they'd saved. It made an odd sort of sense that Mack would be the one to do it. Mack, who'd changed the company mandate back to wellness, who was leading the push for better accessibility to health care for everyone.

"Heads are certainly going to roll," Thomas said, then caught himself. "Metaphorically, of course."

"I would hope so," Krista said in a frosty voice.

She and Tess watched Mack as he visited each stone, brushing grasses and weeds aside and stopping to squint at some, tilting his head at others, his mouth set into a thin line that showed his displeasure.

"Remember to check for ticks when we leave here," Taylor told everyone, curling their lip at the tall grasses. "If there aren't any here, I'm a banana. And I am not curved and yellow."

"You're close enough to being blond," Mack told them. "Over here, Tess. Hey, Taylor, were you blond as a kid?"

"Yes. And so maybe I'm a kumquat if there's no ticks here."

But Mack was done bantering. He was squatting in front of a headstone, the grasses obscuring it pushed aside. He yanked a handful and tossed it aside.

"Who?" Tess asked as everyone gathered round. Well, everyone except Georgie, who had gone to the far side of the cemetery and was taking pictures, his camera pointed at the group.

"Henry? I think. It's hard to read." He pulled at more handfuls of the tall grasses and other weeds that had grown up over the stone.

Taylor stopped him when he started to reach for poison ivy. "You do *not* want to ruin your weekend that way," they said.

"But it's Henry."

"We'll have it taken care of," Tess said, glancing at Thomas and Krista. Logan stood at her elbow, much as Taylor hovered at Mack's, and Tess wondered if she was the one in the wrong, standing beside Mack.

"Is this all that's left on the property?" Tess asked Harald, who stood at the edge of the overgrown part of the cemetery. She wondered if he would take a single step into this section at all. *The master's family*, she thought with distaste. Yet at the same time, they were the Mackenzies. The image of them as horrible people wasn't real.

Bringing peace to Port Kenneth was going to be a long, rough journey.

"There's a house," Harald said shortly. "It's not far. I don't usually go there." He raised his face. Tess was willing to bet the house was in that direction. "Slaves aren't allowed unless summoned," he said and spat toward the gravestone Mack still crouched in front of.

He didn't react.

"I understand," she said, watching Harald with as much empathy as she could muster. He didn't know yet how wrong he was about what had happened here. "If you want to head back, you can. But you've come this far, and—" She shrugged. "Who knows what we'll find?" she asked a little more loudly, intending her voice to carry.

"Another alligator," Mack said, moving to the next headstone. "This one's a woman. Why are you going to be the first Mackenzie wife, Mother, who's going to be remembered at all, let alone favorably?"

"There's nothing in the journals about any of the wives?" Tess asked.

"None seem to have done anything worth talking about."

Harald looked from Mack to Tess. "These are his people?"

She knew she should have told him, but she hadn't wanted to be met with an angry mob. "He has their records, Harald. We should be able to learn about all of these people—in both cemeteries. I think... I think those records will surprise you."

Harald snorted and looked away. "The house is up that way," he said, pointing. "I will wait here."

"You don't have to," Tess said, still softly. "Being witness now may matter as we unravel the whole story."

Harald looked uneasy, shifting his weight and looking everywhere but at Tess. "Will this be unraveled?" he asked.

"Yes," she said. If for some reason Krista forbade it, or Mack couldn't find it within himself to do it, she'd find a way. She'd come too far, of course, but she also felt an obligation to all these people—the people of Woolslayer, the Mackenzies, and the people who'd been involved but whose stories had been lost over the years. This was an important part of Port Kenneth history, and if she was nothing else, she was a child of Port Kenneth. That alone gave her an ownership.

She looked up at Mack and asked, "The house?" He nodded.

She led the way, gasping when the house revealed itself, standing in the center of a yard that, also, looked recently mowed. If the Manor up in Lakeford was a plantation style house, this one... this was an Italianate beauty, with the low-pitched roof, the perfect symmetry, and the square tower in the middle—and the high, high ceilings that made the house taller than it was wide.

The two houses were in the wrong parts of the country, but Tess was reminded of what Krista had said: They were winking at the current Mackenzies, reminding them of the other half of their split personalities. Both Northerner and Southerner.

"How big do you think it is?" Mack asked, breathless.

"Bigger than the Manor," Krista said. She was craning, trying to see first the widow's walk on the top and then around the wide, covered porch that framed the front and seemed to wrap around both corners.

"The Manor's how big?" Tess asked.

"Nine thousand square feet, total," Krista said. "We use much less of it."

"Tess? Got a guess?" Mack asked.

She turned to Red, who held up a total of three fingers, but used both hands to do so. She nodded, agreeing. "Twelve thousand. This is..." She shook her head. "What do you *do* with a house this size?"

"Turn it into a bed and breakfast," Taylor said.

"I would stay here," Gray said.

"Maybe," Mack said dubiously, still looking up at the house. "Maybe we have ten kids, Tess, and fill it."

"You are free to be the one who gets pregnant ten times," she told him, and he laughed, reaching for her to pull her close.

In her ear, he whispered, "Is it okay that I have no idea how to feel about any of this?"

"Yes," she replied. "I'm still trying to figure out what of all this is the Mackenzie treasure."

"That's easy," Mack said and held her tighter. "Me."

She groaned and shoved him away, but he was already moving, leaping up the five steps to the porch and turning in a circle, his arms outstretched, his sense of triumph palpable.

Then he turned to the front door and tossed a grin over his shoulder. "It's unlocked. C'mon, Just Tess. Be the first in with me."

Sixty-Five

T he house was in the same shape as the Piston Building: Recently cared for.

Red pulled Tess aside. "Something about all this smells."

"Like Thomas is letting us have the big reveal?" She waited for Red's nod, but he just cocked an eyebrow at her. "Except he didn't know we were coming out here today."

"He probably knew you'd do it soon, especially once he heard Mackenzie was coming down for the weekend." Red nodded at Mack, who stood in the front room on the left, absorbed in the detail on the fireplace, running his fingers over the carved wood.

Tess nodded. "What do you think is the truth about the bones?" She asked Red softly. "Or the scrubbed records? Do you think it's *all* related, and that Thomas knows about it, too?"

"You'd have to ask."

"How do you just walk up to someone and ask if they know about a random assortment of bones buried under a seemingly random sidewalk?"

"Tess?" Mack asked as Red motioned her to lower her voice.

She took a deep breath and turned to Mack, pasting a smile on. "What do you think?" she asked, gesturing around the room.

He craned his neck at the ceilings. "These are higher than the Manor's."

Red clapped him on the shoulder and left them alone.

"Seriously," she said, reaching for his hands and yanking gently on them.

The look he gave her was somber. "I think that it's a gorgeous house, but everything we've learned... no matter how altruistic Henry was, do you really think he treated *all* his slaves well? And I mean well by *our* standards, not by his."

"Are you worried the house is haunted?"

"No," he said, but his glance around the room was uneasy, uncertain. He took a deep breath. "This is a huge legacy that I've got to undo."

"You do, huh?" She wrapped her arms around his waist and arched backward so she could see his face.

"Well, who else—oh, you mean you're actually sticking around?"

"You really think I'd dump you over this?"

He stared over her head for a long minute. "Yeah," he said at last and put his hands on her waist, holding her steady. "I thought about it, how I'd feel if this was *your* family history."

"And?"

He shrugged. "I'm not you."

"And I know *you*. We'll figure this out. It's not like we're in it alone."

He let out a breath. "I know, but in some ways, it feels like it. This... Tess, it's a huge issue. We're standing in a house that," he paused and looked around, "well, it's in really good shape for its age."

"It's been well taken care of, and modernized," she said.

He gave her a look. "How do you know?"

"The porch lights," she said with a grin and stretched to brush her lips over his. "But I understand what you're saying. This house has history. *You* have history. I bet even PharmaSci does, and that might be the darkest part of it all."

His eyes darkened and he scowled.

Tess figured he hadn't thought about that.

"What do we do?" he asked softly. "How do we fix it?"

"I don't think we *fix* it," she said slowly, trying to sort her words. "I think we acknowledge it, we own it, we show through a series of actions that we *are* who Henry Mackenzie expected us to be. That we see the value of every human being, and we will continue the work to raise them and help them realize their dreams."

"Lofty words," he said with a small smile.

She shrugged. "It's what I've been doing. Just not so deliberately ambitious in this way."

"Emerson?" Krista said, dwarfed by the doorway to the front room. "I think most of us are ready to leave. Logan would like a nap, Taylor is feeling anxious that there is no cell service out here and an office that the five of us have left untended, Thomas and Gray think they are too old for all this excitement, your photographer has run out of memory, and Red is vowing to start work here if you don't chase him out. And I'd like to get back to Lakeford. Port Kenneth is lovely, Tess, and I will visit more often. With a better wardrobe." She picked at her pants.

Tess nodded and looked up at Mack. "And you?"

He adjusted his grip on her and winked.

She ran a hand through her hair and touched the tattoo on the back of her neck. These ashes were still too hot to spawn the sort of phoenix they most needed, but once they cooled, they could teach people about the good the Mackenzies had done—if they had, indeed, done good. Maybe the bird would rise.

They headed back to the cemeteries, through the hole in the fence, and then back to Woolslayer, where everyone drifted off to where they needed to be. Taylor leaned on Tess' car and bent over their phone.

"Miss Tess, this was the best day," Georgie said, "and not just because I got to skip school."

"You still have to finish," she told him.

"Do you think Mr. Red would talk to me about running his own business?"

"How about, when I send you the mentor I've lined up for you, I send you Red's contact information and you ask him yourself?"

"You'd do that?"

She nodded. "Don't be surprised if there's some work for you over the summer, too." She laughed as Georgie leaned in to hug her, so full of thanks he could hardly get the words out.

She watched him head deeper into the neighborhood.

"Before we put you in a rideshare, Taylor, can we make a detour?"

They waved at her, phone glued to their ear. Mack grimaced. "I'm going to hear about whatever that is, I'm sure."

"Come with me," she said and led him over two blocks and down one. A tall red rowhouse stood there, the buildings on either side torn down and left as vacant land. "Janeesa, one of my tenants at the incubator, found this for me. I'm kind of in love with it," she said, looking up at it.

"So buy it," Mack said.

"Buy it? Just like that?"

"Yeah."

"And then what?"

He shrugged and scratched his shoulder. "Fix it up. Isn't that what you do? Fix up old places?"

"I have a place to live."

He was silent for a minute. "But *we* need a place to live. Your condo's fine," he said quickly, as if anticipating that she'd protest. "But it's yours."

"And how do you think you and your bank account will be welcomed?"

"When they realize we're here to live the way they do, to be part of their neighborhood, that we're not changing it? They'll probably be glad to have us. I hear one of us knows people at the mayor's office." He nudged her.

"You'd be happy living in a working-class neighborhood like this?"

"I don't know," he said somberly. "I have this vision of going for a run in the mornings and seeing people who know me and say hi. Who talk to me in line when I pick up breakfast while you sleep in. Isn't that what you tell me makes this place special? That people watch out for each other? That they care about each other? I think that'd be a nice departure from Lakeford and its enforced isolation."

They were quiet for a long minute. "This feels like another of those points of no return," she said.

"We run into a lot of those."

And, Tess thought, they managed to get past them all. "What does life together look like, to you?"

He rubbed the back of his neck as he started toward the car. "I run PharmaSci. You work for Red and take care of the incubator and whatever else you want."

"And who takes care of the house? Cooks? Cleans? Shops?"

He stopped walking and gave her a long look. "We hire someone—someone who'll become part of the family so that when the next Mackenzie appears, it's seamless."

Tess frowned.

"What? You don't want someone else raising your kids? I think I turned out okay."

"I... well, kids. I didn't think I'd have any."

He didn't answer.

"And what if I want to cook? Or do some of this domestic stuff?"

He shrugged, and Tess had the sense she was making too much of nothing. "You do it," he said. "The idea, Just Tess, is that we have the money. So let's bring someone in, treat 'em well, and take the pressure off ourselves. We have that luxury and we're stupid not to use it."

She eyed him. "I need to think about all this."

"But you and me?"

"Suddenly just got a lot bigger than what we had been."

He looked out at something over her head. "Yeah, it did, didn't it?"

"I'm... it's a little scary."

"Yeah," he said, his face as troubled as she felt. "I get that. Are... you going to kick me out and make me go crash with Taylor?"

Tess paused, hopefully out of Taylor's hearing. "We have a couple hours. Want a nap?"

"Only if that's a code for *want to get naked with me for a few hours*."

Sixty-Six

May 31

It was late by the time Mack got back to the Manor, but that didn't stop Krista. She was waiting up for him.

"Oh, goodness," she said when he came into the kitchen from the garage. "You..."

"Haven't shaved, Mother. Men do that sometimes."

"What did Tess say?"

"She said normal men don't shave on weekends."

"Oh, I don't think that would go over well..."

"That's what I told her. Did you stay up to give me a hard time about my facial hair?"

"No, I wanted to welcome you home and thank you for including me in the tours."

Mack snorted softly. She hadn't really given him the choice about whether or not he had wanted her there. She had just taken it on herself to show up.

Truth was, he hadn't minded.

"Emerson, look at what we've uncovered," she said. "Look at the magnitude of it. This goes beyond anything I could ever imagine, and the fallout is... it could destroy the company."

"What we've uncovered, Mother, is that Henry and then his son Everett bought over two hundred people, educated as many as they could, and helped them down a path to better lives. Tess and I spent a large chunk of the weekend going over all the old papers I brought with me. She's going to take them to her expert in Knoxville, but it looks like the story's solid. More than two hundred people—and their descendants—got better lives because of Mackenzies. That's not going to destroy the company so fast. That's the sort of PR gold most companies would kill for."

He tried to school his thoughts away from the idea Tess had floated: that some of those people had been test subjects for the first PharmaSci drugs. There hadn't been any proof of it.

"And Taylor? What did they think of Port Kenneth? It's a lovely city, I must say."

"They liked it. We all went to a museum yesterday and helped them find some people they could start to network a social life through." He didn't need to tell Krista that he'd been nervous Taylor wouldn't like the city. Taylor had said they would go wherever Mack went, but he wasn't so much of a heel that he didn't care if his assistant was unhappy. "Now, if you don't mind, it's late and I'm beat."

"Emerson," Krista said softly, her voice full of rebuke and something else Mack couldn't recognize, "all-night sex marathons at your age?"

He gave her a look. Hadn't he just told her he and Tess had been going over the papers? But then he caught a smile tugging at her lips and he bit one back, himself. "Don't tell me you and Logan don't do it from time to time." He paused. "No, really. Don't tell me. Let me believe that when Tess and I are your ages, we'll still be this hot for each other."

"And here I was thinking you wouldn't want to know your mother has a sex life at all."

Mack crossed the room and kissed her cheek. "I assume you do, and that's the end of this discussion. What Tess and I do, what you and Logan do, stays behind closed doors."

"When you're this tired..."

"Maybe because we stayed up last night talking about what to do with all these houses, PharmaSci's headquarters, how we're going to juggle a couple big careers and Tess' community service work, if we have kids—and we know: There needs to be a Mackenzie heir—her ambitions for the neighborhood she's been working in, if I'm done playing Ultimate and what I'll do to stay sane if I am, and everything else under the sun we could think of."

"Oh. Oh, well, I'm glad to hear that."

Mack nodded and left for his rooms. He sat on the edge of his bed and scrubbed at his scruff. He'd meant to shave it before leaving for the airport but had decided to leave it, if only to torture Krista a bit. Taylor had gotten a kick out of it, too.

They'd had an interesting time, he thought. Up until this trip, they'd both been content to keep things professional. But as the move started to seem like it could happen, he'd realized he had to take care of Taylor maybe more than he did for the average employee—and not just because Taylor didn't fit certain ready-made molds. He had to do it because Taylor was as vital to what he did as the company itself.

His phone buzzed. *You should be back by now.*

Yep. At the Manor, even.

Sleep well, lover.

You too. He smiled. Being with Tess was as natural as breathing. It always had been.

He tossed his phone onto his nightstand. A gleam of gold caught his eye and he picked up Kelsey's bracelet. He hoped she was resting well, that she'd found peace at last, and he set the bracelet back down, sending her a silent thank you. She'd probably only meant to escape the hell her father had created for her, but she'd given him a freedom he'd never expected. And a past, too, as uncomfortable as it was.

In the morning, he'd start to put into motion the renovation of the Piston Building, which really meant getting the board to officially approve it. He was sure the usual ten corporate fires had erupted over the weekend, too, along with the stuff he had known wouldn't get touched while he was gone. Things had been real before, but now, they took on something new, something bigger, deeper.

Henry and Everett had saved people. PharmaSci had been founded to save people. And now, in this day and age, it was time to save even more people, not make them choose between medicine and food. It was time to position PharmaSci to change the entire industry—and he was *not* going to do that without making more enemies.

With a deep breath, he stood up to get ready for bed. And maybe, just maybe, not put off shaving until the morning.

Sixty-Seven

June 1

Tess felt triumphant when she walked into the conference room for the morning meeting. "The Piston Building," she announced to everyone, "is *mine*." She grinned. "But every single one of us is going to have a hand in it."

Red nodded. "I got an early morning phone call. PharmaScience Technologies is the client, folks. It's official."

She and Red took turns talking about what they'd found the previous Friday, and while most people seemed excited about the project and what they envisioned the scope to be, a few grumbles erupted about conflicts of interest and landing a project because of who she was sleeping with.

Red wasn't having it. Neither was she, but she was also smart enough to let him handle it. She had other things to deal with, starting with the incubator and their monthly meeting. And she needed to touch base with Philip. The journals had spoken of the Flaherty family, who'd had no love for the Mackenzies. Maybe they were behind the bones, since Philip and the mayor's office had decided someone had left them there to cause trouble. PharmaSci and the Mackenzies might have left town, but old family grudges could linger.

Philip's eyes lit up when Tess mentioned the name Flaherty. "They owned the city's oldest newspaper—the one brother still does, but the sisters left town to get into TV."

"And would they view the Mackenzies as their rivals?"

He started to laugh. "Undoubtedly. Those two names might have come up in private discussions of this whole thing."

Tess took a deep breath. "Are they going to cause trouble for PharmaSci's return?"

"The mayor's on it. We need a good corporation to headquarter here and anchor the downtown."

Tess gave him a tight-lipped smile. "More for me and Red to renovate." But part of her was thinking that once again, the Mackenzies were coming to the rescue. Only this time, they weren't leaving so fast.

Back at her office, Tess called Krista to ask her to check out this Flaherty dynasty.

"That's an interesting request, and I certainly hadn't known about any bones and an attempt to further sabotage the Mackenzie name," Krista said slowly. "But why are you calling me with this first, dear, and not Emerson?"

"Because... he has PharmaSci to run?" Tess said slowly, less a question than a reminder of what the situation was—she hoped. She wouldn't be pleased if Krista made some comment about Mack only *thinking* he was running things.

"That's true, but what man doesn't like to hear from his partner during the work day?"

"Him. And if we can get away from the gender designations, me too."

Krista was quiet for a minute. "Good for you two," she finally said. "One thing I like about your match is that you respect and value each other's work."

"We both do important things." In the same vein as Henry Mackenzie, it seemed.

"You certainly do. Okay, I'll see what I can learn about this Flaherty family. I may ask Emerson if he recognizes the name."

Tess had expected her to do that, and she confirmed that it was a good idea.

"Tess? Before you go, may I ask you something?"

"Sure," she said cautiously, not sure what sort of zinger Krista was going to hand her.

"This history of the Mackenzies. How do you feel about it?"

Tess paused. "I'd love to know more about the people he saved. Where are their descendants? Do they know the story? If so, how do they view Henry? Do any of them hate him for that initial purchase, which was what set everything in motion for their freedom?"

"I think we may never know for certain," Krista said. "Exercise caution if you and Emerson decide to move into the farmhouse."

Tess paused. "We're going to renovate an old rowhouse in Woolslayer. At least for now."

She waited for the sniff of disapproval, but all Krista said was, "You rebels."

SIXTY-EIGHT

June 25

"Close your eyes."

"Tess, c'mon," Mack said, half-bent to allow Tess to put her hand over his eyes. "I know we're at the field."

"I know you know. But I don't want you to see it as you walk into it. I want you to open your eyes and *voilà*!" She told herself she should have brought a blindfold, then brightened. She had a jacket in the car. She could toss that over his head and he'd have the added benefit of being able to see where he was walking, if nothing else.

He consented to that, and narrated the whole trek down the stairs and into the middle of the field. "I can see the steps," he said. "And look! The bleachers are green... I'd forgotten we'd done that. This is nice concrete," he went on. "Nice and new and not falling apart. I approve."

Tess smacked him but he just laughed and let her continue to lead.

"Okay," she said when they were at the center of the field. "You ready?"

"Just Tess."

"Yeah, yeah. You were born ready. For *this*, Mack. For your first glimpse of Field Emerson."

He pulled the jacket off his own head and paused, mouth open, eyes wide. "Holy shit, Tess," he breathed.

She wrapped her arms around him, moving with him as he turned in a circle to take it all in.

"This is..."

"I hope it's what you dreamed of."

"Better than," he said, returning her embrace and rocking with her in his arms. "It's perfect." He kissed her and Georgie's shutter clicked.

She cleared her throat and pulled away. "And," she said, jogging back the way they'd come and running up to the third row of bleachers. She picked up a disc and held it up, widening her eyes. "I can't toss it. The wind might not be right."

He laughed, one hand on his belly, one hand outstretched toward her. "Yes!" He jogged over to her and she leaned forward and gave the disc an awkward toss; she'd always been steadfast in her refusal to learn his sport, citing the need for him to have something she wasn't part of.

But when the disc landed in his hand, he looked at it and laughed.

She'd had it custom printed. *Field Emerson. Inaugural Disc.*

And the date.

And an alligator rising, phoenix-like, from the ashes of the old field.

About the Author

Susan Helene Gottfried is the heavy-metal-loving, not-disabled enough divorced Jewish mother of two. A freelance line editor to authors of fiction by day, Tales from the Sheep Farm is her offer to her fellow diverse authors to create a world in which all are welcome.

Susan holds a BA (University of Pittsburgh) and MFA (Bowling Green State University) in English Writing and Fiction, respectively. Her older works include the Trevolution series of books and a number of short stories, most of which have been anthologized in various spots. Some are even still for sale!

She lives with a couple cats in the Pittsburgh suburbs, just West of Mars. Visit her at http://WestofMars.com and http://TalesFromTheSheepFarm.com.

Also By

The Trevolution series (short story collections and novels)
ShapeShifter: The Demo Tapes (Year 1) (2008)
ShapeShifter: The Demo Tapes (Year 2) (2009)
Trevor's Song (2010)
ShapeShifter: The Demo Tapes (Year 3) (2011)
ShapeShifter: The Demo Tapes (Year 4) (2013)
King Trevor (2012)

Collected short stories
Permission to Enter (2023)
Broken but Undaunted: Collected Stories (2023)

Short stories
Mannequin: A Short Story (2011; out of print)
Guitar God Numero Uno (With Love Anthology 2011; out of print)
The Taste of Pink Snow (Pink Snowbunnies in Hell Anthology 2011; out of print)
Make a Wish (Bestseller Bound Short Story Anthology—Volume 2 2011)
The Ghost of the Dresser (Bestseller Bound Short Story Anthology — Volume 4 (2012)
Broken (2014; out of print)
Undaunted (Running Wild Press 2018)

Sample Chapter: Populated

Book Two in the Tales from the Sheep Farm Series

There was only one other person who had the key to Delia's place: her younger brother, Leon. That was because Leon was the only person she could trust with it; if she'd given it to her parents, her dad would have come by to paint and change lightbulbs, and her mother would clean the kitchen and do her laundry.

And other than her parents and her brother, Delia didn't have anyone left in her circle. Not anymore.

So when someone jerked her out of an alcohol-induced sleep—not a drunk sleep, but the after-effects of hitting the sweet spot of just enough—she didn't freak out the way she might have if she'd still been seeing Chad. She was safe. She could trust Leon.

And he did have a reason for being there.

"Stevie needs you down at the gallery, like an hour ago."

"Why?" Delia rolled over and put an arm on her forehead. She had no responsibility at the Woolslayer gallery. She made sure new things were delivered as promised and picked up the checks for the old. That was it. Nice and simple.

"You just need to get down there," Leon said and twisted around, looking for, probably, clothes he could throw at Delia.

Too bad for him she'd learned to actually put her clothes away. Even what she'd worn to Journey's End the night before had been summarily deposited in the dirty laundry basket. Or, more likely, the floor in front of her very small laundry machines. Small was better than not in the condo, though. She'd take small.

"Is it really a national emergency?"

"Apparently," Leon said.

When he started opening the drawers in her dresser, she stopped fighting him. After all, he'd come across town, used his key to get in, and wasn't backing off. Whatever this was, it was real.

"Can I shower?"

"No."

"Eat?"

"I'll fix you something. Just put some clothes on and let's go."

He had a package of Pop-Tarts ready for her when she came out of her room dressed in ripped black jeans and a dark purple t-shirt. She was trying to both walk and tie her Docs at the same moment, and that wasn't going so well, so she jammed the laces inside, grabbed the Pop-Tarts, her wallet, camera bag, and then her own set of keys, and followed him downstairs to his car. Like usual, he was in the loading zone out front.

The gallery was hopping, Delia noticed as Leon drove past and turned the corner so he could park. Whatever this was, she thought, maybe it wasn't so bad, even if the gallery was really only open on Sundays during the December shopping season.

As they walked over, Delia decided *hopping* wasn't the right word and that yes, it was as bad as Leon had hinted at. Stevie was in the center of the thick group of people who'd gathered, and she was talking to a cop.

And Tess Cartieri.

"Whoa," Delia said, stopping in her tracks. Leon bumped into her, fumbling as he swung around her body, grabbing her upper arm and starting to tug her forward.

"I told you."

"Yeah, but *Tess*?"

"Nothing happens in Woolslayer without her knowing," Leon said, like it was no big deal.

Rumor had it that Tess had her fingers in the finances of the gallery, like she did with almost every other woman-owned business in the neighborhood. And there were a lot of women-owned businesses these days—thanks to Tess.

"Delia, there you are," Tess said as Leon pulled her through the people who'd gathered to sightsee, most with their phones held up, possibly to get pictures of Tess, although that didn't make perfect sense. From what Delia knew, Tess didn't keep a low profile in the neighborhood. She looked Delia over, then turned back to the cop and made introductions.

Delia paused. She'd never met Tess, but clearly the other woman knew who she was. Or maybe it was that Leon had escorted her through the onlookers and Tess wasn't stupid. Leon had said they were waiting for her.

Even though she knew it was stupid, she was glad Tess didn't react to her clothes. Then again, she was wearing an electric blue oversized hoodie, dark yoga pants, and a pair of sneakers that were probably more expensive than Delia's last grocery run—although, to be fair, Delia still shopped at the discount grocery. Tess' dark hair was down, as always, spilling over the hood and, in spots, into it. It had the perfect look of carelessly messy and Delia would have thought it was arranged except that as Tess turned her head, her hair moved in and out and around the hood.

Delia itched to pull out her camera, but this didn't seem to be the right time for that. She didn't even want Tess' face in the shot. Just that hair.

"I'll let you two talk," Tess said, touching Delia's elbow gently before she turned to Stevie and pulled the other woman aside.

The cop commanded Delia's attention. "Pissed anyone off lately?" he asked.

Delia blinked in surprise. "N-not that I know of."

"Break up with someone? A one-night thing that maybe didn't end the way you thought it did?"

"Just Chad Flaherty, but that was months ago and he wouldn't be caught dead in Woolslayer." In some part of her brain, she heard his disdainful sniff. "What's this got to do with the gallery?"

"Got any fans who've asked you to give them some of your work because they can't afford it?"

"No," Delia said slowly. That question, at least, was worth considering. But anyone who'd asked for freebies, other than her family, hadn't come around since before Chad. That was a year now. A lot of bridges had been burned in that year. "Why are you asking me all this?"

"Someone broke into the gallery last night. They jimmied the door and managed to disable the alarm, then stole all of your items."

"All?" Delia tried not to smile. That was kind of flattering.

"All. And nothing else." The cop wasn't smiling.

It was useless. Delia let herself grin. "Well. I've got a fan."

"Who's committing crimes."

"Yeah," Delia said and managed to erase the grin. "That's not cool. I mean, stickers sell for a buck. Who can't afford a buck?"

Stevie came back over, hugging herself. "Any ideas?"

Delia looked at her, speechless. A wave of sympathy rolled through her. Having the gallery robbed must feel like an invasion on the scale of a rape, she thought. Violent, unwanted, unwelcome. A power play.

"About what I thought," Stevie said. She had dark circles under her eyes, which turned them from brown to almost black, although maybe the thin eyeliner helped with that. Her hooped nose ring glinted gold against her dark brown skin, made even more obvious by the fact that her impossibly dark hair was, like Tess and Delia's, down around her shoulders—which wasn't Stevie's norm. She wore jeans and a patterned shirt that was probably from India, like many of her tops were. She finished it with simple brown ballet flats.

"Whoever it was, they knew what they were doing," Stevie told Delia, then turned to the cop. "Can I show her?"

He motioned to her to lead the way, wrapping his free hand around his utility belt. That, too, would make a great shot, Delia thought, wondering how she could make it happen. Could you ask a cop if you could take pictures of his hand?

She was aware of the cop behind them as she and Stevie walked into the gallery.

"*What*?" Delia gasped when they got inside. This was beyond anything she had imagined, even though the cop *had* said *all*.

The gigantic picture, which had been fully framed and had needed a forklift to mount, was gone, too. It had been a picture of the street the gallery sat on, black and white, gritty, full of people—and definitely not for sale. It had been a gift to Stevie when she'd started carrying Delia's photography.

Stevie put her hands on her hips. "Like I said, they knew what they were doing."

Delia couldn't argue.

"And they must *really* like you," Stevie went on. "That had to have taken multiple people more than an hour to get down."

"Could it have been someone who used to work here, then?" the cop asked.

"It's been me and Georgie ever since I opened."

"Georgie?"

"Not our guy," Delia said. She pointed to another picture of Woolslayer on the wall. "That one's his."

"Professional jealousy?" the cop pressed.

This time, Delia and Stevie laughed.

"Georgie used to follow me around, asking for tips," Delia told him.

"And you snubbed him?"

"Hell no. Kid's got talent. Remember the water main break about a year ago?"

The cop gave her a look.

"Remember the alligator? *That* was Georgie's work. All of it. I helped him sell those pictures to the paper." She snorted. "Jerks weren't going to pay him for them. Trying to pull one over on the inexperienced kid."

"Doesn't mean he couldn't have done this. Or helped whoever did." The cop turned in a circle, as if taking in all the artwork. "Where is he this morning?"

"Probably at church. With his mother," Stevie said and Delia looked down at the floor and scuffed her toe on the spotless surface. So she wasn't the only one annoyed by this cop. Good.

"You think I haven't seen that one before?" the cop asked.

"Have you met Bettina?" Stevie tossed back. "If I have to go get Tess so *she* can tell you, I will. There's no way this was Georgie. There's a reason his isn't a name you know."

"Who else knew how to disable the alarm and get the picture off the wall?"

"Georgie didn't know how to get the picture down."

"Do you need me?" Delia asked. She looked at the cop. "I have things to do, so maybe give me your card, tell me not to leave town or something?"

"It doesn't work like that."

"Well, however it works," she said, reminding herself it probably wasn't a good idea to roll her eyes at a cop. "I didn't do this; why would I take my own things?"

"For the publicity."

"Please." This time, she didn't bother to stop the eye roll. "I'm doing just fine. And I can promise you Georgie didn't do it and if you keep looking at him, someone around here will hit you with a racism charge, and it might even be Tess herself who does it."

The cop glared at her but didn't say anything.

"We don't need to hide behind Tess," Stevie said after the silence had started to stretch.

"You sure?" Tess herself asked. She stood in the doorway with a silver travel coffee mug in one hand and a white bakery bag in the other. "Because I was walking past on my way home and was surprised to see you're still here."

"He thinks Georgie did it," Delia said, tilting her head at the cop.

Tess laughed.

"That's what we said," Delia said. She glanced at Stevie, wondering why she'd gone quiet, and realized she and the cop were still glaring at each other.

Slowly, Stevie raised one eyebrow. "Would you care to listen to *more* reasons why Georgie couldn't have done this?"

"And if I didn't check out *everyone*, would you be satisfied?" the cop answered. His calm manner set Delia on alert.

"Fair point," Tess said. She was leaning against the doorframe, as relaxed as anyone Delia had ever seen. She could have been watching a tennis match, she was so mellow.

"It's one thing to talk to the people with access to the gallery," Stevie said, "and another to pin it on a seventeen-year-old high school kid just because he seems convenient."

"Fair point," Tess said again and sipped at her coffee. "Officer? You're up."

"I don't answer to you."

"Oh, but you sort of do," Tess said with a smile that suggested she wasn't as mellow as she seemed. "Taxpayers and all that." She held up the hand holding the white bag, almost as if she were offering it to whoever jumped for it first. Delia wondered what was in it; Pop Tarts weren't much of a breakfast after a night at Journey's End. "But we understand you have procedures and hoops to jump through. Maybe we should all get out of here, let Stevie close up, let you go poke around at everyone, and we can all get on with our days."

The cop didn't look happy, but Delia didn't much care. This was *Tess Cartieri* setting him in his place, and it was kind of fun to watch. She hadn't pulled on any of her connections, or her identity, or anything. She'd just stated some basic, true facts in a very calm, quiet, reasonable way.

It was an impressive show, an impressive lesson to absorb.

Stevie motioned them out of the gallery. By the time Delia got outside, Tess had rounded the corner, presumably headed to her place.

Delia figured that was the smartest retreat. She pulled out her phone, intending to ask Leon for a ride, and decided to hop the bus instead. That way, she wouldn't have to answer Leon's questions.

Small favors, she reminded herself. Be thankful for small favors.